P9-DHD-888

253

Geoff Ryman

is a Canadian writer, author of numerous highly acclaimed works, now living and working in London and Oxfordshire. He works as Head of New Media for the Central Office of Information. The following are selected responses to his previous novel *Was*:

'Staggeringly original and profound ... All paths lead back to that farm in Kansas – no place like home – but Ryman's message is far from the film's bromide, involving the loss of innocence, fantasy and reality, and a history of America. Extraordinary, wonderful.'
Time Out

'Ryman's imagination and his meticulous care for detail make this an extraordinarily powerful novel which should win him the mainstream critical acclaim that he so richly deserves; at the end of this yellow-brick road, there could even be a Booker.'
New Statesman & Society

'Ryman's depiction of the harshness of frontier life is enthralling and his portrayals of the various characters' childhoods have the bitter tang of truth.'
Daily Telegraph

'Both a moving lament for lost childhoods and an eloquent tribute to the enduring power of art ... a forceful and resonant book.'
New York Times

'Imagine for a moment if Dennis Potter looked behind the legend of the film of *The Wizard of Oz*. The result would be certainly bizarre, and exactly what Geoff Ryman has created as he weaves three separate possible backdrops to Dorothy's adventures in the land of Oz ... The book and the characters will haunt you.'
Daily Mail

By the same author

THE WARRIOR WHO CARRIED LIFE
THE UNCONQUERED COUNTRY
THE CHILD GARDEN
WAS

253

the print remix

Geoff Ryman

 St. Martin's Griffin ✖ New York

Library of Congress Catalonging-in-Publication Data

Ryman, Geoff.
  253 : the Print Remix / Geoff Ryman.—1st St. Martin's Griffin ed.
    p. cm.
  ISBN 0-312-18295-3
  1. London (England)—Social life and customs—Fiction. 2. City and town life—England—London—
Fiction. 3. Subways—England—London—Fiction.
I. Title.
PR6068.Y74A615   1998
823'.914—dc21   98-28602
                                           CIP

First published in Great Britain by Flamingo, an imprint
of HarperCollins*Publishers*. A slightly different version
of 253 has been published on the internet since 1996.

First St. Martin's Griffin Edition: September 1998

10 9 8 7 6 5 4 3 2 1

for Bryan

253

253

(or Tube Theatre)

Beginning . . .

- Why the title?
- How to use this book
- Time span
- Other information

(please choose one)

WHY THE TITLE?

A tube train only has seven cars. Why? It seems an odd number. Eight would be rounder, more comforting. Perhaps it is seven for good luck.

A tube carriage has 36 seats. This means that an ideally filled tube train that was neither overcrowded nor disturbingly empty, would carry 252 passengers plus the driver. This would make a total of **253** people. That's the comforting thing about numbers. However unlikely, numbers are always there for a reason.

On January 11th 1995, a tube train left Embankment Station, in London, England, heading south on the Bakerloo Line towards a station called the Elephant and Castle. (This is what happens to words. 'Elephant and Castle' was originally named after the Infanta of Castile,[1] who was wrongly supposed to have stayed there once. This is an example of the kind of poor

The first helpful and informative **253** *footnote*
1 Another theory is that the Elephant was named after the Cutlers' Company that dealt in ivory at the junction of roads.

Medieval heraldry often showed an elephant with a castle on its back, so that might be a source. Is it any wonder that the English are so obsessed with their fascinating history?

communication that costs British industry billions of pounds every year.)

It was the ideally filled tube train. Every seat was occupied. No one was left standing unless they wanted to. Because the universe is not held together by cause and effect alone, but by mysterious patterns, every one of those people reached an important point in their lives. Some made key decisions. Some attained enlightenment. All except for the driver. He fell asleep.

This book is about those 253 people. That is why the title is **253**. So that the illusion of an orderly universe can be maintained, each section will consist of 253 words, not counting the headings, page numbers or footnotes.

HOW TO USE THIS BOOK

All **253** characters have their own page. Each page is divided into the following helpful sections:

Outward appearance

Do the characters dress well? Do they look like someone you would like to have for a friend? Remember: this book happens in winter. Many of the passengers are wearing thick winter clothing. This hides some of their individuality. For example, few of them are wearing T-shirts with messages, or revealing lycra shorts. Nevertheless, **Outward appearance** should help you to decide if you want to read more about that particular person.

Most of the people in **253** are going to places in and around Lambeth and the Elephant. Most of Lambeth was a marsh until the 18th century. Never guess that from street names like Lower Marsh, would you? In fact, one of the guesses (by Christopher Hibbert) as to how London got its name is because of Lambeth. If Lambeth was basically a shallow lake, the place beside it might be called Llyn Din — Lake City. And I thought it was because the Roman city was called Londinium.

This is the second novel I've set in Lambeth. I work there, and it makes research cheaper than, say, Egypt or Thailand.

Inside information

People are not always what they seem. **Inside information** provides key facts about each passenger. Some of them are very interesting. Others are not.

What they are thinking and doing

Some of them are thinking positive thoughts. Others are up to no good at all. Some of them take decisive actions. Most of them simply sit and think. Whatever happens to them, you will share their London Transport experience.

People and Subjects

How to find a particular individual? The book works its way from the front of the train towards the back, one carriage at a time. Each car has a map, showing who is on that car, and where they are sitting. All passengers have their own unique number.

A **List of Links** at the end of the book details things the characters share, such as:

MARGARET THATCHER: how do the characters view this historical personage?

HAIR CARE: who is a beautician?

LOWER MARSH: who works on this important street?

This feature might help you to find subjects of special interest to you.

TIME SPAN

Every novel happens over a particular period of time. This can present many interesting technical problems. Budding authors may find the following information of interest.

This novel begins as the train doors close at Embankment Station. The journey under the River Thames to Waterloo Station takes roughly one and a half minutes. The train waits there for thirty seconds before leaving. Two minutes later, it arrives at Lambeth North and waits for a further thirty seconds. The final leg of the voyage takes three minutes to reach the Elephant and Castle.

In other words, the action of this novel lasts seven and a half minutes. This means it probably takes longer to read it than it would to live it. This may strike you as absurd.

If so, may I recommend my previous work of serious fiction, *Was*? It lasts 114 years and takes most people considerably less time to read. *Was* is about the book and the film *The Wizard of Oz* and features stimulating characters, colourful locales — and some guest appearances by well-known celebrities.

To order *Was* in the United Kingdom, email me, the author, at:

Ryman. Worksltd @ btinternet.com

In the United States, simply visit your local bookstore and find a member of its Sales and Service team. Ask a team member to order the book for you. Quote the following ISBN numbers: 0–679–40429–5 (hardback) or 0–14–017872–4 (paperback). You should find the Sales Team members very helpful.

If they are not helpful, email me. I will sort them out for you.

OTHER INFORMATION

Nothing exciting happens in this novel. It is ideal fare for invalids or someone wanting a quiet break. Those seeking excitement are advised to read the section called *The End of the Line*.

253 is designed to appeal to the Nosey Parker in all of us. How often have you sat in a restaurant, theatre, or bus and wondered who the people around you are? This novel will give you the illusion that you can know – indeed, that you are Godlike and omniscient. This can be a very pleasurable sensation. But remember that, as soon as you close the book, you are no longer Godlike and omniscient. The author, however, is. This is because the author only exists because of and within the book.

If you plagiarize parts of this novel, I will get ugly and sue. Save yourself the trouble. I am an author myself and understand the need to recycle material. Simply write to me, stating which parts of my novel you wish to purchase. Undertake to provide full acknowledgement in your novel. I will give you a firm quotation that will not change unless your brief changes.

Finally, help us to serve you better. Please take a few moments to fill in the customer feedback form at the end of this novel. Don't think too long about each answer – just give us your first response. Mail the completed form to the address shown. All information is treated in the strictest confidence.

That's all there is. Enjoy your copy of **253**.

For Your Reading Ease and Comfort

PASSENGER MAP

Car No 1

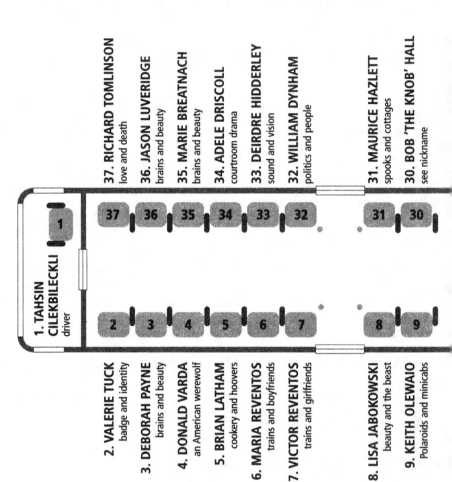

1. TAHSIN CILEKBILECKLI driver

37. RICHARD TOMLINSON love and death

36. JASON LUVERIDGE brains and beauty

35. MARIE BREATNACH brains and beauty

34. ADELE DRISCOLL courtroom drama

33. DEIRDRE HIDDERLEY sound and vision

32. WILLIAM DYNHAM politics and people

31. MAURICE HAZLETT spooks and cottages

30. BOB 'THE KNOB' HALL see nickname

2. VALERIE TUCK badge and identity

3. DEBORAH PAYNE brains and beauty

4. DONALD VARDA an American werewolf

5. BRIAN LATHAM cookery and hoovers

6. MARIA REVENTOS trains and boyfriends

7. VICTOR REVENTOS trains and girlfriends

8. LISA JABOKOWSKI beauty and the beast

9. KEITH OLEWAIO Polaroids and minicabs

THIS MAP SHOWS YOU

☞ WHO is in the car
👉 WHERE they are sitting and
✋ WHAT are their interests and concerns

29. HELEN BALE
ads and medicine

28. FLORA MCCARDIE
departed days

27. DANNI JARRET
sex and pencils

26. PAUL HENNESSEY
wife and grandson

25. ALFRED CUSHWAY
Vauxhall and violence

24. CLIVE KELTON
bathroom paradise

23. YOSHI KAMIMURA
London and Japan

22. TONY MANNOCCHI
wine and spirits

21. JUSTIN HOLMES
holmeslessness

20. JOY HARVEY
one-stop anger

| 29 | 28 | 27 | 26 | | 25 | 24 | 23 | 22 | 21 | 20 |

| 10 | 11 | 12 | 13 | | 14 | 15 | 16 | 17 | 18 | 19 |

10. TOBY SWISWE
Britain and minicabs

11. DOUGLAS HIGBEE
pianos and boats

12. GINA HORST
louts and pooftahs

13. MAY HANMORE
fear and photos

14. PHIL BARKER
dads and knuckles

15. HARRY WADE
rugby and sheep

16. MINERVA NICHOLAS
love and Bosnia

17. HARRIET DAWE
sons and lovers

18. TONY COLLEY
Camilla and good faith

19. EVELEEN DOYCE
melodrama and happiness

At last! The book that thinks for itself!

*How often have you been embarrassed
when serious fiction is discussed at the office?*

Employers expect the modern executive to hold his own during literary discussions. So do discerning social circles. You're at a dinner party. Your partner for the evening says "Forrest Gump is a Christ symbol." You realize that you have missed the point again.

End Literary Embarrassment Forever

253 uses the miracle of information technology to ensure that you can follow the main themes and relationships that link the text. Without even having to remember who the characters are!

Simply purchase an Internet service agreement. Install six separate pieces of software and then configure them. It's so easy there aren't even any manuals. Instant answers to your questions are available from your Internet Service helpline through the miracle of email. Unless of course your email isn't working yet. In that case, just go through your modem, using Hayes modem language.

Voilà! You're ready to 'surf' the Web.

Simply key in **http://www.ryman-novel.com** and if lines are available and the server is working, you will have time to read a few Web pages before the connection goes down. All for the price of a very long phone call!

What could be easier?

Impress Friends and Colleagues!

Just imagine the boss's face when you tell him, 'I've read 253, the novel for the Internet.' He will look at you through new eyes. So will your partner for the evening.

**253 – a world of success and romance
could be yours for the price of a phone call!**

THE DRIVER –
MR TAHSIN ÇELIKBILEKLI

Outward appearance
Like Antonio Banderas in *Interview with the Vampire*, down to the long black hair. London Underground uniform, neatly pressed except the jacket which is slung over the back of his chair. Unshaven, baggy-eyed. His Hush Puppy shoes are worn along one edge.

Inside information
A qualified Turkish political scientist living in Britain with a British wife. He walks splay footedly because his feet were beaten while he was in prison. His name means Perfection With Steel Wrists. Turkish surnames are new this century, added under the rule of Ataturk – Father Turk. Such names sound beautiful to them.

What he is doing or thinking
The train pulls out, Tahsin sighs with exhaustion. Last night he argued with his two best friends about Islamic fundamentalism. Tunc teaches at the School of Oriental and African Studies[1] and is from an old Ottoman family. 'There are only a million modern Turks, but we have all the power,' Tunc said, heavy lidded with superiority. Tahsin's other friend Umut is a failed actor, drinking himself to death. 'There would be no more wine,' Umut complained. 'Umut' means Hope. Tahsin lost his temper with both of them.

Tahsin is from Marash, a town famous only for its rubbery ice cream. His mother and father are illiterate and faithful. 'My modern son,' sighs his father on the phone with pride when told Tahsin is writing a book on a computer. After all the other isms, Islam at least feels native.

His jacket is being crushed. Sleepily, Tahsin hangs it on an available peg – the Dead Man's Handle.

*Another helpful and informative
253 footnote*
1 As a service to our international readers, 253 provides these helpful and informative footnotes designed to point out unusual features of history and architecture. Relax! Imagine you are on a whirlwind coach tour of Britain – only without being trapped for two weeks with people you never want to see again.

The School of Oriental and African Studies became part of the University of London in 1916 and is yet to fully become so in spirit. Its original building is a dispiriting brick nonentity lost in the no man's land between Russell Square and Malet Street. A newer extension (1979) looks like the South Bank. A new building was donated by the Sultan of Brunei in the 1990s to the School. It needed it.

Scholars from vastly different disciplines and cultures who live in the suburbs and commute daily discover at SOAS that they have nothing to say to each other. Proof positive that to have geography in common is to have nothing in common.

In fact, SOAS has a lot in common with tourist group bus tours.

Or perhaps a trip on London Underground.

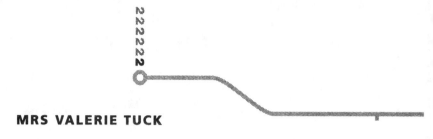

MRS VALERIE TUCK

Outward appearance
Page-boy haircut, green wool poncho over layers of olive and brown. An old-fashioned reporter's notebook on her lap. She chews her pencil.

Inside information
Edits the in-house journal of Otto Beetlehide Ltd, an international shipping company. Valerie's job usually involves buying in freelance journalists to work for branch offices in Cyprus, Denmark, Ipswich.

What she is doing or thinking
Writing an article herself. After a second theft of computer chips, employees in the London office were issued with photo passes. They were sat in front of a camera operated by postroom staff. The results were unflattering blue photographs on badges held by a choice of clip or chain.

The article is called 'What the Well Dressed Beetlehide Employee is Wearing'. Val advises how to wear the badge stylishly. 'Try hanging it down your back from its chain. This is simple, elegant, and less nerdish than clipping it to your front pocket.'

She captions the article's only photograph. 'Bruce Clipping, staff designer, models the mixed approach.' Her raffish assistant wears it clipped to his belt while still held by its chain from a waistcoat pocket. Val recommends spraying the badges lightly with gold nail polish, 'to neutralize the ice-blue, just-arrested look. Younger staff members into punk may wish to clip badges to ears or run the chains through nasal piercings.'

Val sketches elongated people holding the badges like handbags or fans. Like the drawings she did in school, back when she thought she was going to work in fashion.

She smiles as if at her younger self. The article will be fun.

MRS DEBORAH PAYNE

Outward appearance

Young, effective businesswoman. Red crepe blouse peeks out of black coat. Simple but expensive gold earrings. A new leather briefcase crouches like a pet panther at her feet. In job interviews, her face always fits. It is now slightly fragile, lost in thought.

Inside information

Legal assistant for the construction company Mosstains. Currently unattached. Inspired by the suicide of her younger brother, she works nights for the Samaritans.

What she is doing or thinking

She has done a terrible thing: last night her boss rang Samaritans; they were short-staffed so she took the call anyway.

Deborah has never had much respect for her boss. He is capricious, limelight hogging, sometimes generous, always disorganized. He apparently thinks the same thing. 'I want to get out, but I can't, I'm too old. And there's this woman. She's nice enough, but she disagrees with everything I say, and I just don't seem to be able to get through to her.'

Deborah has never thought of herself as a powerful person. She appears to be driving her boss to suicide. That is not her chosen role in life. The whole tumult of his character rolls over her, and she feels horror for him.

At Waterloo, she steps out onto the platform and recognizes him from behind. There are rules against this, but rules are for when you do not know what to do. 'John!' she calls out and runs after him. She takes his arm. 'John, you can leave Mosstains, you don't need to die!' His mouth hangs open in fear, loathing, surprise, rage.

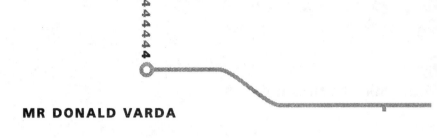

MR DONALD VARDA

Outward appearance
Blond, plump, about thirty. Wears a tight grey suit fashionable a decade ago. Sits in the last seat available. Grins fixedly. The man next to him shifts uneasily.

Inside information
A financial adviser at the Kennington Building Society. Its deposit accounts offer the highest interest rates in Britain.

What he is doing or thinking
Donald is re-imagining the ending to *An American Werewolf in London*.[2] The hero, Harold, realizes only Jenny Agutter can kill him and set him free. He tries to make her take the gun, singing 'It Has to Be You'. She weeps for him. Then, he begins to change. The werewolf chases her through her flat, just as the white-haired expert arrives . . .

Cut to a children's cartoon on television. It features Wile E. Coyote and is followed by a commercial for the American Lycanthropy Society. It shows Harold at work, in a bank. 'We are pleased and proud to have Harold as part of our clerical team,' says the manager. Drugged up to the eyeballs, Harold shakes his hand. His grin is fixed, desperate. 'Werewolves can lead normal, productive lives,' says the expert. 'I should know. I am a werewolf.'

The camera pulls back from the TV. Harold is being made to eat breakfast by his wife. She is not Jenny Agutter. The sound-track plays, 'It Had to Be You'. All Harold's victims surround him, and in their midst is Jenny Agutter. He killed her too. She looks on and weeps.

Where did I get that from? Donald wonders. Then he remembers. He works in a bank.

Another helpful and informative 253 *footnote*
2 There is a library angel who looks after people who write and read books. The most spectacular case for me was when the LA suggested the town of Manhattan, Kansas as the setting for a book. The first reference I found on the town in the *Guide to Periodical Literature* was an article describing a trip through Manhattan taken on a train from St Louis in 1861, lavishly illustrated with photographs taken at the time. Exactly what I needed.

I also know there is a web angel. I wrote this little character wondering what reference his daydream had to 11th January, 1995. Why would someone on a train be thinking of that particular movie? Checking the TV listings weeks later I found out that *An American Werewolf . . .* was screened on Cable TV that night. It was so unlikely, I convinced myself I made it up, and forgot it. Checking again, at the end of 1996, there it was. So Donald has seen the TV listings and that's inspired him. But I didn't know that when I wrote it.

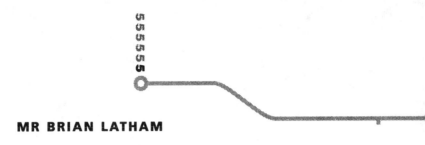

MR BRIAN LATHAM

Outward appearance

Pretty and old – blond hair, cornflower blue eyes. Sits bunched up and turned away from everyone until Donald Varda sits next to him. He then twists back around and segues through a series of extraordinary postures – from Rodin's *The Thinker*, to simply shielding his eyes. Upper lip is sucked into a thin frown, lower lip thrust forward. Wears a blue corduroy suit. No winter coat or briefcase.

Inside information

A broadcaster and cookery correspondent out of work since LBC folded. He now caters for and guests at dinner parties for a fee. Returning to his expensively mortgaged Georgian home near Elephant and Castle.

What he is doing or thinking

Last night he cooked dinner for a bullying ex-colleague who has always terrified him. As a 'friend' Brian was paid to stay overnight and clean up in the morning after they left. Brian knows nothing about cleaning. The poodle left a turd on the carpet. He tried to hoover it up. The vacuum cleaner jammed. He washed the hoover in the sink. The vacuum cleaner shorted when he tried to use it again. The kitchen sink was still muddy with shit. He experienced a blinding rage, and walked out, sink, carpet, cleaner all thick with proliferating turd. He is now appreciating how that will look to his client.

Brian perceives himself to be an essentially tragic figure. You don't like being a servant, he tells himself, but you are a servant. That's what you've become. He pushes himself to his feet at Waterloo, and gets out, to return to Kensington[3] and duty.

3 Kensington is one of those vaguely western parts of London in which rich people live. Therefore very few Brits live there, unless it's in hotels funded by the local council to house those on benefit.

It was a place of farms and factories until the 17th century when mansions began to be built there, including Holland House, Campden House and Kensington Palace. It's called the 'Royal Borough' because a Queen was born there. Only one?

I know nothing else about it. Life is too short.

MRS MARIA REVENTOS

Outward appearance
Twenty-five, black coat, black ski pants strapped under her instep, generous grey scarf. Obviously partnered to the next passenger. She is reading aloud in Spanish from *The London Underground Handbook*.

Inside information
A train fan from Guadalajara, Mexico. Her husband became enamoured of the town's old rolling stock. She became enamoured of him. In the early days of their marriage, she was winsome, naughty, headstrong. He was good, pained, slow. To make up for it, she has come with him on a train-lover's holiday.

What she is doing or thinking
She is fully occupied translating this passage:

> A unique feature of the D78 stock is that it has tube stock sized wheels. Traditionally, surface stock has always had 1067 mm wheels, whereas tube stock has 790 mm wheels. In an attempt to reduce the number of different types of wheel sets in use on the system, the D78 stock has the same type of wheels as the 1973 tube stock.
>
> The D78 stock also saw the introduction of a new kind of bogie . . .

Maria is conscious of a wearisome yearning in her breast. She is an intelligent woman, a school teacher. She wants to see the history of England. Harrods, she wants to go shopping in Harrods and buy tweeds, though they are a bit hot for Guadalajara. Instead, she is travelling on every line of London Underground. She hates the air, she hates the noise, she hates the blackness through the windows, perpetual night.

Then, as the train slows, her husband taps her arm to leave. She looks up in surprise.

18

Outward appearance

He looks like Geronimo – high cheek-bones, long nose, short mouth. He wears a blue-grey jacket of a kind not available in England, a blue and brown checked shirt, jeans, and immaculately white trainers. He sits with an arm behind his neighbour's head, his hand separating strands of her hair. He keeps looking up as if nervous.

Inside information

A train fan and civil engineer from Guadalajara, Mexico. Two days ago, he bought every book in the London Transport Museum Book Shop. Making a daytrip to Elephant and Castle station (1907) to see its famous Leslie-Green-style tiles.

What he is doing or thinking

He finds English women dangerously attractive. His eyes keep flicking up at a girl with a mirror (Passenger 35), and a more mature secretary-type (Passenger 34). Then there is the trendy student with devastating skin (Passenger 33).

Victor was inspired to come to England not only because of London Underground but because during the last Olympics he saw televised a display of synchronized swimming. Two huge English gals with shoulders like walruses and smiles like Rita Hayworth's breasted the waves in perfect unison.

Suddenly he's heard enough about D78 stock. Suddenly, he wants to see English girls swimming. Suddenly he wants to be swimming. He suffers a moment of fannish conversion – a pang of loss, a giddying reversal and a burst of yearning as sudden and delicious as biting into fresh pineapple. He is now a fan of synchronized swimming. He taps his wife on the arm. They get out early at Waterloo Station in search of a swimming pool.

MS LISA JABOKOWSKI

Outward appearance

Mid-thirties, long hennaed hair. A strained but carefully made up face. Boy's black leather jacket with quilted shoulders probably from the 1970s – lots of unnecessary zips. Black jeans, heavy unmarked tan boots. Unusual black leather shirt, low cut to reveal a bony freckled chest. Enters with a dog wearing a spotless new blue body jacket. She sits at end of row next to large bag.

Inside information

Runs a market stall that sells very light, thin silver jewellery – bracelets, rings.

What she is doing or thinking

She is catching a Network Southeast train to stay with her mother, which she does when she runs out of money. She smokes a lot of dope, listens to a lot of music, but still does not seem to have a good time. The dog is her only real friend. She has it sit up on her lap, and gently strokes it. The beast pants with an air of patient forbearance. It is black, but its greying muzzle matches the old jacket.

Lisa catches her reflection in the window. She has always considered herself to be attractive. That is why selling jewellery was an appropriate occupation, why the black leather jacket is a daring fashion statement. What she sees in the pane of glass is an angular woman with a bitter, thwarted air. She sees her mother. Lisa became wild in order to avoid becoming her mother. Fate and genes seem to close in around her. Is this what happens to us, Mum? She begins to feel some extra sympathy. She gets off at Waterloo.

MR KEITH OLEWAIO

Outward appearance
Jovial, mature black man sharing a series of jokes with a friend. Probably African from the accent. Expensive herring-bone trousers slightly mismatch with blue outdoor coat and soft shoes.

Inside information
Staying with his brother, who has a British passport. Jointly owns a minicab with Passenger 10. They are going to collect the car from a body shop located in arches under the railway. Mr Olewaio loves being a driver in Britain. Takes Polaroid photographs of his customers. Hopes in this way to make lasting friends.

What he is doing or thinking
He is telling his partner what happened with last night's fare, a drunken woman who wanted to get to Potter's Bar and was unable to suggest a route. Potter's Bar is just outside the range of *London A–Z*. Mr Olewaio knows nothing of London geography, and did not have a compass. London boroughs usually street-sign cross roads, not main streets. The signs can be posted anywhere on the sides of buildings, and Mr Olewaio needs glasses. He drove concertedly along a main road, finally glimpsing what it was called – 'High Street'.

'North, north,' the woman kept saying. He kept looking for the Thames. Realized he was heading south. Left the woman on a train platform. 'But this isn't Potter's Bar,' she protested. He shows a Polaroid photo of her. She is slumped on a bench, looking very confused. He gave her money for the train. He laughs, but is laughing at himself. Under the laughter, he is becoming coldly determined. I am a fool, a he thinks, until I learn.

MR TOBY SWISWE

Outward appearance
Thoughtful, mature black man, nodding and smiling as his
neighbour tells jokes. They both wear nearly identical herring-
bone trousers. From time to time nervously gnaws his thumb-
nail.

Inside information
Swaps day and night shifts driving the same minicab as his
cousin, Passenger 9. Mr Swiswe arrived in Britain before him,
and is already having to avoid drawing attention to himself for
fear of deportation.

What he is doing or thinking
He's preserving the innocence of Passenger 9. His cousin thinks
the car was damaged in an accident. It was in fact the target of
a gang. Mr Swiswe dropped off a fare at Hammersmith tube
station. There were many cars and people gathered in the glare
and darkness of the forecourt. He drove alone up Shepherd's
Bush Road, to the traffic lights at the Bush. Suddenly, the car
was surrounded by white youths. They shouted at him; he
did not understand. They gestured at him to come out. The
lights were red, he could not escape. They started kicking his
car, and wrenching off the antennae. 'Stay out of it, you black
bastard!'

Mr Swiswe feels he cannot call the police. His cousin with the
British passport advised, 'Stay out of Hammersmith. The gangs
there think they've got a right to all the cab trade. And the
Hammersmith[4] police are the most unpredictable in London.'
Mr Swiswe remembers how Britain first looked to him: calm
and orderly, if slightly deadened. That's a lie, he thinks, it's still
all there, all the shit. He is badly frightened, and wants to go
home.

4 Hammersmith is relentlessly self-improving. It used to have the scuzziest pub in London, *The Clarendon*, now long gone. It is now part of a shopping mall. Squatting over the mall and tube station as if they are eggs to be hatched is the new, huge Coca-Cola building.

Other revamped Hammersmith landmarks include The Hammersmith Palais, round the corner up the Shepherd's Bush Road, which has been a danceateria since about World War 2.

Underneath the M4, The Hammersmith Apollo or whatever it is now called, used to be a great rock venue (in autumn 1996 it was running, Dear Jesus, *Riverdance*, a show). But it was a great place to see rock artists on the way up or the way down including David Bowie and Paul McCartney.

The Lyric Theatre was given a new face, but still looks ornate and gilded inside.

Hammersmith is also distinguished by being ringed round with feed-in roads to the M4, an ecologically friendly building that is quite nice inside called the Ark, and HarperCollins Publishers inspired by, appropriately enough, a Scandinavian prison.

Like many London areas, Hammersmith is a bit difficult to characterize. There are pockets of posh housing, left over from its village days. It has a beautiful walk along the river from its bridge to Chiswick. *The Dove* is one of only about five OK pubs along the river, which also has many rowing clubs. Lots of revealing lycra in summer. The policeman Harry Daley in his autobiography *This Small Cloud* portrays Hammersmith in the '30s as being a mini East End in the West of crime and vice. He remembers the riverside walk as where the lowest order of prostitute massaged tired old cocks in bushes. Nothing much changed there then.

Hammersmith has been a place since at least the 13th century. Then as now it really exists because of its junction of roads. The IRA failed to blow up its bridge in 1996. The explosive didn't go off.

About Hammersmith police, I only know that they are much given to arresting people for walking home at the wrong time of night.

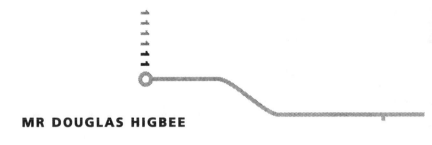

MR DOUGLAS HIGBEE

Outward appearance
Blandly British, about thirty, plump, moustache, no chin. Black trousers, huge winter coat, blue shirt collar. A large overnight case. Appears to be asleep, except that one eye is open.

Inside information
Mr Higbee is the bar piano player on a cross-Channel ferry. His bag contains a change of underwear, a top hat, and home-produced cassettes which he offers for sale on the top of his piano. No one ever buys them. Like Superman, his costume, a tuxedo, is under the ordinary coat.

What he is doing or thinking
He is trying to avoid having to talk to the ship's magician, Passenger 18, who is also in the same carriage. Douglas has nothing against the magician. They have to spend a lot of time in the same bar and cabin being professionally pleasant to each other. You hardly want to be pleasant all the way from Waterloo to Dover as well. Douglas finds it difficult to be pleasant.

It's all right for the magician. *He's* pretending to be riveted by a newspaper. Douglas has no such luxury. He left in a terrible rush this morning. Forgot his book, sponge bag, sheet music. He could always have pretended to read his underpants or his own cassette covers, like he forgot the running order of the tracks.

Instead, Douglas is pretending to be asleep, but only with the right-hand side of his face, the one turned towards his colleague. His left eye is reading the ads in safety.

The underwear in the bag is in fact a pair of his girlfriend's frilly knickers.

MS GINA HORST

Outward appearance
Virulently pink and orange coat, men's blue slacks, brown shoes. Arms folded like a boxer around a cloth briefcase. Short disordered blonde hair, clear bronze skin. Looks either fed up or not quite awake.

Inside information
Owns and manages a gym near Waterloo Station. Has a degree in Leisure Management.

What she is thinking or doing
She is contemplating the oiks who work for her. They are rotund with muscle, so big they have to wear Hawaiian sportswear all the time – nothing else is loose enough.

It's not so much that they want to play dance music instead of George Michael. It's not that they won't repair the exercycles because they think exercycles are girly.

It's their friends. They want the place to stay a club for weightlifting Neanderthals. She dreams of aerobics and sunbeds, customers from St Thomas's, Dun and Old, Pall Mall Oil, BT.

One of the thugs works for Railtrack. Yesterday he boasted how he'd seen off a pooftah in the Waterloo toilets by pouring bleach over his genitals. They roared with laughter. How can she explain that she wants a few pooftahs? They're polite and they pay the bills.

She sees suddenly that it's not her fault. It's not a question of her making the case to them. It's that they don't want the place to change.

She thinks again of the Health Centre on Lower Marsh.[5] It went bankrupt, but none of its members came to her. I could always sell the old one and buy that. Yes, she thinks with growing excitement, yes. I can.

Another helpful and informative
253 *footnote*
5 Two years later, by some strange twist of fate, Gina's first gym was converted to a gay sauna. Equally sadly, the gym on Lower Marsh that Gina bought closed again in April 1996.

MRS MAY HANMORE

Outward appearance
Painstakingly turned out older woman. Flawless make-up, bee-hive jet black hair. A spotless waterproof neatly belted. Sits unmoving and small. Her eyes dart, flicker.

Inside information
Lives near Bow Road, works at Boots near Waterloo, mostly in the photo section.

What she is doing or thinking
May lives in terror of crime. She is convinced that older women are the main target of hoodlums. Chains and locks are no use, they just kick doors down.

Her housing estate is strangely laid out with long balconies on the upper floors. May has to walk through clusters of local children and teenagers to get to her front door. They are beginning to make fun of her.

She is aware with gratitude that it is already getting dark at 5 PM rather than 4.30. All the way home she is in a state, clutching her bag.

She feels unsafe, even at Boots. A shop for violent perverts has opened nearby. You see horrible people all in black with rings. Some of them give her film to develop.

May is unable to concentrate at work. She gets terribly muddled with all those red envelopes. Yesterday a gentleman who had ordered two complete sets of 300 photos of his holiday in New Guinea found instead a range of other people's Christmas parties. May burst into tears. She now fears for her job.

Someone shouts nearby, men move suddenly. Unnoticed under the neat coat, May begins to shiver as if freezing cold. She cannot take this journey any more. She decides to quit her job.

MR PHIL BARKER

Outward appearance
Tiny, nervous, about nineteen. Longish brown hair, brown sports jacket, yellow shirt, green floral tie. A blue sleeping bag coat balloons around his shoulders. Sits slumped into the aisle with his left foot resting on his right knee.

Inside information
Works in the post office near Waterloo Station. Actually 22 years old. Lives with his family in Hackney.[6]

Phil's problem is his father. His father is 38 and still wants to be 22. He works as a bouncer and furniture repossessor, and is big, blond, spotty. His knuckles are tattooed. It's like living with the head of a rival gang. 'How much you bringing home each week?' Dad said this morning. 'You need to get yourself a sideline. Women love villains. I should know.'

Money, women, respect, power to terrorize – Phil has none of these and his father makes sure he knows it.

What he is doing or thinking
As the doors close, a blue blur sits next to him. A tremor passes through Phil, and the sole of his left foot sweeps down the blur's trousers. His neighbour immediately slams back with his knee. Phil's leg is pushed into the dividing panel. His knee nerves buzz like a funny bone.

Phil explodes. 'You do that again and you'll get a fucking knife in the ribs.'

The man stares back at him – he is blond and huge and his mouth hangs open. Then he hurls Phil against the dividing panel. Phil crumples, and swiftly withdraws. He stands hunched in the door area, burning with shame as the train pulls into Waterloo.

Another helpful and informative
253 *footnote*
6 Hackney is poor, gentrified, central, peripheral, ex-sweatshop . . . it's a good example of how London swirls with change. Up until the mid-19th century, it was known for its rural character. It became, with the railways, an industrial centre and an active hub of the kind of business that hires non-English speakers at sweatshop rates. In the early 1980s, many of these businesses closed.

Bordering on gentrified Islington, it has canals along which gentrification spread like athlete's foot. Other parts remained resistant to buyouts, partly because so many old buildings had been torn down to build the swathes of large public housing buildings called, with the typical respect the British have for people with lands who don't work, 'Estates'.

That just about sums up Hackney's history, estates to estates. Given its rough edge, it's actually a great place to live. My clever chum Roz lives there. I had another friend who did some arts work for Hackney Council, which in those days sounded oppressively politically correct.

MR HARRY WADE

Outward appearance

A swollen cherub. Blond, pink cheeked, too big for the train. His huge shoulders push the woman next to him to one side. Conventional dark blue suit, blue-grey overcoat. Battered brief-case has papers scrunched into side pockets. Shifts and fidgets as he sits. His stare is blank and he is chewing the inside of his cheek.

Inside information

A rugby player. On the field he is swift, calculating, fierce. Almost everywhere else – passive and put upon. Works as a tracker for repair calls made by British Telecom. Hopeless at it and about to be made redundant. His mother bought the flat in Pimlico for him.

What he is doing or thinking

Nothing – until Passenger 14 smudges dirt from his shoe down Harry's stale suit. Harry still thinks nothing as his body knee-jerks.

'You do that again, you'll get a fucking knife in the ribs.' Harry stares at the boy, temporarily unmanned. Why would someone swear at him? He was the one who was kicked!

Then the rugby field takes over. Harry is fed up being confused, alarmed. He finds he has seized the little weasel, the little spiv, and ground him like a pretzel against the dividing panel. He sees fear in the little spiv's eyes. He sees him scuttle away, suddenly small. Confused again, Harry feels he has done a wrong.

He thinks about his mother, his childhood. Nothing since then has really made sense. From somewhere deep inside him comes the thought: I want to be a farmer. He sees himself wind-blown on a green slope, looking for lambs.

MRS MINERVA NICHOLAS

Outward appearance

An older woman, face creased by continual despair. She is too short for the seats – the tips of her thick soft blue shoes only just reach the floor. She is an odd combination of the academic and the prosperous. A silver eagle brooch is pinned to her cloth coat, a Hermès scarf splashes pink and black across the collar. She looks as if she were hypnotized, concentric circles of flesh around her eyes.

Inside information

Lives in Marlow. Husband is a Head Teacher in High Wycombe. He takes the car; she has the commute, getting up at 6.00 every morning. The cushioned shoes help with the walk to the station. Works for a mental health charity in Lower Marsh.

What she is doing or thinking

She is remembering a dream from this morning. She dreamt that her house was in Bosnia. She was serving supper, carrying in a dish of Brussels sprouts, her husband sitting at the table.

Something was thrown through the window. In her dream she knew it was a bomb full of ball bearings. She flung herself back into the kitchen; there was a crackling of fireworks.

She can still hear the noises her husband made – like cricket balls dropped into custard, and a horrible dog-like yelp that rose to a squeal. The sudden silence afterwards told her that her unattractive but decent husband was dead.

That is what Bosnia is like. It is real. And now someone has threatened to knife the man sitting next to her. She feels delicate, shivery and wants to get off the train.

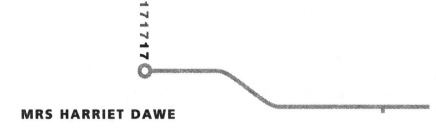

MRS HARRIET DAWE

Outward appearance

Extremely tired woman in her thirties. Bumfreezer black jacket over a bright red dress with white polka dots. Red shoes. Dead blonde hair.

Inside information

Works as a fully qualified masseuse in a Soho basement. Her boss is an older woman with a smoky voice . . . 'We have a *lovely* girl here . . .'

Fat, unshaven Mediterranean men walk in, see two older women and walk out again. Police come for payoffs. Tricks get threatening. Harriet likes doing old gents best; she feels kindness for them and nothing else.

Last night her sixteen-year-old son came in. She heard his voice and her heart stopped. He doesn't know about her job.

She stayed hidden in a curtained room with a handsome, brutish Aussie. She was towelling her hand when she heard Charlotte call, 'You still busy, love?'

'Mmm hmmm,' Harriet said, disguising her voice. She heard curtains close. The trick growled at her, she let him go and stayed hidden. Afterwards, she peered between the curtains and saw only her son's back. Tall, skinny, alone. She wished he had a nice girlfriend instead.

'Fancied the Aussie, did you?' was all Charlotte said. Harriet stared at her over their usual morning cup of coffee and thought: you've had my son.

What she is doing or thinking

What does she do now? She can't go back. There is a Sauna Centre near Lambeth North. That's a bit too close to home – her son would never go there. Harriet decides very suddenly to change venue. Maybe they're still open. She gets off at Waterloo, instead of the Elephant.

MR TONY COLLEY

Outward appearance

Worn, but otherwise well turned out. Coiffed and tinted hair. Dark coat over black pressed trousers. Large case at his feet. Reading *The Daily Express*. A playing card peeks out from his cuffs, and the bag stirs uneasily, all by itself.

Inside information

A magician on a cross-Channel ferry. There is a live rabbit in the bag.

What he is doing or thinking

Pretending not to notice the ship's piano player, Passenger 11, who also sits in the carriage. He tries to absorb himself in news of Camilla Parker-Bowles's divorce. He vaguely identifies with her; he suffers a similar sense of exposure, of ageing, of being in the wrong place at the wrong time. Nothing beats getting a card trick wrong in front of a bored seven-year-old. Nothing beats a set of hardened eyes which plainly say: did we ask you to come to our table and do tricks with coloured scarves?

If it were possible to live in complete good faith, he would tell management that it doesn't work, people don't want a magician. But he needs the money. He has a beautiful little daughter. He never sees her, bounding back and forth from France in a French boat. He hates the fatty food, the iced prawns, the language.

He is suddenly aware of a scuffle further up the row of seats: some bully picking on a little fellow. Life's too short, he thinks.

Then he knows: today he will get off at Waterloo, and turn around, and go home to his daughter. Then he knows that he won't.

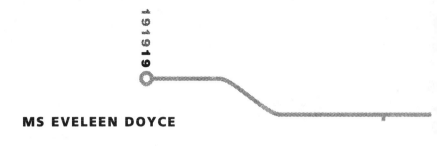

MS EVELEEN DOYCE

Outward appearance

Large black woman over whom gravity has no power. She appears to have been pasted on the seat by computer imaging. All in black, except for a cap edged with gold braid. Her face beams in steady contentment.

Inside information

Made redundant by British Telecom two years ago. Pregnant with her second child. Going to Elephant and Castle Shopping Centre to collect a stereo system. She bought it on credit by claiming she was still on pregnancy leave. They asked for references and she gave her old BT boss, a batty female accountant. The woman must have taken a shine to Eveleen. She told a fib.

Eveleen has a mad, one-armed stepfather who wants to kill her. He phones her day and night to threaten her. The idea of him, one-armed, trying to do her in makes her laugh. She roars at him down the telephone, even at one in the morning.

What she is thinking or doing

A scuffle breaks out. Eveleen frowns in amusement and delicately scratches her head. These white people, she thinks. They are so selfish and it just makes them crazy. The whole world is crazy, spinning round and round. She thinks of her brother who tried to slash the seats at McDonalds. The seats at McDonalds are so hard that people won't sit for long. The seats don't slash, but her brother always keeps on with whatever he's doing. He was still slashing when the police arrived.

This mad world pleases Eveleen, leaves her content. If she were to die right now, she wouldn't mind.

MRS JOY HARVEY

Outward appearance
Polished black woman. Huge coils of hair, like someone out of *Dynasty*. Burgundy business jacket, yellow sweater. She looks enraged and keeps pulling down on her sweater.

Inside information
Works in a one-stop shop for the Council. Today her mobile surgery will be held at the Wasteco Superstore in the Elephant and Castle. The surgery was set up to provide information about local events and the Council's activities. But people want services instead of information. Joy has become a one-stop advocate for the illiterate who have received a final Council Tax demand, the aged who aren't claiming benefit, the young men who can't get a council flat, people who can't get their rubbish collected. Etc.

What she is doing or thinking
She is looking at the obviously homeless man next to her. She deliberately sat next to him in case no one else would. She takes in his stained, rumpled trousers; the tiny woman's coat; the thin shirt; the shoes with white water marks. Poor man, look, he's shaved and washed. He's spent money to clean himself up and he probably could have used it for food. Look at people, wrinkling their noses at him. Aren't they horrible.

'Are you all right?' she asks. He looks around at her in misery. 'Are you all right?' she asks again, touching her new purse.

'No, no,' he pleads, holding up his hands. 'I don't need anything.'

Good, she thinks, that's good. Pride. She receives an energizing jolt of anger that will see her through another day. She pulls down again on her sweater.

MR JUSTIN HOLMES

Outward appearance

Homeless person – ill-fitting, flimsy clothes. His coat is orange with black fur trim, and is too small for him. The shirt is thin summer cotton and is missing a button, showing his pale tummy. His hair is curious – it is disordered but layered.

Inside information

Freelance journalist posing as a homeless person. He has spent the last week in the concourse under Waterloo Bridge round-about. Slept two nights in a cardboard box with an older long-hair who made a pass at him but was easily deflected. Moved to a doorway in the Strand. Last night spent some of the money hidden in his shoe to shower in Waterloo Station. Went home. His flat was dark and locked. The porter came with spare keys. The locks had been changed.

Justin is now homeless for real. He will wash again at Waterloo and go to Lambeth North police station.

What he is doing or thinking

He remembers his girlfriend's face. 'You can borrow my old coat, but don't expect me here when you get back,' she told him. He has no i.d., no keys, no plastic and only five pounds left. When has he ever been fingerprinted? How can you prove who you are?

The woman next to him is talking. He looks around. 'Are you all right?' she asks, about to give him money. A terrible sense of fraudulence comes over him, and he pleads with her to put away the money, the sympathy.

He remembers his girlfriend's face, and understands. He wants to go home.

He thinks of his article.

MR TONY MANNOCCHI

Outward appearance
Worn, sallow, a bit beaky with deeply sunken eyes. Thin lips held in a permanent smile. Thick blue coat still zipped up, maroon sweater showing under cuffs. Hair combed across bald patch. Plays with a heavy set of keys.

Inside information
Proprietor of Roma Fine Wines near Waterloo. It has recently gone bankrupt. His son and his new wife were to inherit the business in a few months' time.[7]

What he is thinking or doing
He is meditating on how everything is replaced, most especially people. There was a time when he would make this same journey and know half the faces – customers, vendors from the market on Lower Marsh or the train station, or just people on the train. He can close his eyes and see 1964. The Brylcreemed hair, the haze of tobacco, a certain kind of hatchet English face that has gone. The jokes, people used to joke all the time in London, it was what kept you going. Replacement people, a bit like pets. One dies, you buy another one for Christmas.

They've torn the heart out of this area. The GLC used to be full of customers, now it's vast and empty, soon to be Japanese. That big office block next to Lambeth North, it was full of very well-spoken people who always bought wine. Even the OPP, that's much smaller now, and not what it was. Dark, dark, we all go into the dark.

My son says, 'What am I going to do?' I'm going to tell him. Get yourself a gimmick. And replace someone.

Another helpful and informative
253 *footnote*
7 In autumn 1996, the shop was still empty. In autumn 1997 it became an Afghanistani grocery.

MISS YOSHI KAMIMURA

Outward appearance

White bulky jacket, lime green trousers, white trainers, pink hair grip. Balances on her lap a glossy pink bag with green polka dots and a plastic shopping bag crammed full of books and papers.

Inside information

Studying English at Bruenwalt International College. Yoshi is now pregnant, addicted to heroin, and moving into her new boyfriend's flat near Elephant and Castle.

What she is doing or thinking

Yoshi lives in a dream. For her nothing in Britain is real – it is outside Japan. There are Italian fascists in the dorm. They hold pissing competitions in their rooms. She made friends with Swiss students. They stayed out late – until 11.00 PM – and sang in raucous voices on Waterloo Bridge. 'London is a wild town,' announced a goggle-eyed Swiss girl. Oh, thought Yoshi. One is wild in London.

In all innocence, she tried everything. She is going to have an Italian fascist's baby. She cannot pronounce his first name and does not know his last. Her new boyfriend has many flats, and she has already turned her first trick for him. But he loves her.

She told all this to the College counsellor who stared at Yoshi for a moment with wide blue eyes and then passed her a pink business card with Japanese lettering. It offered a Japanese counselling service. 'This happens a lot,' said the counsellor.

The touch of Japan was like a hot hand on a frosted window. Everything melted for a moment and Yoshi could suddenly see clearly. Now she wants frost everywhere, on the dark windows of London Underground.

MR CLIVE KELTON

Outward appearance
Fit, middle-aged man. Grey, short hair. Sharp face, no jowls.
Wears new, all-black, casual clothes. Fast asleep.

Inside information
Works in Bathroom Paradise, a massive showroom of fixtures
and fittings located in railway arches near Waterloo. Clive was
once a hippy, living in Devon. He started fitting kitchens to
make money. There was not enough of it in rural Devon. He
moved to London, and ended up in Paradise.

What he is doing or thinking
He is meditating. Over and over he mentally repeats a mantra –
'I-ying-I-ying-I-ying'. This develops concentration and releases
tension. It needs releasing: pain and anger coil in his breast. His
wife feels trapped and lonely and bored and doesn't understand
why they moved back to the Smoke. His two children miss
horses and downs. They don't admit it, but they are afraid of
some of the children in their school.

His boss has it in for him. Clive does not live the Bathroom
Paradise Promise – A Perfect Fitting Every Time. The stuff is too
cheap, it's never in stock. Most people buy their taps or their
shower heads and pay someone they know to install them. Clive
worries how long there will be a job for him.

Only here, on the tube, does he have any time to himself, time
to rest. Then across from him someone growls '. . . you'll get a
fucking knife in the ribs.'

The mantra is broken. He opens his eyes to see two men staring at each other. One of them flees.

What am I doing here? he thinks. Could we go back?

MR ALFRED CUSHWAY

Outward appearance

Ageing male model. Every hair in place, immaculate coat thrown open, brown and black Italian jacket, loosely hanging trousers. The face is handsome, dead in the water, baggy-eyed.

Inside information

An executive at Mosstains. Has not worked on a building site since his twenties. Moved into sales, then account management, dealing with customers. Has a family, a house near Ely, Cambridgeshire. Collects art and antiques. Beats his children uncontrollably.

What he is doing or thinking

Alf has started drinking again and is battling the cloud of hangover across his forehead. He knows he shouted at the kids last night, but is sure, sure that he did not hit them. At least, he can't remember it.

Why does he lose his temper with them? He never does with anyone else. He loves them, gets frustrated by them. They can't hit back.

It's the one flaw in his perfect life; he can feel it like a crack across his face.

There is a bit of argy-bargy. Alf chuckles to himself, some poor kid has bitten off a bit more than he can chew. He looks at the boy's brown jacket, green tie. No dress sense.

Then the chuckle dies. That's me, Alf recognizes, that's me at the same age. He remembers his wedding photograph: transparent mauve shirt, long hair like a truck driver in drag. The embarrassed, grateful eyes.

It's Vauxhall, he thinks. All my life I've been trying to get away from Vauxhall, but it follows me. Hard, sad Vauxhall. Alf looks at the kid and knows: he'll hit his children too.

MR PAUL HENNESSEY

Outward appearance

Near retirement. Impish face with folds of sallow flesh. Watery eyes, a head of snow-white hair. Reading *The Guardian*, folded down to a column's width to keep it in control.

Inside information

Runs the purchasing department of Dun and Old. Member of the Institute of Professional Purchasers. Author of *Tightening the Screws: Purchasing Secrets of Japanese Business*. Commutes from Haywards Heath and writes his books on British Rail.

What he is doing or thinking

He is not reading the paper, but thinking of his wife, Elisabeth. She is 55 and has gradually given up all her interests. Instead of working with the Sunday School, she says, 'They don't want some old lady.' She no longer goes to her art classes – 'I've stopped getting any better.' She only half finishes books and ducks out of bridge evenings.

Their daughter now lives in Cork. She came over for Christmas with their first grandchild. Oh, he is a bouncy babe, blue eyes, a face like an apple. A light of recognition came into his eyes whenever he saw his Gran. He needed to be burped, talked to, petted, tucked in, changed. He kicked and shrieked with laughter. She played for hours with his chewable blue train. Choo choo. Choo choo.

Now they've gone back home to Ireland and his wife is bereft. It's two weeks since they left. Paul came downstairs this morning and saw Elisabeth sitting at the kitchen table in her dressing gown, cradling empty air.

A crazy idea comes to him. Could they adopt? The train slows. He puts the newspaper away.

MS DANNI JARRET

Outward appearance

Alarming. Bright red pantsuit, workman's donkey jacket. Black T-shirt on which Pooh appears to be buggering Piglet. Writing with a pencil in a notebook, and giggling to herself.

Inside information

Works by day for the Department of Health, Elephant and Castle. By night she is a comedian, billed as The Stand Up Civil Servant. She is writing new material. She writes each routine only once, in very clear block capitals, using pencil so she can erase and rework.

What she is doing or thinking

She is aware that the woman next to her is reading over her shoulder and is stiffening with shock.

This is providing Danni with a great deal of inspiration. Sammy the Sperm Cell has just discovered that he's been shot up someone's arse and has been making love to a turd. Danni then asks the audience: have you ever been up someone's arsehole? Tastes terrible, doesn't it? First time I did it, I went home and stuck my face in a bucket of Flash. Whenever I do it now, I get a Flashback. Ho ho.

At that point, her pencil breaks. Sammy will have to wait. It has been great fun shocking someone, but she really needs to write in pencil. Danni stands up to get off at Waterloo and buy a pencil at W. H. Smith. She passes her neighbour, who looks about 50 and is almost certainly a virgin. In a moment of inspiration, Danni pushes her neighbour's nose like a button. 'You keep sticking that in funny places, it'll get bitten off,' she promises.

MISS FLORA McCARDIE

Outward appearance
Looks like an athletic boy with freckles, reddish hair and bags under his eyes. In fact, a fifty-year-old woman in sensible clothes.

Inside information
Works for Christian Aid on Lower Marsh Street. The happiest period of her life was spent in Gabon with an American evangelical mission. Heartbroken when she learned that its charismatic leader was siphoning off funds. Returned to the UK middle-aged and at a loss.

Currently mourning the loss of her good friend, Lavender. Lavender was 75 years old, and produced vowel sounds that have disappeared everywhere else. Lavender was a friend of Flora's guardian and saw Flora through childhood, giving her the nickname Poppet.

Lavender died old, cold, alone. Flora has begun to see a kind of tribe; a chain of steadfast, upright, noble, unloved women.

What she is doing or thinking
She thinks of Lavender as she reads what the girl next to her writes. Poor Lavender, with her faith in decency, progress. Here is an apparently intelligent young woman writing in such a tidy, careful hand such terrible things. I'm worthless, it seems to say, you're worthless, here, eat this.

The girl gets up, and in the thickness of her body Flora sees part of the chain. Then the girl pushes Flora's nose, and insults her. Flora tuts and tosses her head, then remembers that she gets out here too.

On the platform Flora reaches forward and stops the girl and demands: 'Why did you do that to me?' The girl's face is blank for a moment.

Then they begin to speak.

MRS HELEN BALE

Outward appearance
Faded English rose. Merry face, rather rural looking with pink cheeks, long nose, tiny mouth. No make-up. Beige and black scarf, thick sweater, gloves held to her wrists by cords. Home-knitted. She looks upward at something, smiling as if having seen the Light.

Inside information
A mature nursing student doing a study at St Thomas' Hospital[8] into aspects of alternative medicine.

What she is doing or thinking
She is trying to decipher an Oranjboom ad. Along with *Poetry on the Tube*, they are the only objects of interest among the usual January package holiday ads. The joke is that the slogan looks Dutch, until you work it out.

> *Druifes u tooi*
> *Dis traag schone*
> *dous ent et?*

In the back of her mind, her study seems similarly disjointed. Helen has not been able to identify enough patients with similar conditions to be separated into control groups – let alone to discount variables such as age and general health. She is in touch with an American hospital doing similar work, but they are suddenly being difficult about releasing their data. Perhaps they think she is a crank. Or just a nurse.

She tries sounding out the Oranjboom slogan without looking for meaning. It suddenly swims into focus.

> *Drives you to*
> *distraction*
> *doesn't it?*

Helen smiles. Part of the joke is working so hard for an answer that means nothing. She is beginning to accept that her study may not work. Still smiling, she waits for others to pass before standing up to exit at Waterloo.

Not everyone will get it, says the punchline.

Another helpful and informative **253** *footnote*

8 St Thomas' Hospital, according to Christopher Hibbert, dates from 1106, and was named after St Thomas after 1173. It has a long history of fire, rebuilding, re-opening, and re-naming. Dick Whittington, of the old story, added a chamber to it, and noted that it was for young women who had done amiss. For a time, the hospital had a bawdy reputation. It did not have a physician until 1556. The founder of its sister hospital Guy's, Thomas Guy, also part-funded St Thomas' for a time.

In 1859, the site was acquired by the Charing Cross Railway Company for London Bridge Station. A new site for the hospital was found next to Westminster Bridge and the new buildings opened in 1871. Florence Nightingale approved the plans and established there the Nightingale School of Nursing.

The Florence Nightingale Museum opened in 1989 and features in a small space an impressive exhibition of photographs, letters, and exhibits which bring to life exactly what Nightingale accomplished.

Some of the old, grand, towered hospital buildings were bombed in World War II. Others remain, walled off from the riverside walk. A new, airy building stands just south of the Bridge, with a pleasant modern fountain, which is sometimes switched on. It may not have a bawdy reputation, but personal experience suggests that a lot of romance still took place within living memory in the nurses' quarters.

A justly award-winning example of new media exists in the consultants' clinic dealing with rheumatism and other bone diseases. An information kiosk, designed to look like a living-room TV, gently, and with immense tact, helps people understand the implications of their diagnosis. Designed by Dr Julia Schofield in association with a hospital consultant.

BOB 'THE KNOB' HALL

Outward appearance
Skinny seventeen-year-old in black satin jacket with the Nintendo grinning face logo. Jeans, boots. He sits slung across the seat, open legged, his Walkman hissing nervous, rattling drum and bass.

Inside information
Studying print technology at the London College of Printing, Elephant and Castle. On his way to his first class. No books or papers.

What he is doing or thinking
Bob listens to Dub Culture while eyeballing the tightly crossed ski pants of Passenger 6. Latin pussy, yum. He can see the perfect brown flesh, the slit, the hair; he can almost taste it. Shame she's got her boyfriend with her. Number 8's a bit past it and has no tits, but a woman in leather must be a bit pervy. Though the dog would probably get in the way. So it's all the way back to Passenger 12. Blonde. She looks like a bloke, but she's got nice skin. I bet she's brown all the way down. Sunlamps and oil. He can feel her skin under his fingertips, smooth with a layer of fat just underneath the surface.

His cock is wet. He has a shift of affections towards himself. Wanking when you want a fuck is boring, but when you want a wank, there's nothing better. He calculates. Can he stand going through the morning before having a wank? He hates doing it at school, he always thinks people can hear under the partitions.

Suddenly he decides: the clean marble loos at Waterloo. The train slows and he stands up. You're only young once, he thinks.

MR MAURICE HAZLETT

Outward appearance
A distinguished businessman on holiday. Double chinned, grey haired, but in anorak and blue jeans mismatched with heavy brown brogues.

Inside information
A retired intelligence agent who worked for MI5 when its offices were in Lambeth North. Has come up from the country without his wife to help their daughter move. On a sentimental journey to see his old haunts. In the 1940s, he was a lover of Donald Maclean. Many other secrets. He would be pleased to see Passenger 22 from whom he used to buy wine.

What he is doing or thinking
Remembering the old days. The Russian 'export shop' across the road. Spooks would wave to each other in the mornings. The church tower nearby had a pair of nesting kestrels that returned to it every year. All of MI5 birdwatched through their mirrored windows. It was a dull life in a way.

Why am I doing this? he thinks. Everything's closed, the bookshop, the Turkish grocers. Nothing left.

Maurice also remembers the smell of underarms, cigarettes, white linen. Embracing one of the great traitors of the century in a blackout. You gave no sign in those days, it was secret, you were never sure until the very moment you kissed male stubble.

There is a cottage in the toilets at Elephant and Castle. He is, after all, off his leash today – Jenny need never know. He has an image of a young well-spoken man, rather like himself, or Don.

He heads on towards the cottage at the end of the line, unaware that it too has been closed.

MR WILLIAM DYNHAM

Outward appearance

A more mischievous Tony Blair. Impeccable blue suit, grey coat, burnished black shoes, new briefcase. He sprawls relaxed, hiding a grin behind a hand.

Inside information

A Euro MP for a Midlands constituency which he had never visited before becoming a candidate. Lives in the Chitterns, has a flat in London. His parents are decent middle-class people from Kent.

William became a Euro MP to make money. He has. Previous careers include being a bicycle messenger, teacher of English in the Philippines and a professional lobbyist for the Small Bosses Syndicate. Has an appointment at 9:00 with the new Director of the SBS, Passenger 106.

Most people think William went to Oxford and was a businessman. He has one O level. Everyone believes everything William says. For a while.

What he is doing or thinking

He is savouring the uncommon experience of travelling on public transport. He enjoys looking at the people.

For example, he decides Passenger 11, the cross-Channel pianist, is an off-duty policeman because of his black trousers and blue shirt. Passenger 4, the grinning werewolf, is plainly a recipient of Care in the Community, and will be discovered to be a serial killer. William fears that Passenger 5, the broadcaster, may be a constituent. The face is familiar. William has a tendency to forget their names.

Suddenly, down the carriage there is some unpleasantness. A fight! Entranced by the richness of life around him, William reluctantly stands up to go. He has an appointment. Why does he find such things so boring these days?[9]

Another helpful and informative
253 *footnote*
9 William's sense of mischief and adventure could not be restrained by a respectable job for long. In autumn 1996 he announced, as a Euro MP, that he was going to stand as an MP for Sir James Goldsmith's anti-Europe Referendum Party.

MS DEIRDRE HIDDERLEY

Outward appearance
Black crushed-velvet jacket under a coat with a ring of fake fur round the hood. Wiry red hair pulled fiercely back. Round pouting face like Shirley Temple. Headphones, a whisper of classical music. She opens her eyes, closes them, opens them.

Inside information
Arts/music student at Merely College. Lives with her parents in Stratford.

What she is doing or thinking
She is mourning the gradual loss of her synaesthesia. Synaesthesia is a medical condition in which one sense triggers a response in another. Until a month ago, Deirdre could see sound.

The opening of the tube doors used to send delicately coloured soap bubbles wafting through the carriage. The rattling smear outside the windows would trail floating oranges and melted-wax bobbles of purple. The sound of people talking evoked bright, jagged, jerking shapes of yellow, blue, green.

Deirdre's fear is that all modern art has been derived from synaesthesia. Kandinsky, Auerbach, Bacon were synaesthetic, she is sure. She felt like a member of a secret society. Deirdre was never good at school (she is also mildly dyslexic). But she could sing and paint. She now fears that her talent will go, along with the thing that made her special. It is as though part of her had died.

Even music no longer works. She snaps off the Walkman. She begins to hum a tune. She becomes aware of it, something sad, graceful, expressing loss. Whose is it? It's modern, but it's not Pärt or Tavener or Glass.

It's hers. Emotion has been converted into music. She fumbles for a pen.

MRS ADELE DRISCOLL

Outward appearance
Professional woman in crisp blouse, pleated grey skirt, brown coat. Glasses as big as windows with transparent frames. Longish, curved, tinted hair.

Inside information
Works as a Personal Financial Adviser at Lloyds Bank, York Road. Originally from Melbourne, Australia. Today she is returning to work after two weeks' jury service.

What she is doing or thinking
'Interesting case?' people ask her brightly. It was rape. She remembers the man's heavy, thuggish face and the prickle in the air when the charge was announced. The victim, a fourteen-year-old black girl, stood straight, proud, small-voiced. She had been terrorized into going into his flat, too afraid to fight or cry out. Adele felt hatred.

Then the psychiatrist testified. The thug is simple minded, with verbal skills that disguise that he cannot understand the most basic social signals. Afterwards, he had asked the girl if he could see her next Sunday. He was a virgin too. Something he denied in a stumbling voice as tiny and uncertain as the girl's.

But in police tapes, he was a different man: sly, ugly, playing games with the interviewers. 'Yeah, I get around a bit. She didn't look fourteen, know what I mean?'

What was true? Who to believe? To be guilty of rape, he must be in a condition to know what he was doing: when did the girl say no?

God help them, the verdict was not guilty. There was a woman in the court every day. Was she his mother? When the verdict was read, the woman nodded once, yes.

Yes what?

MISS MARIE BREATNACH

Outward appearance

About 22, black hair pulled behind her ears. A sprinkling of spots on her chin. Everything she wears is blue, like a school uniform. Stares at herself in a small hand mirror.

Inside information

Marie is from Northern Ireland and lives with her brother and his wife. She has a steel plate in her head. She was hit by a van when she was twelve cycling in a country lane.

She starts work today in the pay department of Railtrack, Waterloo Station. She forgot until reminded by her brother.

What she is doing or thinking

Marie has headaches and gets confused. She has a headache now. That means she's nervous. And she was such a brave child. She was cycling much faster than her friend Fee, and didn't see the van because she was looking back over her shoulder. She won the race.

She looks at her chin in the mirror and thinks: you'd never believe I used to have a beautiful complexion. Marie is unsure if she is pretty. She would really like to be told one way or the other. The face in the mirror doesn't look like the one she remembers.

She is sure they won't mind her being late in the new job. She will explain that she forgot today was the first day. Then she'll ask for a nice cup of tea.

The doors open and close. Through the window, the sign says Lambeth North. How many more stops to Waterloo? Marie gets out her map as the train gathers speed toward Elephant and Castle.

MR JASON LUVERIDGE

Outward appearance

Late teens, black male. Slumped in green baggy track suit, American sports jacket and baseball cap. Looks resentful, staring ahead.

Inside information

Going to the South Bank Technology Park near the Elephant.

Jason's mother saved enough money to send one of her children to St Paul's School.[10] This is resented by her other children who make fun of him when he wants to hear classical music or watch *Panorama*. He still thinks his mother made the right decision. Jason is academically gifted and wants to study computer science.

Jason's clothes are camouflage. He expects to wear camouflage all his life.

What he is doing or thinking

Jason has been struck with love for Passenger 3, Deborah Payne. He does not know that he will always be attracted to older women. All he knows is that she looks pretty, clever, concerned. He is already dreaming of marriage to her. A wife like that would show what he was – smart, caught between worlds. She's not some daft Sharon, or prejudiced. She'd be too business-like for that. She's what I want, he realizes. A business woman with soul.

He follows Deborah out into Waterloo Station. He is heartsick, hands jammed into his pockets, knowing she would find this creepy.

Then she stops a man on the platform and cries, 'You don't need to die!' Wow. That does it, this woman is special.

'Excuse me,' says Jason. 'I don't normally do this, I'm shy. But. Can I ask you out?' The man and woman stare at him, open-mouthed.

Another helpful and informative
253 *footnote*
10 St Paul's School was, according to Christopher Hibbert, founded in 1509 by the Dean of St Paul's Cathedral. It was at that time the largest school in the country. It had all of 153 students.

It continues its tradition of egalitarianism. It opened its first building in Hammersmith (see footnote to Passenger 10) in 1884, and the school moved south of the river to Barnes in 1968. Famous pupils include John Milton, Samuel Pepys, Field-Marshal Montgomery and G. K. Chesterton. These are healthily outnumbered by pupils who are not famous in any way.

The little second-hand experience I have of it suggests that it was in the late 1980s a great introduction to the rave scene.

MR RICHARD TOMLINSON

Outward appearance

Stocky, middle-aged man, athletic build. Rumpled pink face with pure white hair. Blue jeans, anorak, woolly red hat. He seems lost in thought.

Inside information

He is returning from hospital having failed to convince them to let him die. This is his second bout of pneumonia and he has survived three suicide attempts. One left him in a wrecked car, sick but alive, in the pouring rain at one in the morning. None of his friends know he is ill – except one, Passenger 235, who withdrew from him in fear and disgust. Richard lost heart after that.

What he is doing or thinking

Dying is a full-time job. Politics never let up. Richard had the support of one doctor but, after a battery of interviews, they decided to offer him two more years of declining life.

Richard's anger at the hospital is cold, shaped by logic. It is not for them to tell him that he must live. They have not had anal herpes that feels like a lighted match on an open wound. They have not had the giddy spells, the eye infections, the thrush. As far as possible he wanted a normal life. That is no longer possible.

The best they could do is let him go home. Despite his size, he is very weak and cannot breathe. He has just enough strength left to walk from the tube, and draw the curtains and listen to Mozart and let the pneumonia blossom. An answering machine will take all his calls.

He goes on to Elephant and Castle.

For Your Reading Ease and Comfort

PASSENGER MAP

Car No 2

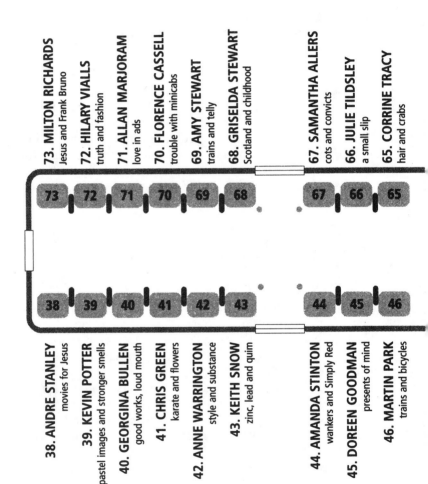

73. MILTON RICHARDS
Jesus and Frank Bruno

72. HILARY VIALLS
truth and fashion

71. ALLAN MARJORAM
love in ads

70. FLORENCE CASSELL
trouble with minicabs

69. AMY STEWART
trains and telly

68. GRISELDA STEWART
Scotland and childhood

67. SAMANTHA ALLERS
cots and convicts

66. JULIE TILDSLEY
a small slip

65. CORRINE TRACY
hair and crabs

38. ANDRE STANLEY
movies for Jesus

39. KEVIN POTTER
pastel images and stronger smells

40. GEORGINA BULLEN
good works, loud mouth

41. CHRIS GREEN
karate and flowers

42. ANNE WARRINGTON
style and substance

43. KEITH SNOW
zinc, lead and quim

44. AMANDA STINTON
wankers and Simply Red

45. DOREEN GOODMAN
presents of mind

46. MARTIN PARK
trains and bicycles

64. MICHAEL LIPKIN
sex and scripture

63. OLIVER MASKEY
last night's burglar

62. MARY AL-MASUD
cats and bigamy

61. MICHAEL JEROME
shoes and snooze

60. DIMITRI BELINKOV
Gin and tonic

59. IGOR KLIMOV
tonic and gin

58. RICHARD MAYO
jobs and slander

57. MAGGIE ROLT
love and capital

56. SAVI GUPTA
fate and mannequins

| 64 | 63 | 62 | | 61 | 60 | 59 | 58 | 57 | 56 |

| 47 | 48 | 49 | | 50 | 51 | 52 | 53 | 54 | 55 |

47. ASHLEY WATKINS
pride and Tammy Wynette

48. OLIVIA PARSONS
last night's burglar

49. MARTIN BELCHER
performance parts

50. RALPH MOLES
courage and KY

51. AMINA KHATUN
sons and insurance

52. ANNIE JEANRENAUD
dead letter office

53. EVA SIMMONDS
beauty in the eye

54. BILLIE HOLIDAY
crossed lines, wrong signals

55. HARRY FREER
graffiti and dopplegangers

Become a writer in your spare time!

In just a few hours a day, you too can become a writer. 253 shows you how.

Every passenger in 253 has a number that is his or hers alone. And every section has 253 words. This means that: each character has his or her own word in *every* section.

Put all these words together – and you have made a monument to your favourite 253 character.

Here's how it works. . .

Let's take passenger number 9, Mr Keith Olewaio.

All you have to do is take the 9th word from each section. If you put together Keith's words for Car One only, it reads like this:

> *Even under short suit sits and of carefully jokes his black brown make brown big she jacket tinted power someone is eyes pink face long face T his rural track haired grey with open ears jacket very.*

Surrealistic!

Do that for each of the seven cars, and you will have a new 253-word section in honour of Mr Keith Olewaio. In the privacy of your own home, you will have:

> * *treated words as things,*
> * *moved them into place*
> * *and counted them.*

That is all that writers do! That's all there is to it. Try it next time you want to write a business letter or instructions for the general public. Write a poem and see if it really is any different from the 253 method. You'll have a fun hobby and will impress your friends. But remember, the one thing you will not do is

Earn big £££££!!!!!

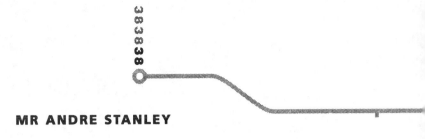

MR ANDRE STANLEY

Outward appearance
Ageing football coach? American letterman's jacket with beige sleeves, black trunk. OSHKOSH INDIANS it announces, NUMBER 22. White Levis jeans, white socks, black shoes, salt and pepper hair, healthy pink complexion. A young person into retro fashion would kill to know where Andre finds his clothes.

Inside information
A minister from an Episcopalian diocese in Wisconsin on a theological fact-finding mission. Andre is particularly bemused by the debate about gay priests. Why the fuss? There are none.

Andre served in Vietnam. He is baffled by all the talk of post-traumatic stress disorder. He piloted helicopters and saw the worst the war had to offer – the blasted bodies of young men – but he has no trouble accounting for the deaths, the destruction. God leaves everyone free, everyone responsible, even Nazis. We are free to wage mistaken wars, mistranslate the Bible, or commit rapes. And we are free to fight back.

Andre wants to write screenplays for Jesus . . . and reclaim the media from barnstorming fundamentalists. He is working on a screen treatment now, about helicopter pilots in Vietnam.

What he is doing or thinking
Trying not to breathe. The man next to him stinks beyond belief. It is an inhuman smell, very pungent, like scorched hops. It reminds Andre of his one visit to the Annhauser-Busch brewery in Los Angeles, which was like a sewer. Do all English people smell like this? Don't they ever wash? Maybe they just don't know about dry cleaning.

Then a woman says in exasperated, fruity tones: 'This is unbearable! Can't you use a deodorant?'

MR KEVIN POTTER

Outward appearance

John Carradine? Elongated, raffish, middle-aged man. An ill-fitting black overcoat. Its velvet collar arches up to his hair line. Bone-thin, hairy wrists. Young person's black, thick-soled shoes.

Inside information

Purchaser for Mosstains and closet novelist. Sits alone in his office and continually rewrites *Pastel Images*, a novel based on a love affair he had in 1967.

Kevin would not recognize himself under the lank grey hair. Being a kind of handsome and full of promise was part of his identity for so long that it comes as a shock to realize he is near retirement, without a published novel or even a chain of mistresses. As if his life were not complicated enough, under the black suit, he is wearing women's underwear.

What he is doing or thinking

Kevin wonders with hurt bafflement why his career has stalled. Colleagues avoid him; salesmen cancel appointments. His PA keeps her window wide open. The office is freezing. 'Do you have to keep the window open all the time?' he once asked. Her face was hard, strange. 'We need the air,' she replied. His nickname around the office is Rotten Fish. All of this is very hurtful. He is a sensitive, creative person.

To his horror the woman sitting next to him erupts, jowls quivering. 'This is unbearable,' she announces. 'Can't you use a deodorant? You smell like a bonfire of old rubber tyres!'

What is she talking about? Kevin can't help sniffing; he smells nothing. Insulted, hypnotized by shock, he stands to get off one stop early at Waterloo.

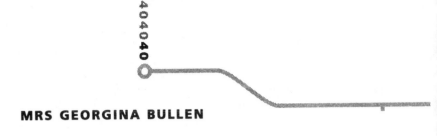

MRS GEORGINA BULLEN

Outward appearance
Rugged old type. Heavily made-up face seems about to smile grimly. Green jersey, grey skirt, clean sensible shoes. It is a surprise to see town shoes instead of green wellies.

Inside information
Her husband was a Captain in the Royal Navy, and turned around his destroyer to propose marriage. It was war time. Georgina now does work for charities and the church. She is a caring, conservative woman, whose heart sings at the thought of Mrs Thatcher, whom she regards as a great force for good brought down by the jealousy of those around her. Georgina devotes herself to church work, her decent romantic husband, and the memory of her one true love – a Pakistani lawyer she met in Quetta in 1941. She has no photograph of him.

Georgina is visiting Lambeth Palace[1] for a briefing on the issue of gays in the priesthood, and will have an embarrassing meeting in 20 minutes' time with Passenger 38. She will assume throughout that he is gay and will address him sympathetically on the subject.

What she is doing or thinking
Feels pity and horror for the man next to her – he may not even know that he stinks. She has stood it since Baker Street and now has a terrible headache. She explodes and says perhaps too much . . . something about burnt tyres.

The poor man flees and she feels terrible. Billows waft from the folds of his coat like a gas leak. Georgina feels the stench in the roots of her teeth.

She has to get off at Waterloo. With him.

Another helpful and informative
253 *footnote*
1 Lambeth Palace is the
Archbishop of Canterbury's official
residence. It is on the south bank,
but walled away from it, across the
main road. Part of its grounds are
now a public park, Archbishop's
Park, which was donated in 1900.

To most of the people who drive
past, aiming for the roundabout by
Lambeth Bridge, or who walk past,
choking on asbestos dust, the great
house might as well be invisible,
walled and churched-in as it is. The
Park is what they can use, with a
play area for children, and tennis
courts.

The Palace's great ecclesiastical
library has its roots in a bequest of
books in 1610 from an
Archbishop. From time to time, the
buildings survive riots – in 1640
from London apprentices or in
1780 by Gordon rioters.
Otherwise, for the most part, its
history is unbelievably dull.

MR CHRIS GREEN

Outward appearance
Shaved temples, dyed blond hair. Earring. White jacket and slacks, bovver boots. Broad-shouldered, slim-waisted. Looks healthy except for old tobacco-stained hands. Reading *Clive Barker's Books of Blood.*

Inside information
A qualified psychologist going for a job interview as a karate instructor at the Multi-Use Resource Centre, Lambeth North. Also rock-climbs and plays in a band.

Chris's last full-time job was in the Personnel Department of Hackney Council. His boss was another idiot. He thought the staff were depressed for psychological reasons. In Hackney? 'They're only depressed because they have to work for peanuts for you,' Chris told his boss and walked out. Then he sent the Mayor a letter detailing why staff hated working for the elected officials of both parties.

He now offers aromatherapy to clients he terrifies; classes in communication to computer geeks at whom he shouts. Saturdays he arranges flowers and delivers them to restaurants. He makes flowers look angry. His clients try to like them, but the exclamations of pleasure die in their throats. They are too frightened to complain.

At least people who learn karate will be more durable. He thinks.

What he is doing or thinking
The stench of Passenger 39 is like what Chris feels most of the time. Nothing works, and he is 34 years old. At college people clustered around him, in clubs everybody used to know him. He knows he's smart, strong, fast, clever. He knows he has something, but it always escapes him, and the world is run by fools whom he frightens.

It should be the other way around.

Outward appearance
Fuzzy black jacket, a sweater that is a work of art – blue, green, yellow angular patterns in different thicknesses of yarn. Red hair in a Beatle cut, green eye make-up, lipstick that matches her hair, tooled cowboy boots.

Inside information
Works as an administrator for the Florence Nightingale Museum, St Thomas' Hospital. Considers her skills to be in style and marketing. Member of the Health Museum Network, which has proved to be counter-productive.

What she is doing or thinking
She is fuming. Dun and Old, the accounting firm, are just across the street. For months Anne has been building a case for sponsorship: a venue for D&O visitors, exposure to the health market. Instead, the Museum of Dental Prosthetics has got the money. It's infuriating. It was Anne who told the dentists that D&O's Public Sector Manager had false teeth. They sent him a giant grinning set as part of their SMILE campaign and promised exposure on every leaflet.

When she first visited the Museum, Anne fell in love with the story of Florence Nightingale. Sad, alone, battling depression, Nightingale exposed a truth that no one else wanted to face: the British Army took everything it could from its men, and then discarded their wounded bodies like burnt bacon. Florence proved beyond doubt that the Army did not care, and that she did. She invented a profession.

Anne wanted to be part of that story. Rivalry and conniving were not what she meant. What next?

You could always, a voice says within her, become a nurse yourself.

MR KEITH SNOW

Outward appearance
Big, blond, soft-faced man in wire-rimmed spectacles and clean casual clothing – brown slacks, tan jacket. Carries a shoulder bag hugged by a grubby, grinning Garfield cat.

Inside information
Keith was meant for the priesthood until faced with a choice between A levels and the school rugby team. Chose the latter. Went to Hull Polytechnic instead of university, where he met and married his similarly religious, gentle wife. Now father of six tidy children.

At twenty-six, he was surprised to write a series of funny pornographic stories about an ancient Greek satyr loose in modern Britain. He rutted people's trouser cuffs. On the strength of the stories, Keith was offered the assistant editorship of *Exposed for Men*. Needed the money. Hated it. The walls were covered in fanny. He lied about his job. They offered him editor and he left. He couldn't face telling people he was fully responsible for Britain's leading dirty magazine.

What he is doing or thinking
Trying to feel the full happiness of his new job.

Keith is now the proud editor of *Zinc and Lead*, companion periodical to *Bibliographical Supplement on Mining*. It has modern offices on Lower Marsh: the walls are covered with mineral crystals. This fulfils an ambition; he studied mineralogy at Hull and often consulted the *Supplement*.

So he's happy, right? So why can he still see the satyr and his grin? Worse than that, Keith is sure suddenly that he can smell him, the goatish, ruttish musk.

He looks around, paranoia in his eyes. He is of course smelling Passenger 39.

MS AMANDA STINTON

Outward appearance

About 22, in black leather jacket and ski pants. Long hair tinged with henna. Her Walkman plays music loudly identifiable as *Simply Red*.

Inside information

Works in the Pay Unit of the Metropolitan Police HQ. Lives with her parents. Both she and her parents think of her as a wild hoyden. 'Fancy Amanda, working for the police,' says her mother, who dreams of her daughter doing all sorts of things she never did.

What she is doing or thinking

Amanda thinks about her affair with a married man in Maintenance. Gary is everything a man should be: masculine, a bit hard. She has to confess that the attraction is mostly sexual.

It was exciting in the beginning. You see this married man and you begin to think: I could have him. But much longer and she'll just be a little mistress, waiting for him to call.

Sunday was the worst. They were supposed to meet up at Gary's mate's. It was so humiliating. She showed up and Gary's friend opened the door and just said, 'Gary rang. He can't make it.' Then he said, 'I'm free as it happens.' Oh please. He's a horrible little wanker as well.

Mick Hucknall sings ... *Maybe some day, someone will come*. Amanda decides. It's going nowhere. She'll end it.

The woman across from her stands up. Oh wow, she's wearing one of those antique slips. People make a big thing about it, but it's just nice lacy material. Amanda salutes her for fashion bravery: more power to you, girl. She decides to do the same.

MRS DOREEN GOODMAN

Outward appearance

Tiny, elf-like black lady. Sits smiling in conservative blue clothes, teased up straightened hair, and padded shoes. On her lap, there is a parcel wrapped in purple with a lavender ribbon.

Inside information

Works in the Corporate Development Unit of the London Emergency Service[2] off Morley Street. The Unit was set up to market the Service after a series of management disasters, particularly a new computer system. A new logo, a Management Accounting System and stringent financial targets were put in place by the new manager, a failed banker. Doreen types her memos and drafts the letters to employees who have been made redundant.

Doreen has always been a quiet soul. She has a sweet slow husband, whose moustache is white and who has retired from his job as a security guard in a bank. They both miss the island they left as children. Doreen will retire soon and then they will go back home.

What she is doing or thinking

She is thinking of the present she has bought for her boss that sits so prettily on her lap. There is a card signed by the entire Unit. They all banded together to buy it, but it was Doreen's idea.

The boss is old, white haired, and knows only money. She has bought him for his birthday a fossilized turd.

It is probably from a bison or other bovine mammal, large, round in sections and petrified a beautiful smooth blue. He'll have to open it up in front of everyone. She can't wait until she sees his face. Birthday boy.

Another helpful and informative
253 *footnote*
2 There is no such thing as the London Emergency Service. I made it up. Think of it as a glorified ambulance service.

MR MARTIN PARK

Outward appearance
Thrusts himself into the carriage as if having beaten his way through bushes. Grey-green trousers crumpled where bicycle clips usually go. Heavy Aran sweater under a duffel-coat. Ill-advised greying beard. Carries a plastic bag full of books, and a bicycle seat. Accidentally hits Passenger 47 with it as he passes.

Inside information
Runs a bookstall along the Embankment in front of the National Film Theatre.[3] Last night found that his bicycle, ringed round with chains like tinsel on a Christmas tree, had had its seat stolen. He is bringing its replacement. The books in the bag are stock. Twenty years ago running a bookstall seemed romantic. In January, in biting winds with few customers, it is a fate that closes in. Last March he developed large purple welts across his face. The doctor said it was the ozone layer: standing outside in winter sunlight has become dangerous.

What he is doing or thinking
He cannot believe the pure hell that is London Underground. Due to the genius of British design, the way out and the way in for the Bakerloo platform at Embankment use the same tunnel. A thicket of blocked, bored people had taken root in it. His bicycle seat caught one woman's bag. She plainly thought he was a thief. Spinning around he trod heavily on a gentleman's foot. The man erupted: 'You people are ruining my shoes!'

'Hey man,' rumbles Passenger 47. He's big. 'Sorry,' says Martin, like a curse. 'Didn't mean it.'

He will arrive to find that, chained to the railings, only the bicycle wheels remain.

Another helpful and informative **253** *footnote*
3 The area of bookstalls is under the arches of Waterloo Bridge, sweeping off overhead across the river. This riverside walk is lined with trees. Joggers wobble past, children sit on the sculptures, and the National Theatre, looking like a temporary facility in a trailer camp, also fits neatly under the bridge, offering outdoor tables and food.

The National Film Theatre is one of the best repertory film theatres in London – though less adventurous than the ICA or than it used to be itself. Part of the British Film Institute, it is the central venue for the London Film Festival and the Gay and Lesbian Film Festival. It has a great bookshop and is attached to the Museum of the Moving Image, which honours television as well as film.

MOMI and the NFT form part of the riverside area called the South Bank. This horseshoe-shaped bend of the river contains the Royal Festival Hall, the Hayward Gallery, the Queen Elizabeth Hall, and on the other side of Waterloo Bridge, the Royal National Theatre and on to the new Tate Gallery in the old power station and the new Globe Theatre.

The Royal Festival Hall was built as part of the Festival of Britain. It is large, many floored and does free lunchtime concerts in its lower floor bar area, next to its free exhibitions. A good place to meet for lunch. Concerts of everything from Argentinian tangos, to Steve Reich, to Franz Liszt (which is what Passenger 53 is booking – her daughter will hate it).

I originally intended these footnotes to be full of bitchy misinformation designed to mislead. I keep losing heart and telling the truth. Losing heart is at the core of all artistic failure. I promise that some of the information in these footnotes will be deliberately, wilfully WRONG.

What other novel will make you that promise? Someone has to maintain standards.

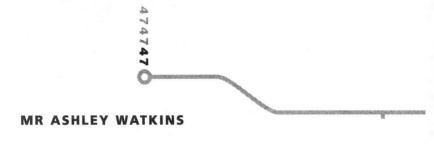

MR ASHLEY WATKINS

Outward appearance
Heavily set black man in woolly hat, army jacket and baggy blue jeans. Hair in braids down behind his head, tied in a pigtail. This looks slightly out of place with his age, bulk and general air of gravitas. Deeply lined hands rest on each knee. Passenger 46 bumps him with a bicycle seat and apologizes. 'Tch' says Mr Watkins, sucking on his teeth in disgust.

Inside information
Runs a stall in the bleak, windswept trench around the Elephant and Castle shopping centre. Everything Mr Watkins sells is black-themed: Egyptian papyrus, towels with leaders' portraits, books by Malcolm X and Louis Farrakhan, and tapes of lectures.

The stall really makes its money from soul, rap and dance cassettes, which he buys in bulk from a supplier who seems to have a limitless source of deleted albums.

What he is doing or thinking
Mr Watkins' dignity is affronted. His white supplier must have made a mistake or he's taking the piss. He is yet to have words. The last shipment of cassettes consisted almost entirely of the Tammy Wynette back catalogue. There were some George Reeves and Slim Whitman cassettes, nine copies of the *Ray Coniff Christmas Album* and two copies of *The James Last Sound Honours ABBA*. There was a single bargain basement collection of the worst of Teddy Pendergast. Mr Watkins does not drink or smoke; he does not pursue women. Women do not pursue him. He labours in the fields of pride, but there is not much harvest from the concrete plains of Elephant and Castle.[4] And even fewer laughs.

4. The Elephant and Castle shopping centre is one of the most beautiful buildings in London.

It is a prime example of the great favour Hitler did in bombing flat many of London's most historic areas. The opportunity to rebuild unleashed a diarrhoea of imaginative architecture.

Nothing in all of London quite takes away the breath like the Elephant. Its attractive maze of underground tunnels affords pedestrians safe passage under one of the most ruthless traffic interchanges in Europe plus ample opportunity for dog-emptying. The doggy results are often criss-crossed with skateboard tracks. Attractive murals mingle with the work of local graffiti artists.

Nothing can prepare the traveller for the first sight of the Shopping Centre itself. It is huge and painted a shade of pink that exists nowhere else in art or nature. Now attractively aged and peeling, it has acquired a patina of genuine London urban angst.

Delightfully set off by Alexander Fleming House, a building that has been closed for years because it made people sick. It used to house the Department of Health.

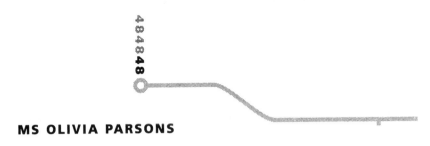

MS OLIVIA PARSONS

Outward appearance
Red-framed spectacles, a hearty plump face, mauve sweatshirt over stretch trousers and a quilted coat. Long, careless hair. Stares ahead of herself chewing abstractedly on one strand of it.

Inside information
A contract tutor and Apple operator at the South Bank Technology Park.[5] Olivia teaches Quark Xpress and Illustrator skills. Also works on the Park's money-making design and publications service.

What she is doing or thinking
Olivia is remembering the terror of the night before. She was working late on the University prospectus, when she heard a noise, a bit like one of the swing windows thumping against its frame. She thought no more of it. Then her door opened.

A young man in sweatshirt and baseball cap stood there. She had time to register that she did not know him. 'Oh shit,' he said, and left, quickly. She went on working for a few moments, and then realized that something was wrong. She stood up, went into the next studio. The backs of the machines were prized open. In one corner was a curl of turd. Her heart started to pound. It was 10.30 P M and she was alone. For some reason she ran back into her own studio before ringing the police. The first the security guard knew of it was when the police arrived.

For a full fifteen minutes, from the questioning, it was plain that the police suspected Olivia of helping. She now fears for her job. It would be so easy for them to cancel her contract, just in case.

And she can still smell the shit.

Another helpful and informative
253 *footnote*
5. To be honest, I'm not sure what the South Bank Technology Park is, except a huge brick building full of computers which I choose to believe is linked in some way to the University of the South Bank.

That is why anyone going to the Technopark could be linked to USB and vice versa.

Full marks to whoever had the balls to call a brick building by the Elephant a park.

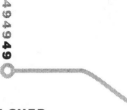

MR MARTIN BELCHER

Outward appearance
Stout, clear-complexioned man about 34, wearing quilted black and red motorcycle gear. Sits with his boot resting on the opposite knee, occupying a fair amount of space. Reading *The Independent.*

Inside information
Manager of Waterloo Spare Parts, a motorcycle supply store. Usually he motorcycles into work, but it's too cold today. The tube gives him a chance to read the paper.

What he is doing or thinking
Man U's paid *seven million* for Andy Cole! Lucky Geordie bastards . . . a Russian journalist has been expelled as a spy . . . Tony Blair having a go at the lefties over Clause Four. And Howard has sacked the Governor of Parkhurst jail after the escape and everyone says he's a scapegoat . . .

Martin reads with satisfaction. Yesterday, a real biker came into the shop. Officer class, posh, not pretentious, he wanted a spare part for a Kawasaki ZX. Martin had to laugh. 'Sorry, we do stuff for couriers . . . You know, little Hondas.' The guy had biked all the way across Soviet Asia to Mongolia. He was planning to bike up through California and the redwoods, up into Oregon. Martin ached with jealousy and gave him an address for high-performance parts.

Martin was just about to feel depressed when, outside the window, the guy looked both ways up the street then nipped into the massage parlour next door. Martin's jealousy burst like an ear infection. I suppose he's got performance parts, Martin thought. He grins, and goes back to his newspaper.

The Indy's got a competition for an Alfa Romeo Spider. Things could be looking up.[6]

Another helpful and informative
253 *footnote*
6 Unfortunately, by mid-1996, the shop was closed, replaced by a vintage clothing store that also moved quickly on. Maybe Martin took off for the redwoods after all.

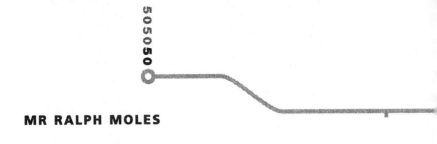

MR RALPH MOLES

Outward appearance
About 32, plaid shirt, no sweater, glossy bum-freezer in black vinyl with fake fur interior. An old-fashioned 1950s hat with earflaps. Retreating hair, thin face, a light beard, black boots.

Inside information
Works as a body-piercing specialist in *Courage*. This is not a brewery but a rubberware and fetish shop. It has a black shiny awning and rubber draperies across its front window. The shop used to be the neighbourhood butchers.

What he is doing or thinking
Ralph is still gently stoned from last night. Jamie showed off his new acquisition, yet another heavy ethnic earring hanging from his scrotum. Jamie works out at the YMCA, has shaved pubes and a spider's web tattooed over his designer-stubble chest. The spider sits on his tit. Stanley and Jane were discussing their investment in an exercise horse, over which to bend people.

For some reason Ralph was unmoved. He excused himself and tumbled into a bed with rubber sheets. Woke up clammy with sweat. Stumbled to the loo and tripped on a leather jock strap. Dazed by the lights, he tried to brush his teeth and found he'd used KY by mistake.

He's sick of everything smelling of old shoes. He now finds nothing sexy about nipple clamps, face masks, chains, diapers. Worrying about what else the kitchen grater might have been used for. Who needs any of it?

Ralph wants clean white Y-fronts and Hayley Mills fully clothed. How long will this alienation continue? It puts at risk his friendships, leisure pursuits, profession.

Is there a counsellor for this kind of thing?

MRS AMINA KHATUN

Outward appearance

A red and orange sari underneath a black coat. Hair enlivened with streaks of white. Dark circles under her eyes. She coughs over and over, hand covering her mouth. The eyes flicker back and forth about the carriage.

Inside information

Her son Imran manages a newsagent opposite Lambeth North tube. She is going to nurse it for him while he renews his passport.

What she is doing or thinking

Who are all these people? Mrs Khatun cannot identify a single customer or family member. She is unused to taking the Underground. Nearly always a cousin or a son will drive her.

Imran's shop is so sad. He has to leave it half-empty because of the insurance. Mrs Khatun likes a shop to be full, the racks bulging with colour. Milk, newspapers, and magazines the wholesalers force him to take are the only things left.

If only Imran would work, bring in business. Of all her sons, he does the least. If he wanted to be a computer programmer, then he should have studied. He still could study.

Instead, he is always going back to what he calls home. It may be home, but things are better here. It breaks Mrs Khatun's heart to see her boy, now fat, not handsome, dreamy, mismanaging the store and fleeing to Pakistan. Oh they make a fuss of him there, they think he is a rich businessman. She curses the insurance company, but what can she do? She coughs again. This cold has not gone, it will not go. It's been with her for years.

MS ANNIE JEANRENAUD

Outward appearance

Frizzle-haired, large lady of about 45 in a long batik dress and oatmeal jumper nearly to her knees. Rifles through a hessian bag. Pulls out a final warning in red, various tube passes, and a letter from a rumpled envelope.

Inside information

Teaches life drawing at Merely College. Loves it, economizes, eats little, remains large, and has many middle-aged boyfriends, which on the whole seems enough. Her large cheekbones, narrow eyes (myopic) and ironic grin make her most natural expression one of merriment. Recently had tests for a lump in her womb. This evening she's meeting the art class for drinks.

What she is doing or thinking

The letter is xeroxed. The salutation and ending are hand-written.

Dearest, Dearest Annie

If you should hear that something has happened, I would like you to have this letter. It thanks you for the years of friendship and support you have given to me and my work. Sometimes life is strange rather than wonderful. Sometimes it is wonderful.

Don't believe any rumours you may hear about me. There are people who will stop at nothing to discredit the author of work that does not express what they themselves see or feel.

Thanks for all the evenings at the Rose and Crown!!!

Love, June

June is a sculptress of Annie's age. Annie sees her thick mop of grey hair, the strange mask of the face after plastic surgery.

Annie knows then: June has killed herself. She leaps up, as if to prevent it. Then she remembers: the letter has been in her bag for weeks.

MRS EVA SIMMONDS

Outward appearance
Middle-aged woman, small, pinched, hairy chinned, a face pulled into itself. Her clothes are beige and clean. Clunky shoes. Chews on her lower lip, arms folded.

Inside information
Eva married her cousin, who is Professor of Jurisprudence at UCL. Everything she has done since has been done equally blindly. What she was blind to was her husband's ugliness. His eyes bulge, his tiny nose is hooked, his chin juts out to meet it, his teeth splay like clumsy feet, he has to suck in spit all the time. He works with his books, mostly at home. He insists Eva stay with him and forbids her to work.

Eva asks questions of herself vaguely, as if about someone else: did she marry him out of pity? Did such supreme ugliness carry a kind of sexual jolt?

Eva once was very pretty. She is dimly aware that somehow, over the years, she has become ugly too.

What she is doing or thinking
In her own way, Eva has rebelled. She is going to the Royal Festival Hall to buy two concert tickets, not for David, of course, who never goes to such things, but for herself and her daughter Harriet.

Three days ago, on Sunday, Eva looked out of their apartment window and saw David and Harriet walking. Harriet slouched until she was almost hunchbacked, wearing boy's clothes, unironed and grubby. David followed her with little pestering steps, eyes glaring at her face. Harriet is fifteen.

Eva is vague about this point too, but something in her said: not Harriet; not her too.

MISS BILLIE HOLIDAY

Outward appearance
Short hair, black trousers and a fluffy fake fur coat. Pink-cheeked, freckles, clear-framed spectacles, AIDS ribbon. Keeps smiling and shaking her head.

Inside information
Her mother was a singer and named her daughter after a jazz great. Billie works in accounts at British Telecom.

What she is doing or thinking
She imagines herself in the pub, telling the following true story:

> The computer tells us we have this telephone number and no one has ever paid a bill on it? So I go through all the records, back to when we kept things in writing. There's no record of any payment.
>
> So I ring the number to check that it works. I hear a dialling tone. It rings and rings, but no one answers. I try ringing at 6 PM, I stay for the late shift and ring at 10 PM. Never any answer.
>
> So I look up the address: 172, Tottenham Court Road. We send out the first threatening letter. 'Payment must be received in 7 days or legal proceedings will be taken.' No answer. We cut off the connection.
>
> We send out a court summons. And another. We send a notice of conviction. They don't pay the fine. Finally, we send in the bailiffs. The bailiffs can't find 172, Tottenham Court Road.
>
> Then we get an angry call from Camden Council about causing a traffic hazard.
>
> We were billing a traffic signal box. It has a telephone number so we can modem timing instructions. I was trying to talk to a traffic light.
>
> Can you imagine if it answered?

SERGEANT HARRY FREER

Outward appearance
Worn, middle-aged man with a blunt but pleasant face: round cheeks, round nose, slight overbite, small rather blue lips. Thinning salt and pepper hair combed in strands over bald top. Black overcoat, black shoes, blue shirt collar.

Inside information
On his way to work at Lambeth Police Station.

What he is doing or thinking
For four years Sgt Freer pursued a local graffiti sprayer. He'd defaced walls all over Lambeth and Vauxhall – the primary school on Baylis, St Michael's School, the ambulance building. Nowhere was safe. People felt threatened, intimidated. Finally, cameras videoed the culprit and he was identified on *Crimewatch* by a local schoolteacher.

As soon as he saw the young man in court (22, unemployed) Sgt Freer had a strange reaction. He felt personally threatened, shaken by the sentence. He hated the thought of the lad going to prison. How different really were his bright sprayed swirls from most hoardings? Sgt Freer had no words for his feelings. He kept a report on the case with a photograph of the young lad paper-clipped to its cover. His name was Tom Gleadal. No previous convictions, no qualifications.

Last night his wife picked up the photograph from the floor and asked, 'When was this taken?'

'Just before the trial,' Sgt Freer replied.

His wife looked confused. 'Was it before you met me? I don't remember it, that's all.' She passed it to him, and he saw.

He and Tom Gleadal have nearly the same face: the round nose, the round cheeks, the overbite.

'It's me in my artist days,' he answered.

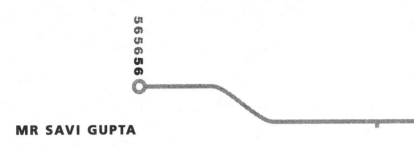

MR SAVI GUPTA

Outward appearance
Fleshy Indian man in loose brown shirt and camel-coloured overcoat. Slightly bouffant hair with waves. Holds a rolled, unread newspaper. Sits sprawled and relaxed, like a laundry basket of expensive clothes.

Inside information
Manager of Emil's Window Displays, a shop selling mannequins. Its front window is crammed with sexless, bald effigies, mostly of children.

What he is doing or thinking
Savi is amusing himself by imagining what the other passengers would look like if they had been born as the opposite sex.

Passenger 50 transforms into a much prettier person, petite with a retroussé nose, the kind of bad girl that produces a naughty tickle. Passenger 51 becomes a nasty customer, the kind of male relative Mr Gupta most hates dealing with: obdurate, religious. Passenger 52 turns into a heavy-cheeked labourer, with broad features and bigger hands wearing two layers of clothes and reading *The Sun* instead of a letter. Passenger 53 becomes a neat, prim, disappointed man with a lined face. Passenger 54 is much improved for being male. Her pink-cheeked jollity would suit an athletic, boyish frame. She would still wear an AIDS ribbon. And the policeman, well, he becomes a frumpy housewife in pastel clothes that are meant to make her look more feminine.

Savi's family were turfed out of Uganda so long ago that he cannot remember, and he runs an unlikely business by accident of inheritance located for no discernible reason on Waterloo Road in London. For him, all fate is arbitrary. His white-faced, sexless dummies await him. He gets off as always at Lambeth North.

MS MAGGIE ROLT

Outward appearance
Short slightly ringleted hair, strong features, bright red lipstick, burgundy suit, crepe blouse, sexy shoes. Soft and voluminous black coat. Hugs a copy of *The Big Issue* to her breast. Rubs her forehead.

Inside information
Investment analyst for Adventure Capital just opposite Waterloo Station. Chiswick homeowner, ambitious daughter, worthy aunt, gurglesome babysitter and MBA.

What she is doing or thinking
Thinking of Pascal, the *Big Issue* salesman. Pascal is large, bronze, dignified and a few years older than she. How did he end up in a doorway at Waterloo Station?

One morning, in exchange for thin coin, Maggie asked him. His answers at first were distant. He was from Switzerland. For years, he took Europeans on tours of Florida, which is why he speaks with an American accent.

He began to ask her about her work and recommend particular articles. Finally, she said, 'This is silly. Let's meet for lunch and talk.' He insisted on going to the cheap Indian across the road, and paying. That moved her. He was still distant. 'I paint landscapes,' he said, making direct eye contact with his Tandoori. 'When I have the money for canvases.' Where does he live? 'I have no family here,' was his only answer. Something came loose inside her, and she wanted to say then, 'You can come and live with me.'

That is what she intends to say to him this morning. But something in her large black coat, the Adventure prospectus, the red jacket is rearing up. Even in rehearsal, the words skitter sideways as if avoiding a gaze.

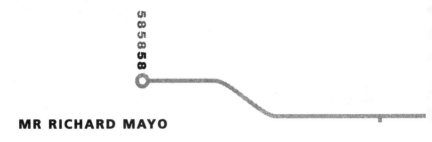

MR RICHARD MAYO

Outward appearance
Frizzy-haired, greying man in tweed jacket, tie and jumper. Sits focussing on something on the other side of the dark windows.

Inside information
An EFL teacher at Bruenwalt International College. He joined the staff in the early '80s when the campus was located outside London and still taught humanities. Now ensconced in an old hospital, Bruenwalt sells three-month diplomas in textile marketing, accounts computing, business English et al.

What he is doing or thinking
He's scared. His face no longer fits; he is a '70s left-over in a school full of young, bouncy Filipinos, Brazilians, Americans who do not identify with him.

He recently sat on an interview board for a new post. George, a contract teacher he likes, was up against the Head of Department's favourite, an MBA with a rodent's cute, sharp face.

His Head lied. He said George had been fired from his last job. Last night, Richard rang George's old employer. Far from being fired, he had been asked to stay, but moved to London to be with his wife.

So how does Richard say to his boss: you slandered someone? Does he say, smiling carefully, uh, you were wrong about George? Only to be told, that would have made no difference to the board's final choice? Does he tell George and violate confidentiality? Rocking the boat loses jobs.

Richard thinks of his divorce, the children grown up. He snatches up his battered brown briefcase to get off at Waterloo and thinks: fuck it.

He'll take it to the Director if he has to.

Outward appearance
Huge, moustached, pink-cheeked, middle-aged. Dusty jeans, tartan shirt under short leather jacket, work boots. Sits holding a large plastic bottle of Diet Tonic. Smiles dimly.

Inside information
Russian visitor working illegally in Britain. Until yesterday worked with his mate Dimi for a Lebanese builder. The Lebanese worries constantly, keeps checking, keeps changing his mind. This leads to fights. Igor speaks English badly; so does the Lebanese. There was shouting. Poor Dimi, who Igor will admit has all the brains, was left out of the conversation. Dimi started drawing on plywood to communicate, which made the Lebanese even more angry. He said he would be happy to have Dimi but not Igor.

What he is doing or thinking
Igor is drinking gin and tonic. He takes a swig of tonic and trades it with Dimi for the bottle of gin. In his current state this makes him feel sophisticated. It is several steps up from potato-derived fermentations.

They have been drinking all night. What else is there to do? Igor has a wife whom he loves dearly. He doesn't want any of the women in the clubs, but he can speak English and chat them up. Dimi is athletic, tiny with a prick as long as his forearm, hates his bitch of a wife but can talk to no one, which leaves him in clubs hopping up and down in frustration.

Igor loves Dimi. Dimi is his only friend, his partner. The gin and the tonic mingle sizzling in his mouth. As long as Dimi can't speak English, he'll need Igor.

MR DIMITRI BELINKOV

Outward appearance
Small, slim but muscular. Short brown hair, jeans, duffel-coat, missing teeth. Trades with his neighbour a bottle of gin for a bottle of tonic.

Inside information
A Russian visitor working illegally as a labourer with Igor Klimov. Mr Belinkov is a qualified engineer who once worked for the Army. In Russia, Igor merely supplies the brawn. Here, he has another role to play. He speaks the English and sticks to Dimi. Dimi understands enough English to know their last employer, Mr Haviri, would have kept him on without Igor.

The two of them once drove to Afghanistan to buy shirts. They drank all the way. You could sell the shirts back home at half the normal price and still pay for the trip. And the drink.

What he is doing or thinking
That Igor is a leech. Dimi laughs to see the huge stupid peasant who has succeeded in sticking to him and taking half his money. It is Dimi who solves the problems, works out dimensions, thinks of new ways to do the same job more simply.

He laughs because what else can you do? At the factory back home, the orders dried up. The Bosses gave the partnership a six-month holiday – with no pay.

Dimi once played football, he had ambitions to be a professional sportsman. He studied engineering. He had hopes. Now he is a spectacle, without respect, drunk on an early morning train. The faces of the other passengers pass him in a swirl and Dimi has no idea what to do, which way Out might be.

MR MICHAEL JEROME

Outward appearance
Tall black man in charcoal clothes and thick-soled shoes. He slumps against the partition, glaring at the drunks next to him.

Inside information
Works as a bus driver at Waterloo depot. Suffering from severe sleep deprivation.

What he is doing or thinking
Michael has lived in the same flat in Camden Town for fourteen years. It is right on Camden Road on a corner over a shoe shop. Everything should be fine. But what happens? The shoe shop puts in a burglar alarm, doesn't it, they have so many thieves. Right outside his bedroom window. So Michael and his wife wake up night after night with the bloody alarm ringing. And nobody comes. They just leave it.

So it's four in the morning. The thing has gone off once before that night. He rings up the police who say they can't do anything if the person with the key won't wake up and come around. Finally, they get the owner in but he slips away before there can be words. Everything settles down, it's all quiet and Michael just about gets to sleep when the alarm goes off again.

Something snapped. Michael went to his tool box and leaned out of his window and hit the bloody thing with a hammer. He banged and banged and finally knocked the thing off the wall. They'll know it's him, but they should have fixed it.

Michael snuggles down into himself and dreams of caressing the smooth flesh of his wife, ample like clouds in heaven. He sinks down into deep and cushioned sleep.

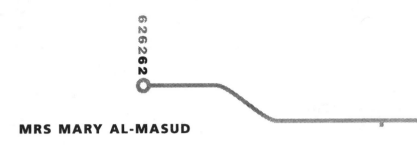

MRS MARY AL-MASUD

Outward appearance

Mid-fifties, old-fashioned East Ender viewed through a lens of money. Cream-coloured coiffed hair, pleated skirt, sky blue shoes. Wide watery eyes and a child's sigh.

Inside information

A bigamist. A Kuwaiti businessman simply made Mary his second wife. They met at a Star Trek convention. He was dressed as Spock. She kept the ears as a souvenir.

Her neighbours firebombed her house. She now lives in Bayswater with the other wife, whom she quite likes if only she spoke English. Mary brought with her eight cats and her dog, Muffin.

She fills her days. She takes opera singing lessons. The other wife listens politely as Mary performs 'Baubles Bangles and Beads' and 'Don't Cry for Me Argentina'. Now going to the Multi-Use Resource Centre near Lambeth North where she does work for the Asian Women's Group who seem not entirely sure why she is there.

Mary walks through life as if on water. Her husband, who loves magic and fantasy, finds this delightful.

What she is doing or thinking

Muffin thinks he's a cat. Nobody other than Mary seems to care. Muffin's hair is starting to fall out. He doesn't bark but tries to miaow. This results in a kind of extended coughing fit.

Her husband's relatives seem to think there is something amusing about it. Mary has tried talking to the ladies in the Asian Women's Group, but couldn't quite make herself understood. She is most concerned Muffin should fall in love with a cat, and . . . you know.

Someone might firebomb the house again.

OLIVER MASKEY

Outward appearance

Small sixteen-year-old. The usual backwards baseball cap and baggy trousers, but instead of trainers he wears tiny, tight climbing shoes.

Inside information

Oliver is a thief. His mum is too. She has special big knickers. She gets past detectors by switching bags or lining them with foil. A friend of the family, Jake, organizes teams of underage lads who break into offices, force open computers and leave with the chips. If they're caught, the lads are too young to convict. Oliver helps out. He's on his way to the Elephant to spend some cash on games.

What he is doing or thinking

He's just realized that the woman sitting opposite saw him on last night's job. Slowly Oliver slips off the baseball cap: he was wearing it then. The woman chews on her hair, stares ahead, and he realizes she's out of it.

Poor cow, she's still scared. Don't you think we're scared too? Why do you think we shit all over the floor? Oliver wonders if she found it, what she thought. She could be his sister. Come on, come on, come on, he tells the train.

At Lambeth North, the doors are on her side. Oliver waits until the last moment before darting through them. On the platform, he's safe. The woman sits with her back to him and runs a shivery hand across her face.

It's nothing personal, Oliver wants to tell her. It's what we do. He knows then he'll do this all his life, and that she will always be on the other side of the glass.

MR MICHAEL LIPKIN

Outward appearance
Well dressed, long-faced man about 35, in grey suit, beige coat, and small round hat. He is reading a sumptuously printed book of Hebrew scripture with gold-tooled lettering. He nods in agreement, thoughtfully prodding a protruding upper lip.

Inside information
Works in the accounts section of Pall Mall Oil[7] as a VAT specialist. The undertaking is vast: tributaries of information about every transaction from catering to cleaning, the staff newsletter or computer maintenance flow into his section. He clarifies policy on each kind of transaction and monitors adherence. It is a sideline.

What he is doing or thinking
The central facts of Michael's life are God and loneliness. He is a naturally solemn man who does everything properly. His work for the company is technically superb and largely unappreciated. He jogs, one might say religiously, every day for the sake of his rangy figure. He thinks a lot.

Michael's father is prominent in London Jewish affairs. Through him, Michael's views on the scriptures are gradually gaining a reputation. Michael's reading is thorough and his arguments, rehearsed in open debate, are authoritative.

Nevertheless, Michael feels continually, completely out of his time. Sage, thoughtful Jews like himself allowed themselves to be herded into camps. New Jews are big, bronzed, crew-cut soldiers who enjoy cunnilingus – and those are just the women. Michael is not a virgin except in his soul, which flowers when he reads scripture – or imagines that he has a wife.

The train stops and he gets out at Waterloo. He bounds long-legged up the steps as if to leap out of himself.

Another helpful and informative **253** *footnote*
7 Pall Mall Oil does not exactly exist.

Imagine, however, a superbly constructed nest of buildings, stone and marble clad, reaching up imperially into the sky.

What you can't see is underground. Snaking around and between the gas mains, the sewers, the storm drains and the tube tunnels for Bakerloo, Northern and City lines is an underground city for Pall Mall employees.

There is a huge gym, with squash courts. There is an olympic-sized swimming pool. There is a supermarket and a cinema for showing corporate films. Most unexpectedly there is a large underground theatre for live performances designed by Cecil Beaton. In its ceiling, tiny lights mimic stars.

There is also a bomb shelter, in preparation for nuclear war.

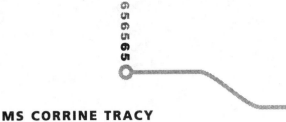

MS CORRINE TRACY

Outward appearance
Stylish black woman, late twenties. Long one-piece dress in a brown herring-bone pattern, brown overcoat with hood, matching flat-heeled boots. Hair short, combed forward, simple gold earrings. Handbag on floor.

Inside information
Works for Winona Hairdressers just behind the Elephant and Castle. She is now the only hairdresser left in the shop, which is seeing hard times.

What she is doing or thinking
Why does everyone assume a black hairdresser can only do black hair? Corrine has photographs of white ladies in her window as well. She's grateful to her black customers, but there aren't enough of them. She spends the better part of most working days staring into space. She is so bored.

She's taken to designing toys, with some success. Leap Frog was a spring-driven wooden toy that jumped. Her brother managed to sell the patent for that. She has been trying to design Scissors Crab, a plastic crab with goofy eyes on springs and pincers that can cut paper. The problem has been safety.

Corrine muses on other useful things the pincers could do – like knit. Suddenly something moves inside her head. She sees the pincers weaving hair, spinning strands, making braids.

People buy cornrows, they spend hours braiding it, it costs a fortune . . . Corrine covers her mouth. Cornrow Crab, the hair-braider! Inexpensive, do it yourself at home. She reaches into her handbag to pull out her notebook. It isn't there. She pauses, then decides. Sod the job, she's getting back to her design pad. She stands up to get off at Lambeth North instead of the Elephant.

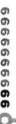

MRS JULIE TILDSLEY

Outward appearance
The last to get on at Embankment, as the doors close. She's youngish, about thirty, but rumpled hair and baggy eyes make her look older and a bit grumpy. She drops down into an empty seat and stares. She wears a shiny white dress.

Inside information
Works for FSD Courier Service near the Elephant. Takes bookings, fills in forms, contacts couriers, gives customers instructions. She lives near Aldgate East – a long way to come, but a job is a job, even one you could do in your sleep.

What she is doing or thinking
Julie actually is asleep. Her morning routine is so established that she dressed herself sleepwalking. She walked on automatic pilot to the tube and changed trains at Embankment without waking up. She is conscious of nothing until Passenger 46 clumps Passenger 47. She thinks: I'm dreaming that I'm sitting on the tube and a man comes in with a bicycle seat and hits a large black man with it. A spooky black lady smiles, nursing something terrible in a parcel. Mick Hucknall seems to be sitting next to the women, singing.

Gradually, Julie realizes it is not a dream. She really is sitting on the tube fingering her white dress. The FSD uniform is a grey skirt.

She's only wearing a slip. Oh my God! she thinks and sits up as the train slows into Waterloo. I'm not dressed, I've got to go home!

All the way to Aldgate East and then walking up Commercial Road, wearing only a slip. But this time she won't be asleep.

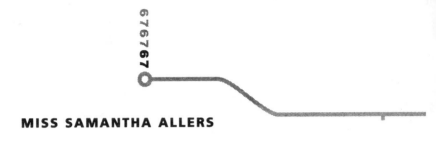

MISS SAMANTHA ALLERS

Outward appearance
Young, carefully groomed. Black trousers, black sweatshirt with Paperchase logo. Pink, puffy overcoat. Burnished bronze hair pulled up into a kind of curly nest on top of her head. Her earrings are the same colour.

Inside information
Sam is late for her job in a sandwich bar on Lower Marsh.

What she is doing or thinking
She's had a bad night. Sam recently moved with her boyfriend into a new flat. She was thinking about wallpaper, carpets, and damp around the windows – until the police called on her neighbour next door. It turns out he's a bit of a villain – and a friend of the three who have just escaped from Parkhurst prison[8] on the Isle of Wight.

They might have turned up just one door along. That's what the police said. They showed her photographs. They didn't look hard, but then villains don't always. They looked squishy and fat – horrible.

As far as Sam is concerned, she and Terry her boyfriend are moving on and up, away from London's past, out to the suburbs, into the future. The whole thing is like finding yourself living next door to the Krays. It's depressing. It's old.

Sam is pregnant. The job is to pay for all the things they'll need. In her mind the new flat and the baby are intertwined. She doesn't want to bring her baby up next to criminals. After months of looking for somewhere to live, Sam becomes determined to move.

Milton Keynes? she wonders.

As they come into Waterloo, there is a waft of a terrible stench.

Another helpful and informative **253** *footnote*

8 The Governor of Parkhurst and his staff did not stay the only scapegoats for the Isle of Wight escape. In October, the Governor General of the Prison Service Derek Lewis was also dismissed. Later described as the highest paid civil servant in Britain, Lewis brought a private case for wrongful dismissal and the High Court judged in his favour in March 1996.

In May of 1997, when the Conservative Party must have felt it deserved a vacation from trouble, Ann Widdecombe, who had been junior minister under Michael Howard, threatened to reveal details of Howard's misconduct during the affair, in a deliberate effort to destroy his chances for the leadership of the Party.

MRS GRISELDA STEWART

Outward appearance

A television granny. She holds a little girl's hand and helps her step up into the carriage. Mrs Stewart is short, round and comfy, grey jacket, tartan skirt, and a tartan shawl perfectly draped and pinned over her shoulders. Carries a picture book.

Inside information

Down from Scotland to see her granddaughter and make sure the little darling is getting enough attention. Her daughter works all hours in local radio, she's split up with her boyfriend, and who can trust childminders these days?

Amy is a picture, in her pert wee bonnet and a lovely blue dress. She's only four-and-a-half but good at her reading. They're going to spend a lovely day out at the motion picture museum.

What she is doing or thinking

Trying to get Amy settled while holding onto her book. There is a real horror sitting on the train, one of those punks. Poor Amy pulls away and no wonder. 'Come on, Amy,' coaxes Mrs Stewart. 'Up you go, onto the seat.' Mrs Stewart opens the book to distract her. 'Read me something, Amy. What's that?' She points, and Amy says, definitely, 'Train.' She's still staring at that frightful creature.

Mrs Stewart thinks: how can you bring up a child in a place like this? Someone sleeps in the doorway of Angie's mansion block. She's getting nowhere in that radio station, and I know she's feeling a bit lost. I'm going to put my foot down. She can come back home. There's Stirling nearby, and Gran to help, and we've got such a lovely school in Dunblane.

Outward appearance

A little girl, pre-school, neatly turned out in a blue dress, and polished black shoes. So pale that there are blue veins in her cheeks.

Inside information

Mum works and Daddy visits on Sunday and takes her out which is nice because she can get away from Mum who needs her rest. They go to the park or the movies, and Daddy always drives her in a car. Her most favourite place is under her bed where the carpet ends. Everyone tells her that Granny Stewart's house is full of nice things, so that is her favourite place too.

What she is doing or thinking

There are all these people with big feet who are in a hurry. Amy doesn't like the tube, and pulls back because she wants to get off. Her Gran tells her to get onto the seat. It's high and if it's dirty it will get her dress dirty, but she wants to do it herself, so she climbs up and there is this man with white clothes and a funny haircut who looks like something from the telly.

Gran wants Amy to read the book to show how much she's learned, but she looks at the picture instead. It shows boxes with rows of faces. 'Train,' Amy says, but it looks nothing like this train. No one looks out of the window in this train. No one waves and smiles. But Amy likes the man who looks like something from the telly, even if he is a bit scary. Television has taught her: everything real is scary.

MISS FLORENCE CASSELL

Outward appearance
Gamine, Italianate, tiny. Olive skin, curly hair cut short, lots of freckles. Handsome coat with black leather sleeves, and diamond patterns of different coloured leather. Picks disconsolately at its surface.

Inside information
Came to England from Kenya when she was a little girl. From time to time people made comments. Manages an Oddbins; shares a flat with a college friend near Elephant and Castle. Has spent the night with friends after a crisis.

What she is doing or thinking
It started with continual trouble from minicab drivers. They would pull over and ask if she wanted to have some fun. One of them showed up on her doorstep and asked her out. She turned him down and he left with reasonably good grace.

Last night the same driver showed up to take her to friends in Queen's Park. She refused to go with him. 'Look, I'm just here for the fare,' he said, affronted. They ended up driving across London in brooding silence. Parked outside her friends' flat he said, 'There. All safe and sound.' Then he said, 'And listen you half-caste bitch, just 'cause you got some white in you doesn't make you any better than anyone else.'

That's all. It was enough.

She spent the evening in the bathroom looking at her face. She had always seen it in her face, but thought her mother would have told her if were true. Why wouldn't her mother tell her? It doesn't make any difference, it shouldn't make any difference. And yet it does, and yet it always does.

MR ALLAN MARJORAM

Outward appearance
Bearded man in a suit and waterproof bunched around his burgeoning body. Oversize head, spectacles, white hands, scuffed shoes. Hunched over *Time Out*, with two different coloured markers. Holds both tops in his mouth.

Inside information
Works in the Foreign and Commonwealth Office Library on Stamford Street. Lives in Harrow with his parents. He is 32 years old.

What he is doing or thinking
Inspecting the *Time Out* personal ads with methodical diligence. His priorities are written on an envelope held underneath each ad. *Red: Short term, pref exotic. Green: Partner, first time advertiser.*

He circles an ad in red.

Attractive Black Woman, 33, graduate professional mature seeks gallant gentleman 33–45, professional, warm hearted ...

He havers. It would be unfair to pretend he was looking for a permanent relationship with a black woman. Besides, he is one year too young. He puts a question mark.

Green Eyes, Red Hair Lady 30 trendy (ish) creative job WLTM sexy man with GSOH for warm nights in. Photo please.

He promptly circles this in green. It meets all his requirements. He's not sexy, though. On second thought, he changes the colour to red.

Allan wishes someone would tell him what a GSOH was. And why did so many people want someone who speaks Chinese or Arabic?

Woman, 32, part-Jewish, sharp tongued seeks someone understanding . . .

That sounded a bit fierce.

Cute half-Italian lady, 35, seeks affectionate, understanding, trustworthy guy . . .

Green. That's all there are. He ranks the greens in order of preference. The train slows and he takes the pen tops out of his mouth.

MISS HILARY VIALLS

Outward appearance

A businesswoman in a TV commercial. Slim in a sharp grey suit. Legs elegantly crossed in sheer charcoal nylons. Small gold hoop earrings, which she fingers nervously. New blue bag, new black shoes.

Inside information

Hilary never thought that she would make 35 without being married. She is cripplingly shy. Works as an administrator at the London Television Centre. Studied the newsreader Gargy Patel, who looked half starved and scraggly at first but became stylish through grooming.

What she is doing or thinking

There is a terrible smell, which she thinks is coming from the man next to her. This stench of male makes her feel giddy. She doesn't quite hate it. It's like a sexual call for help. It fits with what he is doing.

She can't help staring. How can he be so brazen, circling sex ads in public? Those criteria! And the way he changes his mind!

It's also moving in a way. The need is moving. So is the air of hard work. There's nothing lewd about it. He's treating it like an engineering problem.

That is irredeemably male, as are his clumsy baggy body, his fat hairy fingers.

She dresses to attract . . . who? She can't even picture him anymore. Someone handsome, but what is handsome, without a picture? Just a word. This man would need her. She might need him, even if he did treat her like an engineering problem. The train slows at Waterloo and both prepare to go their separate ways.

But she does not fancy the kind of man she thought she did.

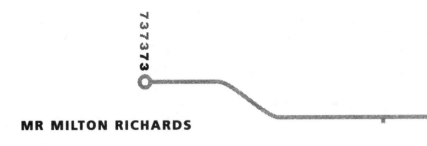

MR MILTON RICHARDS

Outward appearance
Small, neat man in blue trousers, blue padded anorak, cloth cap.
A fiercely trimmed moustache and a general air of rectitude.
One of his sleeves, jammed into a pocket, is empty.

Inside information
Milton lost his arm in an accident at a textile factory in
Hackney. The factory went bankrupt soon afterwards: there
was no compensation. Lives on benefit. The stepfather of
Eveleen Doyce.

What he is doing or thinking
He is sitting with Jesus. Jesus stands in the aisle between the
rows of seats, holding out both whole arms in mercy. Milton
can see the heart of Jesus through the robes of his gown. Jesus
is telling Milton that he must kill his stepdaughter.

She is spawn. Milton has seen her through the connecting
doors between cars, sitting on the same train. By leaning back,
he knows that she cannot see him. Soon, he will kill for Jesus.

Milton loves Jesus. His evil children tell him that he loves
white people more than black people. They do not understand
that he is comparing their own fallen behaviour with that of
bank managers, politicians, the Royal Family, and Andrew
Lloyd Webber. These are the people to emulate, they just happen
to be white. Does he not also instruct them to follow the
example of Frank Bruno? Nat King Cole?

Bruno fights for Britain, and so will Milton. In the empty
sleeve, the knife is hidden. That is why the Lord took away
Milton's arm, to hide the knife, so that he could be His Scourge.

Milton awaits his duty with patience.

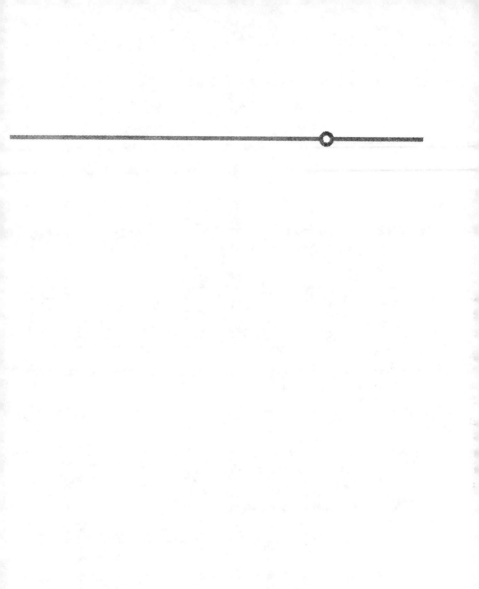

For Your Reading Ease and Comfort

PASSENGER MAP

Car No 3

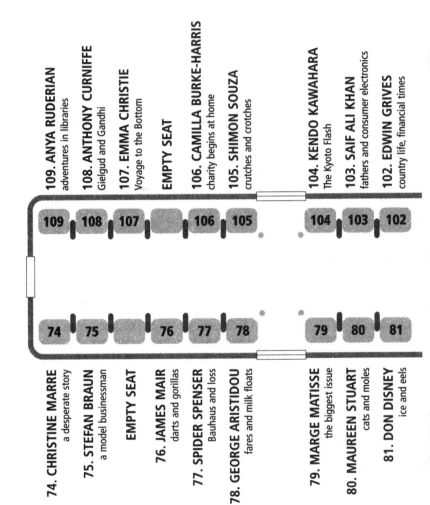

109. ANYA RUDERIAN
adventures in libraries

108. ANTHONY CURNIFFE
Gielgud and Gandhi

107. EMMA CHRISTIE
Voyage to the Bottom

EMPTY SEAT

106. CAMILLA BURKE-HARRIS
charity begins at home

105. SHIMON SOUZA
crutches and crotches

104. KENDO KAWAHARA
The Kyoto Flash

103. SAIF ALI KHAN
fathers and consumer electronics

102. EDWIN GRIVES
country life, financial times

74. CHRISTINE MARRE
a desperate story

75. STEFAN BRAUN
a model businessman

EMPTY SEAT

76. JAMES MAIR
darts and gorillas

77. SPIDER SPENSER
Bauhaus and loss

78. GEORGE ARISTIDOU
fares and milk floats

79. MARGE MATISSE
the biggest issue

80. MAUREEN STUART
cats and moles

81. DON DISNEY
ice and eels

THIS MAP SHOWS YOU

☞ **WHO is in the car**

☞ **WHERE they are sitting and**

☞ **WHAT are their interests and concerns**

101. PAUL LAUNCEY
what's in a name?

100. DIANA DIAMANT
death and Peter Pan

99. SUZE MORLEY
fags 'n' bikes

97. KAREN KEOWN
babies and boyfriends

96. GEOFF RYMAN
maps and mistakes

95. DORIS McPHERSON
smiles all round

94. LAWRENCE TIMMINS
dollars and sense

93. HELEN TIMMINS
present laughter

92. SARA IVANOVIC
youth is beauty

| 101 | 100 | 99 | | 97 | 96 | 95 | 94 | 93 | 92 |

98. BERT HARRIS
bleach and Windolene

91. JAMES BARTLETT
partners

| 82 | 83 | 84 | | 85 | 86 | 87 | 88 | 89 | 90 |

82. THOMAS WEST
fathers and sons

83. GWEN UTLAY
ambulances and ball bearings

84. JASMINE McGOWAN
lamps and Rock-olas

85. RAFAEL DA CUNHA
cakes and cream

86. BERYL BARBER
jokes and history

87. BEN BEVIS
understudies and getaways

88. VITROLA FELDMOUE
fakes and benefit

89. BUNNY TAIT
art and commerce

90. MIGUELA PALLARÉS
Americans and the self

The 253
Personal Ads

WHAT YOU *REALLY* NEED OTHER PEOPLE FOR!

Masculine fruit and veg man, 35, GSOH, going to seed, often wears no shirt seeks female customers to be mildly titillated and buy his cucumbers. Full price list available on request.

Swings both ways ... male or female makes no difference to this post office counter worker who seeks lunchtime relief. Low pay means he's all alone on the afternoon shift. Help him cut that queue! A burden shared is a burden shared.

Dry cleaning shop seeks woman, pref Eastern-European speaking, for below minimum wage employment. Must have unrecognized degree from university in collapsed republic and charming, intelligent, hardworking manner.

Man, 39, told good looking, needs someone to tell him he's good looking. That's all.

Professional male, handsome but ditsy 32, seeks adult to return library books, get printer in for repair, pay council tax etc. Most letters with photograph answered unless lost. Must be prepared to answer all other responses to this ad.

Woman, 40, needs people to mother. Preferably lower class and ignored at work. Let me do everything for you. That way we can never be equals. All nationalities welcome.

Middle-aged woman, non-scene, seeks same for visiting Royal Academy Summer Show, exchanging gardening tips etc. Must drink Earl Grey. No phonies.

Married couple mid-30s seek new friends for safe times at pop concerts. Lightning Seeds, Boo Radleys. Full and frank letter stating preferences gets same by return.

Young 50, isolated, needs devoted listeners for monotone political rants: Clinton a commie, Thatcher destroyed country etc. Willing to travel.

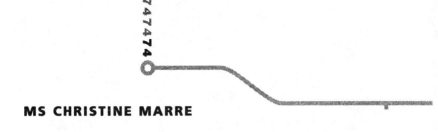

MS CHRISTINE MARRE

Outward appearance
Small freckled woman, flaming red hair, Lucille Ball lipstick, black ski pants, tiny Chinese flat shoes, floral print shirt, floral jumper. Keeps looking urgently over her shoulder, as if pursued.

Inside information
Typesetter for Epik Publications, specialists in gardening and military subjects. She has been telling everyone her husband is an undercover agent who infiltrated the IRA ten years ago. Now, in the ceasefire, they do not know how to get him out safely.

None of this is true. Whenever her phone rings, Christine runs to it as if expecting news. She pastiches fear, tension, drama. Ten local women worked part time at Epik, sorting post, packing books. They started asking things like 'How are you able to tell us this?' When they caught her out with inconsistencies, she apologized, 'I have to mislead you, slightly.'

She's shopped them to the Benefits Agency, anonymously. They've all lost their jobs. She is safe, for a while.

What she is doing or thinking
Christine is acting out several dramas at once, the pursued woman, the citizen against fraud. She fumes against her boss. He was using benefit to subsidize underpaying his workers. It's not her fault he fired them all rather than pay them properly.

There is something empty and gnawing that won't go away. Chris lives alone, in terror of being invisible. She lives in terror of being found out. She lives for the moments clinging in panic to the telephone with other people listening. She looks over her shoulder again. Can people see she is a woman with a desperate story?

MR STEFAN BRAUN

Outward appearance
Polished forehead, tiny nose, craggy cheeks, floppy hair. Broad
shouldered in an immaculate white overcoat and Gucci suit in
patterned olive and brown. Reading the March 1995 issue of
Jacqueline.

Inside information
Professional model being photographed by Passenger 109.
Research shows that men do read this women's magazine, but in
private. The original campaign *Out of the Closets and into the
Streets* was ditched as sounding too gay. Now it's *A Moveable
Feast . . . food, fun, the arts, great suits and pages of beautiful
women . . . what more could a man on the move want?*

What he is doing or thinking
Looking at a piece called *The Prom*. It features grown women
in the '90s dressed up like teenagers in the '50s, driving in a pink
Cadillac in the American desert. Two guys in tuxedos squint
into the sun, or jump up and down. So far, so obvious.

They want teenagers, babyfaces, thinks Stefan. He's old for a
model. It's hard to look like a sleek, powerful businessman
when you're shaky inside and trying to think of the next scam.
He owes the bank money.

When he was a teenager, Stefan made a working model of a
hovercraft out of a vacuum cleaner. He had an instinct for computers: he loved programming. But he grew up beautiful, and
everything was knocked off course by parties, dope, women,
and finally modelling. Deep inside, he's a nerd with a yearning
for a steady job in an IT unit. He can't get back.

Maybe he could teach a modelling course?

'Stefan?' asks the photographer. 'Look up.'

MR JAMES MAIR

Outward appearance
Nicol Williamson playing a farmer. Yellowish, ageing face, red hair, red beard. Clean jeans, rubber-soled boats, green anorak. Tank-like briefcase at his feet.

Inside information
A consultant veterinarian returning home after an early morning call. James has not committed suicide. Many vets do.

What he is doing or thinking
This morning James attended London Zoo to examine an old, sick gorilla. To examine gorillas he has to fire tranquillizer darts at them.

The gorillas have learned what the darts are. They've taken to flinging them back at their handlers. Even more cunning, some of the gorillas pretend to be tranquillized. When the keepers get close, the animals stab them with the needles and send them to sleep as well. All in good fun.

Now the vets call at 5 AM to take the gorillas by surprise. A team of three fire at once from different angles to ensure a hit.

This morning Beefy, an old cancerous male, woke up and saw the team and the darts. Instead of fighting, Beefy slumped depressed onto his haunches. It was strange: he stared at the ground, at his feet. They needed to fire only one dart. It plunged into his arm, and Beefy stayed sitting upright, as tranquillized gorillas do.

When James got near, Beefy suddenly reached up and pulled the dart out of his arm. James scurried back in fear. Then the gorilla, eyes full into his, passed James the dart, handle first. He can still see the old creature's eyes, accusing, ill, angry and sad.

It's that sadness the vets can't take.

MR SPIDER SPENSER

Outward appearance

A diffident librarian coming home from a fancy dress? Skinny, all in black, with traces of mascara and white make-up. Bald on top, with long wispy hair at the back and sides. His shoulders are covered with stray strands. He rifles repeatedly through a black shoulder bag.

Inside information

Works Tuesday nights at the bar in *Etoile*, when it gets called 'Tombstone Blues'. Going home to Lambeth North. Officially unemployed — a Jobseeker, in other words.

Spider is a Bauhaus fan. He used to know people who knew Pete Murphy. He also knows a woman who does publicity for The Cure. Last night she gave him a cassette for free.

What he is doing or thinking

Where's my bloody tape?

It was a copy of *Concert the cure live* from '84. Back then, Spider was new on the scene. His hair was a kind of black fountain off the top of his head. He sat at the bar with his girlfriend Lizzie, who looked like a virgin being buried in her wedding dress. Everyone knew them. They were all ex-punks or Romantics or hardcore Goths or something in between and more interesting.

Some live in Australia now teaching scuba diving. Lizzie married an indulgent businessman *and* went dykey. Now she dresses like Dorothy in *The Wizard of Oz* and is a mother. She looks big. He feels small. They all thought that somehow being fashionable, knowing people, being in the arts would make them rich. Then suddenly they all were gone.

Like that tape. He keeps scrabbling in the bag.

MR GEORGE ARISTIDOU

Outward appearance
Heavy subcutaneous beard. Hair still in streaks from the comb. Big blue duffel-coat with horn barrel buttons, very thick trousers: possibly another pair underneath. Stares fixedly at the empty seat across from him.

Inside information
Mechanic. Used to repair milk floats for a milk delivery company. It was bought by a rival and then closed down. George now works for Lambeth Council's own vehicle repair establishment near Lambeth North tube.

What he is doing or thinking
George is reading an ad for London Transport, one of the latest in a campaign to stop fare-dodging.

A few weeks ago a milkman doing his rounds in Acton was confronted by a pregnant woman. She explained that she was feeling completely exhausted and would appreciate a lift down the street. He helped her into his milk float and took her all the way home. After waving him goodbye, she gave birth to an 8 lb Sainsbury's bag . . .

The text is framed by a surround of white milk bottles. The message is that some people will have to try other dodges now that LT is getting so strict about fares.

George wants to kill someone at London Transport. Don't they realize what happened to the milk floats? Don't they realize how many men lost their jobs, how many men still don't have work, how long it took him to find a job? He pictures some berk in a linen suit in an advertising agency thinking he's clever.

As the train pulls into Waterloo he stands up and tears the cardboard poster out of its frame.

MME. MARGE MATISSE

Outward appearance

String bag, multicolour flimsy dress, grey trenchcoat like Led
Zeppelin fans used to wear. Fiercely proud, much made-up face,
with a swathe of coarse long hair in many shades of blonde.

Inside information

Heiress and descendant of Henri Matisse.[1] Many times divorced.
Marge continues to use her famous maiden name. She lives in
terror of being forced to spend capital. Complains constantly of
poverty and lives on cauliflower cheese.

What she is thinking or doing

Women of a certain age and temperament need love. Marge
believes in simplicity, independence and good taste, and lately
has been very moved by a boy, a young boy, homeless, selling
that magazine, *The Big Issue*.

He looks so handsome, so sad. An uneducated Albanian sea-
man. Lived for years illegally in America, and speaks perfect
English. 'Everyone learns English in Albania. But it is American
English.' There is something so elegant in his distant reserve, his
enduring dignity.

She's going to do something that all her friends will tell her is
very silly, but the heart has its own reasons, mysteries. She has
decided to ask him to live with her. She can introduce him to
books, music, cafés, the spiritual life.

A poor man stands, deformed, and she cannot help but notice
certain other attributes. Again, you see, she has imagination, so
many people would feel mere pity, but she, she can see the man
has a vibrant sexual quality. He perches on two artificial legs,
and she yearns to support him, hold him.

She'll get his name, just in case the Albanian falls through.

Another helpful and informative
253 *footnote*
1 I have no idea if Matisse even
had children. So, to be plain,
Marge Matisse bears no relation to
any of Matisse's surviving relatives.
Marge does not exist, more's the
pity. She'd be a great dinner party
guest, full of spurious stories about
the old man, whom she never
really met. She'd leave thick
lipstick on your cups and not allow
anyone else to talk and need
helping home, declaring 'I only had
one glass of wine!'

The main problem is, despite all
my efforts, she persists in looking
like one of Matisse's paintings.
This means if she came to dinner, it
would be like entertaining a
particularly elegant toon.

Outward appearance

Plump, vaguely hippyish woman in her mid-thirties. Long black hair, loose flowered dress, pink jacket. Broach in the shape of a cat. Holds shut a battered copy of *Duncton Wood*, a novel about moles. She is not reading it, but her lips move silently.

Inside information

Devoted animal rights activist and cat lover. Recently made redundant from a privatized public utility. She gets out of the house as often as she can: she can't stand being cooped up with her unemployed husband, who is rapidly going to seed. Going to the *German Romanticism* exhibition at the Hayward Gallery.

What she is doing or thinking

Composing a letter to the Council about her proposed hostel for homeless cats. A neighbour has complained. Maureen savours each phrase. 'As for noise and odours, Mr Peeling knows nothing about well-run catteries. Cats that are warm, fed, cared for and cleaned are quiet and do not smell. Mr Peeling allows his dog to foul the pavements and to bark. Cats do not, at least, bark.'

The doors open. Maureen realizes that this is her stop, and leaps to her feet. She meant to read her beloved book, but has spent the last half hour, the last six months in a rage. This is getting silly, Mo, she tells herself. She has a vision of her cattery, its concrete floors burnished like metal. She sees herself in the Hayward, reading the catalogue, relaxing in the café. I really am not stupid. I can decide, she realizes, to have some fun. She gets out at Waterloo.

Duncton Wood has been left behind.

MR DON DISNEY

Outward appearance
Man about 50, very tanned, short grey hair, black trousers, heavy-soled shoes, black jacket peeking out from the sleeves of a waterproof.

Inside information
A security guard on his way to work at Mosstains. He has just returned from Christmas holidays in Spain. He always wanted to be in the Army, but only ever made the Territorials. His parents wouldn't sign the necessary papers to let him join at fifteen, so he ended up working in old Billingsgate fish market.

What he is doing or thinking
He remembers the old market, with its arches, its noise, its humour. He remembers the heavy leather boots with the copper toes, and the thick leather hats on which he would balance boxes of fish, or trays of eels.

Don once chained his boss to the stall all day. He had come back having skived off on his birthday, so the lads had made sure he'd stay put. Once a Jap tourist came early to take photographs. He stood up on the barrow which Don pulled, so Don pulled just a bit too hard and sent him flying backwards into the haddock and John Dory.

Life was smart, hard and funny. Now it's grey and corporate. Don wants to live in Spain, and thaw out.

They used to have big metal chests full of frozen eels. The eels would come back to life. The foundations of the old market were frozen solid from the cold store. When they moved the market the foundations thawed, and the building began to fall down. Like Britain really.

MR THOMAS WEST

Outward appearance

Young man in corduroys. Pink skin, red hair, red jacket under a blue overcoat. Soft brown shoes. Going over papers covered with children's handwriting. Suddenly he stops.

Inside information

A teacher at Lower Marsh Primary on Baylis Road. At 24, the youngest in the school.

Tom became a primary school teacher for two reasons. First, he was good at taking care of his younger brothers after his father disappeared. Second, he wants a girlfriend and primary schools are full of women teachers. He is already on his second potential wife.

What he is doing or thinking

Coming to terms with the sudden return of his father. Dad's showed up at Mum's new address with no explanation of where he's been for fourteen years.

Thomas's father had always been odd. He would bring strangers home for supper and put them up. The lawn was never mown; grass grew high around the front door steps. But he sowed wildflower seed, poppies and foxgloves.

He was constantly tearing up floorboards and pipes and then losing interest. Woodworm became an obsession. He took the roof off the house in winter, wrapped it in plastic, and then deserted his family. Effectively a ruin, the house was sold at half price, and the family moved into a flat over an Italian restaurant by the Hanger Lane Gyratory System.[2]

Thomas has always feared that he was like his father in any way. He can't be: he notices children and loves them, and he is charming to women. But last night he saw his father: small, red, round, determined, like himself.

Another helpful and informative
253 *footnote*

2 The Hanger Lane Gyratory System is, despite its fancy name, simply a roundabout. It entangles the North Circular Road with the A40, the major road heading due west out of London.

The Gyratory System is poignant because soon after it opened in the late '70s, the designers admitted that they had made a mistake and it would never work. God knows how you can mistake either of those two roads or which directions they go in.

The result in 1996 is this: a roundabout which is designed to avoid a traffic light snarl-up is now controlled by a carousel of traffic lights. Say you want to turn right: you may have to wait at four red lights as you gyrate. This is instead of the one traffic light the System replaced. The Gyratory System regularly achieves gridlock, which is excellent considering that all the through traffic on the A40 passes under it via a tunnel.

MRS GWEN UTLAY

Outward appearance

Big-boned, with slightly frizzy hair. Red jacket, gold brooch, rust-coloured dress and shoes, large camel-coloured coat and briefcase. Reading a copy of *Management Excess*. She underlines key passages.

Inside information

Gwen works for the NHS Tabulation and Processing Agency in Leeds. She's in charge of their Total Quality Management programme. She is visiting the London office, which shares the same building as the London Emergency Service. Gwen plans to write a report on the success of this related body in establishing procedures and targets. She has been invited by the boss of Passenger 45. He wants Gwen to see his birthday party, and the level of commitment he has from his staff.

What she is doing or thinking

Gwen firmly believes that the entire NHS should have an ISO standard quality accreditation. She was particularly inspired by the example of a ball-bearing factory which held a joint Total Quality Conference with their suppliers. She envisions a national conference of quality stewards from all the NHS agencies and suppliers, to agree industry-wide quality targets.

Gwen is armed with a draft questionnaire for the Emergency Service. It asks ambulance customers if the vehicle was comfortable, the driving of a safe but speedy quality, the staff polite and informative. Did patients have to sit on a trolley for a long time? If they had a complaint, did they receive an acknowledgement? Was the waiting room clean? Did the decor make a friendly impression?

Gwen prides herself on thoroughness. What else might people using ambulances possibly want to comment on?

MRS JASMINE McGOWAN

Outward appearance

Professional shoplifter? Flat tennis shoes, grubby pink trousers, puffy lime-green coat, straw-like untended broom of hair. Plump, smiling slightly, surrounded by shopping bags full of bits of metal.

Inside information

Runs a shop next to Emil's Window Displays. It sells bedsteads, radios, lamps, refrigerators in need of repair, hubcaps from a range of automobiles, old magazines, clothes. It would be easy to mistake it for a junk shop. It is in fact a clinic that cures old jukeboxes and 1960s psychedelic lamps.

What she is doing or thinking

Jasmine left a lamp on all night to warm. The red wax has settled into a sluggish clump at the bottom amid the oil. Sometimes prolonged heating restores its youth. The red bobbles churn once more as livid as a Yes album cover.

Jasmine is also nursing a sick Rock-ola. It's an early '70s model, called *Rhapsody in Colour* because lights flicker within different coloured panels. Jasmine is buddies with the dealer who bought the whole warehouse of Rock-ola spare parts when Mr Rock-ola retired.

She'll be able to keep the Rock-olas and lamps going for years yet. Like the record in the jukebox says: *I Won't Hang Up These Rock and Roll Shoes.*

Jasmine grew up in a trailer in Canada, drifting across another continent with her hippy parents. She remembers pine trees, huge lakes surrounded with rock, flaming autumn colours and winters that left her cold six months of the year. Her dad's still in Canada, near Vancouver, fishing. Her mum's in a home.

She hopes the wax will have warmed.[3]

Another helpful and informative
253 *footnote*
3 Like so many of the smaller shops around Lambeth North, even as the recession ended in 1996, Jasmine's shop was suddenly empty and with metal shutters bolted down over its windows. It is still used for something, however. Sometimes, mysteriously, the shutters are left rolled up. Inside are a few bedsteads, scraps of clothes and notices still pinned to the wall.

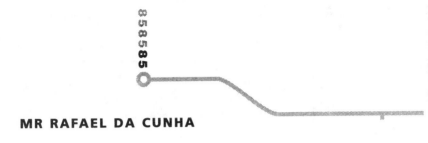

MR RAFAEL DA CUNHA

Outward appearance
Middle-aged man, black moustache and hair, yellow and green slacks, jacket. Throws himself back in his seat, stomps his feet with laughter. Tobacco-stained teeth.

Inside information
A baker at Blands Patisserie, wholesale suppliers of pies and cakes. Blands staff are a mix of regional Spanish, Italian, and Portuguese. Rafael lives alone in a hotel in Seven Sisters.

What he is doing or thinking
A fool peers at the London Underground map over Rafael's head. He doesn't notice when an old lady sits down in his seat. The idiot sits down on top of her. Some dumb American by the look of him. Rafael doubles up.

The idiot looks like the men in the park. Rafael knows no one, speaks little English. He started strolling around Archbishop's Park in the evenings after work and men started to make suggestions. Young folks. He told them, he only did that for money, and they paid him. The young office workers, the boys from the flats, even once a priest, they pay him, old as he is, and become women for him. He tells them he is an Arab, they seem to like that.

If he was home, he would never do anything like that. But working around cakes all day makes him feel sick. He never eats. He used to haul concrete blocks up ramps and play football. He has a big man's body, shrunk back to muscle and bone. He gives them cream, like cakes, and that also makes him sick, but now, now he can laugh.

Laugh at all of them.

Outward appearance

Round-faced black woman. Spectacles perched on the end of her nose. Both feet in a contained parallel. Reading a textbook, *World Peace and Social Change.*

Inside information

At 27 Beryl is many years younger than she looks. Running the family for her mother has left her matronly. Still living with her mother and father, unmarried, a devoted auntie. Works for her overbearing cousin in a theatrical costumiers off Baylis.

What she is doing or thinking

The book is for her evening course at Merely College. It is divided into units not chapters. Beryl hopes that the course, about the history of modern Britain, will help her to understand the people better, why they are as they are. She hopes for that even though the course, and particularly this book, bore her deeply.

Roused by a squall of laughter from the man next to her, she looks in time to see some poor man who has sat on an old lady, stand up, hit his head, and sit on someone else. The old lady laughs, shaking her head. The man he sits on scuttles away, so timid to be sat on first thing in the morning. A pretty girl opens her mouth wide. They all laugh.

Beryl lets the book settle down and laughs too. The man next to her doubles up, like he's done himself a damage.

She wishes she understood. They are all mad. They all enjoy themselves. Underneath everything, the place has as much life in it as home.

Who needs history? She prepares to get off at Waterloo.

MR BEN BEVIS

Outward appearance
An advertising executive from some 1950s sitcom. Squiggly, pockmarked, in a grey suit, pork pie hat, pipe, specs.

Inside information
Professional comedian, organizer and star of *Mind the Gap*, a troupe that stages comedy skits on the Underground for a fee-paying audience. Trying out Geoff, a promising amateur who might fill in when Ben has a better paying gig.

What he is doing or thinking
Ben is jealous. To go ahead and sit on a real passenger instead of the plant was brilliant! And then to sit down on Ben anyway and make it look convincing!

Ben spends two hours, three days a week in protracted ritual humiliations up and down the Tube. He gets in a fight with his tie, and eventually cuts off the ends with a pair of scissors. He gets gum stuck to the soles of his shoe, and from there all over his suit. People roar with laughter. Even for one routine, he misses it.

Then the woman next to him growls, 'This is a put-on, isn't it?' The newcomer hasn't been believed! Ben pretends that he doesn't understand the woman, but a kind of satisfaction settles over him.

It's a brief respite. Police get on. Ben has left the letter of permission from London Transport at home. In any case, it's a forgery. He might have to pay a fine. He has no money. Geoff has a job, he can pay it. Ben decides to make a break for it, first chance he gets. It's every man for himself.

The comedy never stops.

DAME VITROLA FELDMOUE

Outward appearance
Mauve spectacles, henna-red hair, blue denim jacket, multi-coloured ski coat. Leans back, and growls at her neighbour.

Inside information
Famous actress, currently rehearsing *The Way of the World* at the National. Long acquaintance with her own profession makes her impatient with fantasists and phoneys.
She is carrying small arms in her handbag.

What she is doing or thinking
From the moment she got on, Vitrola thought she was watching a show. It was quite fascinating. Either they were very good or something had gone wrong. The way the actor sat down on two people. You couldn't, *couldn't* time a double mistake like that.

But when his second victim, the fake City gent, scuttled across to the seat next to hers, it all began to look rehearsed. She smelled it: failed actor, poncing about for free.

'This is a put-on, isn't it?' she growls at him. He pretends to look blank. In case there is a hidden camera, Vitrola calculates how to raise a laugh and insult him at the same time. She smiles tigerishly. 'You know one of these days they'll stop giving actors benefit, and you'll have to work for a living.'

Two policemen get on at her stop, and she looks back over her spectacles at the actor. She asks with her eyebrows: Are these part of the show too? He's too alarmed to notice.

That tells her: the policemen are real. As real as anything gets. She stands up to go. Her guns clank.[4]

God, she thinks, if only we had a real Conservative government.

Another helpful and informative
253 *footnote*
4 When, in October 1996, the
British Government banned most
handguns, Dame Vitrola emigrated
permanently to the United States in
protest. She became a key
spokesperson for the US National
Rifle Association. 'Britain now lies
defenceless before the seething
masses of Europe!' she declared at
their national convention. Applause
was rapturous. 'Never say: it can't
happen here.' She then repeatedly
fired a .22 calibre pistol over the
heads of the crowd, crying
'Freedom!' with each shot. This
resulted in her prompt arrest.

MRS BUNNY TAIT

Outward appearance
Perhaps Italian? Calm, beautiful, in a Virgin Mary way, about 35. Tan slacks, shoes that appear to be made of varnished straw. Stares unmoving as *Mind the Gap* unfolds around her.

Inside information
Canadian stage manager, part Amerindian. Works in *MtG* for pin money (if that). Introduced Passenger 96 to the troupe. Her husband Julian is an actor at the National, but only gets walk-on parts. His biggest role was masked in a production of the *Oresteia* which was known to use actors normally too ugly to take lead roles. Julian is a lovely man, kind, wise, but now increasingly depressed, haunting their flat, tending the allotment.

What she is doing or thinking
She watches distracted as the routine goes wrong. Geoff's inexperience somehow covers for it. Bunny is more concerned with finding some way to make money. Her friend Judith takes people on London walks, but then Judith has been studying London for years. The Japanese have a plan to start exporting their art and culture. Maybe she could bone up on their theatre or something, start an agency.

The woman next to her is saying '. . . they'll stop giving actors benefit, and you'll have to work for a living.'

It's like the entire country is shrinking. When Bunny arrived in 1978, London's theatres roared, and there were punks and subsidy and yes, the DHSS.

As an Indian, Bunny has the right to live in either America or Canada. She thinks of Julian, whose rich voice would be perfect for radio, the thousands of American radio stations.

She decides. They'll move.

MISS MIGUELA PALLARÉS

Outward appearance
Large, amused woman in her early twenties, dressed in jeans, white trainers, and black leather jacket.

Inside information
Studying hotel management at Bruenwalt International College. Companion for the day of Passenger 92. They are watching a troupe that performs comedy routines on the tube.

Miguela comes from a large Catalan family which shouts its mind, which refuses to budge, which prides itself on never putting on a false face.

What she is doing or thinking
Miguela is studying Americans. It is good for her English. It is good for her understanding. They are funny, these Americans. They never stop performing, like Sara now, perky, sitting up, playing pretty Miss. If she needs to, Sara can play a tough business professional, or tell-me-your-troubles counsellor, or street smart clubgoer in her clean blue jeans.

So who is acting now? The poor guy on show isn't acting: he sits on the old lady for real. The nice American couple, they wear the same clothes. They want to look like bookends. Why?

Police get on and they are all arrested, and the Americans think that is a show too. Sara gleams at Miguela, her mouth wide open in delight. As if we really were friends, thinks Miguela, who smiles back at the effrontery of it.

They have to get off, and Miguela knows that Sara's ego means she will have to do the talking. So she starts being flirty with the old cop, gets him all itchy, and Miguela wonders. You throw on different people, Sara, like clothes. Is there anyone underneath?

CONSTABLE JAMES BARTLETT

Outward appearance

Young Transport Policeman, skinny, red-cheeked. Gets on at Waterloo. Blocks one doorway as his colleague blocks the other.

Inside information

Still in his first month. James's whole family are in the police, including his mother, who monitors surveillance videos. James's first job was with a merchant bank. The computers and columns of figures bored him. It was also a trade for wide boys. He believed he could help people through police work. But he wanted out from under his family, so went into transport security.

What he is doing or thinking

Has he made a mistake? James's partner seems to have come out of an episode of *On the Buses*. Prejudiced, unschooled. He leers at the people, who are obviously a group of tourists. What is the point of trying to scare them?

They get out. Bert glowers at the leader. 'I wasn't aware that London Underground is a theatre. Are you charging money for this?' An American girl tries to explain. Bert fancies her, so he keeps her talking.

It goes on and on. The radio squawks, Bert eyebrows James to answer it.

Did he hear that right? A train has just gone through the barriers at the Elephant. James hunches over the radio and asks, 'Which train, repeat, which train?'

James knows how to stop Bert now. 'Excuse me, everyone, sorry. We've all been very lucky.' James looks at them all. 'The train we were on has just crashed.'

Even Bert falls silent. They stare down the long black tunnel, curving into darkness. A mouse flees along the track.

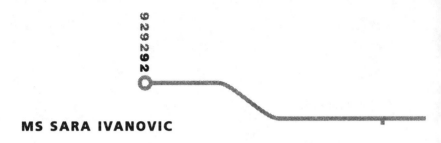

MS SARA IVANOVIC

Outward appearance

Pretty American student. Blonde hair, spotless casual clothes. Eyes glisten with amusement, as a man sits on an old lady, and then on her neighbour.

Inside information

Studying hotel management at Bruenwalt International College. It's important to have experience of other cultures if you want to run a good hotel. European management styles are really weird, but kinda interesting too.

Today was an optional visit to the Radish Edwardian Hotel at Heathrow which is where Sara stayed when she first arrived, so it seemed kinda a waste, so she's watching *Mind the Gap* instead with a girl from her class, Miguela.

What she is doing or thinking

It's really neat. These actors do routines on the tube. They're in some kinda trouble with the fuzz. At the next station, they all have to get out. Sara bounces out onto the platform with Miguela. The Director just runs away up the stairs, looking like an ostrich. The poor actor is left explaining to the police, 'We're a theatre company.' Sara thinks this is the funniest of all.

'It's true . . . it's true,' Sara tells the cop, helplessly giggling, 'Everything this guy told you is true!' She lets the cop have it, full blast, the eyes, the smile, the blaze of being a young American.

The old cop narrows his eyes, like a horny old elephant. Sara thinks: I'm young, I'm sexy, I'll just do this until you get bored and let us go. The radio squawks, his young partner takes it.

'Which train, repeat, which train?' the young cop asks. He sounds worried.

MRS HELEN TIMMINS

Outward appearance

Woman in her fifties, specs, checked shirt, cream slacks, new white sneakers, sky-blue fisherman's hat. Grins in Cheshire-cat fashion, holding her neighbour's hand.

Inside information

On holiday in London with her academic husband. They married in 1960, just before Larry went to college. From 1965 on, Helen was an Army wife. Now she's an academic wife. She does charity work, reads and writes a little. They have one grown-up daughter.

What she is doing or thinking

Present laughter eases her heart. It keeps what is coming at bay. When they get back to Irvine, Helen is going to ask Larry for a divorce.

There's a professor of Hebrew literature, a Russian émigré called Sasha Gnessin. They met at her writing group. She surprised herself that first night; she was a bit drunk; she went to bed with him. As he opened the door to his apartment, she found her knees were shaking. Sasha is small, bespectacled, slightly hunched, her own age (thank heavens), but there's something about him. Lust. It breaks her heart, but she doesn't lust after Larry. Larry is distant from her. He always has been. Despite his size and his masculine image, there is something frail and unsexed about Larry. He is affectionate, but there is nothing exciting in his touch; nothing excited in it either. Sasha awaits, with his sly grin, his books, and his cock that he pulls out of his trousers, and that she kneels to swallow. She never did that before. The image, even now, startles her, shakes her with its power.

So she laughs.

PROFESSOR LAWRENCE TIMMINS

Outward appearance

A big man, broad-shouldered, approaching retirement. Wears a checked shirt, cream slacks, new white sneakers, sky-blue fisherman's hat. Grins in Cheshire-cat fashion, holding his neighbour's hand.

Inside information

Professor of business studies at the University of California at Irvine. To keep his hand in, Larry produced an interactive multimedia training package on producing multimedia training packages. It was a perceived niche market. Treating himself and his wife to a trip abroad on the proceeds.

Played high school football in the jacket worn by Passenger 38.

What he is doing or thinking

Feeling proud that he spotted *Mind the Gap* in *Time Out*.

It's fun. One of the actors whispers to you the next destination and herds you all into the same carriage. Then they start doing their routines. Like asking everybody else directions to Edgware or borrowing another actor's newspaper and cutting out the pictures without asking him first.

Larry gets over to the UK when he can. But it's strange. Things are obviously better since Thatcher took over, but it seems there's less and less reason to come over. Everything's so American, or, like the BBC, the best of it's in America anyway. They can see Andrew Lloyd Webber[5] at home.

Things like this will have to go. Figure they got only four people paying £5.00 each. Twenty pounds for a morning's work? That's only about 30 bucks. There's three of them, so do some of them volunteer or something?

Now there's cops. Are the cops part of the deal too? Larry looks at his wife and roars with laughter.

Another helpful and informative
253 *footnote*
5 Andrew Lloyd Webber is one of
Britain's authentic theatrical
geniuses. His discovery that a
'show' depends neither on acting,
content nor direction but on
staging has meant that his
spectacular musicals are exactly
the same whether playing in Los
Angeles or Singapore.

Serious theatre in London has
benefited enormously from this
discovery. For example *Murmuring
Judges*, a serious exposé of London
legal life, featured real taxis on
stage, fake rain, and recreated
interiors onstage of the Royal
Opera House, Covent Garden, not
to mention a chorus line of full
frontal (male) nudity, greatly
enhancing its message.

To sum up, because of Lloyd
Webber, everything is now a
musical.

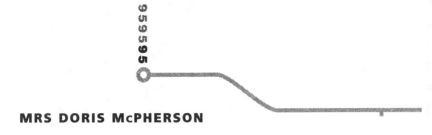

MRS DORIS McPHERSON

Outward appearance
Brown waterproof, brown bow legs, flat shoes, transparent hood tied over a helmet of tightly woven white hair.

Inside information
Winner of the Howick *Evening Gazette*'s London Winter Getaway Prize. It's all laid on. A week at the Savoy. Very nice. Doris is down with her friend Cynthia, who's poorly this morning. Doris is off to see an exhibition at the Hayward Gallery: *German Romanticism*. Not too sure what it is. Doris is a cat-lover whose seven cats are safe back home in a cattery.

What she is doing or thinking
She gets on at the Embankment, only to be sat on by a very tall young man. Well, it was an honest mistake. He gets up straightaway and hits his head, and sits down on someone else. Must be terribly embarrassing for him, poor lad. Everyone laughs. They're ever so cheerful in London, not at all like what everyone says.

Her stop comes up and Doris stands and nods and smiles. 'Any time you want to sit on my knee, feel free,' she says to the young man. As she gets off, a policeman gets on and says hello, so she grins back.

On the platform, amid the gush of people who know where they are going, she is lost. She sees a woman near her own age, Passenger 80. 'Excuse me,' Doris asks, 'do you know the way to the Hayward Gallery?'

'I'm going there myself,' says the woman. By the time they help each other to the top of the stairs, they've got onto the subject of cats.

MR GEOFF RYMAN

Outward appearance

Tall, ravaged, nervous-looking middle-aged man in tourist dress. Stands up to peer at the Tube map opposite his seat. At Embankment, the doors rumble shut and he sits back down on top of an elderly passenger.

Inside information

An amateur actor on holiday from his day job, taking part in a performance of *Mind the Gap*. Paying customers follow the comedians from station to station as they perform. In this routine, he is supposed to stand up from his seat, while another member of *MtG* takes it. The art is to sit without looking backwards.

What he is doing or thinking

To his horror, Geoff discovers that he has sat on top of a real passenger. The man opposite him roars with laughter. Geoff's ears burn. This is the first time he has taken the lead idiot role, and he had not counted on how embarrassing it is. He stands up, hits his head on the rail, and sits on top of Ben, the leader of *MtG*, on whom he should have sat. More laughter.

Then the police arrive. It must have been the tie and scissors routine – that scares people. Ben just sits there. *Ben, say something!*

Questions race. Is this legal? Do LT know? Geoff finds he has no answers. They all have to get off at Lambeth North, and, instead of helping, Ben flees up the steps.

Ben, don't leave me!

'We . . . I'm . . . I'm sure we have a letter of permission.'

'Good,' says the policeman. 'Where is it?'

The train rolls out for Elephant and Castle.

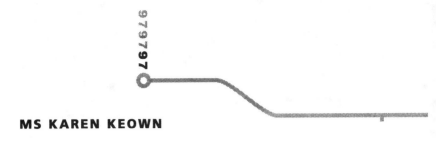

MS KAREN KEOWN

Outward appearance
Pale woman, about 29, wispy hair, fine features cramped by tiny spectacles. Her arms form a circle in front of her.

Inside information
Unemployed woman on her way to St Thomas' Hospital to steal a newborn baby. At home, there is already a nursery with a pram and toys. The neighbours know she is pregnant.

What she is doing or thinking
She is suffocated by a sense of being cheated, of people watching her in order to thwart her. In her arms, she can feel her beautiful baby. There are people everywhere who would deny it to her.

At Waterloo, police get onto the train. Karen refuses to look up, but sees the dark trousers, the blue shirt out of the corner of her eyes. Who betrayed her? Her mind races.

'Do you wish to make a complaint?' the policeman asks. Yes, she answers him in her mind, yes I do, you people should be chasing real criminals. In her mind she must also disguise her intention from him.

The train idles at Waterloo, doors open. If she gets off now, the police will know that she plans to go to St Thomas'. The doors trail shut as if cutting her baby in half.

'I can explain,' the man next to her says. She thinks he is her boyfriend who will protect her. Conspiratorially, she avoids his gaze. At Lambeth North, he lures the police away. Grateful, she decides to make him the father. Karen shifts to make the baby more comfortable. She goes on to the Elephant.

That'll fool them.

CONSTABLE BERT HARRIS

Outward appearance
Fifty, bug-eyed, pot-bellied in Transport Police uniform. Gets on at Waterloo and looms over the end row of seats. His colleague, Passenger 91, blocks the other doorway.

Inside information
Joined Transport Police after a stint in the Army. The job consists of scooping up drunks from platforms, hoisting suicides off the tracks, moving buskers on.

What he is doing or thinking
He's aware that something strange is happening to his mind the longer he stays in the job. You see the worst on the Tube: beggars with hands that won't work properly who stink, whose hair is falling out because they can't wash. He's started to wash it for them, with Windolene spray. The lads caught a poof in the toilets at Waterloo. For a joke they poured bleach on his genitals and he ran screaming out into the main concourse with his trousers down. Bert arrested him for indecent exposure, which was the best joke of all. Animals. Even animals don't do it in toilets. The skin came off.

Now we got some berk bothering people for a bunch of fun-lovers. An old dear is getting off. 'Do you want to make a complaint?' Bert asks her. She just grins at him and gets off. She's gaga. Put her in a home.

'You ought to find yourself a seat, sir,' says Bert.

'I can explain,' says the berk, scared. 'We're a theatre company.'

'I can get your autograph then. When we get out at the next stop.' Officer Harris grins. God, he hates his job. God, he hates the people.

MS SUZE MORLEY

Outward appearance
Young woman pulling a bicycle into the carriage at Embankment. Short hair, a fluorescent coat, safety helmet, and thick legs in track suit bottoms. She flips off a *Viva!* shoulder bag onto an empty seat and stands holding onto the bike.

Inside information
Danni Jarret's sister. Works for the Personnel Office of the Department of Transport near Lambeth Bridge. Devoted to serial monogamy, meaning she only has sex with one man a night. Concerned about the size of her arse, so today she cycled into work.

What she is doing or thinking
Whose good idea was this? It's supposed to be downhill from Camden. A motorcyclist slapped her with his wing mirror at Seven Dials. Trafalgar Square was the most terrifying event of the week, especially when a taxi driver decided to pretend she wasn't there. Now she's sweaty, shaken and utterly puffed. Fags and booze, that's what keeps me in good shape.

People laugh, she looks up. Some comedian has just sat down on an old woman. He jumps up and sits down on someone else. There's no pleasing some people. As the train whines into Waterloo, the old woman gets up and says to him, 'You can sit on my knee any time you like.'

Just let him try it with me, thinks Suze.

A policeman gets on. Just leaving, Officer. The policeman says to the old woman, 'Would you like to make a complaint?'

The old dear just smiles back. You a native Londoner, then? thinks Suze. They both get out without saying a word to the Filth.

MS DIANA DIAMANT

Outward appearance
Woman in early middle age. Denim coat with fake fur collar, cowboy boots, Marianne Faithfull hair, rugged good looks. She should have a cigarette in one hand and a whisky glass in the other.

Inside information
Freelance estate valuer. Works from home which means she can devote more time to Emma, her daughter.

What she is doing or thinking
Emma loves painting up her face and going to parties in character. She lives in a provisional world. If the curtains are drawn at mid-day and it's dark, Emma asks quizzically, 'Is it night?' If they miss a train, Emma sits on the platform and mourns with heaving sobs. Diana is beginning to understand how different Emma's world is and how busy she herself is destroying it.

Diana's best friend Jane died at Christmas. They met at prenatal classes, and visited each other at the births. Their children became friends; Diana or Jane would take care of them both when the other had an assignment. In the hospital, Diana sat smoking by Jane's bed, ducking the nurses and their admonitions. 'You're the only one who hasn't run away,' Jane said.

Christmas was wiped out. As a late treat last night, Diana took both kids to see *Peter Pan*. It did nothing to help little Bobby. 'Look, they're flying,' Diana said to him. He did not respond. In the car going back, he said in a quiet voice, 'Everybody's dead. The Lost Boys are dead. Peter Pan's dead. Tinkerbell is dead.'

'No she's not,' pleaded Emma. 'She's not. She's going to come back.'

MR PAUL LAUNCEY

Outward appearance
Lanky man rising 50, sitting hunched in a rumpled suit. Creased double chin. Bifocals, pink cheeks, balding dome.

Inside information
Investment adviser for Adventure Capital. A Lloyds name and soon-to-be bankrupt man.

What he is doing or thinking
He thinks of his wife and his only child. Benjamin is twelve years old and morbidly shy, hardly able to talk to anyone his own age. He has special tutors. Paul cannot imagine the boy surviving in a state school. That is where he is going.

As for Anne, she is capable, kind, and deserves better. Even though his wife is not a name, her own family money will be taken to pay the debts. Lloyds can take the house, everything else. Alone, Anne would not be in any way liable. They would both be better off if he were dead.

Paul has decided to kill himself. The problem is how. The insurance won't pay out if it looks like suicide. It must be above suspicion, and he must die. The very worst thing that could happen is that he survives as a cripple with debts still due.

He lets his stop rattle past, thinking, thinking, his job now irrelevant. Could he hire someone to kill him? Without anyone knowing it was him? He could buy a new pair of slippery-soled leather shoes and slide helplessly under a bus, scattering papers.

He wants to die. Above all else, cold and angry, he wants the insurance to pay.

He is, after all, insured with Lloyds. The train sweeps him on towards the Elephant.

MAJOR EDWIN GRIVES

Outward appearance

Trim, conservatively dressed, about 35. Sits legs crossed, looking miffed, trying to read the *FT*.

Inside information

Came out of the Army straight into development work for Pall Mall Oil. Knows both Passengers 37 and 235. Travels widely for Pall Mall, always first class. Has family connections in the Far East (as well as a mistress, but he knew her before he married). His wife teaches in the local girls' school. Commutes from a village near Aldeburgh. Lives in a 16th-century farmhouse with a Japanese water garden. He takes the train to Liverpool Street, parking his white BMW at the local station.

What he is doing or thinking

Cursing his local pig farm, which he calls Pig Belsen. When they wash out the tanks late at night, the smell wakes him up. The slurry is so full of chemicals it cannot be used on the fields. It's hauled away in huge lorries marked HAZCHEM.

This morning, however, was beyond imagining. The damn fool lorry driver tried to drive down their lane and got stuck. The valve went and they were flooded with pig swill. Edwin had to drive through it. Sheets of slurry washed up over the windscreen. The wipers jammed. His son Jason had left the back window open. The rear seat was splattered. The stench penetrated everything

The car is still sitting outside the station, a solid mass of drying sewage. The parking lot for several spaces round is empty. Tonight he'll have to drive through the sewage again.

Edwin gives his *FT* another fretful shake. No comment.

MR SAIF ALI KHAN

Outward appearance
Thick-set Asian, about 25, in track suit bottoms, black trainers, baseball cap, jacket with felt lettering sewn on it, lumberjack shirt in blue and white checks. George Michael stubble. Flicks through an issue of *Satellite TV*.

Inside information
Works in his family's hardware business. Married to Amrita, daughter of a business partner. Recently branched the business out into home electronics.

What he is doing or thinking
Thinking about last night. His mother was cooking, hollow eyed, while he talked about his father.

His father came to Britain first, they followed. Saif is convinced his father didn't want them. He would slam doors, slam their mother, slam the two boys. Saif remembers being pulled down the staircase of the council flats by his ankles, screaming, holding out his arms to his mother.

Saif found he could escape beatings by bursting into tears whenever there was trouble. So the father beat the elder brother who blamed Saif. And strangest of all, because he wasn't beaten, Saif thought his father didn't love him.

Saif grew up disruptive, with bad grades and a short attention span. He still finds reading nigglingly annoying, and hates most television. Things bore him. Women bore him, Amrita bores him.

'You still hate your father,' his mother said sadly.

'Yes, yes I do,' said Saif.

He did not see his father standing behind him. 'But I've grown up now,' his father said. It's true. Nowadays he is quiet, gentle, polite.

That's the worst of it. Saif cannot even reach the man who did it. He keeps flicking the magazine pages.

MR KENDO KAWAHARA

Outward appearance

Japanese businessman. Tall and heavy in a grey suit, immaculate white shirt, tan overcoat. Briefcase. Narrow eyes, slightly pock-marked cheeks. Chews gum slowly as if laconically issuing orders. Greased hair.

Inside information

Publisher of a successful magazine for Japanese people about how to live in England during business stints away from home. Also runs a thriving business supplying them with Japanese books, food, music and social opportunities. Mr Kawahara is on his way to a recording session in a small studio operated by Merely College, who provide him with student musicians.

Kendo is an Elvis Presley imitator who releases records of material the King would have recorded if he had lived. His professional name is The Kyoto Flash. The cassettes sell quite well through specialist mail outlets in the United States and Great Britain.

His briefcase contains lyrics and charts for the sessions. The new set is the album Elvis would have recorded in 1991, the year of the Gulf War. The songs include 'Tie a Yellow Ribbon Round the Old Oak Tree', 'You Take My Breath Away' from *Top Gun*, 'Memory' from *Cats*, and Tom Waits' 'Soldier's Things'. This is a great song about war: a friend lists a dead soldier's things at a garage sale. Waits sings it in a dry rasp. Kendo will sing it as Elvis would have done, as a tribute, with a lovely tremolo of emotion and a soaring operatic conclusion.

What he is doing or thinking

Mr Kawahara is planning Elvis's AIDS album. It will include his unique interpretation of Springsteen's 'Streets of Philadelphia'.

MR SHIMON SOUZA

Outward appearance

Small, rotund, dark-skinned man in navy-blue suit. Two walking sticks and a nautical tie clip. He wriggles in place as if doing a belly dance.

Inside information

Legal adviser at the International Maritime Organization near Vauxhall Bridge. Considers implications of changes to International Shipping Law. Of Portuguese/Angolan extraction. Lost both legs as a child when a train ran over him. Won a postgrad scholarship at Harvard. His life is built around independence and dignity.

What he is doing or thinking

Shimon's testicles have caught in the leather harnesses of his artificial legs. Checking to see if anyone is looking, he eases his hand into his pocket to flip them free. The harnesses close like jaws.

He arches his groin up in the hopes of pulling free. His entire genitalia are wrenched around 90 degrees. The most effective thing to do would be drop his trousers and start again. Instead, he gives two hard pelvic thrusts.

This makes him erect. Shimon has always felt that his generous pudenda were a just reward for those with the imagination to sleep with him. Now that very generosity increases his embarrassment. He stands, but putting on his coat reveals the extent of his problem. He whimpers towards the doorway in pain. A woman looks at him in heartfelt sympathy.

Shimon thinks of International Law, safety regulations, important shipping lanes. Rather worryingly, this makes the erection worse.

Shimon waits by the doorway, sweat smearing his brow. It is plainly going to be one of those days.

Until the lady follows him out of the carriage.

MRS CAMILLA BURKE-HARRIS

Outward appearance

Julie Andrews gone British. Short hair, forceful face, pleated grey dress, black jacket, pearl earrings. Holds up wire-rimmed glasses to the light, cleans them, and goes back to documents spread out on her briefcase.

Inside information

Director of the Small Bosses Syndicate.

What she is doing or thinking

Redrafting a paper on the SBS's case against charity shops.

> A review of retailers in Wimbledon has confirmed the effect on small businesses of the five charity shops in the main shopping area. Margerete Tweed, manager of *Dropsilla Fashions,* has recorded a 5% fall in trade since the Aged and Infirm Cancer Benefit Shop opened next door. David Tooth has similar statistics to back up his case against the Wounded Children's Healing Fund.

Camilla writes a note: 'This is all too anecdotal'. Charity shops are, of course, a scandal, undercutting local businesses, but this paper is not good enough. She sighs.

She has a nine o'clock appointment with that wide boy Willie Dynham. It was quite clever what he did to French wine, but Camilla remembers him of old. He simply never tells the truth. Some people seem to find this charming, but as far as she is concerned, he is the sort of person who gives Small Business a bad name.

The train slows into Waterloo. Suddenly a foreign workman of some kind attacks an advertisement. Camilla is outraged. She stands up to him. 'How could you do that to a perfectly good advertisement?' He simply looks blank, resentful. 'That poster creates jobs!'

He's lost for an answer. Such people always are.

MRS EMMA CHRISTIE

Outward appearance
Blue trousers, thick-soled shoes, anorak, pageboy haircut, no make-up. Reads a thick, stapled, mimeographed publication, gone feathery around the edges.

Inside information
Clandestine author of slash fiction, for which she publishes a monthly fanzine. Slash is written almost exclusively by women. It describes in livid physical and romantic detail, love affairs between male television characters. Bodie and Doyle from *The Professionals*, or Sulu and Chekov from *Star Trek*.

Emma's province is *Voyage to the Bottom of the Sea*. The ruined beauty of Richard Basehart, the slightly ageing delicacy of David Hedison, make her heart grow faint. She writes of hidden moments of intimacy snatched between the giant squid or intelligent sea aliens.

What she is doing or thinking
Like a priest caught in a cottage, she is reading her bible for comfort.

The newly released tape of episode 57 has a VERY slashable moment in which the Admiral clasps the Captain's shoulder to give him fatherly advice. Hedison goes all dewy-eyed.

Her husband has found out. He cleaned out the garage, and found a box of 'zines: the scenes of incestuous buggery between Steptoe and Son, a passionate affair among all four of *The Monkees*.

'I understand,' he said. 'You do this because you want to get closer to men. You want to be in love with a man, but as a man, an equal.'

Something in her tremored as he said it, with brown eyes that looked suddenly feminine.

Now, two days later, she understands. Her husband is a cross-dresser. So in a sense is she.

CHIEF INSPECTOR
ANTHONY CURNIFFE

Outward appearance
Blue pinstripe suit, blue overcoat. A broken, disorderly face with heavy nose, lips that curl into a natural sneer, a crown of almost femininely upswept and completely silver hair. Sits still, with a Mona Lisa smile.

Inside information
Chief Inspector of the Metropolitan Police. On his way to his daily work in the bureaucracy of enforcement.

What he is doing or thinking
Remembering yesterday's memorial service for Sir Terence Hobbin, at St Paul's Church, WC2. Sir Terence had been retired for years, but was remembered for a series of administrative reforms in the late 1970s. He was a solid, respected man, notable to the readers of the *Journal of the Police College*.

So even the family were surprised and delighted when Sir John Gielgud climbed into the pulpit to read a poem of John Donne's. It showed an unexpected, but altogether apt, appreciation of a life spent in public service. The rich actorly tones resonated around the roof of the church.

It was even less likely, then, that Sir Ian McKellen also entered and, smiling somewhat embarrassed, began to wave at Sir John. Sir John waved benignly back, and finished his reading. He had been expected in St Paul's Church, SW1.

Every day, walking to the tube from his apartment in Bloomsbury, Chief Inspector Curniffe stops to talk to the statue of Gandhi.[6] This morning the Inspector asked: why did it apply? It was all wrong and all right at the same time. Does God play jokes to tell the truth?

Gandhi just smiled. The answer was a wonderful yes.

Another helpful and informative **253** *footnote*

6 Mahatma Gandhi's statue by Fredda Brilliant is located in Tavistock Square, central London. It was unveiled in 1968.

Anything called Tavistock, Russell or Bedford in central London is or was owned by the same family. There is also a Tavistock Street, Place and Clinic and Bedford Park, Place, Row, Square, and Street along with Russell Square, Street and Road. Basically Bedford Estates included Covent Garden and Bloomsbury. They are also still my landlord.

MS ANYA RUDERIAN

Outward appearance
Mass of curly black hair, black duffel-coat, baggy black turtle-neck, boots. Anya is taking photographs of Passenger 75. Like her, the camera is neat and unobtrusive. She checks the reading, squints, clicks and all without anyone seeming to notice.

Inside information
Freelance photographer famed for her location work. Lebanese-Armenian extraction, married to a handsome, quiet barrister. This job is for a campaign to convince men it's all right to be seen in public reading *Jacqueline*, the fashion magazine.

What she is doing or thinking
If she is not careful, the photographs will look green and horrible and express everything she feels about the Tube: claustrophobia, a taste of something black and gritty between the teeth. The model is wrong too: he looks sulky, not dynamic, not the kind of guy you would want to be.

Yesterday she photographed the inside of the unfinished British Library.[7] It was huge, bare, labyrinthine. The architect wandered off to deal with a wiring problem. Anya was left alone in one of the subterranean chambers.

She got lost. There were no windows, or signage. She wandered for over an hour, calling 'Paul?' Anya doesn't flap (she was able to film in Bosnia). In fact, she found the idea amusing. I could die in here and become its first ghost, she thought. The unfinished corridors went on and on, and everything was coated in white dust. Even now the white dust follows her as ghostly footprints.

Anya says to the model: 'Stefan? Look up.' She decides to take another roll using her handsome husband instead.

Another helpful and informative
253 *footnote*
7 The new British Library is Britain's most famous overrun building project . . . by decades, millions. Plans were approved in 1980 but by October 1996, it still was not open. At one point, after most of the decoration was complete, all wiring had to be replaced. The final cost will be in the neighbourhood of £450 million and it will run out of space by 2000.

It's made of red brick and looks bloody bleak. Next door is St Pancras Station, which was also regarded as an eyesore in its day and now looks like an Alice-in-Wonderland neo-Gothic palace. It doubled as one in the Ian McKellen film version of *Richard III*. Maybe the future will find the new British Library beautiful.

But it will have to open first.

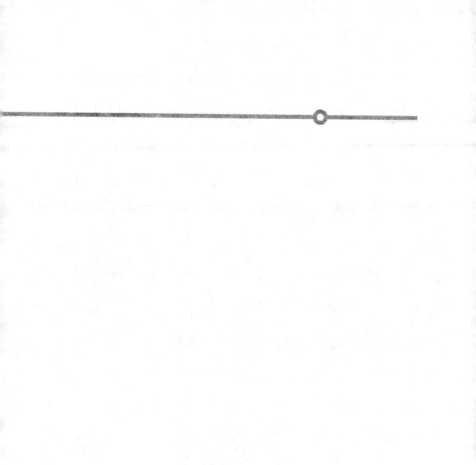

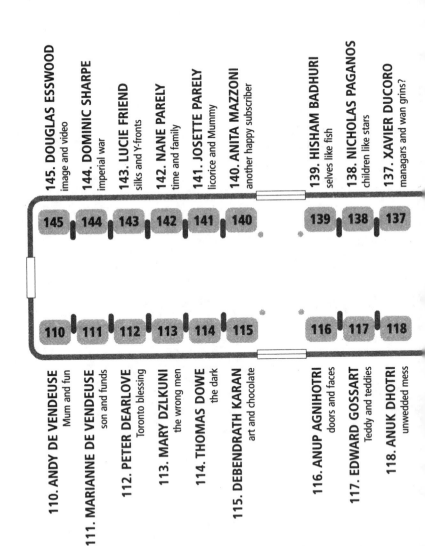

For Your Reading Ease and Comfort

PASSENGER MAP

Car No 4

145. DOUGLAS ESSWOOD
image and video

144. DOMINIC SHARPE
imperial war

143. LUCIE FRIEND
silks and Y-fronts

142. NANE PARELY
time and family

141. JOSETTE PARELY
licorice and Mummy

140. ANITA MAZZONI
another happy subscriber

139. HISHAM BADHURI
selves like fish

138. NICHOLAS PAGANOS
children like stars

137. XAVIER DUCORO
managars and wan grins?

145 | 144 | 143 | 142 | 141 | 140   139 | 138 | 137

110 | 111 | 112 | 113 | 114 | 115   116 | 117 | 118

110. ANDY DE VENDEUSE
Mum and fun

111. MARIANNE DE VENDEUSE
son and funds

112. PETER DEARLOVE
Toronto blessing

113. MARY DZLKUNI
the wrong men

114. THOMAS DOWE
the dark

115. DEBENDRATH KARAN
art and chocolate

116. ANUP AGNIHOTRI
doors and faces

117. EDWARD GOSSART
Teddy and teddies

118. ANUK DHOTRI
unwedded mess

THIS MAP SHOWS YOU

☞ WHO is in the car

✐ WHERE they are sitting and

☞ WHAT are their interests and concerns

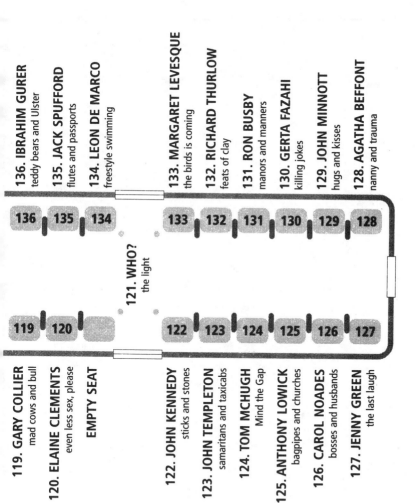

136. IBRAHIM GURER
teddy bears and Ulster

135. JACK SPUFFORD
flutes and passports

134. LEON DE MARCO
freestyle swimming

133. MARGARET LEVESQUE
the birds is coming

132. RICHARD THURLOW
feats of clay

131. RON BUSBY
manors and manners

130. GERTA FAZAHI
killing jokes

129. JOHN MINNOTT
hugs and kisses

128. AGATHA BEFFONT
nanny and trauma

121. WHO?
the light

119. GARY COLLIER
mad cows and bull

120. ELAINE CLEMENTS
even less sex, please

EMPTY SEAT

122. JOHN KENNEDY
sticks and stones

123. JOHN TEMPLETON
samaritans and taxicabs

124. TOM MCHUGH
Mind the Gap

125. ANTHONY LOWICK
bagpipes and churches

126. CAROL NOADES
bosses and husbands

127. JENNY GREEN
the last laugh

The 253 Guide to Homely English

Ashamed by your English?

You're chatting up a bird at the bar. You say "The beauty of the Web is that you can utilize ftp, pdf or even telnet through one interface." She says "Piss off, you pathetic little nerd."

Do you find yourself using words like "prioritize" or "evanescent" in public? Unable to stop yourself using expressions like "Unix file-naming conventions"?

Do you sound like a puffed-up prof, or just like the folks back home? You will know when you use *The 253 Guide to Homely English*

* Simply run 253 of your own words through our Ready Reckoner. Here's how it works!
* Count the number of sentences in your 253 words. Divide 253 by that number. Write down your score. (Hint: the lower the number, the better!)
* Count the number of three-sound words. Try saying the word syllable. See? It's got three sounds! Count 'em and write the number down! (Hint: the more, the worse!)
* Take your first ten sentences. Count all the words in total for those sentences only. Divide by ten. Then multiply the number of sentences by that number. (Hint: the lower, the better)

Add all your scores up. Remember: the lower the score, the better you've done.

Here are some scores we prepared earlier:

Remembrance of Things Past by Marcelle Proust	367.35
The Microsoft Word User's Guide	320.8
Pyramids by Terry Pratchett	233.8
The Sun newspaper	170.37
Oxford Reading Series: Stage One	0

Anything higher than 253 and you're out!!!

Homely English
It's as plain as the nose on your face

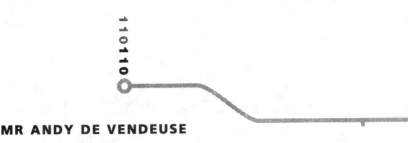

MR ANDY DE VENDEUSE

Outward appearance

Eighteen or nineteen, very tall, wearing blue jeans, black train-ers, blue corduroy coat with fleecy sheepskin lining and collar. Skeletal hands and fingers. Coils of silver bangles around his wrists. Under his coat are layers of green, then red. He has a long, pale, striking face made even more so by thick-stemmed midnight sunglasses and retro-punk spiky black hair.

He pats the seat next to him and an older woman crosses the aisle to sit beside him. He snuggles up to her and puts his head on her shoulder.

Inside information

A musician without a band at the moment. He and his mum have decided to chuck everything in and go to France for a few months. His father is French and the hope is that they will get some of the money he owes them. Andy doesn't want to spend too much time with his father: he works for some kind of bank, and puts waves in his hair.

What he is doing or thinking

He yearns to put his feet on the vacated chair opposite him. His long skinny legs stretch across the aisle. His mum says, 'Andy, don't, come on, darling,' in an East End voice. He has an inspiration. He puts his feet on the arm rest instead. His mum nips the baggy knees of his trousers and lifts his leg. At that moment an old geezer comes to sit down, so he moves anyway. Andy smiles. His mum is great. France, whatever happens, will be fun. He looks over her shoulder at a magazine.

Outward appearance

Brown coat to the floor, delicate scarf in different shades of brown, long soft boots in fake alligator-pattern cloth. Her hair is highlighted but is naturally light brown. Her face, though deeply lined, is somehow also young in attitude: forthright, impatient, open, defensive. She moves next to her son and thumbs through a free recruitment magazine.

Inside information

Works in a friend's plant shop. She speaks impeccable French. Worked in France for many years as a ski instructor, where she met her rich, French husband. Now impoverished, she often nips across the Channel in order to buy cigarettes in bulk to sell in the UK. Sometimes she takes a van if she can afford the rental and buys wine for resale. Sometimes it's cigarettes, which are light enough for the train. She worries about finance, but only for the sake of her son. Otherwise she would live anywhere, anyhow.

What she is doing or thinking

The magazine consists mostly of job ads within a shell of second-hand articles. She hopes to find something that will use her skills in French. 'They all want something I don't have,' she sighs. 'I can speak the language probably better than someone who's been to university, but they all want qualifications.'

'You could get one of these qualifications teaching English to foreigners,' her son says. He thumbs back to the course ads.

Indeed, she could. She smiles and kisses him. Her reward for being brave is Andy. She looks at his black rucksack, with the logo 'Mon Viso 3'.

'My face,' she muses.

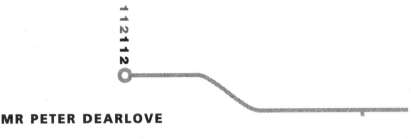

MR PETER DEARLOVE

Outward appearance

Tall nervous black man, gets on at Embankment. Brown leather jacket hangs off narrow shoulders. Green jeans, green socks, wispy moustache, butterfly-delicate ankles. Lopes apologetically to his seat then twitches in place. Charming, childlike and disjointed all at once, like an innocent Martian, or Charlie Chaplin. Keeps clearing his throat.

Inside information

Has returned from Canada, where he accepted the Toronto Blessing.[1] He walked straight from Toronto airport to the church. It was small, ordinary and that seemed right. Peter had to line up for most of a day, but when he got inside, all was as promised. He talked in tongues, thrashed on the floor, and Jesus came and sat with him and held his hand. Jesus said to him that he was to love everyone and everyone would love and forgive him.

What he is doing or thinking

Peter blesses everyone he walks past. He thinks he is about to bear witness, and speak about God's love, but something holds him back. Wanting to speak is an ache inside. Why is he so silent? It feels like shame. The man across from him looks forbidding, the girl next to him is too pretty. Perhaps God will unleash his tongue when the right time comes.

He wishes there were someone here with the Blessing. The Blessing sings like the universe. People with the Blessing hum its tune. Peter may not have a job, but he knows why he is on this train: to bear witness.

So he keeps clearing his throat, and is swept on, towards Elephant and Castle.

Another helpful and informative
253 *footnote*
1 The Toronto Blessing is a worldwide charismatic phenomenon which started in a small church not far from what I think of as Malton Airport (now Lester B. Pearson International). The Blessing sets people talking in tongues. It appears to be passed on from one congregation to another, a bit like a virus.

Worldwide charisma? Canada? It doesn't sound like the country I left.

It's a typical Canadian story. My father was poached by the American head office and, like so many Canadians, we moved south to LA. It was 1962, and we arrived in the middle of the Cuban Missile Crisis, which is another story. I'd grown up in a village that was, in those days, the boonies. My best friend lived on a 600 acre farm that had been in his family since the 19th century. The Credit River flowed through it; you could see deer running the fields. In winter, rabid foxes staggered drooling out of the undergrowth. The farm is now a suburb. The grand old house was torn down.

In 1995, I went back for the first time since 1969. I expected to drive through fields of tract housing. Instead, along the old Highway 10, I drove through skyscrapers. I recognized one barn, alone in their midst. It had a white painted dancing horse on its roof.

The village was even spookier. Its name, Meadowvale, had been hijacked by a suburban development on the other side of Streetsville, and so it was now called Meadowvale Village. A collapsed sign just outside it announced that it was a Heritage Village.

A kind of invisible bell jar had been dropped over it, protecting it from change. This may be because no one wanted to develop land under flight paths. Meadowvale looked as it had done in 1962, except that the faces of the eleven-year-olds I left behind were now as lined as my own.

Meadowvale had been inhabited by the descendants of Scottish immigrants. We used their vowel sounds and said 'aye?' instead of the American 'you know?' I went to a one-room schoolhouse that had been built in 1871, and prayed in a United Church of Canada Sunday School.

I hated it. Canada was a raw country. My schoolmates were tough little kids who wanted to grow up into car mechanics. Toronto was grey, blustery, its port in decline. Many of the people my age have since moved north, deeper into the bush, perhaps to escape the bland gloss of what Toronto became.

Just beyond the border of the Magic Circle was a mound of earth, where the preserving bypass had been built, burying the old 2nd Line West. In the other direction, the road plunges into Toronto's ethnic suburbia. About a mile from my old church, now an evangelical centre, there is a Coptic Orthodox Church. There is a mosque.

Canada was once rich, and monolithic. As someone else said, Canadian artists expressed alienation. Now they express difference: gay Canadians, Coptic Canadians, Armenian Canadians, Italian Canadians. Let alone French Canadians.

Talking in tongues?

MISS MARY DZLKUNI

Outward appearance

Stunningly beautiful black girl, black coat, long red dress with big buttons up the front, left dangerously undone. She stares ahead through narrowed eyes, lips pulled down in a distracted frown. Pokes at her face, unconsciously looking for spots to squeeze. There are some, but not where she is squeezing.

Inside information

A temp, now a receptionist at the Peebrane Trust near Lambeth North. She does not quite know she is beautiful. She feels unloved. Her father and mother split up and divided their six children. Her father took three to England, separating Mary from her twin sister.

What she is doing or thinking

She has just been dropped again. Ken seemed a big, strong, noble man. He visited her father's house, courted her father, booming all the time about his prospects, about his standing back home. Foolish girl, she got carried away, gave in to him and now of course he treats her differently.

The men Mary meets are bold egotists who are confident enough to treat her like a Bastille to be stormed. Being beautiful could be enough to ruin her life.

The man next to her, strange, thin, says gently, 'Do you have Jesus in your life?'

'What? No.'

'If you get to know Jesus, he makes everything all right.'

This is a shy man. It is like talking to a nervous deer.

'I have to get off at the next stop,' she says. 'You can talk to me on the way if you like.'

He does and she does not worry when he gets off with her.

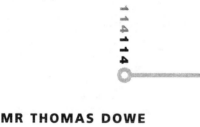

MR THOMAS DOWE

Outward appearance
Balding, rotund man, queasy with sweat in a pistachio shirt and jacket. Pressed white trousers. No briefcase, or heavy overcoat. Body language awkward, twisted, at odds with studied smartness of casual dress.

Inside information
A fireman on long-term sick leave, being treated for depression. Came to London from Northampton after a certain incident that he calls a near miss. Lives alone in a spotless flat. Only companion a female cat he grooms ruthlessly. Has kept secret, even from his doctors, a completely unacceptable sexual longing. On his way to St Thomas' Hospital to request chemical castration.

What he is doing or thinking
The dreams are getting worse, truly terrible. His sexual fantasies shock him, leave him wanting to escape his own body, his own self. But they are there and he knows that now, at 32, they will never go away. They will keep pushing him until, drunk or giddy from his other treatments, he goes under.

He remembers the face of the Northampton girl, her hollow eyes as she realized what he meant to do. He remembers the guilty rush, like a colliding train bearing down the track. He imagines real sex is like that, the rising towards a climax. He turned away that time.

He looks at the girl next to him, her long, vulnerable, fleshy legs. It would be so easy to do it now and be shut away forever. Then the girl begins to speak to the boy next to her. Thank you, Jesus.

The train comes into Waterloo, and unnoticed, he gets up to go.

MR DEBENDRATH KARAN

Outward appearance
Cuddly young Asian man. Knitted ethnic hat with earflaps, knitted coat down to his knees. Frankly fat tummy. Sits with a portfolio and a briefcase. Loosely bandaged thumb.

Inside information
Talented animator who works on the *Asterix* series, and Kia-ora ads. Going to present his work to a South Bank Technopark studio. Confirmed chocoholic who is missing his fix. Bandage from a wound inflicted by a dropped scalpel.

What he is doing or thinking
Dreaming either of a Topic or a Yorkie. He normally has a cup of cocoa for breakfast, but this morning the tin was empty. The thought of Waterloo Station's confectioners tugs at his heartstrings.

At the last possible moment, he grabs his briefcase and gets off. He is going up the long escalator when he realizes – his portfolio is still on the train. His hand hurt, he didn't want to pick up anything with it.

The folio is full of expensive colour reproductions of his best work and will cost 500 quid to replace. Lack of chocolate combines with a sick panic in his tummy. He tries to run up the escalator, but runs out of breath. He rests, leaning on his knees.

At the lost property counter, an elderly lady in line in front of him has lost a clock. By the time he gets to the counter, an old scarecrow of a white man asks him the time of the train. Debendrath guesses. The scarecrow smiles with satisfaction. 'You'll be lucky to get that back,' he says. 'There's been a bit of a crash.'

MR ANUP AGNIHOTRI

Outward appearance
Large man in blue overalls. Beatle haircut, double chin, razor-proof stubble. Briefcase at feet has paint splattered on it. 'Doohrs,' he murmurs. 'Doohrs.'

Inside information
Indian/Ugandan here for many years, running a small but successful electrical contractors. Currently carrying out a small rewiring contract with the Office of Publicity Procurement. Usually takes the van, but all his tools are safe inside the OPP, so he took the tube.

What he is doing or thinking
Looking at the people. It is strange to see how many of them are not English. It is as though he has been locked away in his own world. No wonder his daughter finds him so old fashioned.

Yesterday, one of the managers of the OPP came up to talk to him. What was he doing? The man looked polite, friendly, interested. Anup explained that he was fire-proofing the doors to the main panels. He paints them on both sides with fire retardant.

The man nodded, smiling, friendly, and then asked again. What was he painting?

'Doors,' replied Anup.

'Sorry?' replied the man.

'Doors,' replied Anup. 'Doors.' He swung them back and forth, getting a bit of the paint on his fingers.

'Oh!' said the man. '*Doors.*'

Anup has lived in this country nineteen years and still people cannot understand his accent. He looks at the fireproof paint on his fingers and the nearby faces from around the world. How do they do so well here? He is a happy, outgoing, capable man. How much further does he need to go? Can he go?

MR EDWARD GOSSART

Outward appearance
About 26, suit and overcoat rucked over huge shoulders, ruddy face, jet-black hair. Holds a teddy bear in a Tesco bag.

Inside information
A sales and service executive for Lloyds Bank. Went to Rugby School where he was a star athlete. Will take the teddy bear to Christies at lunchtime to have it valued for his Aunt Ella who needs to sell it.

Teddy speaks estuary English with fluent glottal stops. His job pays shit and he lives in a ground floor flat in Stoke Newington. His aunt lives in a large house in the Cotswolds and thinks the Queen doesn't speak properly. The family made its money running wool mills. The mills and the money have gone.

What he is doing or thinking
Teddy is surprised by the level of resentment he feels. His aunt plainly imagines he drives to work in a BMW. 'Perhaps your girl could take it round for me,' Ella said.

She can't remember where he lives. When friends from work visit, she asks them, 'And how do you like our clean air?' or 'Stoke Newington? We drove through there once didn't we?' When they've gone, she forcefully suggests that Teddy might like to have some more local people around. Jenny Morriat, perhaps. The Morriats owned mills too. Jenny is on heroin.

Ella has no money, and can't shake the flu. Teddy doesn't mind helping her. It's just . . . she makes him feel like such a failure for learning how to live with a changed world.

A teddy bear. Does she really think it's worth anything?

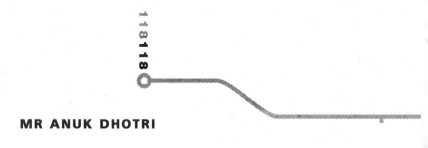

MR ANUK DHOTRI

Outward appearance
Shell-shocked businessman. Black hair in plastered, diving-board angles, dark stubble. Staring, bag-encircled eyes.

Inside information
Down from Solihull for a job interview with University of the South Bank. Spent the night with his bachelor cousin Vikram.

What he is doing or thinking
Anuk is drunk with lack of sleep. He imagines he smells of garbage.

At family gatherings Vik is always immaculately groomed: blazer, brogues, hair-sprayed coiffure. Anuk has only ever seen Vik's London flat once before when Vik had cleaned it.

It is a hell of filth. Vik has a medical condition, and there are used bandages everywhere. The kitchen shelves are coated with dried ketchup. The fridge has mould inside. Outside, pubic hairs are glued to marmalade stains. Eight full garbage bags were decaying in the front hall.

Vik offered Anuk the floor to sleep on. It was sticky and crunchy at the same time. Vikram's cats sniffed Anuk's face and padded up and down him. In the middle of the night he was awakened by a terrible smell. The cats had torn open the garbage bags and coated Anuk in orange peel and discarded curry. He fled to the bathroom to wash. It was in such a nightmarish condition he couldn't use it. He spent the rest of the night outside on the freezing balcony.

Vikram emerged in the morning, cheerful and immaculate.

Anuk can't think straight. The carriage is swimming. To turn up at any university in this state will do him more harm than good.

He decides to get off at Waterloo.

MR GARY COLLIER

Outward appearance
Beefy man about 32, spiky black hair, pock-marked face, black jeans, leather jacket. Scowls broodingly.

Inside information
Works for the Met Police in the Maintenance section. The lover of Amanda Stinton.

What he is doing or thinking
Last night Gary told his wife Toni that it was over, he's leaving her. As she's two months pregnant, there was a bit of a scene. She rang her mum. Mrs Greene came over with murder on her mind. The wife is in the bedroom crying, Mrs Greene is shouting.

'What are you playing at? What's so special about this girl, then? You just get on that phone now and tell her it's over.'

Gary took it for a while and then let her have it. 'I don't have to answer to anybody, let alone you, you old cow. Keep out of it.'

Gary smiles: he has to admit, it was all a bit strong. Mrs Greene is going to do everything she can to make his life a misery. He can't blame them really. You open a jack-in-the-box, you expect it to explode.

The train stops.

Gary gets off at Lambeth North. Two cars ahead, out comes Amanda. He saunters up behind her. 'Boo,' he says smiling.

'Oh. You, is it?'

'Sorry about Sunday. I got something to tell you,' he says.

'So have I,' she says.

They both speak at once. He says, 'I told Toni. I'm leaving her.' She says, 'It's over, Gary.'

Both of them stop, and stare. They don't move as everyone else walks by.

MS ELAINE CLEMENTS

Outward appearance

Young woman, short hair, grim mouth. Felt coat in brightly coloured patterns, like a break for freedom. Reading *Sense and Sensibility*.

Inside information

Works in the British Film Institute Bookshop. It's a gig. She hates movies. At least no one will turn *Sense and Sensibility* into a film.

What she is doing or thinking

Elaine is consumed with hatred for her flatmates. Things were fine until Rita's boyfriend Sedgely more or less moved in.

They fuck like ferrets. Last night, having invited themselves to dinner, they were overcome with passion between the soup and main course. They retired to the bedroom. Elaine made polite conversation over their gladsome cries. Her friends, embarrassed, left early. Quiet descended long enough for Elaine to go to bed. They started again. Their headboard thumps. At 1.00 AM they finally stopped and Elaine got some sleep.

They were at it again in the morning. Elaine put on the kettle, went back to shower, and found that the two of them had migrated to the bathroom and were saving water together. 'Oh God, oh God, I want you inside me!' Rita howled.

Elaine trudged into the kitchen, and drank coffee, her mouth tasting of dead cats. The coffee had its effect. Her bowels started to move. She thumped on the door. 'Oh Elaine!' raged Rita. She and Sedgely stomped out angrily, towels around their midriffs. Rita's glance said: do you think you own the place?

Actually, she does. Elaine wonders: if she threw them out, would it stand up in court?

Knowing Sedgely, something probably would.

WHO?

Outward appearance
Plump, all in grey. Restless, chooses not to stay in his seat, but walks up and down in the doorway area, head cocked sideways in an open, friendly, but somewhat vacant, manner. Iridescent green collar around throat. Pigeon-chested, pigeon-toed.

Inside information
Lost on the Underground system since Baker Street, and separated from his wife whom he misses with a vague yearning. Who is hungry as always. He keeps an eye out for something to eat.

What he is doing or thinking
Investigates a briefcase that smells tantalizingly of proteins, polish, and discarded skin like a corpse in the roadway. Who pecks it experimentally with his beak, but it isn't rotten or crushed enough. Shoes smell inviting too, but they keep moving, and the place where uppers meet soles looks suspiciously like smiling lips over teeth.

Who looks up and sees the lights, as bright as daylight and escape. Leaps up towards them, and pecks at the solidified light, then settles down again. He is no longer mystified by glass. Congratulates himself for being rather with-it, knowing about windows and all. The noise and motion stop, the doors open like jaws, and he scuttles backwards in fear.

Someone tries to herd him towards the doors. Who panics and flies further down the aisle. Suddenly feet, like an avalanche of boulders, move all around him. He flutters up, and people duck. His wings avoid touching their entangling hair.

The doors rumble shut and he is swept on towards the Elephant, and again, he tries to fly upward, towards the light and freedom.

MR JOHN KENNEDY

Outward appearance

Flash git, about 25. Cobalt blue shirt, yellow tie, beige slacks, gelled hair. Looks perplexed.

Inside information

Works at Blote the Bookmakers on Kennington Road. Greets customers like a game show host or computer salesman or boy at Harrods. Unlike his hair, it doesn't gell.

What he is doing or thinking

Yesterday, at lunchtime in Archbishop's Park, John saw an Asian courting couple stoned by kids. At first he thought it was a game of catch. Something arched up into the air and smashed down into a girl's face. Without thinking, John shouted. 'Oi! You! Stoppit!' To his surprise, they scattered, well-dressed lads in slacks. They looked a bit like him.

The girl wept in her boyfriend's arms. 'We shouldn't have been there,' as if God were punishing her for being with a man. She had a Snoopy badge on her coat. They didn't want to call the police.

John went back to work in shock. He told the story, with great drama. Everyone began to laugh, especially at the Snoopy badge. Sharon called out to some regulars. 'Here, John's just seen some Pakis being stoned!'

Why? Why did they laugh? It was as if they were saying: welcome to the big city. He's beginning to understand: it was funny because, specifically, it happened to him. So what is it with him? Under it all, John's a good Catholic boy from the quiet suburbs, who burns candles every Sunday, and confesses minor sins of lust or gluttony. He looks down at his tie and clothes and feels his ears burn.

Outward appearance
Middle-aged man with goatee, russet jacket, collarless shirt, khaki trousers. Sits half asleep, smiling.

Inside information
Middle manager at Mosstains who fancies himself part of the company's young, creative image. Not the kind of person you'd think works there, a good front man. His staff hate him. So do his two ex-wives.

What he is doing or thinking
He's feeling good, on an upswing. Last night he got drunk and sorry for himself. He rang the Samaritans. This acted as a lightning rod for his depression. After ringing, he walked out into the cold night and looked at the stars. It was like looking at eternity. So what if the people at work bypass him, or tell him in taxicabs that they'll fight him every inch of the way and he doesn't have an idea what they want to fight him about? He doesn't want to die, he's just not suited for the job. This mood of philosophical resignation still cushions him.

He gets off at Waterloo and there is a shout. Deborah Payne grabs hold of his arm. 'John!' she says, 'you don't need to die!'

He's still trying to figure out what this means when a black guy comes up and asks Deborah out. She looks stunned. Actually, John always thought he might ask Deborah out, if they ever got along.

'Come out with me instead,' John says trying to twinkle like one of the Musketeers. Deborah holds out both hands: stop. Shaking her head and muttering, she walks away.

And over John, the gloom descends again.

MR TOM McHUGH

Outward appearance

Red thinning hair, pale face, shaving rash on neck. Puffy-eyed from a hangover. Black tie with lurid broken plates of colour, grey raincoat in a swirl on his lap. Lifts up foot to rest on opposite knee. Kicks foot of passenger opposite. Recrosses legs. Pats pocket. Can't find something. Pulls out bits of paper and an opened condom packet (unused). Finds name badge. Tries to clip it onto shirt. The clip won't close. Stands up to put on raincoat. Staggers and steps full onto the foot of the person across from him. Raincoat caught in the belt at back. Struggles with that and steps on neighbour again. Both trouser legs tucked accidentally into socks at back. Shirt untucked. Tries to tuck it in, but pushes raincoat down back of pants instead. Calvin Klein peeks up over top of belt. Picks up case as man opposite stands. Pushes man backwards with his bottom. Staggers to car doors to get off. Vomits copiously.

Inside information

Works for Beetlehide. Tom doesn't know that he is the original inspiration for Ben Bevis's character in Mind the Gap.

What he is doing or thinking

Had been congratulating himself on being so well organized. There he was, preparing early for his exit, sorting out his badge. He wishes he had not drunk so many Pimms last night, but he thought it was lemonade.

He finds vomiting very inconvenient, and a bit annoying after taking such pains. A cloud of hangover descends. He wipes his raincoat with a hanky and prepares to exit at the Elephant.

LORD ANTHONY LOWICK

Outward appearance
Genial older man, short grey hair, grey bumfreezer, polished expensive shoes. Was once perhaps athletic. Sits smiling quietly, cat-like.

Inside information
Full name Lord Lowick of Lowick. His expensive wife is going overripe in the south of France. She lives near their painter daughter who is in the throes of her own divorce. Lord Lowick used to host rock festivals in the '60s; then became a prominent ruralist and friend of Peter Blake in the '70s. Now successfully anonymous.

What he is doing or thinking
On his way back to examine the last of the building work on his new home. It is the tower of the old American Church. The pinnacle has stars and stripes carved into it. The converted bell chamber is huge, with high churchy windows. Lower down, the windows are slits as if for shooting arrows. It is the only completely burglar-proof house he has ever owned.

He will play bagpipes in it. The staircase is wooden and shoots up in one continuous swirl from the ground to the peak. It echoes like a valley. He camped out in the belltower while the work was being done and practised at midnight. He looked out later and saw people gathered below, staring up at the tower with its strange sounds.

No garden to tend, no staff to hide from, the Hockneys and the Blakes safely lining the staircase. Lord Lowick is aware of having escaped many things. The work scared off the nesting kestrels though, and he regrets that. He, himself, will be harder to shift.

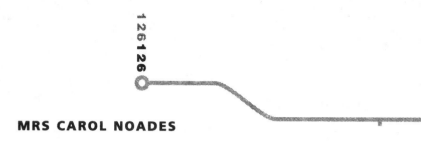

MRS CAROL NOADES

Outward appearance
Nearly invisible. Grey overcoat, blue trousers, stringy hair, a wedding ring.

Inside information
An envelope stuffer at Epik Publications. The Agency found out the staff were working for cash while on benefit. David, their boss, couldn't afford to keep them all on, only some. The girls agreed they wouldn't be divided like that. They all quit.

This is a disaster for Carol. She is illiterate; she survives by deflecting attention. The other women covered for her, reading addresses, matching them to parcels. Where else will she be able to work?

Her husband made her go into work today. Sod the others, he said, we need the money.

What she is doing or thinking
Her husband Billy works as a courier, but it's irregular. He's small and pretty, Billy, and vicious. What are we going to do now? he shouted. It's not my fault! she told him, weepy. He called her stupid, you stupid cow you can't even read. Carol gets on his nerves: he's nice enough to everyone else.

So she's sitting on the train, betraying her friends, but she's thinking: it was wrong of David not to pay us properly and tell National Insurance. He got just as much out of it as we did. Maybe if I go and tell him that, maybe he could charge more for the packing and pay us. Maybe if I told him what it means to me.

So she sits on the train, butterflies in her tummy. But she's going to see the boss and stand her ground.

It won't do any good.

MISS JENNY GREEN

Outward appearance
Red cheeked, twenty, short auburn hair, brilliant red coat.
Bounds in at Embankment, giggling, and peers through the door
between carriages. She waves at someone and starts to laugh.
The train lurches and she drops into the seat at the end of the
row.

Inside information
Works in the pay office of the London College of Printing,
where she met Kevin. Now they live and go to work together
every day. They are both Beatles fans; the music is sensible and
has nice tunes.

What she is doing or thinking
Jenny never had much time for nonsense; straight after school
she got a good job, went out every Friday with the same large
crowd of friends. She knew Kevin was a good thing soon as they
met.

She sees his round pale face, his James Dean hair, through a
screen of splattered grit and dust. She sticks her tongue out at
him. He says, 'You're mad, you are.'

'I'm not having anything to do with you,' she says, and pretends to examine her fingernails. A drunk staggers past her to
stand by the door and that sets her off again.

Then the drunk vomits over her knees. Jenny pauses, and the
ludicrousness of it hits her. Kevin calls, 'That'll teach you!'

She'll have to go home and change. 'I'm getting off here,' she
shouts through the glass. Kevin holds a hand up to his ear. She
leaves the train at Lambeth North, giddy with laughter. The
drunk looks confused. Kevin waves, chuckling, as the train pulls
him away to the Elephant.

DR AGATHA BEFFONT

Outward appearance
A large, round-featured woman with long hair parted in the middle. Everything about her is simple and tidy – from the dark green skirt and jacket to her black coat, all of which a trained eye could see is bespoke fashion. She looks, however, somewhat dazed, her mouth awry in a mixture of amusement and horror.

Inside information
The wife of a junior member of the aristocracy who works in the City. She herself is a member of a major branch of the aristocracy. She works for the Department of Health, Elephant and Castle. Noblesse oblige.

What she is doing or thinking
She is remembering this morning's conversation with her daughter's Nanny. Nanny is attractive, bright, 25 with a delectable smile and good manners. This morning she casually mentioned that she had difficulty with her parents.

'Daddy raped me when I was nine,' Nanny said, brightly. 'I didn't really know what it was. So I dismissed it, I suppose. Except I did rather keep away from him.' Dr Beffont expressed the hope that she did. Did she tell anyone? 'Oh yes, of course,' said the girl. 'That's when he tried to kill me.'

'Kill you!' exclaimed Agatha.

'Mmm hmm,' said the girl nodding happily. 'I woke up with my face covered by a pillow.'

She sounded so cheerfully normal that Agatha left for work. She is only just remembering that most child abusers were abused themselves. And that her daughter is now alone with her. And nine years old.

To make it a perfect morning, someone then throws up on her.

MR JOHN MINNOTT

Outward appearance
Cherubically round man, about 45, in a spruce pinstripe suit and a new blue tie. Grey, flyaway hair. Smiles benignly through slightly piggy eyes.

Inside information
Works in Shipment Traffic for Pall Mall Oil. Once used pins on maps, now works with computers and feels up to date.

What he is doing or thinking
He is thinking of his wife Jean and their morning snuggles. Jean is plump and soft with a vast bottom. Their routine is to wake up at 6.30 every morning for a half hour hug.

It starts with Jean inserting herself under his arm, and resting her head on his grizzled chest. This is called Minging. Then she turns on her side and he hugs her bottom. Then they roll over and she hugs his. It's like toast, you have to do both sides. The climax is the Smumph. He rolls one leg over her and sinks as if she were pillows.

John is convinced that being snuggled regularly gives people an aura. He is sure the old gent opposite is snuggled. So is the laughing girl at the end of the row. Not many other people are, and he feels sorry for them.

He is sure that snuggled people have a broader perspective on life. He could write a book about it: *The Secret of Snuggles*. It would advise long, warm showers afterwards as part of the general cosiness, and give practical advice on what to do if someone farts. (Basically, you ignore it or light a match).

What a lucky man you are, he thinks.

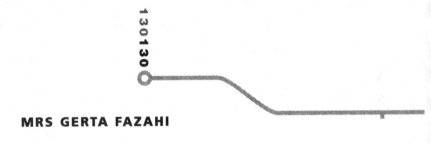

MRS GERTA FAZAHI

Outward appearance

Golden coat, matching scarf, small black shoes and bag. Middle aged, carefully groomed. Smiles to herself, shakes her head, and is suddenly laughing and crying at the same time. Hurriedly wipes her face. No one seems to have seen.

Inside information

Teaches Arabic and Hebrew two days a week at Merely College. Her husband Saul, a lecturer at University College, is dying of motor neurone disease.

What she is doing or thinking

Remembering dinner the night before. Saul has been fitted with a vocalizer, a machine that transforms laboriously typed words into sounds. When it speaks, the machine has an American accent. Saul is Jewish Lebanese. Their visitors were French academics, colleagues who had made a special trip to see Saul before he died.

Saul made light of everything. He started to type in textbook French. The machine burped with an American accent. 'Cesste bun, cesste see deliseeox,' the machine said. 'Jay oon ideeee. Juh voodraize parlezz avek twaaah.' The party took Saul through as many languages as they, in all their cosmopolitan glory, could speak, the funniest being German.

Gerta has just realized that she will never hear Saul's own voice and accent again. He'll still tell jokes. But he's like a tree, falling away leaf by leaf. She wishes it wasn't winter, but spring.

She hears laughter and turns to see a young girl in a red coat, teasing a boy in the next car. Gerta watches them, aching for them. Life is a great rolling wheel, moving on. Sometimes it crushes.

Then a drunk vomits. Sometimes you laugh.

MR RON BUSBY

Outward appearance

Ronnie Kray? Thick-set man, slick hair, cheeks troubled by Marilyn-like beauty spots. Huge shoulders under camel-coloured overcoat. Copper wrist band, gold (?) watch. Going over papers. Sits with one ankle resting on the opposite knee, both arms firmly occupying the armrests.

Inside information

Busby is going to a stakeholders' meeting at Adventure Capital. Runs a deregulated bus company in West Oxfordshire, a cattle feed processing plant, and several homes. Currently developing a property in Little Scam, Oxon.

What he is doing or thinking

Grumpily reviewing papers for today's meeting, still angry at having his planning application turned down. A year ago, he moved into a large farmhouse on the outskirts of Little Scam, redecorated and renamed it The Manor House. The plan was to get clearance to build three new homes in the orchard and sell the entire property with the valuable planning permissions.

Then, attack of the nimbies. Middle-class farts simply didn't want anyone young or non-U moving into their cottage paradise. Road use in the village, no development near the 12th century church, etc. He wasn't given permission. He's writing to Douglas Hurd about it.

Suddenly, Mr Busby's aerial foot is kicked by someone also suspending his foot in the same way. Busby glowers at him. The man's drunk. At Waterloo, both men stand to leave. The idiot bends over and shoves Busby backwards with his bum. Then their briefcases collide. The person sitting next to Busby starts to giggle. Angrily, Busby sweeps away in the opposite direction.

He hates trains. They're full of people.

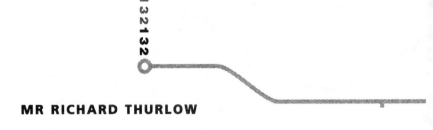

MR RICHARD THURLOW

Outward appearance
Delicate face, stringy, tanned, and ruddy. Narrow shouldered but somehow outdoorsy. Wears a suit and a body warmer without sleeves. Squashed sideways by the bulk of the man next to him.

Inside information
Dick is a champion clay shooter. Works in the York Road branch of Lloyds Bank. Lots of friends in Pall Mall Oil with whom he shoots regularly.

What he is doing or thinking
Wishing his neighbour would shrink. He knows the type: self-made man, thumps around the grounds, arrogant as hell, is a poor shot, but thinks he's a member of some kind of elite.

It pains him to say it, but manners on the grounds are deteriorating. Only last Saturday, he saw some idiot abusing the young scorers. 'I'm not satisfied with the birds!' he shouted. By bullying a youngster, he was allowed to re-shoot the entire stand. It made Dick's blood boil.

Suddenly, Dick's eyes clear: the man next to him. It's him. He's the same one. Dick is about to say something when the man's foot is kicked by the fellow opposite him. Serves you right. Then they both stand and the two of them do a Laurel and Hardy routine, bumping bums and cases. Dick makes a point of sniggering nastily. He catches the man's eye. No wonder you have to take it out on children, matey. Idiots like you scare good people away from the sport.

Dick stands up to follow and sees that this man is too short. He's not the same person at all. But Dick is still mad.

MRS MARGARET LEVESQUE

Outward appearance
Late twenties, neat beige suit, long baby-blue cloth coat. Sits frozen, eyes fixed on Passenger 121.

Inside information
Works in administration for the Tabernacle, an evangelical ministry near Elephant and Castle.

When she was seven, Margaret returned from holiday. On the landing outside her bedroom, something evil waited, small, round, like a mouse without a head. Margaret wailed and it sprang apart and leapt at her face. 'It's just a poor little bird,' said her mum, who always sided with Maggie's younger sister.

Ever since, Margaret has disguised a mortal terror of birds. She and her husband just moved to Theydon Bois. Rooks caw in the trees, jackdaws nest in their new chimney, sparrows feed on neighbours' tables.

What she is doing or thinking
There is a bird on the train. It keeps fluttering upwards. She'll be covered in mites, in dust, in feathers. Her beautiful blue coat will get filthy, she'll choke. She'll itch for hours.

She can't stand it. At Waterloo, she bolts. On the platform, the shaking stops. The guilt comes, then anger, frustration. She'll be late, she's out of control. She's still angry with herself when the next train rumbles in.

Just past Lambeth North, it stops. They all wait. The speakers crackle and the driver announces, 'I'm very sorry to tell you we'll be here for some time. The train ahead of us has gone through the barriers.'

Something without a head jumps again. Margaret remembers the people on the other train and thinks: the bird. It saved me.

So does she like them now?

LEON DE MARCO

Outward appearance
Skinny young man, Italian pallor, 1960s pointed boots, brown leather jacket on coat-hanger shoulders, pink shirt with black bead patterns embroidered on it. Sits scrunched up against the section divider, legs crossed at ankles, face bitter with fatigue. Suddenly smiles gently at Passenger 121.

Inside information
Leon has been out all night. Lives on an estate on Hercules Road[2] with his mum. She will already have gone to work, leaving an anxious note to ring her.

What he is doing or thinking
Remembering last night. Went with his mates to *Wet*, a new club, and stayed 'til 5.00 AM. *Wet* has a temporary swimming pool set up in it. Everyone strips down to their shorts, the girls take off their tops, it's cool, nobody gets hassled. It's just so much fun to dance until you're sweaty, and then to swim. It was sexy but nobody got groped. Well not badly. They all just talked.

He can't remember what it was about, but it was light and heavy at the same time: stars, the beginning of the universe, how good everybody looked. And don't swallow the water.

Then out, feeling glossy, cool, fresh, round to a caff by the market for coffee and doughnuts. They loved each other, at least when they said goodnight, see ya, with the birds beginning to sing in the trees.

He wishes he could hold it in place, build some kind of monument to it. The train slows at Lambeth North and he moves towards the pigeon. 'Come on, little pigeon, go on home,' he says.

Another helpful and informative **253** *footnote*
2 According to Graham Gibberd's
On Lambeth Marsh, land bounded
by the current Hercules Road,
Kennington Road and Cosser
Street was leased by Sergeant
Major Philip Astley in the 1780s.
There he built his own house,
Hercules Hall, the Hercules Tavern,
and also Hercules Terrace, where
William Blake[2a] lived. Until
redecoration in 1996/97 the pub
was a kind of branch office of the
Central Office of Information,
serving fine spirits, hot and cold
dishes and eczema. The Central
Office of Information, on Hercules
Road, is decorated with a crude
mosaic of the labours of Hercules,
doubtless in some ignorance of
Astley.

The Sergeant Major was a circus
strongman, who performed 'Twelve
Trials of Hercules' in his own
theatre, Astley's. The amphitheatre
was on the site of the current St
Thomas' Hospital nurses' home on
Westminster Bridge Road. Astley's
son took it over, and it remained in
operation for many years, part of
the Lambeth tradition of cheap
theatrical spectacle that continues
to this day with shameful excesses
such as the Royal National
Theatre.

Dickens describes the vulgarity
of the crowd and the inferiority of
the spectacle at Astley's in *Sketches
by Boz.*

Astley's went through a number
of name changes, often like the
National called 'Royal', and
remained open until 1893. It was
finally closed, like so many
buildings south of the river, for
being a disorderly house.

Read the tea leaves, National.

A helpful and informative **253**
footnote within *a footnote*
2a On 11th January 1995, William
Blake came back to Hercules Road.

The train, trailing spirits, pulled
him. He arrived staggering forward
as if hurled onto the platform of
Lambeth North tube station. He
swirled, like the leaves the Council no
longer sweeps up, that rattle undead
on the streets year after year.

Outward appearance
He wears a broad, squashed straw
hat and a compress for a toothache.
His jacket is long and brown,
stained, but he wears a new cravat,
snow white. His tan breeches down
to the knee have not been changed all
winter, and the stockings, his silken
best, are splattered with clay and
dung two hundred years old.

It is how he was dressed on 11th
January 1795.

So who is William Blake?
The year just past, 1794, has been his
annus mirabilis. Out of his tiny
cottage he has written, illustrated,
printed *Songs of Experience,* the
Book of Urizon, Europe: A Prophecy
and the *Book of Los.* He is

exhausted. To clear his head, he went walking down Leake Street, under the tossed trees, past cows fenced in the fields of Kennington Manor. Battered by the wind, he was returning when his body was caught up in a mightier gust of the spirit.

What he is doing or thinking
He comes to a stop, and clutches his toothache and looks around him.

It is another vision. He is prone to them. In this vision, people walk through some dim, chattering tunnel. There are black ropes from the ceiling and a terrible smell he cannot identify. It reminds him of the charred odour of the Albion Mill. Dark, satanic, burned in fear and anger by the people, it stinks on in Lambeth Marsh.

A vision of Albion, then, of the spirit of that scorched mill.

The air is dim and terrible. The people scurry as if pursued. He allows himself to be blown along with them, up the tunnel. He wonders: what sad spirits are these? In what echoing bowels of Urizon are they trapped, shuffling? Their clothes are strange. He cannot quite focus on them, the materials, the colours, the cut are so alien to him. But he has learned that in visions detail is all. As in life, the solid details are emanations of the spirit.

He follows two handsome black wenches. So imposing and so spangled with jewellery are they, that it seems to him they must be princesses from some dream kingdom. One talks animatedly. The other, evidently her superior, looks away. Lord, such savage majesty!

They have blue painted on their eyelids! The inferior woman clutches a bag of miraculous tissue that contains, in its satin translucence, useful household objects which Blake recognizes. They warm his heart in a way he does not understand.

They mount steps, into another ghostly chamber, and line up, faces dead, waiting in acquiescence before polished iron gates. Is there fire beyond them?

They are joined by an elderly woman, gazing at flowers. A man, even older, asks her, 'Can I interest you in a further beverage?' His voice is richly grandiose. It is a tone of voice that Blake heard in his own age. He hates it for its aggrandisement. Yet, for all his vocal majesty, there is something glinting and small about this friendly old man. Blake somehow understands that his sonorousness is a final, sad crumbling of former grandeur.

The woman with the flowers looks up, and smiles. Blake realizes that she and all the women here have painted on another face. Has he stumbled on some kind of theatre? The new arrivals all laugh.

A youth joins them, as callow-faced as a Sicilian. His smooth, unharried features are those of a child. Blake peers at him and sees the child is in fact a man in full maturity, though skinny, unbent, with such a delightful expression. The manchild smiles slightly, his face illumined from within by love. Blake wonders if this beauty is to be his angel guide.

Then Blake sees the shoes. The angel manchild is wearing what look like pillows, blue and white. His trousers are heavy and spongy, without warp and weft. They hang like a single mossy deposit rather than cloth. No one ever wore such clothes in Heaven or in Lambeth. Blake begins to appreciate the scale of what has befallen him.

The doors rumble open, as heavily as gates of hell. There is nothing to do but stumble forward.

In clouds of perfume. These people smell variously of mint, sandalwood, almonds, as if the breath of Araby had wafted into this strange carriage with them. They press together in the tiny chamber, the doors close, they are all trapped without a single eye for the wind. But there is no odour of human closeness. The clothes are as spotless as the faces are burnished. The old man bearing whisky laughs with all his teeth intact, as pearly as a young maiden's. A China woman, as if all humankind had called a Parliament underground, is dressed just like Blake's angel, though she is old and female.

The room moves, everything shivering slightly. It is borne upwards, clanking. They are indeed underground, Blake is now sure. There are signs on the walls. They look, at first, like Blake's own poems, portrait-shaped rectangles of melded images and fiery words.

The all-singing musicAL
                    JOLSON

WINTER BREAKAWAYS

The room slumps slightly as if tired. The people shuffle in place, the doors rumble open. To Blake's great relief, there is daylight flooding the tiled

chambers beyond. Blake follows his angel who strides so confidently forward.

Straight ahead there is an arch and a blaze of light on grey. In that winter light, suddenly hurtling past are armouries of metal. They hiss, roar past the opening, in heraldic reds, blues, greens. The armouries are as polished as the people as if the devil had been freshly minting folk as well as coins.

In front of him clattering devices applaud, lights flash, barring his way. *Please seek assistance*

Words of fire? Blake looks around him.

The people disperse, quickly, purposively. They ignore him. Where is his angel guide?

Damn ye, thinks Blake and leaps the barriers. He strides on, following the boy, out through the arch, across paving, onto a polished slate surface. Into a place of permanent winter. Everything grey, everything paved, under stone, as if the people were swept up at night. There is a harsh cleanliness in the air. All the perfumes of Araby cannot make it wholesome. There are no fresh scents of river, lime trees, manure, straw, or laundry airing on the marsh. Instead there is a stench, like tar or oil lamps.

Underfoot symbols zig-zag across the slate. Are they hieroglyphs? Blake stands transfixed in the middle of the road.

Lined up, the armouries have been waiting, rumbling. Suddenly, they all leap forward, heads down, charging towards him. Blake stands dazed, raising his cane against them. All the armouries bellow and beep.

He feels himself grabbed. His angel manchild has him by the sleeve and hauls him up, onto some kind of island of safety amid the slate.

The angel manchild says: 'You all right, mate?' *Please seek assistance* the fire had said.

Blake feels himself to be slack, bewildered, peering at the boy. What hundreds of years could go into the making of that voice? It is a London voice, it is the sound of the mudlark children in the clay flats herding their goats, selling their dung. And yet. This voice is also urbane, polished, fed to bursting as any aristocrat's.

The boy glances at the cane. 'You need a hand across the road?'

'Aye, indeed, or I fear I shall be squashed flatter than a flea between my mistress's thumb and fingernail.'

The boy blinks at him, then chuckles. 'I guess so.'

'Where be we, boy, what place is this?'

'Well, that there's Hercules Road.'

'Herc . . .' and Blake falls silent.

The human mind is not built for logic, one thing at a time in orderly progression. It is built to swallow things whole and leap to conclusions. Blake sees the Hercules Tavern. Amid the roaring traffic he looks down a street whose slight curve is familiar and sees the names of inns: Red Lion, Crown and Cushion. Where he used to drink.

Without logic, full of dread, Blake asks, 'What year is this?'

The boy tells him.

On Hercules Terrace, William Blake lived in a cottage with his wife Catherine, and he gave the place and the spirit of it a name. 'Beulah . . .'

says the old man. 'I . . . I lived here once.'

'Was B . . . Beulah the name of the estate?' the young man asks him.

'Yes,' replies Blake. Here, he and Catherine would read poetry naked but for their hats, and answer the door in that pure condition. 'It was an age ago.'

Leon de Marco stares at the old man and at his dress, and he too is moving faster than logic. 'Are you a poet or something?'

'Or something.' Blake finds the idea both apt and amusing. 'Indeed.'

Leon takes hold of William Blake's arm. 'We used to have a poet live here. A famous poet. They put up a plaque.'

'Did they? Well it saved paying him while he was alive.' As if there had been some kind of signal, all the armouries have stalled, and the boy insists that they cross the road now, by pulling Blake's sleeve.

The Hercules Tavern is now all blue, and square. When did all the world stop building sloping roofs? Along Hercules Road, small trees sigh in the wind. 'Are those cherry trees?' Blake asks.

'Yeah.'

'The authorities plant cherry trees, for everyone?'

'I guess so.'

'The petals fall in spring?'

Leon smiles. 'Yeah,' he chuckles. He's always liked that, ever since he was a kid.

'Mark them well, boy, for that is how we all fall, in beautiful lost clouds, thousands of us as if in an upward fall of snow.'

And Blake remembers the creak of

the windmill as it turned beside the brewery. He remembers the clay flats being mined, the diggers shovelling up clay into the oxcarts, the beasts relishing the mud. Across the pistachio river, up the opposite banks of shale, were the long wooden warehouses in front of the modest Parliament chambers. The market for stone and timber. The sounds of saws and the smells of wood and stone dust reached them even across the river. The long barges rested as if asleep, all in front of the Archbishop's great house.

'Are the mills gone? And the factories?'

'Oh,' said the boy. 'No factories any more. All gone.'

'All gone?' says Blake, overjoyed. 'All gone!' He feels his horsey, ruined teeth are betrayed by his grin. 'Was there dancing?'

Leon smiles at him. 'There's always dancing in London, mate.'

Blake can see him clearly now. Blake remembers the Artichoke Inn, on the muddy lane through Lambeth Marsh, and the village maids and the lusty lads outside it, dancing in a ring. This is not an angel, but a lusty Lambeth lad with spots on his chin.

He sees a woman, in middle age with brazen many-coloured hair, wearing what looks like a new bottle-green coat. Her hard glossy shoes have tiny spikes that make her trip slightly as she battles against the lowland wind. She walks like a lady of promise and stature, alone and undefended on the street. He looks at the jumble of buildings, some shiny like wrapped presents, others like wedding cakes, still others like lavatories with tiles. A mighty age, and a confused and fearful one. What achievements had been squandered here?

'Not quite Jerusalem,' says Blake.

He turns and sees the poet's plaque, on a brick wall that is not altogether out of place amid the Georgian houses. *William Blake Poet and Painter lived here . . .*

Beulah. It is remembered. But why?

There is a gust of wind, smelling of river water, mud, hops, sweat, wool and baked bread. Suddenly Leon de Marco is standing alone in Hercules. In the middle of January, clouds of cherry blossom fall billowing upwards from the single line of trees.

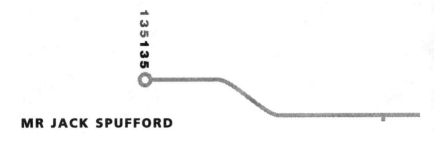

MR JACK SPUFFORD

Outward appearance

Late twenties, casually but neatly dressed, fawn slacks, dress shoes, grey anorak.

Inside information

A part-time classical musician and partner in *If you've got it, flaut it*, a shop that stocks nothing but flutes and sheet music. A year ago, on a concert trip to Poland, Jack met and married Katya. The Home Office would not let her into the UK until they had been married for six months first. So Jack returned alone and they both waited. Then officials said he had to buy a flat before they would let Katya in. He was sharing with three other blokes. Someone said it was because they thought he was gay.

He and finally found a one bedroom place for £59,000. In London that's a bargain. He bought it, but his wife is still in Poland.

What he is doing or thinking

Yesterday, waiting in the immigration court opposite Lambeth North, he met the white wife of a black man. Her husband came here as a student. They are in love, they are married, but he was not allowed to work. She applied for work permits and the officials lost the applications. Now they're saying he has to go home though the marriage is legal. Why? Well, because he hasn't worked all the time he has been here!

An official, another woman, had taken her aside and told her out of kindness to give up – the Agency thought it was a convenience marriage. Nothing she could do would change their minds.

Black or white, if you're foreign, England can be a shithole.

MR IBRAHIM GURER

Outward appearance
Oppressed clerk. Bald, sweaty, plump, in fawn overcoat, grey suit, glasses and briefcase.

Inside information
Turkish Cypriot working in his own travel agency on Kennington Road. Times are hard. This is usually his best time of year and bookings are down. He is a specialist in tours of Turkish Cyprus, which is little help.

What he is doing or thinking
His life is like a nutcracker. His English wife has gone a kind of crazy. The symptom is buying sprees. One room is full of toys that the child doesn't want. Huge blue teddy bears, pink bunnies. Another room is full of clothes and shoes. She buys a CD a day.

He has seen *Absolutely Fabulous* and knows who his wife is: she is the PR lady. That is how other English people see her, almost pretty but gauche, always in pain, always demanding something. She thinks she is a woman of no position. After all, she married a Turk. He can see why she spends: if you spend money, people treat you well. It is not toys she is buying, but respect.

His brother in shipping back home sent Ibrahim a substantial sum to invest. He is doing nothing with it, but let his wife spend. He will be destitute. He looks at the travel advertisements above the seats, they all offer the same destinations. He racks his brain. What else can he offer?

For no reason, he remembers an old Led Zeppelin album cover: the Devil's Causeway.

Of course. *Come see beautiful Northern Ireland.* After all, there's a ceasefire.

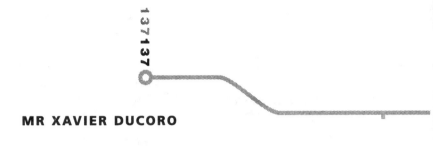

MR XAVIER DUCORO

Outward appearance
Determined young black man. Blue suit, burnished black shoes, beige overcoat. Shaved, short hair with a fashionable Tin Tin flip in front. Stares, his face slack, at a personal organizer.

Inside information
His father was a builder who decided that Chartered Surveying was the profession for his son. His son agreed: it was an attractive mix of professional standing with outdoor, masculine work. Has met at his church the woman he wants to marry, Charlotte. He is courting Charlotte in the classic manner of dates and visits with her parents. Works in an architects' office near the Elephant, serving his apprenticeship to become a Fellow of the Royal Institute of Chartered Surveyors (FRICS).

What he is doing or thinking
He is turning the names of stations on the Bakerloo line into anagrams.

Bakerloo line anagrams have become an obsession. It started when, through a train window, the words 'Oxford Circus' miraculously rearranged themselves into 'X. Ducoro, FRICS'. He took this as a symptom of overwork.

The next day, however, the letters of the word 'Waterloo' swam like fish until they read 'a Wet Rolo', which is what he was eating at the time. It seemed the anagrams only formed when they told the truth. After he arranged a loan, 'Embankment' became 'Met bank men'.

Just now in his notebook, 'Charing Cross' has morphed from 'Char Crossing' to 'Scorch in rags' to 'Crash so ring C'.

If that's true too? What if Charlotte's in trouble? He gets off early at Waterloo to ring.

The signs in the station now read: 'Woo later'.

MR NICHOLAS PAGANOS

Outward appearance
A gangster from a 1930s movie. Plump, groomed, handsome, with slick wavy hair, and a suit and a tie. Curve of his mouth gives a permanently satisfied look.

Inside information
Owner-manager of gentleman's hairdressers on Lower Marsh. Came from Cyprus soon after the troubles in the sixties, when he was just a child. Happily married, one son in university, one daughter taking A levels.

What he is doing or thinking
His third child, twelve-year-old Angelica, has the potential to be a professional tennis player. Her teachers spotted it first. She began to train an hour every day after school, and win weekend tournaments. On Saturdays, the family would watch Angelica play. She looked so small and frail with the huge racket. But her very smallness, hardness, was a kind of strength.

They've been told that now she needs professional, individual coaching. This is different from lessons. This means someone who devotes himself to training her. They are talking Olympics. They're talking prize money. They are talking fees that he can't afford.

Nicholas remembers driving out of Cyprus. There was a terrible smell, and the car crept cautiously into a village. A man in khaki trousers lay in the dust and then his mother's hands covered his eyes. Your life is upended, you change countries, you cut hair, and suddenly you have a chance for your daughter to really achieve something. And she wants it. She works so hard, so small, so serious, her face like a little hazelnut. What wouldn't he do?

Nicholas decides. He'll remortgage his house.

MR HISHAM BADHURI

Outward appearance

Indian movie star? Handsome, broad shouldered. Blue jeans, trainers, baseball cap, brown leather jacket with an American oil company logo.

Inside information

Graduate business student on a trainee placement with British Telecom. First degree from Ein Shamsh University in Cairo. Taught himself English as a part-time tourist guide. Learned other things from them as well. A Muslim fundamentalist dedicated to the destruction of Israel. Poster in his bedsit shows the hand of Islam smashing the star of David against the Dome of the Rock.

What he is doing or thinking

His memories swim like fish in a pool. He sees the old man on the bus many years ago back home. He sees his English girl-friend Karen. He sees his mother in their flat in Mansura, reeds on the floor to repair chairs. He sees the many photographs of himself, handsome in a gelabiya.

He sees Karen's father, big, pink faced, crumpled, white haired, in the showers after tennis. Karen's father's hand on his thigh. Karen's father lying face down on the bed. Karen saying, 'My father really, really likes you. He keeps asking after you.'

He sees the rowboatmen in Mansura. 'You are an Egyptian, why are you taking the side of these foreigners?' And he himself saying, 'It doesn't give you the right to cheat them.' He cheats them himself. He loves them.

He supports a group that aims rifles at them because Islam stands up to Mubarak and his corruption.

What stands up to his own corruption? His many selves swim like fish, on from Waterloo Station.

Outward appearance
Floppy velvet hat, black bangs, red lipstick, Gothic pallor, bovver boots, charcoal stockings. Sits smiling slightly, legs crossed.

Inside information
Works for a small commercials production house behind Merely College. Her boss is an ex-academic who gets nervous in presentations and nervous around her. She likes making people nervous.

She's an unusual girl. She would have been on the *Marchioness* the night of the disaster, but a last minute liaison meant she was otherwise engaged. Her mother dated Mick Jagger, was briefly famous as a model and went out with John Noakes of *Blue Peter* fame. Anita inherited this capacity for effortless notoriety. Her friend Ruth did a portrait of Anita for a degree show. It won a prize, and she ended up on posters all over the Underground.

What she is doing or thinking
Anita loves herself. She is about to embark on another escapade. The *Big Issue* salesman at Waterloo is a real hunk. She's been chatting him up for weeks, getting off one stop early. Today she's going to tell him: don't be homeless, come live with me and be my sex slave.

His name is Antonio. He's from Italy, and is so much more interesting than English men. He's an actor and worked in New York for years which is why he speaks with an American accent. Antonio came over here for a show. It went bust, which is why he's on the skids. Anita knows people who could help him.

She thinks: who else but me would have an affair with a *Big Issue* salesman?

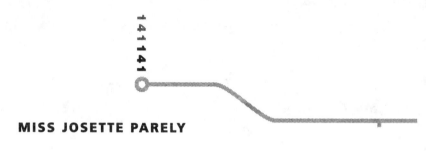

MISS JOSETTE PARELY

Outward appearance
Middle-aged woman, thick pebble glasses on a chain, grey overcoat, brogues. Sits reading with ferocious concentration a *Beryl the Peril Annual*. A young woman next to her reaches across and shakes a pack of licorice allsorts at her. The woman chooses one with great care – a pink square. 'Put the book away,' says her companion, and they begin to pack up for Waterloo.

Inside information
Josette suffers from Down's Syndrome. Her family are French. They escaped the Occupation and stayed after the war. Her mother was a trained nurse who devoted herself to raising Josette. Her younger brother took care of her and defended her if she were teased.

'How come your sister is funny?' children would ask. 'I'm retarded,' Josette would answer. She learned how to manage other children. They grew up. She did not.

What she is doing or thinking
Josette wishes she were like Beryl, looking after herself. But she doesn't because she has Down's Syndrome. They are going to visit Mummy, and talk to Mummy and leave her some sweets. You can't replace a Mummy, she goes away and leaves a hole. You want people to hug you, but no one hugs you like Mummy.

They're going to change trains! Josette recognizes the signs in herself, she could get over-excited and silly. She gives Nane a quick hug, and Nane knows what that means. 'We'll settle down soon,' Nane promises. 'Got everything?'

'Except my Mummy,' says Josette. But that will solve itself soon because Josette knows Down's Syndrome don't live long. She'll join her soon.

MISS NANE PARELY

Outward appearance

Old-fashioned woman in her late twenties. Vanessa Redgrave hair, tan sheepskin coat, Laura Ashley dress. Tends the older woman next to her.

Inside information

Graduate student doing a PhD on Dog Latin and Renaissance verse. Born out of wedlock to Josette Parely when Josette was sixteen.

Josette was always affectionate. One day she hugged the wrong man. No one knows who the bastard was. Nane and Josy grew up like sisters in the grandparents' house. Nane assumed that Gran was her mother. Both are now visiting Gran's grave.

What she is doing or thinking

When Nane's girlfriend asks what was it like to grow up with Josette, Nane says that it was fun. Like having a big sister who was just a bit bigger than other people's sisters. They had friends and parties together. They would make paper crowns and sing. It was easy to scare Josy, with ghost stories or summaries of horror films. 'You mustn't scare me,' Josette would warn. If frightened, she would weep, beg and scrabble at the floor until her fingers bled.

Josette loved putting on plays. In 1981, when Gran was dying, Nane was thirteen. She decided to distract Josy with a production of *Grease*. They and little Christian rehearsed 'You're the One that I Want' between summer visits to the hospital. Their father sat in the garden and wept.

Now he lives in France, with other graves and memories. In her mind, Nane sees him, her girlfriend, her Gran and has a sense of unlikely connections. Time and family. Her sister-mother stands.

MS LUCIE FRIEND

Outward appearance
Going to dinner dance in 1957? Satin top, full black skirt, velvety black high heels, tweed coat with black velvet collar. About 36. Looks across the row and fans out her fingers of both hands. Turns her head· to the left, to the right. Squeezes both earrings. Grimaces showing all her teeth, moving head from left to right again. Licks teeth. Reaches into purse.

Inside information
Works for Beetlehide shippers as PA to the Mediterranean Controller. Unmarried, lives with her mother. The two are very fashion conscious and share clothes.

What she is doing or thinking
Lucie is using the windows of the train as mirrors. She was very impressed once by a description of Mrs Thatcher's[3] grooming. The secret was constant maintenance. Lucie checks out hair, fingernail polish, and teeth, for any signs of breakfast. From her colour-coordinated purse, she gets an i.d. badge, and tries out various positions which combine modesty and assertiveness.

Lucie knows her workmates are spreading vicious rumours. They say she has fallen in love with the Mediterranean Controller. That is because she must restrict access to him, protect him. Others are out to undermine him, and so target her as well. Naturally, a woman devoted to her work is devoted to the man. She keeps a picture of his two children on her desk. She sends them birthday cards and presents. She gives him presents: mugs, pens and, once, a set of six white Y-fronts.

Armoured for the day, she walks early to the doorway, rustling from silks and girdles underneath her skirt.

Another helpful and informative
253 *footnote*
3 Margaret Thatcher is one of Britain's greatest fashion and entertainment icons.

She is perhaps best considered in the light of the 1985 pop video 'Dancing in the Street' which starred Mick Jagger and David Bowie, the other great British national figures she most resembles.

No one who has seen documentary footage of David Bowie's final performance as Ziggy Stardust at the Hammersmith Odeon in 1973 can doubt his influence on Mrs Thatcher. She appropriated Ziggy's make-up and general air of warm androgyny.

Consider also the parallels with Mick Jagger. Both are first generation university-educated people of exceptional achievement. Their last names are both easily understood derivatives of verbs that became professional designations (a jagger being a thief or highwayman). Both became widely loved and hated at the same time, and Mrs Thatcher took over from Jagger as one of the public figures most often appearing in people's dreams. Both of course are sex symbols. 'The eyes of Caligula and the mouth of Marilyn Monroe,' said François Mitterrand of Mrs Thatcher, a description that applies equally to Mick Jagger.

Finally, and of course most importantly, all three conveyed a similar social and political message. 'Calling out around the world are you ready for a brand new beat?'

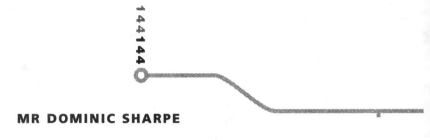

MR DOMINIC SHARPE

Outward appearance
Old soldier in green camouflage jacket and blue jeans, hiking books, tartan beret with a regimental badge on the side. Red beard streaked with grey. Matching scarf. He looks pudgy, pernickety, gruff.

Inside information
An unemployed Munchausen, who imagines he was a soldier. On his way to the Imperial War Museum,[4] where he talks to visitors about his wartime experiences at the Battle of the Bulge. If challenged by a foreigner for being too young to have served in World War Two (Dominic is 55 years old), he pretends to think they are German and yells xenophobic abuse at them. If they could not be taken for German (for example, black Americans) he thanks them for being too kind, and says that he is sure he looks every one of his 77 years.

If challenged by a Brit, he winks and admits he is an actor paid to enliven the exhibit. This is also untrue but it is close to what he tells himself – that he is an unpaid display.

Then he asks for money.

Has just sold his volume of wartime memoirs for an undisclosed sum.

What he is doing or thinking
Fuming over the size of the advance. The book took years to write, the product of bitter experience. The incompetence of his commanding officers, the heat, the dust, the loss of young life. The book will blow the lid right off the scandal of that fiasco. What do they know about it, snug in their publishers' offices?

What happens if they ask him for proof he was there?

Another helpful and informative
253 *footnote*
4 The Imperial War Museum
seems to be impossible to find.
Anyone who plainly cannot speak
English and is walking along
Westminster Bridge Road with a
map will ask you where it is.
'Directional Questions not
answered,' says a helpful hand-
lettered sign next to the *Evening
Standard* kiosk in front of Lambeth
North station. The Imperial War
Museum is to blame.

I have never succeeded in
entering it. It costs a reasonable
sum of money to get in, and it
never struck me as being
worthwhile to pay it for a quick
lunchtime scan. It is set in a
surprisingly large, surprisingly
open park, with an annoyingly
inconvenient fence all the way
around it. No one ever sweeps up
the leaves. You realize in late
summer that the leaves on the
ground are last year's or the year
before's.

It was founded by an Act of
Parliament in 1920 and opened at
the Crystal Palace, moved about as
London institutions do, and ended
up in a hospital building. It was
closed during World War Two,
since they had a real war to muse
upon.

Its park is called the Geraldine
Mary Harmsworth Park in
memory of the mother of Viscount
Rothermere. Now who could
forget her? The pub opposite used
to call itself after Charlie Chaplin,
who at least drank in the vicinity.

MR DOUGLAS ESSWOOD

Outward appearance

Middle-aged man, prematurely grey, bustles into the car. Heavy grey suit, clean beige overcoat. Briefcase and smaller cloth bag probably containing laptop computer. Passenger 110 moves feet so he can sit down. Nods to the kid then settles in more pensively, index finger pressed against the line of his mouth.

Inside information

Sales Director of Effective Buggers Inc, an American company. On way for third presentation to the Met Police. Douglas's company offers realtime image enhancement to video surveillance systems.

What he is doing or thinking

Pondering Britain. A kid like that back home would be a punk, here he's sweet and polite. This is such a nice country, but all anyone talks about is security – job security, locks, CCTV. Douglas knows his product works. It enlarges, clarifies but it's being called upon to do new things.

Because, to put it bluntly, it's illegal to spy on people in America. A visit to New Scotland Yard left him exhausted. A very pretty woman his own age simply switched channels from flyovers to alleyways, shopping centres, main streets. The whole country is wired. In a department store in Oxford Street, the cameras followed a man the operators didn't like around the shop. After he left, they warned other stores by radio.

Then cameras followed him down the street, saw him get on a bus, and videoed the bus to make sure he didn't get off. The English live in *1984* and don't know it.

Still, it's good for his business. As long as nobody tries to do the same to him.

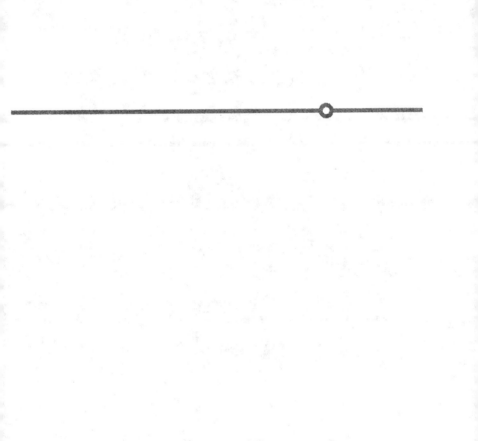

For Your Reading Ease and Comfort
PASSENGER MAP
Car No 5

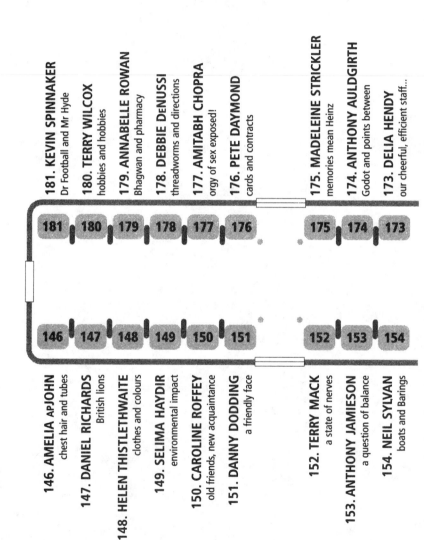

181. KEVIN SPINNAKER
Dr Football and Mr Hyde

180. TERRY WILCOX
hobbies and hobbies

179. ANNABELLE ROWAN
Bhagwan and pharmacy

178. DEBBIE DeNUSSI
threadworms and directions

177. AMITABH CHOPRA
orgy of sex exposed!

176. PETE DAYMOND
cards and contracts

175. MADELEINE STRICKLER
memories mean Heinz

174. ANTHONY AULDGIRTH
Godot and points between

173. DELIA HENDY
our cheerful, efficient staff...

181 | 180 | 179 | 178 | 177 | 176   175 | 174 | 173

146 | 147 | 148 | 149 | 150 | 151   152 | 153 | 154

146. AMELIA apJOHN
chest hair and tubes

147. DANIEL RICHARDS
British lions

148. HELEN THISTLETHWAITE
clothes and colours

149. SELIMA HAYDIR
environmental impact

150. CAROLINE ROFFEY
old friends, new acquaintance

151. DANNY DODDING
a friendly face

152. TERRY MACK
a state of nerves

153. ANTHONY JAMIESON
a question of balance

154. NEIL SYLVAN
boats and Barings

THIS MAP SHOWS YOU

☞ WHO is in the car

WHERE they are sitting and

WHAT are their interests and concerns

172. LISA MUIR
gotcha!

171. VICTOR DOWIE
Shoot! Shit!

170. LINDA SCRALG
cats and mating calls

169. ESTELLE IRTIN
The Apparatus of Yearning

168. GURDEV DHOLLIN
instant dharma

167. PAULE WRIGHT
other people's offices

166. MARY LENEHAN
'Orrible murder, horrible lies

165. MEL McKINNEY
keys and brothers-in-law

164. BILL McREADY
Scotland and Ascension

| 172 | 171 | 170 | | 169 | 168 | 167 | 166 | 165 | 164 |

| 155 | 156 | 157 | | 158 | 159 | 160 | 161 | 162 | 163 |

155. IRIS KRAUSHAAR
she's leaving home

156. SONALI SHETTY
young love and big bums

157. PAUL BINYON
gardener's question time

158. TINA RAVON
Chums R Us

159. CLIVE SIDDEN
flying the flag

160. SASHA BINGHAM
inside housing

161. PRU WAVERLY
'Orrible murder, 'orrible lies

162. STEFANIE PARASHAR
smiles and villains

163. SUNIL KURASH
attack of the Were-duck

on the train? Order your copy now of...

do on the Tube

- Twiddle your earring round and round through your ear until someone wails: 'Please! Stop!'
- Nibble your hair.
- Check for split ends.
- Clean your ears with a biro top.
- Sweat.
- Take surreptitious notes about your neighbours – the lurching train will make them illegible.
- Read the Blistex ads and marvel that anyone could publish illustrations that bad.
- Spot the foreigners. They are the ones who:
    - hold onto each other instead of the handrails when the train lurches.
    - crowd on in a panic, holding the doors open.
    - smoke.
    - bellow across the aisle trying to talk over the noise.
    - have to get off laughing at the next stop, going the wrong way.

Yes, hours of fun await you on London Underground...with 253!

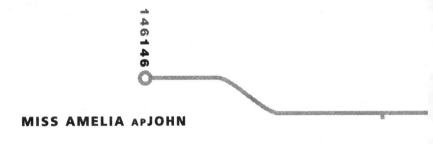

MISS AMELIA ᴀᴘJOHN

Outward appearance
Early twenties, small, sturdy, sits on tiptoe as the seat is too high. Black stockings, stubby, soft black shoes. Tan overcoat with corduroy collar. Blue dress peeking through underneath. Sits looking at the rings on her fingers. Begins to take them off, one after another.

Inside information
A trainee nurse at St Thomas' Hospital.

What she is doing or thinking
She is not allowed to wear rings or wristwatches at work and so is removing them.

Amelia hates being around sick people. She dislikes the old, particularly old men. She didn't know that men's body hair continues to grow, on their shoulders or chests. It gets very long, and then it goes white, a grizzled mat over withered dugs. Their arms look like crepe paper. Their lips go thin, their ears fat. She didn't realize they get covered in little brown spots. She has to plug colostomy bags or feed gurgling pipes down into their bellies. Old men make her feel continually sick.

A fine time to find that out; after you've decided to become a nurse. Yesterday, an old man collapsed in the toilet, and Amelia ran out to fetch the ward sister. 'You can't panic like that,' said the ward sister.

'It's not panic,' Amelia said before she could stop herself. 'He's just so . . . UGLY.'

'This isn't a beauty contest,' said the sister.

Amelia became a nurse with images in her head of healing the pathetic, the young, the sad, the handsome. Something clicks. It's young hunky soldiers she wants to heal.

She could always join the Army.

MR DANIEL RICHARDS

Outward appearance
Small, slim, young black man. Thick-framed glasses. Short, white overcoat, dark suit, blue shirt with white bordered squares, black and yellow tie. Shoulder bag made of tan leather, slumped between feet. He prods chin thoughtfully, reading *Coningsby* by Benjamin Disraeli.

Inside information
Works for Dun and Old. Should be studying the documents in his bag on qualifying for tax accountancy, but sometimes the soul gravitates to what it truly needs.

What he is doing or thinking
Coningsby's a bloody awful novel, but its siren call is this: Disraeli was a Jew who decoded Britain enough to rule it. Daniel has not had an easy life. He's small, not physically strong, and comes from a family of robust brothers. They are proud of him now. They used to beat him up. When he was a child, his favourite bible story was Daniel in the Lions' Den.

When Daniel was ten, his calm and funny mother collapsed while the boys were at school. No one told them she was in hospital and their father, not a resilient man, disappeared from grief. The boys were left on their own to cope for a week. Little Daniel emerged as the brightest. He decoded the cookbooks; he found where Mum was; he found the way to the hospital. When both parents finally returned, Daniel was head of the family.

His brothers defended Daniel after that. He found that wit could marshal strength. He is still small, still in the Lions' Den, still learning. Daniel has a vision of Britain, one in which he fits. Rules.

MISS HELEN THISTLETHWAITE

Outward appearance

As slim as Audrey Hepburn. Wiry red hair in careful disorder. Clothes all black except for the raincoat. It looks like a shopping bag, lime green with huge white dots.

Inside information

Works in *Horse(clothes?)*, a shop on the Cut that specializes in restrained fashion - beiges and blacks, usually long, knitted, and baggy.

Helen's sister Pearl has been missing for twenty years.

What she is doing or thinking

Helen is shamed by the raincoat. It's cold today and both of hers were being drycleaned. She found this in her closet: she thinks it's her mum's.

She looks at the sleeve and can't help but think how different fashion is now. This must be from the early '70s. Even in mid-winter, women went about the streets in miniskirts (though they wore long, long boots when it was really cold). They were either cheerier, bolder or stupider.

It was about then that Pearl disappeared. She was six years older than Helen, a teenager, with long hair and tight-ribbed sweaters. Helen lived through Pearl: boyfriends, fashion, fun.

She disappeared, no news, no body. Mum never gave up trying to find Pearl: mediums, sniffer dogs. Arrested serial killers got a letter with a photograph, pleading to end a mother's suspense. Nothing ever did.

For the most part they never talk about Pearl, though her photograph is on top of the telly. Helen has only just been able to leave home, and Mum has never thrown out the old clothes.

Neither one of them ever wears strong colours. Something lurches.

This is Pearl's coat.

MISS SELIMA HAYDIR

Outward appearance
Nearly middle-aged, beaky woman, with neatly tied scarf over her head, wearing a suit that the Queen might wear: navy blue with white polka dots and a pleated skirt. Flicks through *Introduction to Assessing Environmental Impact.* The tops of the pages have been stamped, 'University of the South Bank'.

Carries an empty cloth bag. A printed panel on it shows a hand draped in the American flag holding a bouquet of Planet Earths. *The Ninth International Conference of . . .* it says, *July 1995.* The main word is an unintelligible hippy logo.

Inside information
Well-known Bosnian film critic. Selima's career has suffered a certain amount of disruption. Her father is prosperous and has paid for her to do a degree in safety in Britain.

What she is doing or thinking
Selima aches like a loose tooth that needs to come out. Her home city is under siege, the landscape of her childhood is being blown up. Is that Environmental Impact enough? Films bore her, everything makes her feel like a coward, safe, away.

And alone. Her English, which everyone told her was excellent, is fine on theoretical matters, but she doesn't know words like 'bicarbonate of soda' or 'mushrooms'. The embassy has no work for her. Her father has gone underground, and the Muslim men she meets are all Arabs. The bag is empty so that it can be filled with shopping, which she will eat alone. The conference it refers to is for Peace. It has not happened yet.

What she really wants to do is pick up a gun.

MISS CAROLINE ROFFEY

Outward appearance
Discreet black coat, brown suit, dress a bit short. Honey-highlighted hair, luxurious make-up. New, slim leather case. Badge just visible on inside jacket. Reading the *FT*.

Inside information
Director of Training for Pall Mall Oil.

What she is doing or thinking
Scanning the paper when she senses something out of kilter next to her.

'Caroline! Hello!' says a deep, rich, posh voice. Looks up to see a grey-fingered, grey-faced man with unwashed locks spilling over a re-stitched jacket collar. He asks, 'How're things at Pall Mall? Still doing the training?'

Who is this? An ex-colleague? Pall Mall has downsized twice. Caroline frantically tries to place him, re-imagining him in clean clothes and short hair. 'I'm fine thank you, how are you?'

He bellows, 'Couldn't be better. You know I'm working on the Internet now? In fact, I was speaking yesterday at the Marketing on the Internet Conference.'

'What a coincidence!' she says. 'I was at that conference.' Back, very far back, at university Caroline knew the band Genesis before they made it. She is beginning to wonder if this is one of the original members – one who left too soon.

He pats his pockets. 'I used up all my cards yesterday. Do you have one of yours?'

Something tells her no. She chuckles. 'I used up all mine too.'

She gets out at Waterloo and walks quickly away in case he follows. She feels sorry for him and awful about her reaction. I used to know him, she thinks. Who, who, who?

And why?

MR DANNY DODDING

Outward appearance

Filthy middle-aged man. Uncut hair and beard, Frankenstein boots. Suit repaired with thick white thread. Enters at Embankment, scans the carriage, and promptly sits next to a woman.

Inside information

Begs for money and travels all day on the Underground to keep warm. Grew up in Barnado's and drifted ever since, buggered off as he puts it, except for a brief period in university. Danny studied philosophy. Proved to his own satisfaction that it was illogical to wear shoes.

He is to be seen in summer walking along country lanes. Likes to talk to people, but has to scheme to gain and hold attention.

What he is doing or thinking

What a pretty woman, the kind he went to university with. He spots a forgotten conference badge on her jacket. *Marketing and the Internet*, it says, Caroline Roffey, Training Director, Pall Mall Oil. Oil huh? Well all the trendy little girlies went into business and became like their dads only not bald and fat.

'Caroline!' He greets her like a long lost friend. He would like to take her for a six-month walk, show her the stars from under a hedge. He would like to put his hands on a fully operational warm radiator. He might just get her card, if he asks.

But, no, her caution is automatic.

'I'm in the book,' he calls out as she leaves. Her smile looks clear, unforced. That was all he wanted. He sits back content.

Then the man opposite sits forward. Oh good, someone else to talk to. His lucky day.

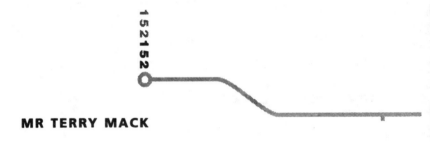

MR TERRY MACK

Outward appearance
Small, handsome man. Kindly face, red moustache. Green jacket, bilious sweater, hiking boots. Holds open *The Daily Express*, but his eyes are fixed elsewhere.

Inside information
A member of the IRA posted to London during the ceasefire to recruit Irish men who already live here. The mission has changed. A friend has identified the wife of an informer.

Terry is tailing Passenger 74, Christine Marre.

What he is doing or thinking
He knows Christine will get out at Waterloo to work in Epik. He has seen the way she travels, nervous, looking over her shoulder. She's an informer's wife all right, in a permanent state of nerves.

He's been in her flat, looking for photographs or letters. She's thorough. Obviously trained - not a letter anywhere. She must read them and eat them. He looked through the wastebin for torn paper. He looked at her phone bills, from Mercury, itemized. No Irish calls. Everything in the flat looks temporary, like she doesn't really live there.

He wants to fuck her. She's the kind of woman he likes; there is something delicious and theatrical about her face. He wants to have an affair with her, and find out all about her husband. And then one night, with his dick up her, he'll tell her: I'm a Provo.

That will make her come; he knows that from her face, from its avidness, its blank stare. She'll be terrified, thrilled. Middle-class British bitch.

He decides. Today on the platform, they'll meet. He stirs himself as the train slows, ready to catch up with her.

DR ANTHONY JAMIESON

Outward appearance
Grey hair, but young, pink face. Aran sweater, black trousers. Voluminous, shiny overcoat. In boisterous conversation with his companion, legs apart, apparently holding an invisible cup of coffee.

Inside information
A GP with an enthusiasm for boating. He and his companion crew together. Both are visiting Buntleys Coachworks to hire a trailer to haul a very particular boat to The Boat Show.

What he is doing or thinking
Telling his friend about a video conference from on board a ship in the Fastnet boat race. The chairman kept lurching in and out of the picture. Tony mimes it. 'He kept disappearing out of shot. Then he'd swing back in and start talking about sponsorship.' Less experienced participants were flung about in the background. One of them suddenly leant overboard and vomited in shot.

'But there was this one old man. Nothing fazed him. He just stood there like this, absolutely unmoving. He looked a bit like a drunk, only he had a cup of coffee. And he stood there drinking it, like this . . .'

Tony mimes a superior looking man, with his coffee tacking back and forth across the air in slow progress towards his lips.

'He never said a word, he just kept looking at all these berks trying to have a serious business meeting in the middle of a boat race.'

Tony's wife is a serious middle-class woman tormented by the children's education and ecological issues. His work consists of prescribing happy pills to lonely old people.

'So,' he suddenly says. 'What's our next little adventure going to be?'

MR NEIL SYLVAN

Outward appearance
Balding, fit, chinless. Brown sweater, trousers and boots, but his tartan shirt collar is in vibrant colours. Neil nods, laughs, crumples forward as his companion completes his story.

Inside information
Analyst for a City merchant bank, who captains Passenger 153. They are selecting a trailer to haul one of Neil's boats to The Boat Show at Earl's Court.

It's all a bit of a laugh. The boat is a six-foot dinghy from an old cruise ship. They have entered it in the Classical Yachting ex-hibition. It is, after all, by definition a classic boat. They've had a lot of fun pretending to be insulted that the Show doesn't want it. Now the Show has agreed to exhibit it. They can't wait to see the look on people's faces.

What he is doing or thinking
His chum asks: so what's our next adventure? 'The Club Supper,' Neil replies.

'Oh, you're joking,' says Tony. 'I said adventure, not a wake.'

'You haven't heard about our outfits,' says Neil. 'I reckon tuxedo tops. Tailored shorts. And yellow wellington boots.'

'With waterproofs?'

'And Sou'westers,' says Neil. 'Very elegant.'

'Now what will the wives wear?' They exchange a gleam of understanding. The real reason for being a sailor is to get away from patients, bosses, aggressive barrow boys, wives, spreadsheets and diaries.

This could be the last year for Neil. Running a boat costs money. Things at the bank aren't good. Something funny seems to be happening with some of their futures in the Far East. Mind you, nothing they haven't seen before at Barings.[1]

Another helpful and informative
253 *footnote*
1 In case you live on the moon or somewhere similar such as West Los Angeles, Barings Bank, the guarantor of David Niven's trip *Around the World in 80 Days* and less salubrious imperial activities, met its end at the hand of one of its own traders, Nick Leeson, the next month. It was one more nail in the coffin of the 1980s, but very far from being the last. Those nails fell like rain.

MISS IRIS KRAUSHAAR

Outward appearance

Elongated thirteen-year-old, brown hair pulled back, wrap-around tartan skirt, powder-blue stockings with socks rolled down around ankles on top of spongy brown loafers. Braces on teeth. The whole effect is curiously 1940s. Listens warily to the girl next to her.

Inside information

A ballet student who gets two mornings a week off from St Paul's girls' school to attend dancing classes held in the Merely College studio. Grandparents are German refugees who escaped Hitler's Germany. Father is Financial Director of a large pharmaceutical company.

What she is doing or thinking

That Sonali is trying to tell her she's got a big bum. They were supposed to have a truce. Neither one of them is exactly a dancer yet. Iris tries to talk instead about a favourite teacher.

Sonali keeps up the attack. 'Well, she's got the reverse problem. Tiny legs.'

Iris delicately rubs the tip of her nose. Sonali is the nearest thing Iris has to a friend. This new jealousy, if that's what it is, is some kind of last straw.

Maybe Sonali is put off by the big house in Bishops Drive. Iris is. She wants out from under her family. Above all else she wants to be a dancer. She knows she is shy, slow to make friends. And dedicated.

She decides, very quietly. She'll leave, go to a boarding school with a proper dance programme. To begin work in earnest. To grow up.

'Tiny legs or not, she's a good teacher,' Iris chuckles. 'She's just a bit demanding for people who are too young.'

MISS SONALI SHETTY

Outward appearance
Thirteen years old. Raw silk top, white slacks, green cloth coat
with fake fur collar. Short hair, which she keeps tossing out her
face. Gold earrings, and make-up. Strains upward to talk to her
taller companion.

Inside information
Ballet student given time off from St Paul's to practise in studio
at Merely College. In love with the girl next to her.

What she is doing or thinking
Everyone knows that she, Sonali, is prettier than Iris and looks
are important if you're a dancer, so why is Iris so superior all the
time? Is it money? Well Sonali's family have money too.

She's trying to help Iris. 'You have to have a good silhouette.
A large bottom needs long legs. You can get away with it if you
have a high waist and a good carriage.'

Maybe this sounds a bit personal, Sonali thinks. But you have
to be objective about such things.

Suddenly, Iris is talking about their teacher Miss Boniface,
who Sonali is sure fancies them both, and that makes Sonali sad,
angry.

'But she has the reverse problem, tiny legs,' Sonali says. It's
her problem, too. She thinks her own legs are small, bandy,
nearly misshapen.

Iris wipes her nose in that prissy way. Iris! Notice me, not
your bloody teacher!

'Also, the legs are thick, just here in front,' Sonali says, continuing, sensing that something has veered out of control. She
hates Miss Boniface.

It's not like that when the music plays, and they strip down
to work and they are like horses, running. Running together.

DR PAUL BINYON

Outward appearance

Ageing art student? Facial stubble, pony tail, black corduroys. Desert boots, ethnic waistcoat, white jacket. Looks disgruntled, hands shoved into armpits.

Inside information

Young Turk of the gardening establishment, those authors and presenters who provide advice and inspiration to a nation of gardeners.

Dr Binyon is the author of *The Exploded Garden*, which advanced a radical approach to garden design. *Forget Man* advocated a non-anthrocentric approach to gardening, putting the needs of wildlife and fungi above people. The BBC are talking to him about presenting a final episode of *Arena* on the radical gardening movement.

What he is doing or thinking

Dr Binyon is contemplating ecological catastrophe. The New Zealand flatworm has finally appeared in the heartland of British gardening – the rich southeast who buy his books.

The flatworm encoils the domestic earthworm, liquefies and then drinks it. Like one gardener to another.

No one seems to be recognizing the scale of the disaster. It's on a par with grey squirrels. The extinction of the soil-draining earthworm would mean a return of low pastures to marshland. There needs to be a national day of action. Out of the lounges, onto the lawns. Seize specimens now! His lecture today at USB is devoted to it. Is it the kind of thing that will mobilize young people?

More important, will it make good television? Can a non-anthrocentric radical gardener be seen to be campaigning against a worm? Dr Binyon considers. In fact, the imported flatworm is a prime example of human interference. Radical! He'd better talk to the Beeb fast.

MISS TINA RAVON

Outward appearance
About 24. Red jacket, jeans, a skimpy white T-shirt, showing pale, limp tummy. Explosion of curly hair, Irish-fresh face and merry eyes.

Inside information
Student at RADA, club organizer, and business woman. Visiting a temp agency for tips. Her real name is Monica.

Got into this car to avoid *Mind the Gap*, with whom she used to work. Tube theatre was fun but was never going to make any money. Tina took the basic idea and came up with a few scams of her own.

First she hired out student actors for parties. The actors insulted the hosts who had pre-arranged scripts with brilliant replies. But that required the hosts to perform. Some of them sounded like they were reading. Others forgot their lines. Some of them didn't pay.

So Tina eliminated the host. Instead, her actors staged blazing rows in the middle of dinner parties, breaking sugar plates over each other's heads. It was trendy for a while.

What she is doing or thinking
Tina looks at the faces around her, the strain and exhaustion. These sad people, she thinks. I should hire them friends.

The idea takes hold. No one to invite to your wedding? Hire some attractive guests. Rent a jolly best man who can deliver a genuinely funny speech. Embarrassed by your parents? Hire some others. Told the boss that you went to Oxford? Hire yourself some old classmates, every one guaranteed genuine Oxbridge.

Friends: the ultimate fashion accessory.
Chums R Us.
McPeople: fast & tasty.

In three years' time, Tina will be a millionaire.

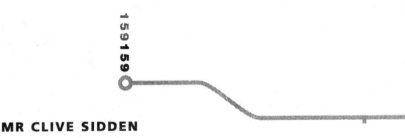

MR CLIVE SIDDEN

Outward appearance
Grey and pink and creased, in a crumpled brown pinstripe suit. Scuffed old briefcase.

Inside information
Retired information officer of the General Education Funding Body, late of York Road.

The Funding Body was broken up into four separate organizations. Three moved to Carlisle, Norwich, and Okehampton. A rump body to be renamed the Office of Educational Finance moved to a vacated floor of the Civil Servants Union. There, for a month, the old GEFB flag flew.

What he is doing or thinking
Of how loyal he used to be. The Government Information Directory listed his home phone number in case he was needed. He commissioned a GEFB uniform for exhibitions. The GEFB flag and motto were his ideas.

He thinks about how he grovelled to his bosses, and how he boasted of his relationship with them. 'And the Director said to me, "Clive," he said, "I trust you to do the right thing." '

He thinks what a fool they made of him. He supervised the move; briefed his successors; they suggested early retirement; he said goodbye to what was left of his staff.

And then in the winter darkness, he climbed up onto the roof and he cut the cords of the flagpole with a stanley knife. They won't be able to pull down the GEFB flag. They'll have to shimmy up the flagpole or build some scaffolding.

In the end, it's the thing in his life he's proudest of doing. No one knows. He's going back now, to take a photograph. Then he'll salute the GEFB, the old world, himself.

Outward appearance
Woman about 25, blonde hair, David Bowie face - pretty, angular, sardonic. Brown pinstripe trousers mismatched with a fluffy collared, slightly grubby sheepskin coat. A large handbag doubles as briefcase. She flicks through an issue of *Inside Housing* as if angry with it.

Inside information
One of many financial advisers for the Peebrane Trust, a housing association near Lambeth North. The Peebrane buys properties, acts as a landlord, works with the Prince's Trust, and matches a £30 million government grant with private capital. It is now raising a further £70 million by debenture stock issue.

What she is doing or thinking
She thinks she is scanning the news. Her mind is blocked by unacknowledged anger. Her last two jobs were with merchant banks and it was made plain in each that her services were no longer required. She ended up working for a business that masquerades as a charity. It's just not honest enough to admit it.

It's happening again. The gossip, the politicking. Her boss is a nice old gent on his last legs. They liked each other, Sasha knew he saw her as new modern woman, a kind of progeny. One night drinking late, he told her he had cancer.

Wasn't she supposed to tell anyone? Look, your main fundraiser is ill, just when you need him most? Wasn't telling the Trust about him a kind of loyalty? Launching a debenture is not easy, do they want someone who's on heavy medication?

So why is nobody talking to her?

They'll think better of it when she's given his job.

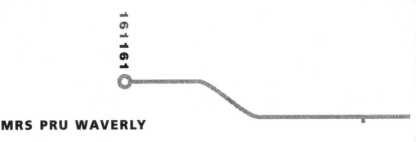

MRS PRU WAVERLY

Outward appearance
About 40. Blue suit and black and white tweed overcoat. A firm, dour face, rumpled around the mouth. Untidy, dyed hair. Eyes watery, round.

Inside information
Switchboard operator at Buntleys Coachworks. She is posh to customers, robust with staff. Yesterday, over a crossed line, she heard a murder being planned.

What she is doing or thinking
She feels shaky inside, exactly as though she'd eaten something off. She's been telling her friend Stef about it: the red light came on for Mr Gray's extension. He was busy, so she picked it up. The line was dead. Then two women came on, nothing out of the way about them.

Except that one of them said straight off: 'We'll get her, then.' She was talking from a payphone near traffic. You could hear it roar and hum.

There was a silence and the other woman said: 'You mean what I think you mean?'

The other one sniffed. 'You know what I mean. We talked enough about it.'

'She *is* such a bitch,' the other one agreed. A baby was screaming. She told it to shut up, then she said, 'He'll stop us doing it. He's not up for that sort of thing.'

'Him? Won't be anything he can do. When she's dead.'

Pru slammed the phone down. What does she do now? Stef says: nothing, you don't know who they are, who they're talking about.

It was the noise that got her. It was just the noise of humming traffic, but at first it sounded like voices, thousands of them, singing. In hell.

MISS STEFANIE PARASHAR

Outward appearance
Tiny, foreign woman, with a lively face, lipsticked mouth in a seemingly permanent smile. Volumes of spidery dressed hair piled up around a seashell grip. White shirt, black slacks, very stacked heels.

Inside information
Clerk at Buntleys Coachworks. Shares office and often lunch with the woman next to her. Shares drinks and often a lot more with the lads. More than anything else Stef likes a laugh.

What she is doing or thinking
Trying not to smile. It was a bit naughty of the lads, but Pru can be bossy at times, so to send her up they made this tape. Even Mr Gray was a sport about it, letting them play it through his extension.

They all thought Pru would make a fearful fuss, call the cops, demand action, all of that, make a right idiot of herself, and then they would tell her. Instead, she went all quiet. She sat and stared, hand over her mouth. The lads peeked in through the door window and she didn't even see them.

They'd found a weak place in tough old Pru. She looks like she's been kicked in the stomach and you can't blame her.

Pru says, 'It was horrible, Stef. It just made me feel sick.' She's really worried. She really thinks someone is going to die.

It's not funny, Stef tells herself. And then she thinks of Andy and the boys with their tape recorder and wants to giggle.

'And their voices, Stef. They were so mean. You know how horrible people can be.'

'Yeah,' says Stef, and smiles.

MR SUNIL KURASH

Outward appearance
Tall, prim gentleman sitting upright in grey suit and overcoat. Another passenger, swaggering, deliberately kicks his briefcase. It is Sunil who apologizes.

Inside information
Works alongside his solicitor brother for a law firm that rejoices in the name of Kurash and Steal.

Sunil is the model of polite behaviour. His politeness annoys people. He apologizes for arriving late or early or dead on time. He apologizes for talking to people or not talking to people.

When he was a child, Sunil had a terrible temper. He would leave the table in a high dudgeon. His father warned: 'If you smash your sister's new fire engine I shall punish you,' and Sunil did smash it. He would howl and rage and kick.

But now when Sunil loses his temper, something worse happens. He starts to talk like Donald Duck. Exactly like Donald Duck. Wharr wharr warraraa. He finds this mortifying.

What he is doing or thinking
Sunil can't believe that he apologized. The old man, red-faced and drunk, feints at the case again as if it were a football and drops into his seat. Sunil finds his soul prickled as if with a rising of feathers. He can almost feel them under his skin.

'Scotland Forever,' the drunk says.

Sunil struggles to suppress his inner Donald Duck. His soul is filled with wordless anger in a language from beyond childhood. He yearns to lisp and spray and throw things.

Instead Sunil clenches his paper into folds, picks up his case, and gets off at Waterloo.

Sunil cannot speak any Asian tongue.

MR BILL McREADY

Outward appearance
Short, grey-haired man in red Adidas shirt, denim jacket and jeans, rubber-soled bovver boots. Makes a football kick at someone's briefcase.

Inside information
A sailor in the merchant marine docked at Chatham for the last time. Drunk and lost in the underground system. Has a semi-derelict home in a Glasgow suburb. No wife or family.

What he is doing or thinking
Last night's bender has induced a kind of euphoria. Bill hears all around him the roar of a football crowd, thousands of people singing: *You'll never walk alone!*

Bill loves footie. He played a lot when he was younger. He couldn't resist taking a swipe at the gentleman's briefcase.

Bill feels friendly towards him. 'Scotland Forever,' he says, meaning, you and me, we're not one of these English cunts. Bill spent six years of his life anchored off Ascension Island. He remembers the chief of police from St Helens. He was black, a great little striker.

His tanker never moved. It was filled regularly with oil to supply the Beeb, the Yanks, the RAF. During the Falklands War, the sky was filled with planes. At night on the beaches, giant turtles would lay their eggs. You'd take motorboats to go ashore, and you had to duck the flying fish. The island was blistering hot - red, black, and beige from different kinds of lava. But the top of the mountain was emerald, like a memory of the heaths of home.

How he wanted to be back home. Now he wants to be back on Ascension. The crowd roars.

MRS MEL McKINNEY

Outward appearance
Late twenties, drifting off to sleep behind huge specs. Ill-assorted clothes: black leather jacket with a flimsy green dress bunching up behind her knees.

Inside information
Her husband Bill is the caretaker of St Michael's RC school. Their flat is stuck on top of the scruffy, modern brick building. The roof terrace deserves tricycles and building blocks, but they have no children.

Mel's husband is away on a conference. Last night, Mel popped out for a loaf of bread. 'We are trying to keep this door locked and secure,' says a hand-lettered sign on the school door. Mel remembered halfway to the shop that she'd left her keys behind. She had to stay the night at her sister's.

What she is doing or thinking
Mel is dreaming of her brother-in-law, Ray. Shy, sweet, he has high cheek-bones, a snub nose, and black hair that keeps its comb marks. Her sister Sandra has blonde slightly spiky hair. She has two kids and a ring through her nose. Mel showed up, apologized, was given the usual lecture. 'Honestly, you'd think you'd learn!' The two sisters don't get on.

Years ago it was Mel who brought Ray home first. He wasn't quite her boyfriend, but he was going to be. Sandra as usual wanted something someone else had. She's got him now.

But Ray still likes Mel best. His eyes go all soft when he looks at her. All of Mel goes soft for him. Asleep now, she dreams of the taste of his tongue, of having his babies.

MRS MARY LENEHAN

Outward appearance
Pixilated and prim, pursed lips, purple hair, slithery lapis dress, and shoes with diamanté buckles. Fills in a typed sheet, smiling.

Inside information
Now works as an EO in the Department of Transport office near Lambeth Bridge. Used to work with mass murderer Donald Nielsen. She has consented yet again to answer questions for another book.

Mary has two boyfriends, both 50, one to pay the bills, the other a well-hung Serb. They don't know about each other. She plies the first with drink until he passes out. Then she sees Marco and, after a bit of the other, she gets him drunk too, and slips back home.

What she is doing or thinking
Mary is writing terrible lies about Donald. She says that he slept in a coffin imported from Hungary. She writes that he brought curries for the office Christmas party in large pots, the very ones in which he cooked the heads of young boys. She smiles, thinking: this is a lie. It is in fact the truth: she's told the story so many times she now thinks she made it up.

Mary dropped in on Donald one night to find him very embarrassed. A sleepy young man grinned on the sofa. He was drugged, about to be killed. At the time, Mary was pleased that Donald had a sex life at all. Shame. Rather pretty.

She decides to tell the researcher that Nielsen was addicted to absinthe. Sometimes she confides giggling to friends that she didn't know Nielsen at all. But she did.

He reads what she writes.

MRS PAULE WRIGHT

Outward appearance
Tired, middle-aged black woman. White track suit bottoms, white trainers. Brown and green coat with a 'Lake Louise' logo on it. White shirt in Matisse patterns, pink and black.

Inside information
Lives on a Hercules Road estate. Returning home from a cleaning job. Her husband who worked as a clerk in a bank for years was made redundant, so Paule went back to cleaning offices.

What she is doing or thinking
Has Charley remembered her birthday? He was asleep when she left. She imagines a card on the table, a red rose. Charley is so casual about birthdays. In Paule's family, birthdays were big.

Paule gets out at Lambeth North. 'Hello, Paule!' someone cries and her heart sinks. She turns to see her friend Mary, looking like she just left the beautician's, with an artfully arranged scarf and a hairdo like Jackie O's.

'What you doing out this time of the morning?' Mary asks.

'Out early doing my birthday shopping,' chuckles Paule.

'Have to do your own? What about that lazy man of yours?' Mary asks. They laugh sociably all the way to the lift, Paule on tenterhooks.

Mary asks, 'Your husband still in banking?' but doesn't wait for an answer. She talks instead about trouble with a noisy neighbour.

Paule is relieved. She and her husband came here 30 years ago to make something out of life. She doesn't want anyone to know she's gone back to cleaning.

It is not until they are outside, saying goodbye, that Paule suddenly thinks: what's Mary doing coming back at this hour?

MR GURDEV DHOLLIN

Outward appearance
Tough, perhaps sour, middle-aged man. Black hair streaked with white. Jacket, shirt with broad blue stripes, no tie. Light blue-grey trousers, too tight. Briefcase.

Inside information
Runs a small dry cleaning shop on Kennington Road. Lets his staff do the work while he goes through his business papers. He has a phone in his briefcase and one plugged into the cigarette lighter of his car.

Grew up in the Punjab, where his family are now. Has carefully mapped out his return in five years' time.

The money from the shop is enough to finance property developments in his native state. His eldest son runs the casino in one of his hotels. The other runs a series of housing developments, building homes for the new middle class.

What he is doing or thinking
Dismayed by the invention of Hindu fundamentalism. Where does this come from? The term Hindu refers to geography not belief. No one in India calls it Hinduism. It is the dharma. People can worship Rama or Durga. All religions are individual and personal.

Gurdev blames the failure of politics in India, and he blames that on corruption. He intends to return and enter politics for the Congress party.

India should be a number-one country. It has the resources and the people. Why are they licensing foreign car manufacturers? Give the contract to Indians.

But the image in his mind is this: a slow, sluggish river winding through a hushed, hot landscape, patient, heavy, like a pregnant woman; and a giggling boy shimmying up a tree: himself.

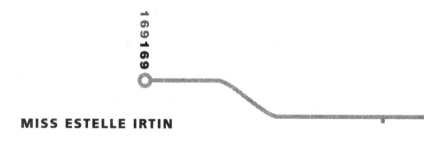

MISS ESTELLE IRTIN

Outward appearance
Large woman in her early thirties. *X-Files* T-shirt, tie-dyed gown, leather coat with Indian fringe. Generally pugnacious air, softened as she reads a leather-covered book.

Inside information
Since 1991, Estelle has been in love with Saddam Hussein. The *Saturday Independent* ran a photograph of him swimming. His delighted smile seemed to stare up at Joy itself, his bare shoulders promised an exotic body. Estelle desires his olive skin, his dark and dancing eyes, his cheesy grin. Saddam makes Estelle feel like a loosened girdle.

Her husband used to masturbate at night next to her when he thought she was asleep. He was small, pale, and pretty, and left her for a man. She became obsessed with Saddam: his terrible childhood, his beatings with tar-covered sticks. Part of her thinks she could make him good through love, kissing his closed eyes. Part of her can see his penis, very clearly.

What she is doing or thinking
Estelle has found a rare volume - *The Wit and Wisdom of Saddam Hussein*. This is one of the jokes: what thing does a rich man keep wrapped in cloth, that a poor man throws away? Answer: the results of a blown nose.

Saddam called his secret police The Apparatus of Yearning. That is tattooed on Estelle's smooth, white arm. His political prison was called the Palace of the End. He made building-size statues of broken hearts. People paint portraits of him in their own blood, out of devotion.

At home, Estelle has a canvas waiting, a brush and razor blade.

MRS LINDA SCRALG

Outward appearance
Silver blonde hair, white T-shirt, loose black coat and jumper, very tight jeans.

Inside information
Designer at Broad Brush, a small design agency. Recently married to a hulking New Zealand farmer who is also an Olympic high diver. He is to say the least very different from the men she met at St Martins. He's called Heathcliff.

What she is doing or thinking
That the marriage won't do.

On Sunday, Heathcliff burned her cat. Verity was a beautiful all-white Persian. She was a famous cat. She'd starred in a series of Broad-Brush greeting cards.

Linda was looking out the window at Daddy's herbaceous border, and saw Heathcliff throw Verity, stiff as a board, onto a bonfire. She'd died of a heart attack; it was the shock of seeing a farm. Heathcliff couldn't understand why Linda was upset. 'It's just a dead old puss,' he said.

Then she had some friends round to lunch, and he insisted he could imitate a bull's mating call so well that the cows would be fooled. There was her new husband making urgent, guttural, bovine noises. The worst of it was that the cows did come crowding round. 'Is that how you and Linda met, then?' Livvy asked. It was so embarrassing.

She's left him down on the farm. The terrible thing is Heathcliff and Daddy get along wonderfully. They sat up 'til three in the morning talking about her. Daddy thinks he's found someone to inherit the farm.

Heathcliff's going to be terribly difficult to get rid of. Just like the others.

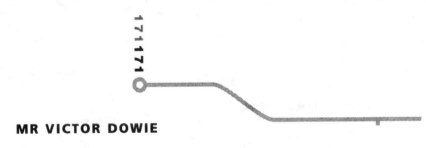

MR VICTOR DOWIE

Outward appearance

Short, athletic black man in mid-twenties, sleepily slumped, grinning, occasionally shaking his head in amusement or disbelief.

Inside information

Works as a secretary and sales assistant for *Sarf London Security*, a shop specializing in locks, bolts, bars and alarms. It's owned by Sanjay Kumar, but managed by Victor's mate Ian, who got him the job. Ian's a fellow Arsenal fan and lets Victor use the shop's computer to lay out his football fanzine. It takes the piss out of the professional football magazine *Shoot!* It's called *Shit!*

What he is doing or thinking

Thinking of his next issue. He's just come up with an article called *You are the Ref*. The reader has to call unusual football violations such as invasion of the pitch by Morris Dancers, or misbehaviour by the giant styrofoam arrow that keeps pointing to the ball. *Spot the ball* has photographs of football players in showers, shorts etc.

Say Cheese is a more regular feature. It asks for examples of readers' worst ever football memorabilia. Last week a photograph of the Esso 1970 World Cup Coin collection was sent in by novelist Jeffrey Archer. Victor rang the publishers, and it's true. 'I think you need to know that Mr Archer threatens to send you,' the publicity executive continued, 'his collection of football star jam jar lids.'

Fame at last. Vic eases out of his seat, still grinning. He's just had another idea. He's going to run a story on Jeffrey Archer memorabilia.

It would be nice if there was a way to make money doing this.[2]

2 Following the closure of *Sarf London Security*, Victor's fanzine went – briefly – professional. He was talent-spotted by British comedians Skinner and Baddiel and ended up on the writing staff of *Fantasy Football*.

Jeffrey Archer made a guest appearance.

MS LISA MUIR

Outward appearance

Fawn overcoat belted over brown corduroy trousers, yellow sweater, fawn jacket. Thick, fur-lined gloves in pocket. Large cloth bag laden with papers. Reading *Exchange and Mart.* Mid-thirties but first impression is ten years younger.

Inside information

A property developer. Does up properties or supervises building work under contract. The recession made her life easier. It weeded out the cowboys and made everyone else grateful for work. Her previous jobs have included reviewing feature films for airlines, selling car insurance, and writing template tenders for corporate identities. Knows contract law backwards.

What she is doing or thinking

Getting a rough idea of property prices this week. Smiling slightly to herself because she has sprung a trap.

She showed up yesterday at a flat being converted on King Edward Walk. It was 4.45 and the house was empty and dark. One of the mates showed up, claiming to have just stepped out for fags. She pretended to believe him; and casually let him know her car was being serviced today.

This morning, she'll let herself into King Edward Walk with a small electric heater, some letters to finish and some reading to do. She'll be there for 8.45. It will be interesting to see when they turn up. Any time after 10.00, and they're fired.

She likes it when their faces fall, and they suddenly realize that this slim pretty woman knows what she's talking about and that she has no problems with fights and firings. In fact she rather enjoys them. She has enjoyed them for these last fifteen years.

MRS DELIA HENDY

Outward appearance

Camilla Parker-Bowles? A white sporting jacket with a thick, accordion collar over a brown sweater and a white sailing shirt. White towelling trousers, thick-soled, clean trainers. Waterproof bag printed with bamboo imagery and a stamp 'Forbidden Cargo'. Stares shell-shocked at a form, then writes.

Inside information

A professional domestic carer, contracted to Lambeth Council. She visits the infirm, cleaning their flats and cooking them lunch. The Billericay Building Society has just found a new way to make her homeless.

In November she bid for a house that the Billericay had repossessed. She won the auction fair and square, for £34,000. Guess it wasn't enough. They exchanged contracts, and the Bill told her the completion date would be January 12th.

She went and sold her flat didn't she? Exchanged contracts. Then her solicitor got a letter saying the Billericay ('Feel Dicky with the Billericay') were pulling out of the deal.

Delia rang and the girl cheerfully admitted that they had reneged. She kept calling Delia Mrs Henry, despite being corrected. 'It happens sometimes,' the girl bubbled. 'We will be paying you compensation for any inconvenience caused.' Delia is now sleeping on a client's floor. You call that inconvenient?

What she is doing or thinking

The Bill has sent her a customer satisfaction questionnaire.

Does she like the decor of her local branch? How long does she have to wait in line? Do staff smile? She has responded positively to each question. There is no opportunity to do anything else.

Suddenly she writes at the bottom, 'But I hate you.'

MR ANTHONY AULDGIRTH

Outward appearance

Old blind man with a white cane and carefully maintained suit. A few wisps of red hair over his head. The bald skin is mottled with age spots, which have gone crusty. His hands are frail bundles of tendon and blue veins. He sits patiently, quietly, waiting.

Inside information

His name would have been well known to readers of *The Times* during the early 1950s. Became a friend of Samuel Beckett's at Trinity College, Dublin. Saw *Godot* in its earliest production and realized then his friend was marked for greatness.

Misses his wife Elizabeth beyond endurance. In New York, Norman Mailer once said of her: 'This is a woman you can talk to on any level.' Elizabeth died of cancer in 1985.

What he is doing or thinking

Remembering his first meeting with his wife's best friend in 1934. Daphne lived in a house right on the banks of the Thames. She wore a green bathing suit. Anthony was shy: all he could think of saying was 'Elizabeth tells me you stand on your head.' Daphne promptly did so, and walked back into the house on her hands.

Daphne's son Thomas is now 50 years old, running a business in Australia. Thomas knows nothing of the house near Reading, or of how beautiful his mother once was. As a schoolboy in the 1950s, Thomas would come to stay, bringing his friend. In consequence, here Anthony is, in the 1990s, going to visit that friend in West Square with Elizabeth's daughter. The consequences go on and on.

The people don't, of course.

MRS MADELEINE STRICKLER

Outward appearance
Instant 1960s. Long auburn hair, brown overcoat, left arm across tummy, right hand in 'Thinker' position, both resting on top of Acorn computer bag. Contemplates the old gentleman next to her.

Inside information
Freelance editor and journalist. Lived for many years in the Orient, then America, where her children now live. Converted to Buddhism along with her husband. Lives with her father who is sitting next to her. They are visiting a family friend near the Elephant.

What she is doing or thinking
She is remembering a day on the tube in 1957. They were going to a wedding, so she and her sisters were all in ribbons and white. Daddy was in a morning coat. People travelled on the tubes like that in those days. There was an advertising campaign for Heinz on underground posters. Each poster told you which of the varieties a particular Heinz product was: tomato soup, no. 2, brown pickle, no. 37. If you collected all 57, you won a Christmas hamper.

Daddy was a freelance journalist: they needed the hamper. She and her sisters ran up and down the cars dressed for a wedding, squealing. They changed carriages at each station, calling like seagulls, 'Forty is spaghetti in tomato sauce!'

Then they bumped into teenagers doing the same thing. After that, to keep the secret, they whispered or passed notes.

Madeleine can't remember if they got the hamper. But where are the children running now? The white dresses? The top hats? She takes her father's hand.

'This is the last stop, Daddy,' she says.

MR PETE DAYMOND

Outward appearance
Trim man in his thirties, blue jeans, white trainers, thinning blond hair. Two plastic bags full of something square-cornered. Eyes keep looking up.

Inside information
Poster sticker, sometime dope dealer. Returning from work, pasting girls' cards in phone booths.

What he is doing or thinking
He's scared and knackered. He hates putting up the cards. You do five or six girls at a time. You have to leave the bag outside the booth, put your money in and phone home. While it's really ringing, you paste the cards, receiver under your chin. Just in case someone checks you're making a call.

You work from 6.30 to 8.30 AM. There's enough people around in case of aggro, but not so many that they get a good look at what you're doing.

There's rival groups, and some of them are not very nice people. They don't particularly like it if you paste in what they think is their turf. But you've got to post where the punters are. Kings Cross, Tottenham Court Road, all round there.

Pete was sure he was followed into the tube. At first, he thought it was Passenger 151. Then he saw the state of it. Bet he could use some dosh. Sub-contracting would be good for my health.

'You looking for some work, mate?' Pete asks.

'I'm an Internet trainer,' the man says, grandly. Well maybe.

'This is part time, just mornings.' The man's eyebrows rise. 'Where you getting off?' Pete asks.

He shrugs. 'The Elephant, I suppose.' Going nowhere.

They get off at Lambeth instead.

MR AMITABH CHOPRA

Outward appearance
A tiny middle-aged Asian gentleman, slim, in a green suit, white shirt, red tie. Sits reading a magazine with the cover folded over.

Inside information
Works in the Sweet Shoppe in Waterloo Station. Hates chocolate. But it is a clean and orderly environment. Has to control feelings of shame that he does not run his own business at his age.

What he is doing or thinking
Reading what he thinks of as a dirty magazine: the February 1995 issue of *Stardust*. He deliberately sat some distance away from other Asian men to prevent being discovered. The cover shows a pretty girl taking a sudsy bath in a bikini and floppy hat.

SEX it shrieks. Then, tiny letters: *the industry's*. Then huge: ORGY
tiny letters: *of immorality exposed*.

Mr Chopra loves Bollywood movies. *Stardust* is devoted to them, in over thirty countries. *Sanjay-Raveena* STRIP *each other*, it promises, with Sanjay and Raveena both in tummy-revealing pervy leather glowering into the camera. MAMTA ACCUSED! *How Aamir Faked his Illness to Save his Marriage.*

It's a magazine for scandal-soaked women. Amitabh loves the movies, and wants to read about them. He extracts from the scandals news about movies like *Karan-Arjun*. In between there are ads for skin lighteners, wedding dresses, movie-star address finders, Bombay Jungle mix Bollywood Fever and AT&T.

Where does he fit in? Amitabh has always been a dreamer. In his mind at night he sees gods and heroes, riding elephants besaddled in red and gold. He hears the sweeping sounds of orchestra and voices.

MS DEBBIE DɛNUSSI

Outward appearance
Glamorous red lipstick, long red hair. Floor-length coat made of black leather. Black beret perched on the side of her head. Blue jeans and patent leather, alligator-pattern shoes. Tiny dangling earrings with a Dracula-eyed glint of light in each. Clutches a tiny purse. Keeps standing up, looking at the map, peering through the window. Takes out a personal organizer and keys in a question.

Inside information
An American film maker following English instructions to the Royal Pharmaceutical Society, where she is to be briefed on the making of a new film about threadworms.

What she is doing or thinking.
Where the hell is she? They told her to walk from the tube station to the Church Tower and then cross to the blue pub called the Hercules and go down that street and then turn right. Can't miss it.

But which tube station? She looks at all the people getting out at Waterloo. The willowy woman next to her saunters out. It must be nice to be that confident of where you are going. No one gets on, and Debbie starts to get worried. What if she's going to a bad part of town?

At Lambeth North she gets out. She looks at the dingy platform, and at the wall map, and sees the next station is the end of the line. That must have been why they didn't tell her. You can't miss the station at the end of the line.

She hops back on just as the doors rumble shut. Whew, she smiles. Just made it.

MS ANNABELLE ROWAN

Outward appearance
Woman about 40, wearing black trousers which show a well-preserved figure. Cloth coat with extravagant fake fur trim. With stately calm, reads Jeff Noon's *Vurt*.

Inside information
Receptionist at the Royal Pharmaceutical Society and ex-devotee of the Bhagwan Sri Rajneesh. Sits all day surrounded by a collection of 19th-century pharmaceutical jars. They are nearly as tall as she is, translucent with ornate labels and filled with green, blue or red fluids.

What she is doing or thinking
Calmly waiting for the moment when she has to tell the Publicity Chair that his film maker will not be showing up. She printed a map with instructions, but he insisted on giving directions over the phone. No one in England can give directions. That is because there are no reliably placed street signs. We direct people to the local Tesco then on past the off-licence and wonder why foreigners stop us in the street for help.

It was one of many things Annabelle learned in Oregon.[3] The Bhagwan told her: life is a joke. Always land on the wrong airfield, buy as many cars as you can. Imelda Marcos's shoes are a great joke. One must be calm and laugh. For a woman as highly sexed as Annabelle, it was paradise, for there were handsome men, beautiful women, and they all made love rather as cats must, in complete security.

The bottles surround her, historic, preserved, huge, and highly coloured as if her own past were bottled in them.

I wonder what this film maker would have been like?

Another helpful and informative
253 *footnote*

3.   Oregon is the ugliest state in the union. It used to be one of the most beautiful. When I was a teenager, my parents and I used to take long drives along its coast. It seemed to be one long beach state park, with sandy cliffs, blackened driftwood, banks of wild blueberries, and small, isolated fishing hamlets. I remember one blissful week at Christmas, staying in a motel, making friends with a bunch of guys, one of whom read a girly pop star mag. 'It's the only way I can find out about the music,' he said. He was right; articles about the Kinks, the Beatles, the Stones. BRS - before *Rolling Stone.* I remember there was a tiny store in walking distance, with record racks: Patty Page, Perry Como . . . not a single pop album in the racks. 'No call for that kind of thing here,' said the old gramps behind the counter.

In 1996, I did the drive again with my parents on my way to Clarion West. Had the state parks become a haven for hippies? Did dope-smuggling boats land at night on the isolated coast? Did the bottom fall out of the Monterey Jack cheese market? For whatever reason, the state parks are gone. In their stead is a chain of what looks like badly built used car lots, a string of motels built right on noisy roadways, small supermarkets, or gas stations that straggle out from, and disguise, the old villages. Northern California is far wilder and less spoiled.

The development trails along a great length of coastline with a 35 mph speed limit. If you drive any faster, you will certainly get one or more tickets. If, in desperation, you turn inland, you are likely to find the stubble-covered hills that resulted from previous decades of tree-felling.

Oregon: fly over it.

MR TERRY WILCOX

Outward appearance

Fawn raincoat, blue suit, soft shoes. Balding in the middle of his head so that his hair makes wings. Florid face a bit like Albert Finney's. Opens up a slim leather case stuffed full of magazines, and pulls out a DTP document.

Inside information

Manager at the Wasteco Supermarket, Elephant and Castle. Terry's hobby is hobbies - matchbox toy cars, rare records. His jazz collection is complete, except for a few Stan Kenton LPs, and a rare Brubeck. All 4,500 records are catalogued and hardly played. The walls are insulated with video tapes of his favourite movies: he's missing a few Deanna Durbin classics. For a while, he was in an Iron Age recreation group. He wore hessian tunics and collected replica maces and battleaxes.

His two new enthusiasms are picture phonecards and becoming an umpire for American baseball.

What he is doing or thinking

Reading the rules. Baseball moves faster than cricket. You need to have eagle eyes. It all comes down to whether the man on base catches the ball before the runner gets there.

Baseball's a kind of fantasy: Coke, hot dogs and hot summers. It's neither as bruising as football, nor as fast as basketball, the real American National Sports. Baseball belongs to the 1890s.

Whereas phonecards . . . It really is extraordinary how fast they have become collectors' items: Star Trek phonecards, Disney phonecards. Wasn't there something in the last issue of *BT Card Collector* about special phonecard storage furniture? Complete with indexing and retrieval? He puts down *The Umpire Strikes Back* to look.

He likes to keep active.

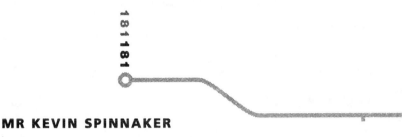

MR KEVIN SPINNAKER

Outward appearance

Tall, round faced, wears black with black dressed hair. Yelps with laughter. Stands up and makes faces through the window between the cars.

Inside information

Works for the Pay Unit of the London College of Printing. Wanted to be a professional football player. On the field, he transforms from an easily pleased, nice-enough bloke, to someone demanding, aggressive and quick. It is the one area of life where he can be so. Boyfriend of Jenny Green.

What he is doing or thinking

Waving through the window at Jen. To tease her, he told her she was getting plump, so to get her own back, she changed cars. She sticks her tongue out at him. He loves her humour. He loves going to gigs or Formula One with her.

He doesn't love having sex with her. He has managed to hide this from Jen by effort of main will. He's young and fit, but it takes him forever to come because he's so unexcited.

She misreads this. For her, a man who takes half an hour to come is a hero.

The man she loves is the man his friends sometimes call gormless. She doesn't know the man who forces balls past goalposts as if by concentration, who feels implacable hatred for his opponents. She doesn't know he hates her lack of make-up, her ordinary body, her ordinary face. Sweet, nice Kevin does know, but it is this Kevin who won't be able to tell her.

So he mugs and smiles, and waves through the separating glass as if saying goodbye.

For Your Reading Ease and Comfort
PASSENGER MAP
Car No 6

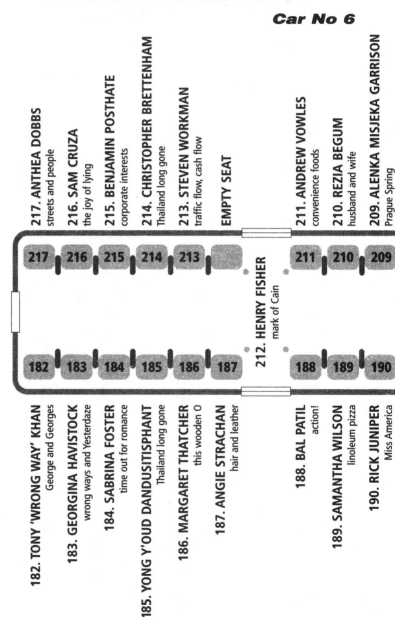

217. ANTHEA DOBBS — streets and people
216. SAM CRUZA — the joy of lying
215. BENJAMIN POSTHATE — corporate interests
214. CHRISTOPHER BRETTENHAM — Thailand long gone
213. STEVEN WORKMAN — traffic flow, cash flow
EMPTY SEAT
211. ANDREW VOWLES — convenience foods
210. REZIA BEGUM — husband and wife
209. ALENKA MISJEKA GARRISON — Prague Spring

212. HENRY FISHER — mark of Cain

182. TONY 'WRONG WAY' KHAN — George and Georges
183. GEORGINA HAVISTOCK — wrong ways and Yesterdaze
184. SABRINA FOSTER — time out for romance
185. YONG Y'OUD DANDUSITISPHANT — Thailand long gone
186. MARGARET THATCHER — this wooden O
187. ANGIE STRACHAN — hair and leather
188. BAL PATIL — action!
189. SAMANTHA WILSON — linoleum pizza
190. RICK JUNIPER — Miss America

208. DAVID OFFSEY
snip!

207. ANGELA DOWD
image

206. MICHAEL HANSHAW
things go better with...

205. DODIE McGINLAY
defenders and benders

204. HARRY MIGSON
Carpenters' fan club

203. LEONE SKERRIT
Golden Girls

202. MARYAN ELLIOTT
The Knowledge

201. 'BERTIE JEEVES'
going through the motions

200. ROSEMARY OLIVER
Good Food Guide

| 208 | 207 | 206 | | 205 | 204 | 203 | 202 | 201 | 200 |

| 191 | 192 | 193 | | 194 | 195 | 196 | 197 | 198 | 199 |

191. SANJAY KUMAR
taken to the cleaners

192. JAMES WHITTHEAD
espresso snoro

193. LORRAINE HANT
Attack of the Puppet People

194. MARY WALLIS
antique antics

195. HARRIET ZINOVSKY
fake and reality

196. TONY 'PEEWEE' HATCHET
birthing *Beowulf*

197. JIM HAIGH
serving Anita

198. BEVERLY TOMPSET
to love or love up?

199. STAN GRAY
Y-fronts and murder

Crimestoppers Textbook

THE PROFESSIONAL WAY TO DESCRIBE CRIMINALS

You can never tell when you might witness a crime. Any detail that you remember, however insignificant, may clinch a conviction and put a villain behind bars. You must be ready to describe exactly everyone around you.

Do they sit pigeon-toed or knock-kneed? Do their fat, short, stumpy legs mean they sit on tiptoe? Splay-footed? Do they have long shanks? Unfashionably short trousers revealing bony ankles? Diamond pattern socks?

The woman opposite you with blood red nails covers her mouth: does she always yawn when she has something to hide?

Do they wear wedding rings? Have they removed wedding rings? Look for tell-tale puffiness on the third finger left hand. Can an alert observer note that their ears have been pierced?

Are they behaving suspiciously in any way? For example, do they seem unusually fixated on the people around them, staring at them intently?

Use the **253** description code: Categorize people!

Are they
- [ ] puny: (short and thin)
- [ ] squat: (short and fat)
- [ ] fat: (medium to tall but bloated)
- [ ] scrawny: (tall and skinny)
- [ ] apple on a stick: (skinny with a pot belly)?

Is their hair
- [ ] permed like a poodle
- [ ] crisp with gel
- [ ] blue with rinse
- [ ] bacon-streaky with tints?

Are their faces
- [ ] oblong,
- [ ] round,
- [ ] square
- [ ] or kumquat-shaped?

Do they suffer from
- [ ] receding hair
- [ ] facial scars or other disfigurements
- [ ] grey anoraks?
- [ ] pink and purple anoraks?

REMEMBER: THE PRICE OF VIGILANCE IS ETERNAL FREEDOM.

Shop your neighbours!
Use the 253 Interpersonal Description Guide!

MR TONY 'WRONG WAY' KHAN

Outward appearance

Angular, handsome young man in a tuxedo and white scarf. Sits in angry silence next to a young woman who looks at him mournfully.

Inside information

The son of the Pakistani lawyer beloved of Georgina Bullen. Tony's father moved back to Britain in 1979 when his English wife became homesick.

Just returned from a wedding in France. Went the wrong way from Waterloo, heading north on the Bakerloo line. Changed at Embankment, and is now heading the right way.

What he is doing or thinking

Why does everything go wrong? He met the woman next to him, Georgina, on the Shuttle on his way to the wedding.

'I'm going to a wedding too!' Georgina said, pleased. 'What's your friend's name?'

'George,' was the answer. 'So's mine!' she cried. It was in the same town. They bought Shuttle champagne on the strength of it. They laughed all the way under the Channel, through Paris and to the country train station.

The taxi driver smelled of sweat and couldn't find the address that Georgina gave him. They arrived late and embarrassed. The French bride pressed them with more champagne.

Anthony couldn't find his friend. 'Have you seen George?' he kept asking. Georgina replied, mystified, 'He was just here.'

Finally, she dragged him to George. He turned out to be Georges, and French. Anthony was at the wrong wedding. Another taxi ride. Anthony's George had already gone by the time he arrived.

No one bought champagne on the trip back. Now at Waterloo, Georgina stands up to go. 'Goodbye?' she says.

It's a question.

MISS GEORGINA HAVISTOCK

Outward appearance
A glum fairy? Pretty, plump woman in a pink dress, all lacy pleats like a ballet tutu. Veiled 1950s hat over short black hair.

Inside information
Part-owner of Yesterdaze, a shop near Waterloo that sells vintage magazines and clothes. Her partner is her ex-boyfriend. Things are a bit tense.

Just back from France on the Shuttle. Has followed her neighbour first north from Waterloo, then south.

What she is doing or thinking
It always seems to happen. She's never had so much fun as yesterday, all done up, taking the train to France.

And meeting Anthony. She thought he was gorgeous the moment she saw him. He was so much fun as well. She would like to remember just one of his jokes. Maybe they weren't that good; maybe you had to be there. Maybe you had to be going to someone else's wedding by yourself, a bit tipsy, and relieved to meet someone so nice. Who was going to the same wedding as you.

Only he wasn't. Her hands rise and fall with frustration. She's already lost her temper with him for blaming her for taking him to the wrong wedding. 'I wasn't blaming you,' he said mysteriously. So why isn't he talking to her?

At Waterloo, Georgina says, 'Goodbye.'

He looks up, surprised. 'You get off here? Why did you take the tube north?'

She shrugs. 'To stay with you.'

'I'll call you,' he says.

On the platform Georgina sees an older woman who looks firm, settled. Georgina wonders: will I ever be as tough as that?

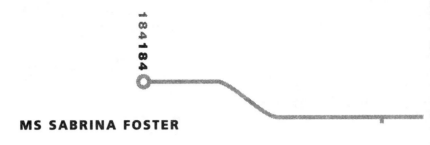

MS SABRINA FOSTER

Outward appearance
Brown suit, tan ribbed jumper, long brown coat. Piled up,
M-People hair. Hands held criss-cross over the top of a letter.

Inside information
Teller at Kennington Building Society. Advertiser in the same
Time Out personal ads being scanned at that moment by
Passenger 71. Reading her first batch of replies.

What she is doing or thinking
It was a mistake to advertise as a black woman. It would have
been a mistake not to. Right now a crab-faced white man with
a grizzled beard is leering up at her from a photo-booth nightmare. His letter keeps talking about his car and house. Glancing
sideways first, Sabrina looks at the next letter.

And quickly, she covers it. Attached is a tiny photo from a
contact sheet of a man in the nude. Not to be unkind, but she
would need a magnifying glass anyway. He looks doe-eyed and
sweet, dumb enough to think that a full-frontal would turn a
woman on.

What she wants is a mature, intelligent black man who is in
stable employment that does not cost him his dignity. There
must be one somewhere?

Her next correspondent is white, pockmarked, with a pony
tail. His letter is amazing. He plainly thinks women advertise
for one night stands. The next reply is an outright proposal of
marriage from Zimbabwe.

Sabrina pushes the whole mess into her bag, and goes. On the
platform, she thinks: I'd settle for someone nice, fat. Like the
big, suited pillow who just pushed past her.

Well, maybe next week . . .

MR YONG Y'OUD
DANDUSITISPHANT

Outward appearance
Neat, middle-aged Asian man. Thin, inward-turning mouth. He rocks slightly in place, and then slowly lowers, hangs, his head.

Inside information
Owner of Cow Tom's Thai restaurant on Westminster Bridge Road. Was given a work permit in 1984 as a specialist chef. Soon discovered that England offered little of the smiles, hand greetings and gentle good grace of his own country.

After ten years, saved up enough to open his own restaurant in an unpromising locale. It proved to be an immense success. Married Sanam, one of the waitresses, and is now a proud father. He often trots his son Sammy around the restaurant, teaching him to walk.

What he is doing or thinking
Fearing for Sammy. He is huge for his age, but has not begun to talk. His cheeks are covered in a rash. His mother keeps laughing and says the rash will go. It's spreading. The boy's chin has swollen, while his head stays narrow.

Last night Yong Y'oud took Sammy for his usual walk. He kept stumbling and falling, vacantly, without crying. Indulgent customers pretended to be charmed. They asked how old he was, and when Yong Y'oud said 22 months, their smiles grew shadowy, strained.

Sammy is ill. Yong Y'oud thinks of how Sammy used to love hanging upside down from his knees, or hiding under the bamboo chair, grasping at his yellow duck as if at a mystery. He sees his wife Sanam's thin face, its smile too wide, and wonders how he can make her accept the truth.

England suddenly seems smaller.

MRS MARGARET THATCHER

Outward appearance
Short-haired woman in workman's jeans and donkey jacket. Reading *The Marriage of Cadmus and Harmony*. Understandably, looks bored.

Inside information
Mrs Thatcher is a thatcher, currently working on the roof of the new Globe Theatre.[1] It's traditional straw and reed, fireproofed and hiding a sprinkler system.

Margaret has lost her car keys. This is particularly poignant as her husband Dennis has just lost his.

What she is doing or thinking
Margaret is reasonably certain that the keys fell out of her pocket while she was on the scaffolding yesterday. If so, they will be bundled up with the thatch.

The scaffolding has moved. She can ask the works supervisor, but he's hardly likely to re-erect the scaffolding just for her. Or allow her onto that steep roof without it.

She's had the keyring since she was in university. The medal, in the shape of a panda, says on the front, 'Sold to assist the World Wildlife Fund.' On the back it's engraved, 'Awarded to Margaret Thatcher for excellence in canoeing.'

She imagines 500 years from now, when they tear down the Globe. The beams are held by wooden pegs; the walls are horsehair and lime. They'll think it's the original theatre, and as it falls, they'll find a keyring with a panda. A World Wildlife Fund? Pandas? In Elizabethan Britain? Awarded to Mrs Thatcher? The Prime Minister? In Elizabethan Britain? Why was she canoeing? Was this a traditional Thames pastime for politicians?

History's just a myth anyway, something we make up to reconcile evidence. Margaret leaves with a smile.

Another helpful and informative
253 *footnote*
1 The New Globe Theatre is real, it exists. I've seen *Two Gentlemen of Verona* played on its stage. It changes Shakespeare. The scenes were written for that stage; they fit. The balcony is a convenient height for handing down notes. The kiosk centre stage makes hiding easy; the enforced simplicity of the staging makes changing from tempest sea to island sanctuary quick and simple. A comic character wanders on with a real dog, and what is slightly tiresome banter at the National or on the page, becomes a crowd-pleasing comic turn. The plays become gigs, broad and barnstorming. The modern audience somehow knows that it's all right to shout back at the actors.

The world is as full of coincidence as **253**. Standing amid the groundlings in front of the stage was a tall, grey, benignly smiling man. I saw him hitch his shoulder in a way that meant his left arm was withered.

I recognized him. This was the Englishman who taught me Shakespeare at UCLA. He was young then, and for North Americans a baffling mix of what would have seemed shyness to Americans and a kind of wild Englishness. On the day of a major earthquake, he showed up in class wearing fluorescent disaster gear and a construction worker's orange hard hat.

I didn't remember his name. Later, I tried to find him but he was lost among the crowd streaming out through the doors like commuters from a train.

Just a splinter of the past. I wonder if his last name was Thatcher?

MRS ANGIE STRACHAN

Outward appearance
A certain age, trying hard. Ribbed white jumper, white leather jacket, long flowery dress. A cloud of wispy blonde split ends down her back.

Inside information
Has worked in front-of-house for ten years at Anderson Imports. Travelled to Singapore and Turkey for the company. Lately, has been subject to offers of further trips, not especially for business purposes, with the MD.

What she is doing or thinking
Angie is considering the MD's offer. He is portly, second-generation Lebanese, aggressive. He goes around the world bartering for hides. He smells of them. His attentions are demanding, but in a slow way that works under your skin. 'The offer stands,' he says, every day. Angie has admitted to herself that she dyed her hair for him.

Tommy, her husband, is a tall, thin and acerbic Scot, whose bitter wit is often turned on himself or on her, especially when drunk. Tommy works in a car showroom. He sweats with nerves, is covered in freckles, makes love in hard quick jabs.

Someone jumps past Angie to get off at Waterloo. His metal watchstrap catches in her wispy hair. She is jerked sideways and yelps with pain. She sees the man's pale, pudgy face. He is panicked, needing to get off. He keeps yanking.

'You're pulling my hair!' she says. He doesn't stop. She gives him a light little punch. The doors shut.

He drops his hands in dismay and that also jerks her hair. He doesn't even apologize.

'Do you have a pair of scissors?' he asks.

You could hate men.

Outward appearance
Delicate man, his moustache and thicket of silver-flecked hair overwhelming his face. Grey dust in the crevices of his shoes. Endlessly twirls uncut hair round a finger.

Inside information
A maker of memorial stones for Heritage Stone and Marblecraft, near the Elephant. It is not an occupation for a person of caste. His father made a living carving figures for temples. His father gave him the image of Hanuman the monkey that hangs around Bal's neck.

Bal's own son has qualified as an airline pilot; his daughter is a solicitor. In this sense, Bal feels his life has been accomplished.

What he is doing or thinking
The carving of names is an unnecessary call by the dead, who are free, on the living, who are not. But it is something the English believe. Lately, the company has gone from restoration to selling old gravestones as new. Mr Harris comes back with covered lorry loads sold to make way for roads or new development.

This has left Bal with a bad conscience. He shaves exfoliating granite until there is something like solid stone. Sometimes the stones, like toast sliced too thin, collapse.

Yesterday, through one grey window, the sun came out, and in a sideways light, a vanished name emerged from the stone. *Virginia . . . 1839.* It was like a face. Bal is an imaginative man, and saw Victorian dress, hair, eyes.

A native Marathi speaker, Bal keeps a bound volume of Ramdas open on his table. Ramdas abjures us: don't talk, act. This is wrong. The hair twirls faster and faster.

MISS SAMANTHA WILSON

Outward appearance
Dishevelled young woman in black overcoat, clunky shoes, red sweater, grey suit. Balances a huge, rebellious bag full of papers. Firm, sensible face undermined by an almost drunken wooziness. Starts playing with a strand of her hair.

Inside information
Teacher at Lower Marsh Primary School. Inamorata of Thomas West.

What she is doing or thinking
At a very deep, lower level of her brain, the spiralling gesture of the man next to her mirrors two things: her love life and her stomach.

She was up late last night marking papers and forgot to shop. There was nothing in the fridge except her flatmate's frozen pizza. Potato and Garlic – 'You'll never fear vampires again'. The pizza was still cold and doughy in the middle when she ate it at 12.30 AM. She spent the night writhing with indigestion, burping bubbles of garlic and basil.

Tossing on the bed, all the terrors of her life tossed with her. She was 26 and had no boyfriend, not a trace of one. Amid the bicarbonate and the fear, something happened.

Thomas West. In her mind, in garlic gas, he transmogrified from a dumpy carrot-top, to a big, masculine man. She saw his green, steady eyes. Why was she turning him down all the time? How had he seemed so small? Mingled with the burning, linoleum pizza in her belly, he seemed looming, inevitable.

She wonders how Thomas will look in the flesh, in winter, at a primary school. Hands occupied, exhausted as if from multiple orgasms, she cannot cover a huge and garlic yawn.

Outward appearance
Young businessman in a blue suit and Frank Church shoes, sits shell shocked, staring. Starts twirling his hair and yawning.

Inside information
Recently promoted to Four-Colour Manager at TipTop Printing, east of Waterloo. All was fine until his current assistant, Lola, started work.

Lola is possibly the most beautiful woman in the world. This is not good for Rick's composure. Lola is married, American, in Britain for a year while her husband finishes his postgrad work. She's like a filled-out Audrey Hepburn: leggy, brunette, confident, jolly. And given to wearing skin-tight black leggings.

What he is doing or thinking
He'll resign. He's just not suited for the job. He can't control his own space. Jools, the Dutch guy, sits on Rick's desk, ignores him, and jokes with Lola for hours.

Clients call to see how their work is progressing. Lola gives them coffee. They stay all afternoon, in gradually increasing numbers, flicking ash. Rick's boss hangs mournfully over Lola, reminiscing about his days in a rock band. He gives Rick basilisk stares and asks why he doesn't have any work to do.

After a drunken lunch, Bollocks (an amateur rugby player) actually stuck his hand up Lola's skirt. Rick threw him out. Lola chuckled at him. 'I don't need you to look after me.'

Anybody else would politely but firmly see all of them out of his room. Rick has to get up at 6.00 AM to catch the train from Peterborough and is seriously wondering if it's worth it. He yawns and retreats into a quiet snooze.

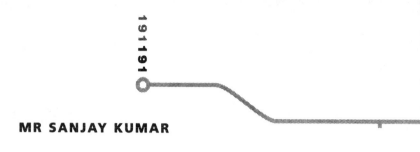

MR SANJAY KUMAR

Outward appearance

Broad-shouldered man, balding, all in grey: jeans, shirt, jacket, scuffed boots. Between his feet is a grey bucket with washing up liquid and window wipes. He appears to be asleep. His hands, clasped in front of him, form an arrowhead shape with his index fingers. They point to the bucket. A large keyring weighs down his belt.

Inside information

Owner of four businesses around Kennington Road near Lambeth North. The locksmith, chemist's and police uniform supplier are in difficulty. His dry cleaning shop was doing well. Now that's in trouble.

What he is doing or thinking

Sanjay is resting but not asleep. He takes advantage of the tube to close his eyes. He thinks of his businesses.

Another dry cleaning shop has opened on the parade. It's part of a large chain. The manager, a Punjabi, offers swingeing discounts. 'Your second item free. Half price discount for all items brought in before 9.00 A M.'

Such pricing is not sustainable. It's an attempt to drive Sanjay out of business, backed up by the stability of the chain. They are relying on his other losses to pull him down. Whenever they pass on the street, the Punjabi, sleek with his mobile phone, grins at Sanjay.

So Sanjay washes his own windows, hoovers his own floors and racks his brains. He sees the faces of the staff he might have to let go, in the security shop or pharmacy.

Can he offer customers something else? Loyalty vouchers? Personal delivery? He sees himself carrying hangers in plastic bags, running up office[2] stairs.

Then falling.

2. Mr Kumar escapes the crash, only to go to the end of the line in the way that his subconscious foresees. On April 15th, 1996, he was running up the stairs in the Office of Publicity Procurement, delivering two pressed pairs of trousers. He seemed merely to lose his footing on the polished black stone steps. As he slid down onto the landing between floors he began to feel a rending pain across his chest. He lay on the landing for nearly fifteen minutes before being noticed. His chemists shop had by then closed. Sarf London Security followed shortly.

MR JAMES WHITTHEAD

Outward appearance

Plump, bullish man in a white shirt and smart, patterned black-and-white suit. Crumpled in a heap, fast asleep. Starts to snore.

Inside information

Meet the contented man: the Branch Manager of the Kennington Building Society. Considers himself a kindly, hands-on manager. Recently had to let someone go. Carol (what a terrible name for a man!) really wasn't suited to finance. He kept doodling on documents. James protected Carol until he found a job in the Health Advice Centre in the Cut.

James looks older than his 35 years, which has so far been a help in his career. Still plays midfield in the branch football team. Everything in his life, from his wife to his two beautiful young children, is as he would wish . . . except for his espresso coffee machine.

What he is doing or thinking

Making the same noises as the coffee machine that haunts him. Snort, gurgle, steam. He inherited it from Carol. It was a beautiful present, gleaming and metallic. Maybe a little lime-caked inside.

It went proudly into Jim's office, dribbling out small, cold cups tasting slightly of de-scaler. Then the Building Society Interest Group visited. James proudly turned on the machine.

It produced steam in a mounting, volcanic rush, but no coffee. It began to whistle. His important guests stirred uneasily. To his horror, James heard the thing begin to creak. He pulled it out at the plug just before it exploded.

James snorts loudly and stops. He blinks and wakes up.

Surely Carol wouldn't have given it to him deliberately?

MISS LORRAINE HANT

Outward appearance
Young, long blonde hair, freckles, layers of blue clothes, jeans, trainers. Gazes at the row next to her as it snores, yawns or twiddles.

Inside information
A policeman's only daughter. His stories have made Lorraine distrustful of black people, dance music, clubs, etc. Does church work on Sundays, where she met her fiancé Dominic.

Temporarily works in a warehouse for a minimum-staff retail chain. She counts the sheets, the pillow cases, the toy trucks, as they arrive. It will do until she is married.

Yesterday in the lunchroom, the conversation turned to crime. Lorraine told them what her father said about single mums and the decay of the black family. 'In some areas, people just aren't very nice,' she said.

'Well bugger off somewhere where nice people are,' said Jennette, a black woman of whom Lorraine has always been afraid.

'That's not very nice,' said Lorraine, and they all roared.

What she is doing or thinking
Is there some kind of virus that makes people act alike? She can't explain why nobody likes her at work. It was spooky the way they all laughed at her.

She has watched the twiddle, the yawn, and the snooze spread down the row like a disease. She tries tapping her foot. Involuntarily, the foot across from her jerks. Lorraine gasps. The man next to her gasps and wakes up. Experimentally, Lorraine whistles George Michael. As if annoyed, the black man across from her starts whistling too.

So that was it. People follow each other, don't like anybody different. Not like her and Daddy.

MRS MARY WALLIS

Outward appearance

Well-turned-out older black lady. Shawl with sequins in zig-zag patterns. Examines items from her bag: a clock, a wooden frame the size of a pocket calculator, something with a wooden handle and a long metal prong.[3]

Inside Information

Lives on a Hercules Road estate. Friend of Paule Wright's. Has invested some of her husband's redundancy money in a small antiques business. Returning from Camden Passage's Wednesday morning market.

The metal prong is a device for firing pills down horses' throats. The wooden frame is for storing playing cards. The train eases into Lambeth North; Mary puts away her acquisitions.

What she is doing or thinking

She sees Paule on the platform and calls. Paule freezes and almost walks on. She doesn't want to be seen. Has she got a boyfriend? 'What you doing out this hour of the morning?' Mary teases and instantly regrets it. Paule's had to be taking up cleaning again. Mary tries to change the subject to Charley, but that's a bit sensitive too since he's been fired.

Mary feels terrible, and gossips about neighbours. Outside on the street, she makes excuses, and darts off towards the Cypriot bakery. Oh Mary, love, you got to watch your mouth.

Then she thinks: I could have told her about my antiques. I could have asked her to join me. I need someone to help run my stall when I get it going. Still feeling remorseful, Mary turns and runs after her friend.

'Paule!' she calls. 'Paule. I got an idea!'

Paule walks on, pretending not to hear.

Another helpful and informative **253** *footnote*
3. 120 years into the future, this same antique article of animal husbandry will be lovingly preserved by a family of Restorers, a virally-selected working group. See the author's description of this future time, *The Child Garden*.

MISS HARRIET ZINOVSKY

Outward appearance
Slightly plump businesswoman in brown trouser suit and long overcoat. Keeps rubbing her thumb and fingers together.

Inside information
Miss Zinovsky has a Russian father and an Israeli mother. She speaks three languages and has a first in Organic Chemistry from Cambridge. She is 23, but older people, particularly academics, feel comfortable around her. Recently began her first job at the Science Museum in Kensington.

Harriet organizes interactive exhibits. By interactive she means people get to touch real things. She calls it RR – Real Reality. Her current project is Fakes: children get to touch real fur and fake fur, costume and real jewellery. She is on her way to a leather warehouse in the Elephant and Castle.

What she is doing or thinking
Remembering her first visit. The warehouse smelled like a cross between an abattoir and a jar of vanilla sugar. Pale bales of leather, all undyed, were in shaggy rolls like giant pastry. You could tell what country the skins came from by the scars. From Western countries, there were close stitch marks around cuts. From others, there were fat ribbons of scar tissue.

Is she going mad? She remembers that one of the skins had a tattoo. It's possible that people tattoo the skins of sheep some- where in the world. But a rose and a banner with the name Maria?

Harriet has a nightmare vision of a third world so poor that it has started to sell human skin for leather. She shakes herself. It must be false memory syndrome.

It isn't. She goes on to the Elephant.

TONY 'PEEWEE' HATCHET

Outward appearance
Tiny, older man in T-shirt and sneakers. Continually massages a salt-and-pepper beard.

Inside information
Film editor for LWT and director of an educational film version of *Beowulf*. It is his final effort to be taken seriously as a film maker.

What he is doing or thinking
That he's accidentally made the sequel to *Monty Python and the Holy Grail*. OK, it was low budget and had some bad luck.

The flooded quarry looked perfect for Grendel's lair. Beowulf needed to stride boldly into the waters. Unfortunately, the waters were only three feet deep. In one shot, Beowulf dives in and doesn't sink. In the second, he wades in already dripping wet.

Then there were the horses. Well, ponies. They refused to ride up a hill. Then Beowulf made a John Wayne noise: 'Yeee-ha!' The ponies bolted. Their bareback riders dropped spears, scattered shields, and fell off, swearing, 'Whose fucking bright idea was this?'

The flame thrower for the dragon didn't work. Peewee doused Beowulf's shield with petrol and flicked matches at it. The rushes show vapour trails of matches. The shield never caught.

Beowulf's funeral pyre did. Halfway through the scene, the corpse jumps up screaming. They had no more wood for a retake. Saxon warriors wore wristwatches and spectacles. Mobile phones rang during undubbed dialogue.

There is not a single saveable shot.

All his life, Peewee has aimed at dignity. All his life, people have clutched their sides. He is unfailingly funny. His soul aches.

OK, he tells the universe, next time I make a comedy.

MR JIM HAIGH

Outward appearance
Young, with floppy hair shaved at the sides, blue jeans, blue-tartan shirt, big new soft boots.

Inside information
Administrative gopher for Nexus Productions.

Jim is not ambitious. All he wants is a regular job that will give him enough money to buy some clothes, some dope, some free time. He keeps trying to plan a trip to India. He doesn't remember much about the last one.

What he is doing or thinking
Fuming about a woman at work, Anita. Jim tries to be friendly with everyone. He was pleased when Anita suddenly said, 'Jim, you go home by Dillons don't you? Do you think you could pick up a book for me?' He thought she was asking as a friend, and was happy to help. He went to Dillons and bought the book with his own money.

Yesterday, when he gave it to Anita, she didn't even look back around from her desk. He told her the price, and she said, 'Well, claim it from expenses.'

He was so surprised, he just walked away. His own boss refused as it's not out of his budget, and Anita's boss said she knew nothing about it.

Anita was too important to do her own shopping. She tricked him into being her gopher, and she plainly won't pay him the money unless he nags her. He remembers as he walked away that she smiled with satisfaction.

Being nice doesn't work. Did he ever think it did? He prods the numb spot in his soul that doesn't want anything and fears for his future.

Outward appearance

Worn, middle-aged woman, bright red hair, green overcoat, black jeans, loafers. Reading *The English Verb*. The lettering is 3-D and emerges from the distance, like the opening of *Star Wars*. LTP, it says, as if that were something thrilling.

Inside information

Lecturer in commercial sociology at Bruenwalt International. Her foreign students tend to speak textbook English. They cannot fathom English verbs, which are modified out of recognition by prepositions. 'To beat' is different from 'to beat up'. Beverly is yet to find a textbook that adequately explains this.

What she is doing or thinking

She is thinking of Attila, the homeless *Big Issue* salesman outside Waterloo. She wants him to lecture her students on English. He's a Cossack but his English is flawlessly American and colloquial. Perhaps he could explain prepositional verbs to them. As it happens, there is a lad on the course from the old Soviet Republics. Beverly is sure that it would be a relief for Attila to talk to someone from home.

She thinks of her lovely, plump, pallid husband. How can she explain to him or herself that she is in love with a wild Cossack who worked many years on American merchant vessels? Beverly has spent her life banishing romance, all that novelettish stuff. She can banish it again.

But for now, surely it's all right to dream a little bit of being swept up in firm, brown, young arms? She lowers the book and sighs.

In the meantime, she can at least get him work. Again, she lifts up *The English Verb*.

MR STAN GRAY

Outward appearance
Carefully groomed older man, wavy silver hair, computer-salesman grey suit, rotund tummy. Sits frozen with a smile pressed so tightly that it's almost a frown.

Inside information
Owner of Buntleys Coachworks and Pru Waverly's boss. He may just have successfully framed one of his employees for murder.

What he is doing or thinking
Would it have happened at all without Andy? He came up with the idea for the joke, a tape of two women planning to kill another and played so that Pru would think it was a real crossed line. Stan's ears pricked up at the word murder. 'I'll go along with it,' Stan said. 'If you supply the tape.'

Stan wouldn't have gone ahead if the tape hadn't made plain it was a woman who would be killed. One of the women talking on the tape was Andy's wife.

Stan had two days to steal Andy's things: a cigarette lighter with his initials engraved on it, and the 27-inch waist Y-fronts from his workout bag.

They'll be found under the sofa and behind Stan's own bed on which his wife will lie still, after lunchtime today when he nips home with wire and tape. After he rings the police tonight.

Will he be able to weep for the cameras? Will he hell. He lies about sexual or drinking binges. He's found, our Stan, that he can do anything necessary.

And Andy, or his wife, or both, will go down. Stan allows himself to grin.

On the platform he is able to say, lightly, 'Hello, Pru.'

MRS ROSEMARY OLIVER

Outward appearance

Striking woman, early thirties. Mediterranean complexion, fragile face. Short tousled black hair. Blue, tousled, furry jacket. Legs as thin as wrists, and elbows thicker than her hands, huddle in the seat as if cold, or crowded by the huge man next to her. Her thinness makes her look tall: her feet reach the floor only on tiptoe. She smiles.

Inside information

A professional key-cutter and full-time anorexic. Works at Stanley's Key Bar on the Cut. Her workmates are all male, and bully her, they think, for her own good. She has just had her day of vengeance.

What she is doing or thinking

So she hates eating. That's her business. They keep dumping food on her desk – oh Jesus! – greasy hamburgers, or lumpy health food Spinach and Vegetarian Cheese Pasties, or pink cheap cakes.

So. Yesterday, she bought some HobNob biscuits, which look like a kind of pressed sawdust floor tile. Then she melted chocolate Ex-Lax on the little one-ring cooker. See how domestic I am? *Pour liberally over biscuits and let cool and harden in fridge for half an hour.* It was like being on one of those nightmarish cooking programmes.

When her workmates were tucking into their laxative biscuits with afternoon tea, she took out her brand new crusher. Rosemary shot garlic over her colleagues. 'Isn't it delicious?' she cooed.

She's been thinking of new recipes all night. Salt instead of sugar icing. Steak and kidney pies lurking under a smothering of Bird's custard. Used coffee-ground pasties.

The Anorexic's Cookbook. See how it feels?

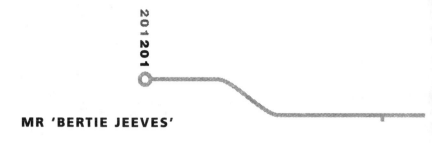

MR 'BERTIE JEEVES'

Outward appearance

Huge, loose-limbed black man with no. 1 trimmed beard and head, in blue track suit and Planet Hollywood, Beijing cap.

Inside information

Real name Andre Chambers. Manufacturer and retailer of own-brand ice cream. It is a top quality product, which is why its trademark is a snooty Englishman with a monocle. Bertie's vanilla uses real vanille from France. It is full fat, no air. 'Like me,' Bertie always says. He insists on being called Bertie Jeeves. His wife, Frances, drew the line at the monocle.

Bertie plays tennis every lunchtime at Archbishops Park, rugby every Saturday and works out every other day. He has developed a rather embarrassing health problem.

What he is doing or thinking

Bertie is suffering from ice cream poisoning. His motions have turned white.

Bertie slips into the giant fridge to cool off after sport and can't stop himself eating ice cream. It's cold, it's liquid; he's hot and thirsty. Before he knows it, he's eaten an entire tub of Real Walnut or Canadian Maple or Surrey Strawberry.

His wife Frances has noticed that stock is missing. She's had to raise the price by ten pence in the pound. She's harangued the staff for theft.

'When I find out who's been spiriting the stuff away, they'll be gone, too,' she warned them, 'to jail.' She tells Bertie. 'You're too easy on people.'

Bertie lives in dread of Frances' rage. He lives in terror of forgetting to flush the toilet and her finding the evidence.

There are times, he thinks, when I wish I were anorexic.

Outward appearance
Tiny, plump woman wearing a black shirt printed with gold leaves. Sits with a handwritten list on her lap. Eyes closed, she recites.

Inside information
Maryan emigrated from Armenia after marrying a British tourist. He looked big, clear-skinned, blue-eyed – the model of a Soviet citizen. Back in Britain, he simply looks fat. He's a taxi driver.

Maryan's father was an economist. Her mother, heavily made-up in orange silk, frequently visits Britain, looks stricken, and lobbies the embassy to see if they can give her daughter a job. After months of applying for research or translation work, Maryan took a job in a new dry cleaning shop.

Two days convinced her that she needed to do something else. She decided to become a taxi driver.

What she is doing or thinking
Maryan is studying The Knowledge. To be a taxi driver you have to pass a test to prove you know the streets of London. So, with Charlie's help, she is memorizing London.

She spends weekends driving up and down roads, to learn what they look like from all angles. She has to know every no-left-turn sign or one-way street.

She can feel her brain being colonized. Sections of it feel weighed down, as if lead were being poured into a filigree mould. At night, as she goes over the names, the streets spread in her mind like frost.

Maryan will be one of the few people who know what London really looks like. She will never again stumble on anything new by accident. She recites.

MS LEONE SKERRIT

Outward appearance
Leonine older woman, with a mane of streaked hair. Carefully made up. Red jacket. Small suitcase. Glances at her watch.

Inside information
Leone was a Bond Girl. In *Goldfinger*, she lounges around the Miami pool and lowers her sunglasses as hairy-chested Sean Connery[4] walks past. She was in *The Liver Birds*, two Carry On films and *Confessions of a Window Cleaner*, playing an ageing masseuse. She calls herself a one-woman barometer of the fall of the British film industry.

Late in life she showed a talent for understanding technical briefings. Today, she demonstrates cellphones at a temporary stand in the concourse of Waterloo Station. Special offer: only ten pounds for the phone and your first three months of non-international calls free.

She is nearly late, but elegantly as always.

What she is doing or thinking
About her grandchild who is coming to stay for the weekend. It will give her daughter Jemima and her new man a rest. Which is what Leone will need herself when the weekend is over.

Leone lies about her age: she says she's 45 which is old enough. She's 52. At the end of the day, grinning at potential buyers, she feels like a death's head. Her feet ache, her knees hurt.

Jamie will want to walk in the park and be taken to see *The Lion King*. He is a bright, pretty little spark, and makes her feel grateful for what she's got.

It's all been worth it. Jemima has just landed a small part. She's a Russian bar girl in *Goldeneye*.

Another helpful and informative **253** *footnote*

4 One of the key considerations of any Web professional such as myself is the downloading times of files and ensuring that the reader needs to download as few files as possible.

For that reason, **253**, the Internet version, made this promise about footnotes: not only did I promise that all footnotes are likely to be misleading and false, I also promised there will be no more than one footnote dedicated to each passenger, no matter how much I wanted to say.

The result was some very long footnotes. This single footnote deals with the following subjects:

- The *Confessions* series
- Sean Connery
- *The Lion King* and English accents

Confessions
Confessions of a Window Cleaner really did exist as a film. It was terrible, but not as bad as its sequels. The *Confessions* films were meant to be similar to the Carry On series, only cheaper and dirtier. They starred Robin Askwith, a beefier version of Peter Noone of Herman's Hermits. I think he was meant to be a kind of identification figure for thuggish beer-swillers. He certainly was ugly enough with a small enough dick.

The absolutely lowest moment of the series was in, I think, *Confessions from a Holiday Camp*. The title has been blotted out of my memory. The target of Askwith's unbridled lust was a black woman. The script was so racist that plainly no attractive black actress could be found to stoop so low as to take the part. I seem to remember the camera focusing on a butt in hot pants while Askwith's voice-over went something like: 'The jungle rhythms of her body pounded a primitive beat into my brain . . .' Yes folks, in the 1970s, you could still make films with dialogue like that.

The only actress they could find to accept the part was fully Askwith's equal in terms of physical charms. It's hard not to be unkind, but she was not qualified to take the part of an attractive person of either gender. The effect was strange: it was almost touching that ugly, loutish Askwith was drawn to women who were his match.

Films were the bane of my existence in the early '70s, because I had to see them. I was a trade reviewer; it was unprofessional to leave. It was a privilege, after all, even to be admitted to trade showings. It was a privilege to sit next to Marge Bilbow of *Screen International*. It was a privilege to

listen to the *Sight and Sound* completists read full credit lists into tape recorders, spelling out all the foreign names; it was a privilege to be next to the deadbeats who managed to talk their way in as journalists, like the mad Czech with staring, delighted eyes who couldn't see why people were so shocked by the bugging devices in *The Conversation.* Or Smelly Derek, someone whose devotion to films meant he forgot to wash, scrape the green from his teeth, or find accommodation. I last saw Smelly some time in the 1980s, leaning against a wall in Soho. He was plainly staring at the ruin of his life, at the top of the buildings, muttering. He didn't answer when I said hello.

In addition to the superb company, it was the 1970s. No other medium in history has accepted material as bad as the dying national film industries of the 1970s. Spanish Westerns that did not star Clint Eastwood, extraordinarily badly dubbed kung-fu movies, the first vituperatively women-hating slash nasties, increasingly feeble British horror movies or laugh-free versions of TV series like *On the Buses*, British rock movies like *Slade in Flame* or anything starring David Essex, low budget American 'thrillers' starring Susan George. Such films simply never hit screens any more unless in the straight-to-video market.

It put me off movies for the rest of the 1970s. Except for *Robin and Marian*, even Sean Connery was having trouble in the 1970s.

Sean Connery

Proof positive of the unrequited love affair the English have for Scotland. Not only was James Bond, the only post World War Two English national film hero, played by a Scot, but research shows that the English trust people with regional accents more and people with Scottish accents most. The person the English would most want to hear at the end of a helpline is someone who sounds, specifically, like Sean Connery.

He is, of course, a Scots Nationalist, who wants to free his country from the colonial yoke of the Sassenachs. That's what the English get called on a good day. The Scots hate and loathe the English. The English dream of hard, tough, straight-talking folk who you would trust your life savings to. Having dreamt of them, they decided that they must be Scottish. The current (1997) success of the Labour Party is due in part to the Scottish accents and regional accents, of Robin Cook, Gordon Brown etc. and the putatively Scottish origins of Tony Blair.

The English don't feel this degree of admiration for the other Celtic peoples. They see the Welsh as little, nittering, harp-playing elves with a strong line in double-dealing. To paraphase for a moment. They cordially regard the Irish as forelock-tugging peasants who are either at your feet ('Top-o-dah-mornin-to-yah!') or at your throat (bombs). In return, the English are seen as murderous at worst, at best snobbish and devious, imperialists. At least the feelings are mutual.

The Scots, however, are seen as hard headed, forthright and reliable. All of which shows that racism, even when it says positive things, is still racism.

Which brings me to my next topic.

The Lion King and English accents
I'm not alone in noting how anyone not very nice in American movies sprouts an English accent. In the *Lost World*, you can finely grade how approving Spielberg is of Richard Attenborough's family by their accents. The nice grand-children talk American, Attenborough who is misguided but loveable is Scottish; while his villainous nephew is a posh Brit. Similarly, the evil cats in the Fievel series are English, while the nice cat is American. Spielberg's *Empire of the Sun* turns Ballard's epic

novel into a story of how an English kid wises up and becomes an American. In Disney's *The Lion King* the nasty, faggy uncle in a family of American lions is British for no reason other than his decadence. In *Pocahantas* all the evil Englishmen sound English and the nice ones sound like Mel Gibson.

Mel is smart. He's an Aussie, but he now gives interviews as himself with an American accent. Most Americans think he is American too and Mel knows that's how they like it.

The simple fact is that America is another unrequited British love affair. The Brits think Americans like and respect them. They, in turn, patronize the Yanks, but have made up another race of people to love: friendly, polite, energetic and likely to open fire at any moment.

Brits fondly imagine that they have a special relationship with America. Most Americans don't think about Britain from one decade to the next, and have the most peculiar notions about the place.

When I migrated to Britain, an American saw I had an issue of *Esquire* magazine and warned me in all seriousness that I should hold on to it carefully: the British didn't have nice magazines like *Esquire* and might be driven by lust for glossiness to steal it.

Americans moan continually about the British loss of Empire; something that Brits never talk or think about as most of them weren't born when the Empire collapsed. They simply want to get on with making money and become as successful as Belgium.

There is another problem. Despite their wealth, their air of sophistication and their confidence, Americans are curiously certain that they will be snubbed by the Brits. They fear that the Brits will be smarter and more erudite than they. This is pretty rich when you compare the educational achievement of the two countries and the relative quality of the newspapers.

Thinking someone is smarter than you is bound to make you dislike them. English voices make Americans feel creepy. Whenever Americans wish to indicate high-toned prejudice, over-wordy pomposity, over-nice precision, they edge towards a British accent. For them, the accent is the embodiment of closed and corseted, twisted emotions. They are right, of course, about that. But emotional constipation is not the same as villainy.

I felt the same thing when I first arrived in Britain. I was billeted in a medical school and bubbled with pre-emptive loathing of the very smart people in British universities

who were bound to snub me. Instead, they rapidly became friends or lovers, their response conditioned by the mask of Americanness that I wore. They were disappointed to learn my parents were English. 'So you're really just a Brit,' said one of them glumly.

All right, spit it out. A lot of Brits have a sexual kink for Americans. They went off me very slightly when they found out I wasn't. See what I mean about positive racism?

The British think they would love to live in America. What the Brits don't know is that there is no freedom in American life. Everything is ruled by the dollar and its logic and there is no escape. Just great movies and great manners and terrible religion to mask the imprisonment, and get people through to the end of their lives.

What Britain is now achieving is the commercial slavery of America, but with no movies, no religion except possibly Islam, and the worst, most sullen manners in the world.

And the people they love least in the world are themselves.

Question: The term 'Brit' specifically abuses the English, and yet technically includes the Scots and Welsh who are, of course, also British. Does this derive from the assumption that Britain really is run by the English?

MR HARRY MIGSON

Outward appearance
Bulky, youngish man with teddy-boy hair. Purple, broken veins map his cheeks. Corduroy overcoat with fake fur collar. Soft shoes masquerading as office shoes rest on a large cardboard box tied with twine to form a handle.

Inside information
Record dealer. He and his brother Terry run two separate cut-price CD stalls and supply numerous others. Friends in warehouses supply them with returned job lots. What'll cost you fourteen quid in a shop, Harry will sell you on Lower Marsh for £9.99, or he'll get it for you. It's a cold job this time of year.

Today, his brother's got the van to make a collection from Polygram (and to keep Rufus, their bull terrier, with him and out of trouble).

Going through stock this morning, Harry opened up a cardboard box full of reggae and Jamaican imports. He has a terrible feeling that Ashley Watkins got the box meant for a Carpenters Fan Club Sale.

Now on his way to swap boxes.

What he is doing or thinking
What he is going to say to Ashley. Sorry, mate? Ashley always looks so long-faced and grim.

Nothing personal? Got to see the funny side, don't you? Somehow Harry doesn't think Ashley will.

Maybe, thinks Harry, I should go into classical. Different kind of clientele. After all there's that second hand shop by Waterloo. They do all right, and the same places will supply job lots of old Nigel Kennedy stuff. Three Tenors and all that.

He decides to talk to Terry when he gets back from the Elephant.

MRS DODIE McGINLAY

Outward appearance
Professional woman, all in black, knees neatly together. Shiny, childlike shoes with buckles. Large legs in black tights. Slightly straggly face between gold spirals of hair.

Inside information
Works in Pall Mall Oil, supervising orders and invoices for the company's helicopter fleet. Her eldest son Dave wants to be a helicopter pilot. So does she.

Dodie is Captain of the Netbusters women's football team. They are top of their league and have a big game this Saturday.

Dodie has pulled Catherine, an ageing player, out of the starting line-up. Last season Cath was scoring brilliantly. In the game against the Girl Pipers, Dodie fed her, Cath dummied, cut inside the Pipers' defence and bent a superb shot round Relper into the top corner.

But Cath started doing benders of a different kind, burning the candle at both ends, and her game went right off. A spell on the benches might just focus her thinking.

What she is doing or thinking
Wondering what to do. Cath and Dodie have been an item. Cath's a big, raw Irish girl with a mouth, and she warned Dodie in no uncertain terms.

If she's pulled, she'll bring a case of sexual harassment.

Dodie considers her husband. He plays in his matches while she plays in hers. A peck on the cheek, teenage children: it's a settled life.

She imagines the scandal, the embarrassment. She has just learned that football is the most important thing in her life. But she'll have to betray it for that life.

Glum, she stands, admitting defeat. Cath will start.

MR MICHAEL HANSHAW

Outward appearance
Slim, youngish black man. Grey slacks, red-striped sweater, elaborate jacket in art deco knitted patterns and leather panels. Starts to whistle edgily, in competition with the woman opposite.

Inside information
A 27-year-old telephone engineer with British Telecom. The job is skilled and well paid. Mike spends his days out on call. Lunchtimes, he lifts weights with two guys from work. He has a wife and a one-year-old baby daughter. Going to an appointment with a private South Bank clinic for drug abuse.

What he is doing or thinking
He's down. The world is shrivelling like a bad apple and he feels like he's wading through glue.

Coke doesn't change him; it makes him more himself. He sizzles through work, jokes with his friends, pumps iron, goes home and makes his wife giggle. The world seems full of love.

He remembers the first time he took it, at a party full of people he only half-knew and half-liked. His cousin Colin laid it out for him. That night, kipping at Colin's, Michael had a dream. It was more like a vision. All his friends were beyond the bedroom door and they made a light that shone under it, concentrated and searing like a star.

Michael loves cocaine. He's signed a piece of paper that acknowledges he will be injected with a drug that reacts to it. If he uses coke, the drug will make him ill. The contract says it could even kill him.

He thinks of his wife and daughter. And the light.

MISS ANGELA DOWD

Outward appearance

Battered orange leather jacket with diamond-pattern shoulders. Black tights with a hole in the thigh, motorcycle boots with elaborate shin pads and rows of undone buckles. Ring through nose, black T-shirt with the logo 'Misbegotten'. Long hair with pink highlights. Takes out mirror, examines her eye. Starts to read last night's *Evening Standard*.

Inside information

Part-time art teacher and band member. Was part of the Dublin scene for years. Knows Bono. Friend also of Annie Jeanrenaud.

Eighteen months ago, the band got a gig in Paris. With all their gear, they took a minicab to the airport. At check-in, Angela realized that she'd forgotten her passport and dashed back home.

Only to find the cab driver standing embarrassed in her sitting room, hugging her stereo, jiggling it up and down as if it were a baby.

Angela teaches art at Wormwood Scrubs. Yesterday, that cab driver showed up in her class. He stared embarrassed again.

What she is doing or thinking

Keeping her cool. She checks out her split ends: long hair doesn't really suit the image anyway. She examines her eye: she's got a stye coming.

Actually, it's kind of cool to be in a situation where you're training somebody who robbed you. Why else did she volunteer to teach art in prison? She picks up the *Standard*. And puts it down.

Because she's fucking angry. She's angry because she missed the plane, missed the gig; the police treated her like the criminal. And because at night, alone in her house, she's not cool at all.

MR DAVID OFFSEY

Outward appearance

Precise-looking gent of a certain age in a traditional suit. Newspaper held awkwardly high. Sits legs wide apart, a large bandage over his nose.

Inside information

The maître d'hôtel of the Britannia Club, near Waterloo. Appearances are important for the job.

David was trimming his hedge when he noticed blood on the leaves, on his trousers. It seemed that he had cut off the tip of his nose with the gardening shears. His wife asked him why he was on his knees. 'I'm looking for my nose,' he replied, testily.

She drove him to the clinic. 'You can't park there, sir,' said the porter.

'Oh can't we?' replied David, sounding as if he had a cold. He removed his hand from his face. The porter went white.

They repaired the nose by transplanting his foreskin.

What he is doing or thinking

It was a painful operation. Why aren't people sympathetic?

At breakfast, his son Peter smiled. 'I always knew you were a dickhead, Dad.'

'It'll certainly change how I see a kiss on the cheek,' giggled his wife.

On the train platform, smelly Vince insisted on talking loudly about circumcision. 'It's like having an eyelid removed. The tip is that sensitive. You walk around bow-legged for days.'

The people at work were equally flippant. 'So you'll be like Pinocchio then,' said Billy the bellhop. He mimed a massive facial erection.

'Brings a whole new meaning to the expression Nosey Parker, doesn't it?' mused Dora behind the desk.

David rattles the newspaper. Can't see the humour in it at all.

MRS ALENKA MISJEKA GARRISON

Outward appearance
Fierce-faced, well-built, middle-aged woman. Hair in a professional bob. Under the bulky coat, her white suit displays devastating cleavage.

Inside information
Alenka's husband is nice, handsome, and works constantly to keep her happy. For Christmas he gave her a Ford Sierra. Alenka works constantly at being friendly with her fourteen-year-old step-daughter. She is a civil engineer for Dobbs near Blackfriars. Unusually for a woman in an engineering company, she holds a senior position.

Until 1968, Alenka's father was a notable figure in the Czech government. Alenka remembers giving wrong directions to the invading Russian troops. The Foreign Ministry helped her family escape by giving them holiday visas for Tunisia. They lived in Tunis for four years, then were granted entry to the UK. Alenka changed countries at fourteen and eighteen. She now habitually restages such catastrophic migrations.

What she is doing or thinking
The season has changed. Alenka will get off at Waterloo and instead of turning right for Blackfriars, she will turn left for the Shuttle to Paris.

To lose her too-nice husband whom she pictures unloading clothes from a laundry basket. She sees his trusting daughter. Learn, Alenka tells her: life is not for trusting.

Her computer full of notes and research; her closet full of clothes and shoes; the flat full of photographs from this life; especially the Christmas Sierra. She will lose everything. She will be stripped of it, as if naked. That makes her feel engorged. In a dream, she gets off and walks towards the Shuttle.

London Spring.

MRS REZIA BEGUM

Outward appearance
Bolt-upright, older woman wearing orange pyjamas, long peach top, and a gilded shawl. Her face is rigid, as if carved out of polished wood.

Inside information
Rezia's uncle married her to a distant cousin in the UK. It was a magnificent match. She went from a village in Bengal to Brick Lane, and from there to Harrow. Her husband runs a restaurant in some place called Lamabett. She has never been there. Rezia only knows its name and that it's on the Bakerloo line.

Her husband did not come home last night. She is going to the restaurant to find him.

What she is doing or thinking
After 30 years, Rezia misses her mother. She buys dresses from strangers. It is not the same as your family making them for you. Her sister writes tearful letters about the good life Rezia must be having. Could she send more money?

Back home, Rezia would have lived with her husband's mother, who would now be dead, leaving her to run things. Even 20 years of mother-in-law would be better than the huge English house on two floors with its gardens and silence. All three of her children have left home. Rezia wears silence like a cloak. Sometimes it does not seem worth getting up in the morning.

Now her fat, handsome husband has disappeared. She sat up all night; he did not telephone. If he died, who was there to tell her? Would she have to bury him alone?

Lamabett. Where is that?

The train pulls out of Lambeth North.

MR ANDREW VOWLES

Outward appearance
Tall, pudgy black man with long hair brushed straight down his back. Conservative brown suit, worn but expensive shoes. Carries translucent shopping bags full of unlabelled tins. Along with a tin opener.

Inside information
Qualified industrial caterer and past nominee for a Foody Award (Industrial section). Teaches at the Education Authority's Catering Training Unit, a homely bungalow in a Peebrane Estate near Waterloo.

The bags contain prototypes for a new product – ready-prepared West Indian dishes. Andrew has a theory about why Indian restaurants prosper and West Indian don't.

White people aren't frightened of Asians. Working-class Brits, intimidated by posh eateries, feel at home with a curry and lager served by a small polite brown man to whom they can still feel superior.

But they're frightened of Caribbeans. And there are Caribbeans who would be buggered if they'll be waiters to anyone.

So how to get the British eating West Indian food? The answer is to serve it to them in non-West Indian environments. Andrew's *Typically Tropical* line of prepared food would be served in Italian restaurants, Thai restaurants, even Indian restaurants. He hopes to premiere his new product at this February's IFE 95 show.

What he is doing or thinking
Rehearsing his pitch. He pictures the bank manager. Did he know that chicken tikka is the second most popular British sandwich after egg mayonnaise? Did he know that Thai and Tex Mex are now the fifth and sixth most popular forms of cuisine? The British have developed a taste for spicy food.

But not, evidently, for spicy people.

MR HENRY FISHER

Outward appearance
Tall, hefty, raw-fingered ex-public schoolboy in conventional pinstripe suit and sensible shoes. Standing up, eyes closed, smiling. Purple port-wine stain across his forehead, right eye and cheek.

Inside information
Civil servant working in the MOD. His normal exit is Embankment. Got on the tube at Paddington, which was packed. He fell asleep standing up.

What he is doing or thinking
In a reverie of Jenny. They met at a party of his cousin's and knew each other for quite a while before he got the courage to ask her out. Finally, his cousin told him to get a move on. To his surprise Jenny replied yes, without hesitation.

It was like the torment of university all over again. Henry didn't know what to do. He ended up taking Jenny to the Savoy,[5] with its mirrored dining room over the river with the hundred-year-old dance band in the corner. Jenny said she'd always wanted to see it, and with a pixilated grin, toured its bars, hat-checks, and theatre lobby. The bill came to £200.

After that, he treated her to nachos and movies. Nothing else. All his life, you see: his face.

Last night, Jenny coaxed him back into her flat and they made love. Henry was still a virgin, but it made no difference. Pent-up energy or something. They seemed to roll all night long in clouds of each other.

A woman shouts, 'Leave it!' Henry jerks awake: Good Lord, Lambeth North.

He jumps through the doors just in time. And thinks of Jenny.

Another helpful and informative
253 *footnote*
5 I once went to the Savoy. I was walking back along Waterloo Bridge, Westminster on one side, St Paul's on the other. We were cold, hungry, it was Christmas, and who knows when friends would see each other again?

So, like Henry, we blew £200 at the Savoy. The art deco overhang as you drive in, all polished silver deco metal shapes, is stunning. Inside, the deco is replaced by a mishmash of styles – Greek columns, mirrors, old carpet, palms.

The hotel was built in 1884 to adjoin the Savoy Theatre, home of Gilbert and Sullivan opera. The theatre was the first public building in London to be lit with electricity. The hotel had electric lights and lifts. Ritz was the manager, Escoffier the chef, Bernhardt nearly died there, Caruso sang. It was big news. It is less big news now. But you still have to have a tie and jacket.

The theatre, the hotel and the surrounding gardens are on the site of the old Savoy Palace, which was built in the 13th century. It was rebuilt between 1345 and 1370 by Henry, Duke of Lancaster. Geoffrey Chaucer was married in its chapel. It was said to be the finest house in Britain.

History repeats, and repeats.

MR STEVEN WORKMAN

Outward appearance
Plump, milk-white, 35, in a grey suit, a tie that turns sideways, black Oxford shoes, and black Oxford hair complete with dandruff.

Inside information
Freelance systems analyst. Steven never fitted into corporate life. On time for an appointment with Adventure Capital.

What he is doing or thinking
Rehearsing his presentation.

'The technology exists to give every driver in the country instant knowledge of (cue Powerpoint slide)
- where on the map they are
- the best way to get to their destination
- traffic problems en route.'

Scotland Yard's traffic monitoring unit has agreed to lease Steven their information. Traffic flow, cash flow.

'I call the system,' he will say, 'The Knowledge. Every car could have its own personal taxi driver.'

The doors open at Waterloo: his stop. Stumbling out, Steven catches his watch in a woman's hair. He tugs, thinking it will come free. The woman yelps.

The doors close. Damn. Frazzled hair is clenched between the sections of his metal watchstrap. Anyone could see, the only way is to pick it free strand by strand. Why isn't she helping?

Instead, she shouts. 'It hurts!'

'Do you have a pair of scissors?' he asks.

'What?' Her eyes tear up; her arms fold.

He explains: 'I've got an appointment.' He starts to take off his watch.

'Will you stop that!'

They're already at Lambeth North. 'Look, I've got to get off.'
'That's too bloody bad,' she says.
He gestures in frustration; her head is tugged again.
'Leave it!' she says. The doors rumble shut. Both of them are
swept on to the Elephant.

MR CHRISTOPHER BRETTENHAM

Outward appearance
Tall, graceful man, older than he looks. Longish red-blond hair, open countenance, donkey jacket, jeans and boots. Looks up from a book by Patrick Leigh Fermor to peer across the aisle.

Inside information
Stage hand at the Royal National Theatre, South Bank. Has survived all the contracting out. No longer actually helps build sets, instead determines budgets and badgers the contractors to stay within them. Loves travelling and has visited the Yemen, New Guinea, Pakistan, the Andaman Islands and, in 1985, Thailand.

What he is doing or thinking
He has recognized Yong Y'oud from the airplane voyage back to London ten years before. Christopher has never forgotten him.

Chris went to visit a friend who was working with Laotian refugees all along the Mekong. He saw a Thailand tourists to Pattaya, Bangkok or Chiang Mai never see. In places it was like the wild west, with anti-communist private armies. But employers took an interest in their employees' children, and bought them gifts, and found work for the protégées of their protégées.

On the airplane, Chris was friendly to Yong Y'oud. He said something simple like 'What will you do in England?' Instead of being rewarded with a delighted smile, there was an awkward, bitter smirk. 'I live there,' Yong Y'oud said.

Christopher knew then: this one has lived in the West. This is what we do to them. To each other.

Chris thinks of the monks under trees, the women serving soup from corner carts, the beautiful children in uniform. He decides: it is time he saw Thailand again.

MR BENJAMIN POSTHATE

Outward appearance
Fiercely red, thinning hair over pinched red face, grey suit, metal-edged square briefcase.

Inside information
Communications officer for Sum Total, the insurance company which insures Amina Khatun's store. On his way to express his unhappiness with the Cut Health Centre, a one-stop health advice shop.

What he is doing or thinking
He'll withdraw funding from the Centre if they don't shape up. People do not understand that it's not his job to do good works, but to promote Sum Total. The Centre seems ashamed of being sponsored. ST's logo is hidden away on the lower corner of one window; ST's health leaflets are not given precedence in displays. There's nothing that says: Sum Total paid for this.

He'll tell them straight. Either ST's event contractor takes over the design and stock control of the Centre or he'll demand compensation.

It's not as if there aren't plenty of venues. That very nice girl he met from the Florence Nightingale Museum, for example. Now, she had her head screwed on. She knew exactly what was wanted. Corporate entertainment facilities with priority booking for sponsors; a permanent exhibition of ST's role in health care, a constant flow of visiting health professionals plus students just entering the insurance market . . .

What if the Museum were a better deal? This would be the time to cut the Centre off.

He gets off one stop early at Waterloo, and looks up her mobile number. Warrington, that's it. He dials.

A far better bet. Easy on the eye as well.

Her phone seems to be switched off.

MR SAM CRUZA

Outward appearance

New York taxi driver? Translucent, polished complexion. Wild black hair, little moustache, clean but worn clothes, grubby shoulder bag full of uniform slices of paper. Smiles to himself, cupping his hand around the left side of his face.

Inside information

New York taxi driver. Came to London for some fun, plus he needed to duck out of a drugs rap. Some guys he knew got caught. Now he sells *The Big Issue* and shares with some Americans he met coming over. He eats their food and does not replace it.

He's got all these women dancing, man. They think he's from all over: Arabia, Turkey, Romania, places he's just seen on a map. He tells them all kinds of stuff.

On Charing Cross, he saw every one of them go past in the train windows. So he went into this car, and one of them was here too. So he's sitting low-down at this end of the carriage.

What he is doing or thinking

He's not really ready to introduce all those ladies to each other just yet.

He wants the rich businesswoman most, only 'cause she's the coldest piece of ass. Beverly is sentimental – but she'll be good for cash. The spent old broad who says she's Matisse's granddaughter, she keeps saying she's poor, but who knows – maybe she'll give him a painting. Anita is dangerous. She's smart; she could turn on him. Sam's a little afraid of Anita. Her, he would like to hurt.

All in all, it's probably best just to cruise on down to the Elephant.

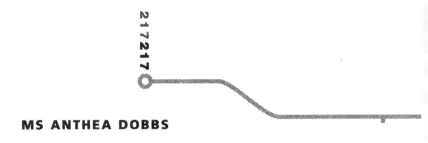

MS ANTHEA DOBBS

Outward appearance

Tinted, straw-like hair, black knitted shawl, billowing printed brown dress and scuffed brown boots. Beautifully made up. Sits with small personal organizer, but is not looking at it. Very suddenly, she stands up to exit at Waterloo.

Inside information

Partner of Joy Harvey in Lambeth Council's information surgery. Regards herself as the more technical side of the partnership. On her way to Wasteco at the Elephant and Castle.

What she is doing or thinking

She looks at the silent people around her and remembers the tube strike of 1989. Everyone walked to work. It was summer, and London was suddenly a festival of people. There should have been banners. The streets, instead of being deserted, bustled. Even the evenings were better: the shadows long, the sun golden. People said what the hell, and went to the pub. They walked in chains with hands on each other's necks. Pretty girls in halter necks, large bouncy men with Jewish hats. You saw faces everywhere, and the message of those faces over time was this: we are for the most part hard-working, decent, pleasant people.

She has read recently of an alarming fall in numbers of people volunteering for charities. It is not due to overwork, since it is busy people who have continued to volunteer. The reason, the article claimed, is habitual isolation. It breeds mistrust and cynicism.

She almost thinks there should be a two-year moratorium on cars, tubes, TV. She suddenly yearns to be out on the streets and abruptly decides to walk to the Elephant from Waterloo.

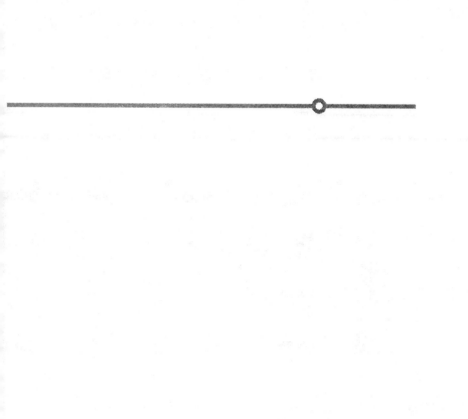

For Your Reading Ease and Comfort

PASSENGER MAP

Car No 7

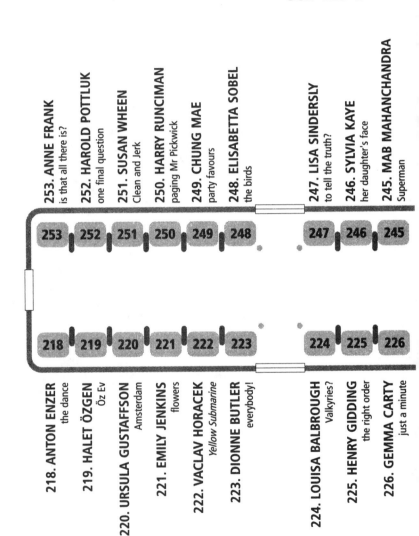

253. ANNE FRANK
is that all there is?

252. HAROLD POTTLUK
one final question

251. SUSAN WHEEN
Clean and Jerk

250. HARRY RUNCIMAN
paging Mr Pickwick

249. CHUNG MAE
party favours

248. ELISABETTA SOBEL
the birds

247. LISA SINDERSLY
to tell the truth?

246. SYLVIA KAYE
her daughter's face

245. MAB MAHANCHANDRA
Superman

218. ANTON ENZER
the dance

219. HALET ÖZGEN
Öz Ev

220. URSULA GUSTAFFSON
Amsterdam

221. EMILY JENKINS
flowers

222. VACLAV HORACEK
Yellow Submarine

223. DIONNE BUTLER
everybody!

224. LOUISA BALBROUGH
Valkyries?

225. HENRY GIDDING
the right order

226. GEMMA CARTY
just a minute

244. SUSAN REECE
important kitchens

243. MARINA PENSBURY
a sympathetic ear

242. HOKIKO McTAVISH
possessing a home

241. MARY SHERRATT
The People of the Book

240. STUART COWE
Dear Diary

239. CHERL JONES
my beautiful nose

238. CHARLES WRIGHT
pleasing Paule

237. BILL HAVERS
personal chemistry

236. JULIE GLUCK
still life

| 244 | 243 | 242 | | 241 | 240 | 239 | 238 | 237 | 236 |

NO EXIT

| 227 | 228 | 229 | | 230 | 231 | 232 | 233 | 234 | 235 |

227. ELSPETH WORLDIDGE
Dunroamin'

228. BECKY PATTERSON
mice cream

229. NANCY KRESS
attack of the jam jars

230. GRAHAM WADDLE
taking care of Stanley

231. THOMAS MILEY
helping hands

232. PETER MORSE
Hallelujah!

233. MALIK BEGUM
laundry service

234. PAUL HENRY
unsavoury pies

235. TRISTAN SAWYER
it's good to talk

The 253 Way to Knowledge

Learn the Secrets of the Ancient Canadians

Since 1995, Canadians have known that the universe is a binary-based system. The 256 binary digits of the ascii code are an accurate Mandelbrot reflection of the universe.

The ascii code can also be used to direct you to the 253 character that reflects your situation. Say you are a sixteen-year-old boy, troubled by acne.

253 is here to rescue you!

Take a humble penny piece. One side has the number 1 and counts as 1. The head of state is the zero. There are no accidents.

Warm the coin in your hand. Concentrate on your question: why am I covered in purple spots?

Flip the coin eight times and record the ones and zeros to form a binary number. Say this was the result:

Value of digit	128	64	32	16	8	4	2	1
Digit on or off	0	0	0	1	1	1	0	0

Add 16+8+4. Your 253 character is 28, Flora McCardie. In what way does a prim, elderly lady resemble an acne-scarred youth?

Consider: Flora is troubled by sex, by loneliness. Could not loneliness and sexual anxiety be the cause of your acne? In which case, the oracle is clear. You must find your number 27, Danni Jarret.

The significant other digits

If you cast all zeros: go to *The End of the Line*. Cast again, for 4, 2, and 1 to find the car that best describes your fate.

If you cast 254: go to *Another One Along in a Minute*, and cast again.

If you get 255: cast again until you get the number of a 253 footnote.

253 – *who will you be today?*

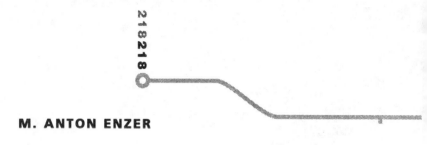

M. ANTON ENZER

Outward appearance

Rail-thin young man, clear complexion, shock of black hair, outdoor overcoat, black suit. Stares at a white card.

Inside information

Returning to France for his father's funeral.

At the age of seventy, Anton's mother asked his father for a divorce. The shock triggered a stroke. When Anton's mother learned that her husband might die soon, and that she had been written out of his will, she tried to declare him insane.

Anton persuaded his father to sign a statement that he was content with his treatment. Anton used this to block his mother's attempts to re-examine his father with her own tame doctors. The divorce and the will went through.

His father married one of his graduate students, a dull woman Anton thought would take care of him. She waited until his will was changed again, and then declared him incompetent. Morose, confused, his father died in care, leaving both Anton and his mother disinherited.

What he is doing or thinking

The invitation invites contributions to an Alzheimers charity. Anton's stepmother is implying that her husband died of Alzheimers. His father was bitter and acerbic, but deserved better.

An old lady, some drunk, asks Anton to dance. He waves her away. She starts to sing. A black woman joins her, and demands, 'Everybody!'

Why the hell not? Anton stands up and bows. 'May I have this dance?' The old woman's face crinkles into a smile. They waltz up the aisle and Anton decides: he does not approve of this funeral. He will not go. He dances on past Waterloo.

MISS HALET ÖZGEN

Outward appearance
Sophia Loren? Strong-featured young woman in black business dress.

Inside information
Turkish business graduate working, like her father, for Beetlehide shipping. Just back from enforced return to Istanbul. Beetlehide have twice tried to get Halet a work permit. They have just re-advertised her job, tailoring it for a Turkish speaker. It is her last chance.

What she is doing or thinking
She cannot go back to Turkey. In Istanbul, she went to a friend's party, head uncovered in Western evening dress. Their car was repeatedly rammed by a rented jeep driven by a man with a beard. Another car eased between them and they escaped down an off-ramp.

A week later, she was in a taxi that was stopped by police. Using the polite plural form of you she asked what the taxi driver had done wrong. 'You are on the side of the guilty!' the policeman said, using the singular. 'Are you my father or a relative?' she replied, insulted. He grabbed her wrist, flung her to the ground. She woke up sobbing in the back of another driver's cab. The driver said, 'You cannot be Turkish, to help a taxi driver.'

The next day she was followed home by catcalling men. They hated her loose hair, her clothes, her manner. They wanted her back in purdah. Halet needs that work permit.

An old crazy lady is singing, 'Is that all there is?' Halet likes the song; there is something Turkish about its mournfulness. A black lady starts to sing it too. Suddenly everyone is dancing.

Including Halet.

MISS URSULA GUSTAFFSON

Outward appearance

About eighteen, blonde, heavy faced. Tan corduroys, black shoulder bag. Looking at a *London A-Z.*

Inside information

Swedish visitor from the town of Ostersund. Missing the first week of college to visit an English boy she met in Amsterdam.

What she is doing or thinking

Amsterdam had been the best thing in her life. She met Chris in a café; they just started talking. He was handsome, outgoing. He took her to a church where a German conductor was recording the King's College choir in a piece by Bach. The conductor smiled so kindly. He really liked Chris. She thought Chris must be part of the choir. 'No, I just met him,' Chris said, not explaining further. Together, they watched this beautiful music being recorded.

She fell in love with him. They visited the Rijksmuseum, they ate meals, they talked and when they said goodbye at Amsterdam station, he waved, she wept. She wrote and told him she was coming.

'Would you like to dance?' an old lady asks her, in a European accent. Ursula shakes her head. She sees herself when old.

Chris never answered her letters. He may have moved. He may not want her to come. A sense of feeling foolish or betrayed rises as she gets closer to Lambeth North.

Now the old women gets everyone singing. Ursula isn't singing. A young man gallantly asks the lady to dance. Suddenly there is a party.

Oh well, thinks Ursula, take what you can. Grateful, awkward, she stands up and traces patterns of dancing in the air alone.

MRS EMILY JENKINS

Outward appearance
Mid-thirties, old-fashioned long hair in sweeping curls, blue jumper and slacks, navy blue coat, flowers by her bag. The flowers are brown at the edges. Writing in a card with great deliberation.

Inside information
Housewife. There still are some. Her husband is the manager of a Renault dealership. Going to St Thomas' Hospital to visit her sister. Her sister is dying, but doesn't know it.

What she is doing or thinking
It's taken Emily all the way from Harrow to write the card.

My dearest Rhona
Wishing you all the best, my darling, on your 28th birthday.
I hope you have an absolutely fab day and year. It can only
be better than the last one!

She wants to write, I remember you as my pretty little sister. I remember taking you to see *Starlight Express*, and your eyes going big and round. I drove you up to university and I was so proud of you, Clever Clogs. Emily wants to write: Mum and Dad still live in the '60s; I don't like my husband; you're the only one I can rely on, Pet.

She had to buy the flowers at the station in a hurry. They're dying too.

'Would you like to dance?' an old lady asks someone. And someone agrees. The gentleman opposite takes out a bottle of whisky.

'I'd love some,' says Emily. The whisky is harsh and warm in her throat. Somehow Emily goes past Waterloo. She gets out at Lambeth North, laughing with the old man. She looks at the flowers.

And they're fresh.

MR VACLAV HORACEK

Outward appearance
Healthy old hippy? A cloud of tangled honey hair and beard, rumpled pink cheeks. Ochre trousers, a natty polka-dot cravat, a grin of crazed enthusiasm. A plastic bag full of cloth and string.

Inside information
Czech theatre producer going to the Old Vic to force them to interview him. He is the director of a puppet version of *Yellow Submarine*. It was a big hit, only the second Beatles show in Prague. It had wonderful songs, a tourist audience, and Vaclav's papier-mâché creations.

What he is doing or thinking
The British don't like the Beatles. No one is interested at all at all in *Yellow Submarine*. They keep talking about this thing copyright. It is very frustrating.

An old woman comes up to him, hunched and small and smiling. 'Would you like to dance?' She is desperate woman. You get them also in Prague station. If he wasn't also desperate Vaclav would give her money. But Vaclav can only afford one meal a day.

The old woman starts to sing and someone else says to all join. Then a young man starts to dance with her. Ah! This is why Vaclav dreamed for years of coming to London.

Vaclav pulls out his puppet of John Lennon dressed as Sergeant Pepper. He makes Lennon totter and starts to sing . . . 'Pah, pah, pah . . .'

That is not a Beatles song he is singing. He has to think. It's 'Papageno' from *The Magic Flute*. That is no copyright. Vaclav's pitch changes.

A puppet *Magic Flute* starring the Beatles and Charlie Chaplin?

Lennon dances.

PROFESSOR DIONNE BUTLER

Outward appearance
Elegant, but slightly down-at-heel, black woman about 45. Very tall, so her long brown flared trousers extend into the aisle, showing thick-heeled but scuffed shoes. Huge, new fawn anorak, low-cut black sweater.

Inside information
American academic and ex-student of Angela Davis's at UCLA. Dionne emigrated to Nigeria ten years ago and now teaches at the University of Lagos. In London at the invitation of SOAS to lecture on African literature. En route to visit MOMI.

What she is doing or thinking
Since getting on at Kilburn, Dionne has had her eye on the old lady in the corner, who kept looking around her, horror stricken. She has just stood up and asked a young man to dance. People's faces froze, they looked away. Oh come on, she just wants some life! She hasn't asked you for money. People cough and shift.

Then the woman starts to sing: 'Is that all there is?' and Dionne understands.

Dionne first heard the song when she was seventeen, and it seemed then to sum up America; something sad and disaster-bound about it. Even then, it was the loneliest country in the world. One reason why she lives in Africa.

And people look as if the poor old dear has said something obscene. She's singing!

Dionne stands up, and with her strong clear voice, joins in. Her eyes fix all the frightened people in turn. 'Everybody!' Dionne shouts and links arms with the old woman, who looks up at her with comprehending gratitude.

The young man bows. The dance begins.

2 2 4 2 2 4

MRS LOUISA BALBROUGH

Outward appearance
Craggy woman with cropped grey hair. Her trousers are tartan
in front, yellow with red polka dots in back. Wistfully reading a
yellowed letter.

Inside information
Antiques dealer returning from Camden Passage. Divorced,
recently lifted up by a love affair with a tall, craggy man called
Peter Wolffe. Her father, an ex-Army officer, recently died, leaving her his letters.

What she is doing or thinking
Reading words written in 1946 from Germany to her mother.

> My darling, I'm so proud of you and baby Louisa. The
> photograph is beautiful. We are still sweeping up the mess
> made by this war but I will be home soon.
> There is one thing darling I never told you. I have another
> child, a son. His mother asked me to help; she could not stand
> her husband, who does not know. I've never seen the little
> fellow, but both of us need to remember, for Louisa's sake,
> that his name is Peter Wolffe.

Louisa had never experienced anything like meeting Peter. His
rangy body, the life etched into his face – she saw him and
thought: 'That's the one'. Peter said later he felt the same thing.

It's the Siegmund Syndrome – in the Wagner opera a brother
and sister meet for the first time and abandon the law from love.
Peter lives simply in East Anglia, selling smoked fish. She wants
to live there with him.

Louisa watches dancing people. She thinks: I'm 50; there can
be no children, there are no Gods to enrage. She folds the letter
away, smiles, and joins the party.

MR HENRY GIDDING

Outward appearance
Scuffed boots, jeans with an open fly over another pair of jeans, bumfreezer jacket over thick Aran-isle sweater, knitted hat, creased face, black beard. Head thrown back. Snoring loudly.

Inside information
Display Operative for EyeFeast Ltd. He puts up three-sided outdoor rotating signs. They come in nearly one hundred separately printed slats, about nine foot high by four inches wide. He and his mate Mark usually do ten a day.

They have spent the last two days doing the same one. And the last two nights doing the other nineteen.

What he is doing or thinking
Seeing slats in his dreams. Over and over, he and Mark have tried to assemble the three-sided sign. It's like a giant jigsaw that won't come right.

One of the ads is for the National Power/Powergen sale of remaining shares. 'An impressive release of power,' it says, over a volcanic eruption, all red and black speckly bits that are absolutely indistinguishable. On the back of that is, 'Share the power' – a clever tie-in from the Billericay who are a share shop for the offer. It's all red and black too.

In his dream, it's bloody cold on the scaffolding and he keeps dropping the slats. They fall and impale passers-by.

Then Nick Berry, Britain's highest paid television actor, steps in, dressed as a bobby. He starts passing Henry the slats in the right order, and Henry sees that yes, for real, this is the right order.

Then someone shouts, 'Everybody!' With a snort he wakes.

The right order scatters.

MRS GEMMA CARTY

Outward appearance
Woman in mid-thirties. Fawns, pinks, browns merge to form a business-like presentation. Orange lipstick matches her short hair. Reading a document, shaking her head slightly.

Inside information
Conference Director of the Britannia Club. Gemma balances the needs of Club members with sales to other customers. She referees when catering, marketing, AV, and finance all disagree.

What she is doing or thinking
Currently reading minutes taken by her new secretary and pondering the mysteries of the human mind. She was told that Suschita, an Indian girl adopted by Swiss parents,[1] would be a very thorough notetaker and not to be alarmed by her methods. Gemma was appalled at the first monthly sales meeting. Suschita spent the entire time drawing circles, arrows, zig-zags, and Dumbo the flying elephant. Her ex-employer Mrs Hofer soothed Gemma's fears.

And here are the minutes, typed from circles and arrows.

Mr Gestetner emphasized that the brief for the new audio visual equipment was a matter for the presentations team. Miss Buxton replied that it was typical of the AV team to try to do marketing; Mr Gestetner replied that it was typical of marketing to think that equipment did not need specification. Mrs Carty resolved the issue by deciding to include marketing in the tender team.

Gemma can't send that to people. It's too accurate.

People on the carriage begin to sing and dance. There are puppets and party favours. Getting out at Waterloo, Gemma thinks: what a strange and miraculous species we are.

Then she thinks: I'll send it just as it is.

1. The real Suschita Jungblot was murdered a few days before 11th January, 1995 in the town of Dunstable. She was a twenty-year-old au pair studying English with the Hofers. In this fictional world, things worked out differently.

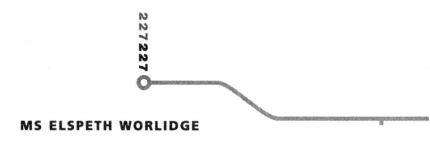

MS ELSPETH WORLIDGE

Outward appearance

Very suitable girl, dressed like an ad for sherry in a 1967 *Sunday Telegraph* colour supplement. Hermès scarf tucked around neck, yellowish blouse, carefully combed brown hair, simple black business suit, clean coat with fake fur collar. She stares ahead frozen in horror, her freckled hand jammed into her orderly hair.

Inside information

PA to the Director, Public Sector Services of Dun and Old, the accountancy and business consultancy.

What she is doing or thinking

Everything has just fallen into place. The tenders for consultancies to the nearly innumerable government bodies (4,000 on their mailing list) fall like autumn leaves onto her desk. They want corporate strategies, sales strategies, efficiency savings, marketing plans. She photocopies the documents and sends them to the same ten people in Dun and Old, and sets up a tender meeting. Sometimes she reads them.

The tender in her bag is headlined 'General Policy Direction and Application: tender for long-term consultancy and evaluation contract.'

She read it several times before it made any sense. It kept talking about long-term targeting, horizontal and vertical analysis followed up by monitoring and corrective actions.

The sense it has just made to her is this: the governance of Britain has been put out to tender to the private sector. The United Kingdom will be run by a consultancy. No wonder Dun and Old has built a mini-Whitehall just across the river. No wonder her boss danced a little jig and then rang to thank Larry.

They are in competition with three other companies. Are any of them European?

MISS BECKY PATTERSON

Outward appearance

Raw-boned, hearty girl wearing an iridescent jacket in a pattern of roses and leaves. Glossy peppermint-pink lipstick. Lady Di honey hair, grey slacks, red sweater. Takes out a torch from her bag, rifles through jump leads, and takes out a wiring diagram.

Inside information

Daughter of third-generation Zimbabwe farmers, with a degree in Tibetan. Assistant librarian in the British Library's oriental collection near Blackfriars. Planning the rewiring of the flat she has just moved into with her partner Bill, a burly schoolteacher.

What she is doing or thinking

Bill turned out to be English, after all. He's so wimpish about everything. She'll have to do the rewiring herself. He's scared and wants an electrician.

It's like their bathwater. All she says is that it's wasteful to use the water only once. He gets to be first; and she's stopped using it a third time for the dishes. If only he'd remember to use biodegradable soap, like he promised, she could use it to water the basil.

He's never had to transport all his water by truck in barrels. He's never had to save and reuse everything. Why not reuse good fat? All the different things it's cooked add to the flavour.

She admits: it was a shame about the mouse. OK, so it fell into the fat jar and she didn't find it until months later. Doesn't he know what gives wine its bouquet?

That's the trouble with Westerners; they're just too clean. They don't develop their immune systems.

She sniffs, having decided how to rewire the flat.

MRS NANCY KRESS

Outward appearance
Checked jacket, white shirt, long red dress. Reads *The Telegraph* with beady focus. Her blue shoes are patchy with stains.

Inside information
Customer liaison at IBM, mother of three, proud cook. Nancy's life is a whirlwind.

What she is doing or thinking
Maybe she's doing too much.

The kids had finished their breakfast, Bill had taken them to school, she had her car keys in her hand, about to go, when she saw that a jar from last night's marmalade session was still unlidded. She screwed on the lid, and held the jar up to the light.

Baking the jar sterile must have cracked the glass. The bottom fell out. Marmalade poured over her keys, her suit, her shoes, the floor.

To sweep it up would ruin her broom. She tried pushing the dustpan into it, which was only partially successful. She went to get newspapers and heard the kiss of sticky shoes on carpet.

She took off her shoes and cut her foot on broken glass. Scraped up jam as best she could, flooded the floor with water, and covered it with newspaper to soak it up. Went off to change clothes and stanch bleeding.

Came back to find that the mixture of marmalade and water had flyposted the newspapers to the pine floor. Used the egglifter to scrape them up.

Ran to car, and jammed keys into the ignition along with a chunk of orange peel. Abandoned car.

She has just remembered that she didn't have time to wash the jars. The marmalade will taste of homemade pickled onions.

MR GRAHAM WADDLE

Outward appearance

About 26, skinny, spotty, with a big nose, no chin, and huge teeth that threaten constantly to push his mouth into a smile.

Inside information

Van driver for Buntleys Coachworks. Very quietly keeps the company functioning. Its stock control system is faulty: the computer system needs too much feeding. Graham knows what parts are running low and what is being repaired, and collects what's needed before it's even ordered. Gives staff and customers lifts, deals with the MD.

What he is doing or thinking

Never a dull moment at Buntleys. Graham needs the loading bay for the van, but Mr Gray parks there overnight. Graham just has to laugh. The number of times he's pulled in with part of a chassis, or an exhaust, only to find Mr Gray's car there.

Graham's become quite an expert on the MD's movements. He says he's popping out for a sandwich, but takes his car. One lunchtime, Graham saw the MD's car parked in a residential street in Clapham. That would be some sandwich.

The two black guys who'd had their car kicked in: Mr Gray told Andy to use an old panel. Graham slipped Andy a new one instead. He saw Mr Gray filch Andy's lighter out of his bag. And there was that joke on Pru.

So all in all, Graham's decided. If Mr Gray says he's going out for a sandwich, Graham will follow him. And if he goes to some bird's house, Graham will make sure the lads all know.

And he'll ask Andy if he got his lighter back.

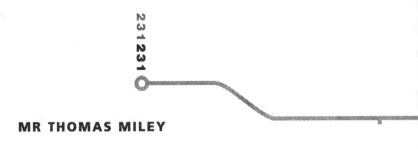

MR THOMAS MILEY

Outward appearance

Casual labourer? Striped shirt, bulging tummy, jeans, orange anorak, thinning hair. Reading some kind of briefing document. Sticker on brown briefcase says 'Temporary Pass London Weekend Television.'

Inside information

A professional mentor. He coaches middle managers, giving them advice on office politics or career strategy. To do that he must gain access to their places of employment in the guise of being a potential customer or supplier. Currently pretending to be a camera assistant in order to advise a producer at LWT. The terrible truth is, the producer isn't very good.

What he is doing or thinking

Reviewing the proposed charter for a new professional body: the Institute of Mentoring ('to guide, advise, and nurture'). Some thorny professional issues are being faced.

> If a Member discovers that mentoring one individual brings the Member into the position of potentially advising against the interest of another client, the case will be referred to a second Member.
>
> Members are encouraged to become experts in the cultures of particular companies. This is to limit the need to access company realities under false pretences.

The bloody puritans are saying that the clients should openly introduce their Mentors to the company. But the whole point for clients is that their Mentor is a secret weapon. And, they're ashamed of needing one.

If the Institute tries to make Mentoring open, it will create a second, secret profession. Like Thomas, it will gain entry under false pretences.

On the other hand, how else are they to get a Royal patron? And what is he going to tell his client?

MR PETER MORSE

Outward appearance

Young black man. Hair close-cropped in zig-zag patterns. Under an index finger, he hides a grin.

Inside information

Dishwasher at the lower staff canteen in Pall Mall Oil. Peter fires a hose of steaming water at the crocks before they're run through the main dishwashers.

Mr Cerbasi, the manager, has been trying to take the canteen upmarket. Customers can see into the dishroom. The dishroom staff talk and joke. That is not upmarket. So Cerbasi has put a bloody great chunk of lavender plywood across the tray window.

This reduced the space through which dirty dishes can be pushed by about two-thirds. Instead of resting on shelves, they avalanche either forwards into the dishroom or back over the canteen floor. And since there is no flow of air, the dishroom is a regular 45 degrees.

What he is doing or thinking

Yesterday, Peter heard a crash of trays the other side of the window. Mr Cerbasi, fat and pale, ran in, grabbed the hose and tried to prove that if you worked in a continual panic, you could, just about, keep up with all the trays. Sweat poured off him.

Peter shrugged, walked off, peed, and came back.

'Where were you?' Cerbasi demanded.

'I'm allowed to pee,' Peter replied. Cerbasi left.

Inspiration struck and, to the tune from Handel's *Messiah*, Peter began to sing, 'Hallelujah! Cerbasi! Cerbasi! Hallelujah!' Everyone in the dishroom joined in. It was quite merry. Then Peter rang the Health and Safety Executive and shopped the canteen.

He's looking forward to today's talk with Cerbasi.

MR MALIK BEGUM

Outward appearance

Handsome businessman, dark suit, camel-hair coat. Black hair rolls back in waves. Deep circles under his eyes. Rubs them, seems to crumple, then sits up straight, in power again.

Inside information

Owns The Sharma Restaurant, near Lambeth North. It is well appointed, with glass panels frosted with Hindu motifs, though Mr Begum is Muslim. The restaurant is almost always empty, but keeps large numbers of people in employment.

It launders money for gentlemen in Soho. Last night, they took Mr Begum to dinner. It went on too long, he became suspicious; they tried to get him drunk then they asked him to work through a ludicrous sum. His percentage would keep his family in comfort – but he didn't know what would happen if he refused.

It's such a risk. No one will believe that sum for food, table-cloths, maintenance. He spent all night trying to work it out and decided: the only way the business would move that much cash was if it were sold. He has to close it. Then that will be it, he promises, he will have no more dealings with them.

What he is doing or thinking

Mr Begum gets out at Lambeth, and to his horror sees his wife in the next car. The doors close, and the train pulls away.

What does he do? The platform is in strange disorder. People from his own car blow party favours. At the far end, two police-men interrogate some tourists. Their radios squawk. They all suddenly look down the tunnel in the direction his wife has gone.

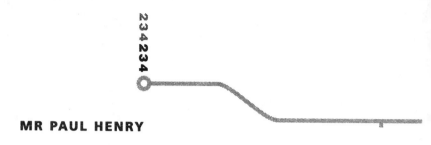

MR PAUL HENRY

Outward appearance
Pretty man in his early thirties. A puff of blond, thinning hair. Brown winter coat, olive suit, brown wool tie. Stares smiling.

Inside information
One of the managers of the Queen of Tarts bakery on the other side of Waterloo Road. Lives with his mum. The only survivor of Donald Nielsen's attentions.

What he is doing or thinking
Paul is wondering why the meat pies don't sell. People buy them once, shudder, and ever afterwards order the spinach and aubergine.

A boyfriend ate one once and said it tasted like burnt tyres. Paul can cook every other sort of pie, even savoury cheese. But not meat.

He has this weird notion that he is somehow tainted. He liked Donald Nielsen; he was older, stable, kindly. Nielsen cooked him dinner, and plied him with booze and then Paul woke up underwater in the bath with a tie being tightened around his neck. Donald apologized, helped him out of the bath, and dried him down. It was only the next day that Paul began to think that someone had tried to kill him and that he had allowed someone to get away with trying to kill him. Paul stayed silent, until he saw the papers. The police were thunderstruck. Why had he waited until now? Paul still doesn't know.

Donald Nielsen cooked him meat pies. He cooked other things as well. The train stops at Waterloo. Paul gets out and a woman in blue, head held high, sweeps past him. For some reason, the platform sways underfoot and Paul has to sit down.

MR TRISTAN SAWYER

Outward appearance
A once handsome face emerges from folds of fat. Grizzled hair. Has his *FT* out, but isn't reading.

Inside information
Financial forecaster for a large corporation. Used to be a colleague and the best friend of Richard Thompson. Works late most nights. Has the confidence of the Managing Director. At dinner last night the MD asked Tristan if he knew why Richard had left. Tristan didn't say.

What he is doing or thinking
Thinking he really should give Richard a call. Tristan was very angry with him for getting himself infected. Silly trollop, there were plenty of nice men who would have fallen all over themselves to have a relationship with him. In his younger days.

The Corp sent them both out to the Falmouth office, and they had to share the company flat. It had been fun, getting drunk, pretending to be het. He really needed watching over, that boy. Overdid the sauce at times.

It was pathetic after he resigned. He didn't realize he no longer had the same hold over people he once had: not as pretty, not as successful. It really was a bit difficult introducing him at dinner parties: this is my dropped-out friend Richard.

He's as strong as a horse of course, and will be fine. Anyway, Tristan has to fly out to Brunei next week. Maybe he'll give him a call after that. Just to show he isn't avoiding him or anything.

Tristan suddenly sees Richard's face as it was in Cornwall: happy, bold, smiling, beautiful. He tries to dismiss it, and can't.

MS JULIE GLUCK

Outward appearance

Stylish woman in late middle age. Skin like a walnut, honey hair wrapped in a slinky patterned scarf, clean blue jeans, brown nylon stockings visible in cleavage of tiny shoes. A painting is turned to face the wall. Canvas has been left unstapled at the back; the wood is badly joined.

Inside information

Runs No Bars Gallery, a space on Lower Marsh. Friends stage openings, drink cheap wine, skittishly look for critics who never arrive, and then leave the pictures on the walls for two weeks in the locked and closed ex-café. Nobody bothers to steal them. It's called art.

What she is doing or thinking

Wondering how she can face carrying the painting through the streets. It is an impasto portrait of female genitalia.

'I'm a heterosexual Mapplethorpe,' said the artist, Jeremy. Some hope. He's always been a sad little fuck, the kind of kid who gets beaten up. Julie has always found him physically repulsive; she didn't know that he was obsessed with prostitutes.

What faces the wall is quite simply the worst single thing Julie has ever seen in her life. Muddy with paint, hideous to look at, poorly mounted, it involves an inserted and lit candle and is called *True Love*.

'I wanted to celebrate the endless variety of whores,' says Jeremy. Sure. That's why all the paintings look the same.

The train whines into Waterloo. Julie stands, adjusts her headscarf and suddenly realizes she's not going to carry that thing out. With an air of delicate nonchalance, she turns and leaves it to its fate.

MR BILL HAVERS

Outward appearance
Burly man, mid-thirties, curly hair, in slacks, soft shoes. Reading *The Daily Mail*.

Inside information
Pharmacist for a small chemist's shop in Kennington Road. Has been troubled by a series of unskilled, unfriendly shop assistants. Until Bertie arrived.

Bertie is nineteen, from a family in the garment trade. She isn't pretty, but she is remarkably cheerful and energetic, with a blunt nose and freckles. For some reason, their senses of humour mesh. She tells jokes about her boyfriends or family. Her uncle Joe is an unapologetic Stalinist who still hopes for a return of Communism. Her aunt Ruby saw off thieves by chucking her stock of fruit and veg at them.

They even went out together to see Diana Ross. Bill's wife was worried until she met her. 'I was wondering why you were so much more cheerful lately,' his wife said.

Bill replied, 'It's just nice working with such nice people.'

Bertie's brother was convicted of causing an affray. The original charge was assault. He's big, cheerful, but loses his temper. Bertie asked if Bill couldn't try to get him a job in the shop. Something told him: no.

What he is doing or thinking
He's agonizing over it. He would hate to turn Bertie down, and hate even more to lose her friendship. But someone with a temper dealing with customers? He can't imagine what Mr Kumar would say. He can't ask. It's not right.

The train slows. He's going to have to say no. With a sense of loss, almost of doom, he folds away his paper.

MR CHARLES WRIGHT

Outward appearance

Unshaven, plump older black man with twists of silver in his hair. Green track suit bottoms, working-class cap, trainers. Sits holding a W. H. Smith bag with a CD in it.

Inside information

Took early retirement from Lloyds. The payout wasn't quite sufficient. Has worried too much about finances since. He's distracted.

This morning he woke up and realized that he had forgotten his wife's birthday. Paule makes such a big fuss over occasions. He pretended to be asleep, as she got ready to go out to her cleaning job. He waited until he heard the door close and then got up, ill with the earliness, did his morning chores, and nipped out of the house.

He went to the concourse at Waterloo Station to buy some chocolates. The confectioner's was closed. Then he thought: I'll buy her a CD single for a card and say I'm getting tickets for a show. But Our Price was closed as well. In a panic, he headed across the river, to Charing Cross. He had a coffee until W. H. Smith opened. Saw nothing she might like. Bought *Now That's What I Call Music 30*.

What he is doing or thinking

Getting back on at Embankment, he saw his wife flash past in Car 5, followed by her friend Mary Wallis in Car 6. Finally made it into Car 7.

Which means he'll have to get out at Waterloo, or they'll see him. He'll have to run all the way home and hope that Mary and Paule will stop to talk.

Happy birthday.

MISS CHERL JONES

Outward appearance

About 24, hair in stripes of different shades of blonde pulled back by hair grip. Black jumper, red bodywarmer, blue suede hiking boots, all spotless. Large cloth bag with ROCK GEEK logo.

She sits like a stack of precariously balanced china. She seems to be looking permanently upwards because of the tilt of the tip of her nose. Her upper lip looks numb.

Inside information

Dental nurse. The gear is a disguise. She'll bounce back into the practice and breathlessly tell them she just got off the train from her especially long skiing holiday in France. In fact, she is returning from plastic surgery.

What she is doing or thinking

She is completely occupied simply with sitting on a train. She feels exposed, as if the top layer of skin has been peeled away (it has). Are people looking?

Cherl is convinced that she is now extraordinarily beautiful. She glances sideways in the reflecting windows and has this confirmed. She looks just like Sharon Stone. She feels nervous and joyful all at once. Her chin used to jut out towards her long and downward turning nose. She looked like a nutcracker.

Now she wonders if a career in modelling might not be possible. She crosses her legs and holds her hands aloft in the air, to judge the effect. Her whole life will change.

She only wishes her face wasn't so cold and heavy. She stands up at Waterloo with a flourish. Her feet pluck a pathway down the aisle, as if she were being married to a new self.

MR STUART COWE

Outward appearance

Pale, ageing man, grimly chewing gum. Ribbed white pullover in stretched ruffles around the bottom edge. Shoulder length blond/grey hair. Grey woollen hat with row of red stars. Lumpy silver ring on finger. Sits like knock-kneed schoolgirl, a bloated hardback notebook on his lap.

Inside information

A compulsive diarist. Stuart cannot help himself writing down every aspect of his life. He feels something akin to terror if he cannot, as if life is leaking away. The current notebook is two weeks old.

Works in a cramped electronics retailer east of Waterloo. Gets up at 5.30 AM to record the previous evening's events.

What he is doing or thinking

Has recorded the morning's ironing and television news, and has moved on to his train journey.

Dear Bill

it says at the top of the current page. Every page starts like a letter to fool anyone who sees him writing.

> Sitting opposite me is a rather pathetic specimen of manhood very skinny with bulbous nose and buck teeth in a blue shirt with diamond patterns and clean blue jeans probably married. Trainers have grease mark along one edge. My tummy is burning from the bacon. I got off schedule and wolfed it down. This is because I did not sleep with worry. I sit here fuming about bloody Ian reorganising my shelving, but there is no communication at that place. All this angst is such a waste of energy . . .

Unlike his diaries.

The woman next to him is leaning over the page. He rears back, snorts, and snaps the book shut.

MISS MARY SHERRATT

Outward appearance
Woman, late twenties. Stretch cord slacks, pointy lace-up boots, enormous fluffy blue hat, matching blue scarf, art nouveau brooch. Hair short, black, in a feather cut.

Inside information
Works part-time for the National Dysphasia and Dysgraphia Society, an underfunded room in the ex-nursery of a housing estate behind Westminster Bridge Road. An accident prompted a small stroke: Mary is dysgraphic. She cannot turn speech into writing. She also has a slight dysphasic speech impediment. She's good at accounts, fashion, make-up and shoplifting. She knows precisely how pretty she is, and how much of the prettiness is contrived. Part of her feels even the prettiness is false.

What she is doing or thinking
Trying to solve the mystery of what the man next to her is doing. What it must be like to read and write. What on earth can he find to write about on a train? Is it for work? He must have to work very hard. She feels sorry for him and wonders if being dysgraphic means she has escaped some hardships.

Suddenly, the man snaps the book shut and bloats like an angry bullfrog. She wants to tell him: it's all right, I couldn't read anything. He flounces off; she looks around for something to do . . . and hears a merry wheezing sound.

A Chinese lady is blowing a party favour. A bottle full of brown fluid flashes between people along with plastic cups. Who needs boring old words . . . and boring old people? There's a party! Mary moves up the carriage to join in.

MRS HOKIKO McTAVISH

Outward appearance

Young Japanese woman. Crisp, plaid jacket, white blouse, black skirt. Everything looks brand new. Reads a letter with calm deliberation.

Inside information

Hokiko was a lecturer in business law at Moshiba-Electronics University in Kyoto. While doing research at Adventure Capital, she met William McTavish, a fleshy, aggressive analyst with blond hair.

Her mother finally persuaded Hokiko's father to accept the marriage, and frequently visits England to make sure Hokiko is happy. Hokiko wonders if she is.

What she is doing or thinking

The letter is from the Billericay Building Society. They are about to forcibly repossess her home.

Last year the Billericay began to write to a Mr Shum and a Miss Fritt at Hokiko's address, reminding them that they were missing mortgage payments. Hokiko replied several times explaining that neither of those people lived at 92 Harrow Court, nor had the property ever been mortgaged to the Billericay.

Further letters were addressed to The Occupant. 'If you are not Mr Shum or Miss Fritt, do you rent from them? Do you know where they can be contacted?'

Today, the Billericay has served notice of repossession. William thinks it's a huge joke and laughs. Hokiko is afraid to come home and find the flat locked and empty. She is ashamed: they have as good as called her a liar.

How, Hokiko wonders, does a company manage to mortgage a property without knowing its address? How do they manage to mortgage it to non-existent people? And why do they never read letters?

Rude, stupid, bewilderingly incompetent: it's what her father says.

MS MARINA PENSBURY

Outward appearance

Corkscrew hair, age somewhere between early and late thirties. Woollen tan matching jumper and skirt, large tan overcoat. Listening intently to her neighbour. Then a sudden, withdrawing shift of body language.

Inside information

Works in HM Customs and Excise, well north of Waterloo. There is something in Marina's timeless looks, professional dress, and sympathetic manner that means she is forever receiving confidences. People tell her about their anal warts; their snoring, their dislike of colleagues, how they changed their names when their father was convicted of child abuse.

Her workmate Susy was desolate after her husband left her. Marina invited Susy to stay, to talk. That was four weeks ago. Marina now knows everything about Susy's sex life, childlessness, and pets. Susy's mother has come to stay as well.

What she is doing or thinking

Marina listens to Susy rejoice: her husband wants to come back. Susy can get rid of her mum and go home to some comfort.

Susy's mum announced, 'I've decided to clean that oven of yours,' the day after Marina cleaned it. 'I've thrown out all that old food from your refrigerator. I brushed Susy's cats. Sorry about the fur. I'll deal with it later.'

Susy's mother drinks. She snoozes on the staircase. None of this has bothered Susy. 'At last the old bag will be out of my hair,' she chuckles.

Susy still has not thanked Marina. Not once in four weeks has she expressed concern for anyone else. Marina can understand why Bill left.

The real question is: why do I keep asking for this?

MRS SUSAN REECE

Outward appearance
Heavy on the slap. Ruby cheeks, vermilion lips, long polished boots. Clutches a black bag, leaning sideways, confidentially, towards her neighbour. Talks, stops, leans sideways again, adds something else, looks away, is moved to speak again.

Inside information
Works in HM Customs and Excise. Workmate of the woman next to her, with whom she has been living since separation from her husband. The rat has asked to come back.

What she is doing or thinking
She feels vindicated, enraged, and can see that Marina feels the same on her behalf. She really doesn't know how she'd have got through it without Marina, especially after Mum stuck her oar in.

'I've told him, if he does come back then we'll have a contract in writing about what happens to the property. If I play my cards right I'm sure I'll get my new kitchen out of it. You remember the one I showed you in the catalogue?'

She leans back, absorbing the sense of victory.

'The white counter tops with the built-in stove? I mean the least he can do if he's coming back is finally do something around the place. It's a tip. The whole house will have to be redecorated, and that's a promise.'

She leans back. She wants a fag. A white Kleenex is wrapped around her thumb, in case she starts to cry. 'Oh God,' she says in despair. 'I'm sure I'm being too nice again.' She looks into her companion's eyes, then at her silver fingernails.

'I'm sure you're not,' says Marina, tartly.

What?

Waterloo.

MR MAB MAHANCHANDRA

Outward appearance
Plump, brown, sharp. Short, greased, standing-up hair. Thick overcoat in zigzag black and white pattern. A green suit that seems to flow like the sticky plastic from which squidgy toys are made. Cobalt-blue tie. Reading a *Superman* novelization.

Gives the party in the car one gimlet look and joins it.

Inside information
Anglo Indian. Degree in computer science. Writing cyberpunk novel. Loves dance music and helps a friend convert his stuff to MIDI files. Folded in his jacket pocket is a business plan for a consultancy to get small firms online. He is en route to the SBS, to present it to Camilla Burke-Harris.

A free man in the new Britain. Mab fancies Dean Caine. He fancies Lois. He fancies anything. Already a father: his girlfriend gave birth at home. Even his bewildered parents don't know about it. His various occupations mean he spends most daytimes taking care of the infant. Works on his programs in the evening until ten o'clock, then goes out 'til 3.00 A M.

What he is doing or thinking
Right now, Mab is thinking of Dean Caine's body in his own new suit. It's by Tom Gilbey, it's green, everyone else is in blue or black. Mab is the bee's knees and knows it.

The dance begins. 'Everybody!' Mab jumps up, swings the black woman around. She recognizes a fellow spirit and roars with laughter. He kisses her on the cheek. He shakes his plump tummy, hands over his head. Then they all spin off the car at Lambeth North.

World, meet your future.

MRS SYLVIA KAYE

Outward appearance
Plump, red-cheeked woman in grey raincoat, scarf, good black shoes. She looks at the floor, the lower half of her face continuing to sink.

Inside information
A beautician in a salon on Kennington Road. Sylvia and her husband are 38, but he looks years younger. He left her for an exciting 25-year-old. Peter has always been outgoing, but weak. He lets their daughter Diana go clubbing with him. They smoke dope together. Diana comes back and abuses Sylvia. This morning Diana hit her. The red cheeks are bruised.

What she is doing or thinking
What do you do when your daughter continually calls you a bitch? When you ask her to turn down the music and she tells you to fuck off? When you ask her friends to leave at 2.00 AM and they all just laugh?

This morning Sylvia had enough. Diana called her bitch again, and Sylvia grabbed her arms and spun her around. Diana slapped her, hard on the face. 'Keep your fucking hands off me!' The girl's face was a mask of hatred. Sylvia broke down in tears.

Sylvia remembers her baby daughter's merry little face. How did it happen? Di was always cheeky, but it made people chuckle. There was no malice.

Sylvia stares glumly at the party in the car. Crushed by a sense of weakness and failure, she is immune to it. Right now laughter is for other people.

My daughter hates me, and I can't cope any more. The only question now is: how do I get her to leave?

MS LISA SINDERSLY

Outward appearance
Chunky young woman in loose ethnic trousers, bulky sweater, AIDS ribbon.

Inside information
Contract data processor for USB's Technopark, working on a project measuring differences in male and female brains. Last night, the patterns came together.

What she is doing or thinking
Lisa is remembering her father, a big slow kindly man obsessed with order. He trainspotted, recording engine numbers. He would travel overnight to Clapham via Carlisle. His travel bag always held a campstove for boiling water.

Lisa remembers her autistic cousin Annie. Annie loves bank interest and counts it obsessively. She plots the stars. She has a system for recording her own learning process using fruit gums, paste-on architectural symbols, and electrical wiring.

Autism is produced by damage to the cerebellum, which controls movement and mimicry of movement. Mimicry of movement allows us to recreate other people's feelings, to understand them. For Annie, people move too quickly to be read. She is subject to rages, especially when someone disrupts her systems of order.

Lisa's data has proved that men are born with a differently functioning cerebellum. Men are mildly autistic. Their elaborate systems of logic, their narrow focus, the lack of emotional understanding are symptoms.

What happens when science proves that a group of people are limited? Do we love them more, like Annie who has learned at 35 to say sorry and mean it? Lisa likes fast cars and raunchy bars. She likes men. She loved her obsessive father.

A young man bows, offering to dance with an old lady out of kindness. Lisa has her answer.

MRS ELISABETTA SOBEL

Outward appearance
Middle-aged woman festooned with symbols of beauty: rings, a brooch of a cat, a bracelet of semi-precious stones. Enters at Embankment, fingermarking her place in the *Journal of the Royal Society for the Protection of Birds*.

Inside information
Wealthy volunteer for the RSPB. Her family were Italian Jews who escaped the war by fleeing to Chicago. Her parents are dead; her cousins scattered to Chile or Israel. Her nephew has cancer.

Much troubled by peacocks. Elisabetta loves birds, but banshee wails from neighbouring Wimbledon Common plague her all night. Peacocks line up like fluorescent ghosts outside her window, peering in, demanding. They follow her footsteps, pecking at them. This morning they lined up across her drive, inflating their tails all at once in a phalanx, saying: remember?

What she is doing or thinking.
Remember?

When Elisabetta was seventeen, her synagogue put on a production of *Fiddler on the Roof*. She wasn't pretty, so they put her in charge of the lights. The hall was to be in darkness, until the first line. Elisabetta couldn't find the right switches. The hero entered a badly lit temporary hall, and said, 'Let there be light.' Elisabetta plunged the hall into darkness.

Like the birds, this unnerved her. What had been meant to be beautiful had become terrifying: there was no light even from God. Why else would so many of her people have been killed?

The carriage begins to dance like a nightmare; the party favours shriek like peacocks. Elisabetta has never understood: the pain in the lament sets it free.

As a bird.

MRS CHUNG MAE

Outward appearance

Tiny, rumpled Chinese lady in khaki anorak, tartan lining inside the hood trimmed with green fur. Lenin-style cap, black jeans over the top of her trainers. Carries various cheap plastic bags. Pink objects with yellow feathers are pressed up against their sides.

Inside information

Granny imported from Hong Kong. Worked for years in the kitchen of a Lisle Street restaurant. Got too old for the hours and the physical demands. Now runs a stand at the Elephant selling party novelties. The season for novelties has just passed.

What she is doing or thinking

Her bones ache, she will be cold, but it's better than sitting behind a till in a steamy shop. The family keep trying to pull her back inside. They don't understand: she likes being on her own, with the little money she gets. Everything else in her life is work and duty.

A strange woman is singing. Suddenly people are dancing; out comes a puppet. Mae doesn't understand. The man next to her offers her a glass of whisky. At first Mae is suspicious. Is it poison?

It is a party. Why else does she have party favours? She takes out a whistle and blows it. It unwraps its pink and feathery length, squeals, and people applaud. 'How much?' asks the whisky man. Mae understands that. Two more people buy them, and blow them, warbling.

The train stops at Lambeth North. Mae hesitates as they all tumble out, having so much fun. Just before the doors close, the strange old lady pushes Mae out. The party continues.

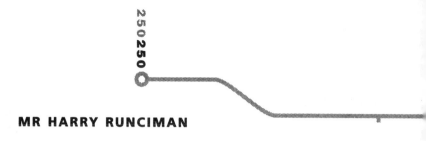

MR HARRY RUNCIMAN

Outward appearance
Plump, Pickwickian gentleman in un-ironed striped shirt, plaid green jacket, grey trousers, greenish Burberry.

Inside information
Lecturer at the new Electronic Polymer Unit at the University of the South Bank. Has had to wear the same clothes since Monday.

What he is doing or thinking
Facing up to the fact that he must indeed go shopping for clothes. Shopping is something that seldom enters his purview. Harry does not shop. A market researcher once thought she had found a prime AB. She questionnaired Harry. How often do you buy the following: CDs? What are they? Oh, you mean those compact tape things. Televisions? Don't have one. Video recorders?

He does his laundry on Sunday nights. Last Sunday night, he smelled smoke. He thought it was his lovely log fire. When he finally went downstairs to the basement to unload his laundry, he was amazed to see smoke pouring out of the washing machine. Flame circulated round and round inside it. It was only eighteen years old.

All eight pairs of underpants, four shirts, four string vests and three pairs of drip-dry slacks were burned to ash. He has nothing to wear. It's depressing because he knows from past experience that he won't be able to find exact replacements.

An old woman is asking people to dance. Harry loves eccentrics. He begins to giggle as she starts to sing. Then, to his surprise, people join in.

Harry just happens to have a bottle of whisky in his briefcase, and plastic cups. You never know when there will be a party.

MS SUSAN WHEEN

Outward appearance

Conventional student: blue donkey jacket; limp sweater in streaks of ochre, pink and beige; clean jeans. Sits upright, avidly reading the bestseller about female weightlifters, *Clean and Jerk*. Shakes her head in wonder and delight. The cover features huge sweaty breasts.

Inside information

Friend and occasional employee of Tina Ravon. Helps pay for her drama course at RADA by hiring out her services as a new form of advertising. She rides up and down the tube visibly reading particular books for money.[2] Sometimes the publisher pays for a friend, and Susan reads aloud to her. Today, she's working the Bakerloo line alone, shuffling back and forth all morning from the Elephant.

Susan calls this 'reality editing'. She invented it herself. Instead of using media that are understood to be bought and paid for, this new advertising changes reality to carry the desired message.

What she is doing or thinking

Acting. She has not read *Clean and Jerk*, in case it interferes with her performance. Instead, Susan focuses with professional rigour on communicating different kinds of reading experience: rapt attention; shock at a plot turn-around; being overcome with emotion, tears filling her eyes. Sometimes, she manages to say to someone convincingly: 'This is such a wonderful book.'

She's getting increasingly annoyed by an old woman singing loudly. It's a distraction from her own performance. When someone shouts, 'Everybody!' and people start to dance, Susan knows she's beaten. Better to work another car heading north. The bookbuyers all get off at Waterloo anyway.

Glaring at the dancers, she stands to exit at Waterloo.

Another helpful and informative
253 *footnote*
2 I sincerely wish I could claim to
have invented this. Unfortunately
it's true. I mentioned to someone in
the trade that I saw a phenomenal
number of people on the tube
reading a particular bestseller. That

book was known to have been
promoted in this way; indeed, the
advertisers worked in pairs so that
one could read aloud to other from
the book as if moved by sheer
delight.

But I thought that would stretch
credibility.

Outward appearance

Tiny, about 28. Grey slacks, white shirt, no tie, shaved black hair. Rubber-soled Doc Martens mutated towards respectability. Writes on a clipboard.

Inside information

A market researcher for London Underground.

For the last six months, Harold has listed people on carriages by age, gender and racial background. He then selects individuals to interview, using demographic criteria. He asks them about the length of their journey and things to improve. This is the last car on his last day.

What he is doing or thinking

Busy finishing his draft report. It ends with a list of those people who do not travel on the trains: the infirm, infants, men with cars. He identifies the need for further research. Why do so few children go to school by tube? Why are there more women than men until you pass Lambeth North station?

Working on the tubes, Harold has witnessed two suicides, one busking quick-change drag artiste, and one successfully completed sexual act. When the bag lady next to him starts to sing 'Is that all there is?' in a voice like Lotte Lenya's, he is merely mildly pleased. When she succeeds in persuading other passengers to dance, he thinks: that's a nice send-off, one final fling on the cattle trucks.

Harold sees them all, sitting inside their fates like eggs in cartons, there through an inexorable logic of age, gender, genes, character, their time in history, luck. He sees their faces like insulation wrapped around boilers. Their stories wheedle out of them like escaping steam. Mostly unheard.

Like his own.

MISS ANNE FRANK

Outward appearance

Elderly woman in a donkey jacket and old grey trousers. Lumpy bandages under stockings are visible over the tops of her scuffed shoes. She scans the rows of faces, stricken. She smiles sweetly, and says to the young man across from her, 'Would you like to dance?'

He stares at her and doesn't answer. She looks at the foreign business woman, at the sad blonde girl, at the nervous old hippy. Anne starts to sing, 'Is that all there is?' She starts to dance alone.

A tall black woman stands up, joins her, demands, 'Everybody!' The young man approaches and bows. In the aisle he and Anne begin a sedate waltz. A Chinese woman shrugs, takes out one of her party favours and blows it, unrolling it with wheeze. Out comes a puppet of John Lennon that starts to pump its feet. Someone passes around the whisky. By Lambeth North, the car is having a party.

Inside information

She is Anne Frank, the famous diarist, but she doesn't know that. She has wandered Europe for the last 50 years. She sometimes sees the face of a child in bookshop windows, and knows enough to be happy for her. That child got what it wanted. It is not what Anne wants.

What she is doing or thinking

Anne thinks she is still on the train to Auschwitz, and that she is trying to make people happy one last time. She thinks she is sprinkling joy from her eyes, with her voice. *If that's all there is my friends, then let's keep dancing.*

Imagine!
Your advertising message
in this space!

Suppose there was a miracle.

Suddenly, you know who everyone is. Outside the tube station, a pedestrian waits for the lights. She's an industrial designer, working on a prototype intelligent shopping trolley.[1] Standing next to her are two old ladies, Anglo-Irish sisters. During the Troubles, they lived next door to Eamon de Valera. He would slip over their garden wall to avoid the secret police.

At work, the security guard says hi. He repairs vintage cars and wants to get into your knickers. A woman from the IT Unit walks past you glowering. She loathes you. Someone has been telling her you are a racist, someone you thought was a friend.

At lunch, ten large men crowd into the bar. In the grip of the miracle, you are hounded by knowledge: they are policemen, off duty, boisterous, veering out of control. They will fail to pay their bill.

Back outside, you are overwhelmed. Passing cars gnaw at your attention like gnats. On the fifth floor of the old MI5 headquarters, a drunk squatter is sprawled, unable to stand, desperate to pee.

"Why?" you ask God. "Why break all the rules just to do this terrible thing to me?"

And God answers. God has a small voice, tiny and sweet. His testes have not descended. He doesn't have testes. He giggles a lot. The voice of God when you finally hear it sounds like a cross between a sparrow and Marilyn Monroe.

"I'm sorry," God coos. "Now you know why I hate miracles too."

Another helpful and informative 253 *footnote*

1   I am not making this up. There are intelligent shopping trolleys that count up the cost of your groceries as you go around the shop and even charge you as you leave. Market research shows people love them. No studies have yet been conducted comparing the intelligence of the shoppers and their trolleys.

The End of the Line

Sensation

and violence

at last! Discover

the horrible end

of the carriage of

your choice !!!

Eveleen's stepfather **Milton** erupts through the door between carriages, knife between his teeth like a buccaneer. **Eveleen** sees him and howls with laughter. **Joy** starts to pull off her jacket – to muffle the knife.

Richard Tomlinson leans back to look out of the window. The train should be slowing down. The platform of Elephant and Castle station is hurtling past them. He jumps up.

So does **Maurice**. There is a brake. He can't find it. The brake has gone as well. He sees blue tiles flash past the window and thinks: I'm going to die because of that cottage.

Richard beats on the driver's door, shouting 'Stop!'

Marie drops her mirror as the car buckles under her. She looks up, and sees the van coming for her again. She has time to think: this time there won't be a plate.

Yoshi looks up to see a fist of metal come for her. How strange, she thinks with mild curiosity, how strange this England is.

Crushed in the driver's cabin, **Tahsin** is alive, unconscious, dreaming.

He dreams he is in the ice cream shop in Marash with his father, who looks young and glad to see him. The big icebox is still outside, the man with the moustache is still milling ice cream in strange machines. The walls of the ice cream shop are lined with books. The books are bound in green leather and gold-tooled lettering that glows not in modern Turkish, but Ottoman script. The glowing words say: Love. Freedom. Peace.

Florence Cassell glances up as the man nearest to her suddenly moves. The doors between the carriages swing and she hears a roar of laughter from the next carriage.

'We're going too fast!' says **Olivia Parsons**, her voice rising in panic. Don't be silly, she tells herself, you're too . . . NERVOUS.

Michael Jerome wakes up blearily, to see tiled walls rushing past the window. Coming into the station, he thinks. Then suddenly the station is whipped away from them like a scarf.

No, thinks Olivia, no don't be silly, something terrible can't happen to the same person two days in a row.

Florence stands up. Suddenly **Milton** is pitched, flying backwards through the doors into her and she is knocked off her feet. She screams. Under her fingers comes a terrible vibration.

Dimi Belinkov looks up drunk, and sees crumpled metal advance along the carriage. It devours the young woman in black leather. I'm going to die, he thinks, die with that bastard Igor, drunk. He looks back. **Igor** still grins foolishly, with something sad in his eyes. He leans forward and kisses Dimi on the lips.

Ashley Watkins has not moved, his hands on his knees. I will have never spoken, he thinks, I was never given a chance to speak.

Milton Richards is enfolded in the steel arms of Jesus. They wrap him up, they cut him like knives, and Jesus says, 'You failed me, Milton, you failed me all your life.' Milton welcomes the pain, and the night, and the release.

From the rush of the tiles past the window, **Karen Keown** is sure she is making a break for it. She hears shouts. The hospital staff have discovered that she has taken her baby. She looks down at its face, it smiles up at her, full of love. At last, she has something to love her.

Paul Launcey is telling himself it can't be happening. This is the answer to his prayers, to die indisputably in an accident. He holds in his mind the image of his wife and son. I love you, love you, love you, he tells them. He sees their future: secure, provisioned, alone.

Stefan Braun is conscious at first that he is no longer being photographed. **Anya Ruderian** has broken into a run along the aisle. White dust footprints follow her like a ghost's. The posters in the station flash past, full of models. **Stefan** looks at Paul's face. It glows with love and hope. You must be a happy man, Stefan thinks. The train plunges into darkness.

And Anya? At the end of the carriage, braced against the sectioning, she holds her camera, set to automatic.

The train stops and all weight shoots forward. Anya's arms are flung out, but she holds onto the camera as it goes, flick, flick, flick. One end of the carriage puckers, then erupts like a volcano. The two men are lifted up as if on lava, and Anya surfs the buckling floor, still corresponding from the front line.

Salvation through art.

Tom McHugh's vomit cleared the carriage at Lambeth North. Tom waits alone by the door, still trying to clip on his badge. He hears fluttering and sees **Who?** beating his wings against a fluorescent panel.

Tom thinks of the bird as an extension of himself, somehow a product of the Pimms. Tom is permanently distracted, his access random. He sends out his thoughts like messages on the Internet only to find they get gummed up in his lack of bandwidth. They stall at some unknown domain, fluttering like pigeons in realms of light and noise.

Then he crashes.

The entire floor rises and tilts. **Debendrath Karan's** portfolio shoots down the length of the car and breaks open. The lights die.

Tom was feeling ill anyway, so he sits down. The car squats with him, to half its normal height, as if wanting to chat. The doors open in a new way, by bursting.

Everything is still and dark. Tom steps out of the doorway and falls seven feet, collapsing onto rails. There is no platform. The carriage sits flattened on top of two others. Muttering about the level of service, Tom brushes himself off and walks down the tunnel towards the Elephant. The contents of the portfolio settle around him: forests in France, or an English cottage seen at rabbit-level amid lettuces. The pictures blow along the tunnel: a circus, dancing birds, and a view of a hill on which a holy fool once sat.

Who? shoots past him towards the light.

Debbie DeNussi wonders why the train is going so fast. It shoots past the Elephant; she must have misunderstood the map. She thinks: I'll never make that fucking film.

Selima Haydir knows exactly what has happened. She begins to shout over and over: no, no, no! She should have stayed and gone down fighting.

Paul Binyon blinks. The whole end of the car has blossomed like a flower in time-lapse photography. Its petals unfurl, sucking in the roof. The car collapses. The lights fail. Didn't he have a TV show to present?

Terry Wilcox imagines a beautiful stack of phone cards, an ordered collection, thrown in the air, forever scattered. **Kevin Spinnaker** is grateful, partly. Jenny has escaped; Jenny will think he loved her. Part of him dies cursing her.

The darkness crushes **Bill McReady**. He dreams he is climbing up the green hill of Ascension, past cactus, through farmland and heath, to a crowning grove of bamboo clattering like flutes. He can see his ship.

Anthony Auldgirth can only tell from the rush of sound that something is wrong. It sounds like his life, Ireland, Dublin, the wars, the years in America, New York, London, Elizabeth. Blind, he sees it whole.

His daughter **Madeleine** still holds her father's hand. And suddenly both of them are in wedding dress, and herself as a little girl comes running down the carriage with a candle. 'It's not reincarnation,' the little girl says. 'It is like the flame passed from old candles to new.'

Bodhisattva.

The passengers in car 6 only have time to notice that the train is hurtling through the Elephant before it ploughs underneath car 5 and is flattened in a breath. Their spirits shoot forward.

Sam Cruza sits in the New York Metro. The other passengers look up from their papers; they are all cab drivers; they are all him: Albanian, Romanian, Greek. They all start to exit, taking parts of him with them.

London taxi drivers swarm around **Steven Workman**, shaking his hand. His uncertain smile freezes. They are pleased he's dying – his knowledge will be crushed with him.

Steven is still wound up in **Angie Strachan**'s hair. She imagines she is travelling to the warehouse. Life is so short, she thinks, wistfully, and makes up her mind to go with her boss to the Lebanon. She sees it – shimmering spires, bullet holes.

Harriet Zinovsky has somehow landed in that warehouse full of skins, only now they all have tattooed names; they are people.

Harry Migson hears the theme song from *The Avengers*, and from *Dr Who*: he is a child again, in the dark, with the sounds.

Rezia Begum is the only one who knows what has happened; she is conscious, wrapped around a metal pole, breathing dust.

For **Bal Patil**, everything spins like his hair. Swinging down the handholds comes a monkey, wearing a spangled crown. It is Hanuman, strength. The Monkey takes Bal's hand. Together they swing up the carriage, away from illusion which exfoliates like stone, towards the airy real.

The last of the laughing people leave. **Anne Frank** knows where they have gone; they have been selected. She knows who **Passenger 252** is. He is the officer who makes the lists. She goes up to him, asks. 'Would you like to dance?'

The officer looks up and says pleasantly, 'No thank you.'

'Why not?' she asks him. 'We have so little time together.'

He smiles. He loved the dance, but the more quickly he finishes this report now, the more time he will have to be himself.

Anne pleads, 'This is a matter of life and death.'

The train roars through the Elephant. All at once, the car collapses from one end, squeezed flat like a toothpaste tube someone has stepped on. Everything stops.

Sandwiched between metal, Anne seeps. Her arm pops back into its socket, her fingers flow back together. From between the torn sheets of metal, she pulls herself out of the car.

A bloodied hand offers her the list. She takes it. It is the list of useful people who will survive:

> the unemployed
> the sick
> the retired and elderly
> the mentally subnormal
> prisoners
> pre-school infants
> children driven to school
> people with cars
> housewives
> nuns . . .

Anne knows such lists. She knows all the names, the millions of names. She catches up with Tom McHugh and takes hold of his hand. Together they walk up the tunnel.

Anne is murmuring the kaddish now, for the dead. She wanders and bears witness. She cannot forget them, nor can she die.

Become an Author in Your Spare Time!

contribute to the new novel

ANOTHER ONE ALONG IN A MINUTE

Unlike authors, God is inexhaustible.

God fills not just one train, but one after another, and the station concourses above, and the towering buildings on the streets overhead, floor on floor.

Immediately behind this train is another. It is stalled in a tunnel, like so many of us are in life. The passengers wait, wondering why the train is not going forward. No one can leave, no one can enter. It sits still for five minutes.

This makes a total of three hundred seconds. Interactivity replaces curiosity about time with curiosity about space (though both are ultimately the same thing). The question is not what happens next? but where will we go next?

ANOTHER ONE ALONG IN A MINUTE pays tribute to stalled time by describing each character in 300 words, one for each second of time.

Together, we are inexhaustible. Populate Internet with people you imagine. Click here to email your 300-word contribution to:

Ryman.Worksltd@btinternet.com

What will your characters do in that five minutes? Talk to neighbours? Read their papers? Complete their crosswords? Imagine that there has been a nuclear attack?

No money will be made from this sequel. Copyright will rest with you. The editor reserves the right not to publish, or to suggest amendments. You must undertake that no one will be libelled by your text and accept full responsibility for the material you submit.

Thrill to the adventures of these new characters in the 253 universe. Connect to:

http://www.ryman-novel.com/another/home.htm

TAKE THE *PAIN* OUT OF SERIOUS FICTION!

Why tax your memory remembering who's who in a work of fiction? The print remix of 253 brings you all the ease and convenience of the original interactive novel, as presented on the World Wide Web.

These are *the original links*. Just like you were online and connected!

What do the characters have in common? Do they interact personally? Do they share a common employer or locale? Do they share other interesting or novel characteristics?

How it works

Each character is listed under key headings, by car and seat number. For example 2/99 means car two, Passenger 99.

To save you time, some links are left out. Passengers who merely sit near to each other are not included. Similarly, linking people because they were gay, black or Asian seemed pointless as linking people because they were white or straight. For charactors who die, see *The End of the Line*.

Next steps in the information revolution!

As skills of memory and interpretation fade, all older fiction may need translation.

For example, an interactive version of *Chinatown* might highlight and explain all the imagery of water. *Casablanca* could have its cage/prison metaphors helpfully pointed out, along with its similarities to *Waiting for Godot*. Verbal exchanges could be clarified and subtext options listed.

In the case of 253, metaphors for life and death could be signposted by userfriendly icons — such as red flashing warning lights; skull and crossbones; or other easily recognized graphic images.

Let us know if you think this would be helpful.

253 – The Application of MODERN Science to MODERN Readers

11th January 1995

8.35 AM to 8.42 AM

All characters in this novel ride on one particular train on this date, during these minutes. To be clear, there was no crash on London Underground on this day. 11th January, 1995 is the day I learned my best friend not only had Aids, but would die within days.

ADVENTURE CAPITAL
Hokiko McTavish 7/242 met
  husband
Steven Workman 6/213
Ron Busby 4/131
Paul Launcey 3/101
Maggie Rolt 2/57

AGEING SCENE MAKERS
Spider Spenser 3/77
Chris Green 2/41

AMERICAN CHURCH,
LAMBETH
Lord Anthony Lowick 4/125
Maurice Hazlett 1/31

ANOREXIC
'Bertie Jeeves' 6/201
Rosemary Oliver 6/200

ARCHBISHOP'S PARK
'Bertie Jeeves' 6/201
John Kennedy 4/122
Rafael da Cunha 3/85
related to

ARCHIBISHOP'S PALACE
Georgina Bullen 2/40
Andre Stanley 2/38

ARMY (BRITISH)
Amelia apJohn 5/146 will
  join it
Major Edwin Grives 3/102
Officer Bert Harris 3/98
Don Disney 3/81
Martin Belcher 2/49 is
  ex-Army, no time to say so,
  envies officer who comes
  into his shop

AUSTRALIA
Anthony Auldgirth 5/174
Adele Driscoll 1/34

BEATLES
Vaclav Horacek 7/222
Jenny Green 4/127

BEAUTICIAN
Sylvia Kaye 7/246
Corrine Tracy 2/65

BEETLEHIDE SHIPPING
COMPANY
Halet Özgen 7/219
Lucie Friend 4/143
Tom McHugh 4/124 also via
  name badge has link to:
Valerie Tuck 1/2

is saved by talking to Peter Dearlove 4/112

Marianne de Vendeuse 4/111 is mother to Andy de Vendeuse 4/110

Anya Ruderian 3/109 is photographing Stefan Braun 3/75

Camilla Burke-Harris 3/106 has an appointment with William Dynham 1/32 and Mab Mahanchandra 7/245

Camilla Burke-Harris 3/106 attacks George Aristidou 3/78

Shimon Souza 3/105 is observed with interest by Mme Marge Matisse 3/79

Major Edwin Grives 3/102 is friend of Tristan Sawyer 7/235 but doesn't know he's a fag

Suze Morley 3/99 is sister of Danni Jarret; 1/27 Danni was married

Bert Harris 3/98 gets the hots for Sara Ivanovic 3/92

Bert Harris 3/98 asks Doris McPherson 3/95 if she has a complaint about Geoff Ryman 3/96

Doris McPherson 3/95 becomes friends with Maureen Stuart 3/80

Lawrence Timmins 3/94 is husband of Helen Timmins 3/93

Lawrence Timmins' 3/94 old jacket is worn by Andre Stanley 2/38

James Bartlett's 3/91 mother has met Douglas Esswood 4/145

Jasmine McGowan 3/84 has a clinic for sick jukeboxes next door to Emil's Window Displays, owned by Savi Gupta, 2/56

Milton Richards 2/73 father of Eveleen Doyce 1/19

Amy Stewart 2/69 and Granny Stewart 2/68

Granny Stewart 2/68 takes against Chris Green 2/41

Dimitri Belinkov 2/60 and Igor Klimov 2/59

Amanda Stinton 2/44 is impressed by Julie Tildsley 2/66

Georgina Bullen 2/40 tells Kevin Potter 2/39 he smells and will accidentally insult Andre Stanley 2/38 at a church gathering

Richard Tomlinson 1/37 feels deserted by Tristan Sawyer 7/235

Maurice Hazlett 1/31 bought wine from Tony Mannocchi 1/22

Flora McCardie 1/28 befriends Danni Jarret 1/27

Clive Kelton 1/24 decides to leave London and May Hanmore 1/13 quits her job after fight between Harry Wade 1/15 and Phil Barker 1/14

Justin Holmes 1/21 is offered money by Joy Harvey 1/20

Tony Colley 1/18 works on the same ferry as Douglas Higbee 1/11

May Hanmore 1/13 lives on same estate as Samantha Allers 2/67

Christine Marre 3/74
Marie Breatnach 1/35
Paul Hennessey 1/26

James Whitthead 6/192
Sabrina Foster 6/184
Donald Varda 1/4

Sylvia Kaye 7/246
Harry Runciman 7/250
Bill Havers 7/237
Maryan Elliott 6/202
Sanjay Kumar 6/191
Victor Dowie 5/171
Gurdev Dhollin 5/168
Ibrahim Gurer 4/136
John Kennedy 4/122

Anthea Dodds 6/217
Delia Hendy 5/173
George Aristidou 3/78
Joy Harvey 1/20

Harriet Zinovsky 6/195
Angie Strachan 6/187

Richard Thurlow 4/132
Edward Gossart 4/117
Adele Driscoll 1/34

Kevin Spinnaker 5/181
Jenny Green 4/127
Bob Hall 1/30

Gwen Utlay 3/83
Doreen Goodman 2/45

Thomas Miley 7/231
Tony 'Peewee' Hatchet
6/196
Hilary Vialls 2/72

Julie Gluck 7/236 (No Bars
Gallery)
Harry Migson 6/204
Georgina Havistock, owner of
Yesterdaze, 6/183
Nicholas Paganos 4/138
Samantha Allers 2/67
Ralph Moles 2/50
Keith Snow 2/43
Flora McCardie 1/28
Minerva Nicholas 1/16
May Hanmore 1/13
Gina Horst 1/12 new gym
extends to
THE CUT
Benjamin Posthate 6/215
(going to Health Centre)
Rosemary Oliver 6/200
Helen Thistlethwaite 5/148
Horse(clothes?)

Samantha Wilson 6/189
Timothy West 3/82
Harry Freer 2/55

Harold Pottluk 7/252

Delia Hendy 5/173
Gwen Utlay 3/83

complete our

READER SATISFACTION SURVEY

Help us to serve you better. Please take a moment to fill in and return this form to:

St. Martin's Griffin
Reader Feedback Service
18A Ridgmount Gardens
London
WC1E 7AR

**1. I found the way this novel was
organized (by car, numbers etc.)
(tick one only)**
- ☐ clear and easy to use
- ☐ a good idea but needed more work
- ☐ boring as hell
- ☐ a good joke, but surely postmodernism requires that (attach essay)
- ☐ huh?

2. The cover and design were
- ☐ brilliant, lots of fun
- ☐ looked OK
- ☐ nearly put me off eating

**3. The typefaces in particular were
(tick two boxes)**
- ☐ nice and big – even I could read it
- ☐ too small by half
  and
- ☐ disgusting and old fashioned
- ☐ sleek and inviting

4. How easy was the novel to find?
- ☐ Tell the HarperCollins reps to get off their butts: I had to look in ..... (number of) bookshops
- ☐ I had to order it and even then, they didn't seem to know about it
- ☐ Easy – my friend loaned it to me
- ☐ Easy. I stole it (please fill in name and address below)

- ☐ It was in a few big city bookshops
- ☐ Wow! Can you guys rep books, this thing was like herpes ... on everybody's lips

5. What are your views of the author
- ☐ tell Geoff not to give up his day job
- ☐ tell Geoff it was OK, but couldn't he do a few more (delete as appropriate) dragons/beautiful women with catlike or metallic eyes/big-breasted babes/happy endings
- ☐ I am currently organizing an SF convention, book signing, birthday party etc (please specify):

....

....

and am prepared to offer Geoff a fee of (please specify below) to attend:

....

....

- ☐ tell Geoff I lust after his body and want to have sex with him (please fill in name and address below, ALAWP)
- ☐ tell Geoff that I am prepared to offer him a living stipend of £20,000 per annum or equivalent (please fill in name and address below, attaching proof of fiscal solvency)

....

....

....

....

....

6.) Fill in this section ONLY if you have ticked either or both of the last two boxes in question 5:

Name...

Address..

Town...

Postcode..

Country..

Email ....

Fax ....

Physical description (or enclose photo)............

....

....

I hereby certify that I am over 18 years of age

Signature...

7.) As I understand it the significance of 253 is (one answer only, please):

☐ as a metaphor for impending death as we live life

☐ as a tribute to the hidden fascinating truth behind each face if we could but find it

☐ as a tribute to the infinite variety of London life

☐ as a deliberate mockery of interactivity, feedback forms etc.

☐ that some of it is mildly amusing

☐ that Geoff had a contract.

Attach essay if absolutely necessary.